THE FORGE

T. S. Stribling

WITH AN INTRODUCTION BY
Randy K. Cross

THE UNIVERSITY OF ALABAMA PRESS

Library of Congress Cataloging in Publication Data

Stribling, T. S. (Thomas Sigismund), 1881–1965.
  The forge.
  1. United States—History—Civil War, 1861–1865—
Fiction. I. Title.
PS3537.T836F65 1985   813'.52   84-24053
ISBN 0-8173-0248-4
ISBN 0-8173-0249-2 (pbk.)

INTRODUCTION

Randy K. Cross

THOMAS SIGISMUND STRIBLING was born on March 4, 1881, in Clifton, Tennessee. It was in this small Tennessee river town—and at the home of his maternal grandparents near Florence, Alabama—that Stribling grew up surrounded by veterans from both sides of the Civil War, by former slaves, and by the anti-Northern sentiment that prevailed in the post-Reconstruction South. These hill people made a great impression on Stribling, and many of them would find their way, years later, into his fiction. Their speech patterns, their beliefs, the intricacies of their everyday lives, are presented in photographic detail in Stribling's works. Yet Stribling was more than a mere regionalist; his characters are motivated by universal emotions intensified by the upheaval of the Old Order.

Early in his life Stribling knew that he wanted to become a writer. However, at the insistence of his father, a practical-minded businessman, Stribling studied law at The University of Alabama, graduating in 1905. After a brief and undistinguished tenure in the law office of former Governor Emmett O'Neal of Florence, Stribling chose to give up his legal practice and follow the literary life. In the years to come, he would publish scores of short stories, a collection of detective fiction (*Clues of the Caribbees*, 1929), and fourteen novels. His realistic treatment of the South would garner praise from Northern critics (in 1932 the *Boston Evening Transcript* would proclaim him "The Novelist of the South") and draw fire from offended

Southerners. Yet, for all the diversified reaction to his work, Stribling would receive the Pulitzer Prize in 1933 for *The Store* and end his career as the best-selling fictionist to write between the world wars.

In 1906, Stribling joined the staff of the *Taylor-Trotwood Magazine* in Nashville where his duties consisted not only of writing, but of keeping subscription lists and typing office correspondence as well. While in Nashville, Stribling began writing stories for Sunday school magazines, an outlet to which he would devote much of his creative energy for nearly a decade. His stories sold well, so well, in fact, that Stribling left the magazine and devoted his efforts to the production of these moral tales. While these stories did not tax Stribling's abilities as a writer, he felt, nevertheless, that they did serve as a profitable literary training ground for him: "I can say this about Sunday school stories, and I am sure I have written ten thousand, they allow a far wider latitude of thought and philosophy than any one dreams of who has not followed that market."[1] Perhaps equally important to Stribling, the stories allowed him to earn his living solely as a writer, a goal which he had established for himself years before. At the end of this remarkable ten-year apprenticeship, Stribling, now a reporter for the Chattanooga *News*, expanded one of his stories into a juvenile novel that was published in 1917 as *Cruise of the Dry Dock*. His career as a novelist had begun at last.

In the years immediately following the publication of his first novel, Stribling contributed regularly to various pulp magazines such as *American Boy, Argosy,* and *Adventure.* In 1921, *Century Magazine* serialized *Birthright*, a book that was, according to Stribling, "the first realistic novel of Negroes written in this country since Opie Read produced *My Young Master.*"[2] Although Stribling originally planned to write a trilogy with *Birthright* as the first volume, poor sales discouraged him from completing the project. He would, however, return to the theme of racial prejudice in the South throughout his Southern novels.

While Stribling's next three novels are set in the Orient and South America, in 1926 his native Tennessee hills become the setting for his first best seller, *Teeftallow*, a bitter satire of small-town life. Although *Teeftallow* brought Stribling almost instant fame in the United States and in England, it likewise brought down the fury of many leading Southern critics who objected to the book's realistic depiction of the social and political inequities in the South. Stribling touched on these same themes again two years later in *Bright Metal* (1928), the tale of the enlightened Agatha Pomeroy of New York whose marriage brings her to live among the backward-pointing citizens of Lanesburg, Tennessee. At about the same time, *Teeftallow* was dramatized on Broadway as *Rope*. Northern critics had praised the novel for its realism and objectivity, but the drama critics were less enthusiastic: the play ran for less than a month.

Throughout his career as a novelist, Stribling continued to receive favorable reviews from Northern critics, but his Southern novels, ironically, offended some of the Agrarians at Vanderbilt who ignored the universal implications of his work. These Agrarians felt that Stribling exploited the South through his realistic pictures of the social, economic, and political ideals of the time. Their argument in favor of a Southern society based on the agrarian ideal and its resulting economy found no support in the works of T. S. Stribling. He refused to romanticize the social and political immobility of poor, uneducated Southerners, black and white. Instead, he chose to emphasize the poverty, prejudice, and greed that often are born out of such a stratified social order. Stribling's portrayal of the South is not always complimentary, but it is fair.

Yet for all his social observation, Stribling's purpose was not that of social reformer. He was a fictionist, a teller of tales, an astute observer and recorder of the life around him. The plots of his novels, though well developed and often intricate, never seem contrived or forced. His narratives unfold naturally, creating believable characters in plausible situations. "The great charm of a fine story," Stribling wrote, "is that it utterly conceals its art, and the would-be writer trying to probe its mystery slides down its finish like a wasp on a windowpane."[3] The greatest test of Stribling's technical skill as a novelist came with the writing of his trilogy, a work that follows the transformation of the South from the antebellum period through the turn of the century. Stribling worked for six years on these novels, and his labor produced a trilogy of epic proportions.

The idea for the trilogy had occupied Stribling's mind for many years, but it was not until 1928 that he began to outline the books and begin work on what was, even to one of Stribling's skills, an enormous task. He approached the project as a single entity, structuring all three novels simultaneously, planning, at first, to publish them in a single volume. In addition, Stribling managed to publish three new books during this period: *Clues of the Caribbees* (1929), plus two novels, *Strange Moon* (1929) and *Backwater* (1930). Although these "pulp novelettes," as Stribling called them, were hastily written and cannot be compared favorably to *Birthright* and *Teeftallow,* they did allow him the financial freedom to continue work on his trilogy. During this period, Stribling became engaged to Lou Ella Kloss, a native of Clifton and an accomplished violinist and pianist. They were married at Corinth, Mississippi, in 1930.

Although Stribling had traveled widely in Europe and South America as a younger man, now at age fifty, he focused his energies on the work for which he would best be remembered. The artistic techniques which he had refined over a twenty-year period as a professional writer could now manifest themselves in a theme worthy of his talents. Years later, while writing *Laughing Stock*, his posthumously published auto-

THE FORGE

IN MEMORY OF
MY FATHER AND MOTHER
AND THAT BRAVE, GAY GROUP FROM WHOM
THESE MEMOIRS WERE TAKEN

biography, Stribling would discuss the motivation behind his trilogy:

> It may be an odd feeling, I don't know, perhaps many persons have felt so before me, but the thought of death doesn't disturb me personally very much. I would, of course, like to see how things come out, but things don't come out. They go on and on and on, world without end, and if one should live forever, still one would never see how things came out. No, personally, immortality or annihilation don't interest me so very much, because the show will never come to its final curtain or the novel to its finis. The aspect of death that appalls me is for the whole generation that surrounded my boyhood and youth utterly to disappear. To think of those poetic figures just after the Civil War, their world, their ways of life, their insouciance, their kindness, their charm, for this particular group to vanish from the world of men, utterly forgotten, lost in the abyss of death— that to me is a tragic and almost unbearable consummation.
>
> I know well enough that all persons have their childhood's world and that it is lost; that each generation looks back to its forebears with poetry and romance, and all in turn disappear; and that the third and fourth and fifth generations know nothing whatever of the first, save a few half-attended tales. And when one goes beyond these immediate descendants into hundreds and thousands of years, then the lives that ordinary people lived are as forgotten as their dust. But all such reasoning had no weight with me. It was my impulse to stave off death as best I could from my mother's people, and the dwellers of Gravelly Springs and Florence whom she knew, who exerted such a charm over me, that I always had planned, when the time was ripe, to write a story which would preserve as long as might be that beloved world.[4]

The story which Stribling resolved to write eventually took shape and was published as *The Forge* (1931), *The Store* (1932), and *Unfinished Cathedral* (1934).

For these novels—which mark the climax of his career as a

novelist—Stribling drew on the scenes, the events, the people
that inhabited his own past. Taken together, the trilogy com-
prises a social and historical document that follows its characters from the antebellum, agrarian South of *The Forge* to the
triumph of the mercantile New South in *Unfinished Cathedral.*

Stribling's desire to "stave off death" from his mother's people motivated him to write *The Forge,* the story of the Vaiden
family of north Alabama during the period of Civil War and
Reconstruction. The lives of Stribling's fictional Vaidens closely
parallel those of his actual relatives: James Waits, Stribling's
grandfather and a local blacksmith, is embodied in the character of old man Jimmie Vaiden; two of his uncles, Lee and
Shelt Waits, appear as Polycarp and Augustus Vaiden; Amelia
Waits, Stribling's mother, is fictionalized as Marcia Vaiden. In
this way, Stribling sought to preserve "those poetic figures just
after the Civil War, their world, their ways of life," and in so
doing, he is true to the spirit of the age. In 1934, Theodore
Dreiser wrote to Stribling that *The Forge*

> is the only novel of all those attempting to cover either the
> Southern or the Northern point of view, that I think is worth a
> straw. By that of course I do not imply that yours is in anywhere
> near the straw category. As a matter of fact, it is as fine an
> American realistic novel as I know of. There is something so
> truly human and real about every line of it. More than that, it is
> fair to life and to the individual in the South who found himself
> placed as he was at that time. Really, it is a beautiful book—
> dramatic, amusing, sorrowful, true.

The truth contained in *The Forge* derives from Stribling's accu-
rate depiction of the changes forced on life in the South by the
war and its aftermath, not from any rigid presentation of historical fact. "A great novel," Stribling wrote, "should remain exactly what it is, a tale, not an imitation of a literal transcript from
life."[5] This dictum applies in *The Forge.* While the book is

honest in reflecting the times, Stribling often manipulates factual events and dates in favor of artistic creation.

This restructuring of history is most evident in the Civil War sections of *The Forge,* all of which point toward Shiloh, the final battle in the novel. General Forrest, for example, encounters General Sturgis in Mississippi at an impossible time (1862), while the Yankees attempt to cut the Baltimore & Ohio Railroad, the main supply line for the Confederates encamped at Corinth (p. 205). In fact, Forrest would not fight Sturgis until two years later at Brice's Crossroads near Baldwyn, Mississippi, in June of 1864. Furthermore, it was the Memphis & Charleston Railroad, not the Baltimore & Ohio, that served Corinth. Later, Stribling's armies fight at Okolona, Mississippi, months before the battle really occurred (p. 213). Although Stribling correctly identifies Forrest as commander of the Confederates, he places the Union forces under Sturgis instead of their actual commander, General W. Sooy Smith.

Still again, Stribling reverses the order of battle when his characters fight at Vicksburg before Shiloh (April 1862). As Augustus is being released from the Confederate hospital at Lauderdale Springs, Mississippi, he overhears talk about the new arrivals who have served under General Pat Cleburne: "General Pat lost men but he gained victories—he ought to have been in control of the defenses of Vicksburg and Corinth" (p. 228). The siege at Vicksburg, however, would not take place until 1863, and the only permanent defensive positions ever established at Corinth were held by the North in October of 1862, seven months after the Battle of Shiloh.

These and the other historical inaccuracies contained in *The Forge* were of no consequence to Stribling. As Howard Bahr has pointed out, Stribling "was not interested in the mathematics of history. For Stribling, history was a convenient stage upon which characters could move in all their diverse humanity, where an author could shift the flats according to his own design."[6] Stribling's aim in *The Forge* was not to produce a historical novel in the strict sense. Instead, he sought to document the spirit of an age and to preserve the memory of his forebears and the inhabitants of north Alabama, caught as they were in the destruction of the Old Order.

The Lacefields represent that segment of the social order most affected by the economic upheaval that occurred in the South. Before the war, their plantation is lush and prosperous, a symbol of wealth and aristocracy:

> Field after field stretched away, with here and there a clump of ornamental trees. At wide distances apart great brick manors flanked by whitewashed slave quarters dominated the landscape. Over all lay the soft blue-and-lavender haze of spring. Aloft floated the clouds in great scrolls and strata. It seemed to Marcia that the clouds over the Reserve were more magnificent than anywhere else.
>
> A faint, almost incorporeal chanting began to grow in the air, as if the scene itself exhaled a haze of music as well as moisture. The black workers were quitting their labors for the day. Far away, Marcia could see them unhitching their mules and leaving their plows sticking in the furrows. They leaped astride their work mules and started home yodeling to the jingling of their trace chains [p. 66].

This romantic view of the Lacefield plantation stands in sharp contrast to the scene which Miltiades encounters four years later:

> Briers and sumac were rank in the fence corners. Small trees had grown up along the way in the fields that had lain fallow. The road itself was grass grown with an occasional mud hole here and there, almost as bad as the public road.
>
> A little later he came within sight of the manor itself. Its silver poplars were thinned to raggedness. The white rows of slave cabins were gone, and in their stead were only a few irregular shanghai huts without any whitewash. The barn was gone. Rails

of the cross fences had fallen into decay. Three or four lean work
mules grazed in the meadows where Prince and Madelon and
Brown Hal once played. From the road he could see that the
glazed flower pit in the garden was a ruin. The office in the front
yard where he had slept had been burned and honeysuckles
had shrouded the scar. The old manor itself, which once had
gleamed whitely through the trees, was weathered to a wasp's-
nest gray [p. 422].

The Lacefields, stripped of their free and unlimited labor and
despoiled by Federal occupation and Reconstruction, become
pathetic remnants of a vanished time.

In contrast to the aristocracy are the former slaves, burdened
by the responsibilities inherent in their new-found freedom.
The Vaidens' slaves—like the other four million across the
South—have no place to go. Survival itself becomes their pri-
mary concern. When Lump Mowbray attempts to explain the
theory behind their emancipation, Columbus asks only one
question: how will they eat?

> "We-all stan' on de same plane now. Abraham Lincoln done lif'
> God's chillun up."
> "Yeh, but he ain't gwi 'sport nobody aftuh he lif' 'em up," said
> Columbus gloomily.
> "Oh, Brothahs, oh, Sistahs, what do de Bible say?" chanted
> Lump. "Hit say, take no heed of to-marr'; sufficient unto de day
> is de ebil dar of."
> "Yeh, but ebil ain't grub," complained Columbus. "You can
> 'pend on there bein' plenty of ebil eber day, but how 'bout de
> grub?" [p. 399].

Like their former owners, the slaves must now create new lives
for themselves and their families in an unfamiliar world.

Although *The Forge* touches on the lives of aristocrats and
slaves, its emphasis is on the Vaidens, a family of yeoman stock
much like Stribling's own ancestors. The Vaidens do own
slaves, but they live a meager existence nevertheless, depend-

ing on a few poorly farmed acres and credit at the local store for their livelihood. The patriarch of the family, old man Jimmie Vaiden, personifies the agrarian ideal. His indomitable spirit brought him, as a young man, to the wilderness of north Alabama where he cleared his land and built his home. A blacksmith by trade, he erected a forge where he shod horses and hammered out plowshares that carved the wilderness into a habitable land for himself and his neighbors. Then came "stables, barns, a cotton gin, slave quarters: a progressive building to house the lusty reproduction of his stock, his negroes and his own body" (p. 1). Thus, the way of life which the old man builds for his family is grounded in the values and traditions of the Old South.

In a futile attempt to cling to the past, old man Jimmie returns, finally, to his run-down forge, a symbol of the Old Order forever gone. After several unsuccessful efforts to build a fire, his frustration and anger precipitate a fatal heart attack. As the old man dies, Gracie, his former house servant, embraces him and reveals that she is his own daughter:

> The old man made a great exertion, put up a hand and pushed away the face of the woman who held him.
> "You—nigger," he panted, "lay me down—lay me back down—in the dirt—" [pp. 524–25].

Unlike his father, Miltiades accepts the fact that life can never be as it was before the war—nor does he wish it so. As overseer on the Lacefield plantation, his only opportunity to advance socially and financially lies with his forthcoming marriage to Drusilla. When she forsakes him for the aristocratic Emory Crowningshield, Milt responds to Marcia: "Well, . . . this ends six years of work and hope. . . . Everything I wanted was back there—beauty, taste, station" (p. 150). Ironically, Milt fights during the war to preserve the way of life that has kept him in subservience; only after the South is defeated can he rise above his inherited social position.

Miltiades's determination to secure his niche in the New Order is reinforced by General Beekman's prediction of the future economic structure in the South:

"And incidentally, gentlemen, from now henceforth you are going to have to obtain the products of negro labor by round-about methods, chicane, finesse, and not by simple force. In other words, you will cease to be gentlemen and become traders, landlords, and business men. In fact, you may fall to the low estate of Yankees and be forced to use your wits all the time" [p. 493].

Now bankrupt, and without means to secure credit, Miltiades realizes that he can succeed only as a member of the mercantile class:

It flickered through the head of the rider that if the negroes had become free legal agents, with the right to make contracts and do business for themselves, then the man who bought from them and sold to them would be the man in all probability who, finally, would receive their earnings. . . .

A twitch, almost of mirth, went through Miltiades. The reins of power in the South would be transferred to tradesmen, to shopkeepers, to men like Handback, or even to such a grub as Alex BeShears. . . .

He was suddenly a free soul. He would take up things as they were and do with them with the utmost wisdom he could summon for the benefit of himself.

As he pursued this line intently he thought again of Alex BeShears and, a half second later, of Ponny. The image of the big, blond, comely girl, who one day would inherit whatever her grasping father had accumulated, brought the rider up at sharp attention.

The question came to his mind: if he meant to take up and use the most suitable weapon at hand . . . what of Ponny? [pp. 510–11].

The war had given Colonel Vaiden his title of honor, but it is his marriage to Ponny that ultimately delivers into his hands the

reins of power as a member of the New Order, the rising mercantile class.

Thus, in *The Forge*, Stribling accomplishes the task that he
had set for himself, "to write a story which would preserve as
long as might be that beloved world" of his ancestors. Through
the lives of the Vaidens and their milieu, the work captures the
essence of an age. Old man Jimmie, who refuses to accept the
changes brought about by the war, and Miltiades, who profits
from them, are symbolic of the diverse attitudes present in the
South at the time. Yet the novel is much more than the chronicle of a family. It is, in fact, the chronicle of the Old South itself,
the story of an entire race caught up in the disintegration of
their world.

NOTES TO INTRODUCTION

1. Charles C. Baldwin, *The Men Who Make Our Novels*, rev. ed.
(New York: Dodd, Mead and Company, 1924), p. 471.
2. T. S. Stribling, *Laughing Stock*, ed. Randy K. Cross and John T.
McMillan (Memphis: St. Luke's Press, 1982), p. 165.
3. Ibid., p. 57.
4. Ibid., pp. 192–93.
5. Ibid., p. 129.
6. Ibid., p. xi.

CHAPTER ONE

O LD MAN Jimmie Vaiden's home was half a house and half a fort. It was built of hewn logs with high narrow windows that were lineal descendants of portholes.

The thundering old man himself was not aware of this martial kinship of his dwelling. It was thus that log houses were fashioned in Alabama, years ago, when he and his family and his slaves had immigrated from South Carolina; therefore he had built his home so, with the unplanning certitude of a wasp.

The pioneer, James Vaiden, added other structures to his holdings from time to time. Across the rutted public road from his dwelling house stood a forge, because he was a blacksmith by trade before he became a landed man. After the forge came stables, barns, a cotton gin, slave quarters: a progressive building to house the lusty reproduction of his stock, his negroes and his own body.

All this ebullience of life was not prosperous in the American sense of that term. It was not arranged and focused on the merchantable. It was a fecundity quite as unplanned as the shaping of the houses. With the Vaidens all things followed the casualness of Nature: their cows calved, their sows littered, their mares foaled, their fox hounds pupped when they listed. The black women on the place produced by hap and chance certain small gurgling, cooing articles of merchandise which later might have been traded but never were.

Old man Jimmie Vaiden's wife, Laura Vaiden, had had

ten children. Six were born at brief intervals before and after the Vaidens had settled in Alabama. Then came a seven- or eight-year truce with the stork, after which, rather surprisingly, four more babies were born. These sets of children were almost as isolated from each other as parents are from their children. Any child in the younger set expected dissympathy and criticism from any brother or sister in the older set, quite regardless of the nature of the project it had in hand.

However, this attitude of perpetual derogation was not so irrational as it sounds. It was based, subconsciously, on the law of averages. The elders arrived at a prompt and monotonously correct judgment when they condemned all activities whatsoever among their younger brothers and sisters.

Take for example Polycarp and Augustus Vaiden, *ætat.* sixteen and fifteen respectively. These young gentlemen had swung two cats by their tails over the lower limb of a black oak which grew in the yard. This provoked instant and frantic hostilities. Beneath the exhibition four or five of the younger set of the fox hounds leaped and yelped at the cats which were just out of their distance. The older dogs, bony and sophisticated, lay curled up in the April sunshine and cracked a single bored eye at the leaping pups and shrieking cats, then closed it again and tried to sleep, or got up and moved awkwardly away after the manner of stiff old fox hounds.

Suddenly, in the midst of this uproar, the pups abandoned the cats, and every hound on the place bolted over the fence with a waving of slim tails and deployed up the road howling to a key more melancholy than ferocious.

The next instant out of one of the slave cabins flanking the big house toward the south ran a negro man. As he came through the front yard he called out:

"You, Gus and Carp, I'm a-goin' to tell ol' Pap on you, hangin' up them cats . . ." then, without a pause, he ran to the fence, climbed astride the top rail, and vented resonant threats:

"You, Roxana! Come on back here, Hyder Ali! What you mean, Bulger! You low-down whelps! Come back in this yard or I'll bust yo' haids."

This vituperation was automatic as the black man peered up the road with the lively interest of a rustic to see what wayfarer the fox hounds had scented.

Four minutes later when a horse and rider rounded the turn of the long red road the negro distinguished nothing more than a certain proportion of white and bay in the horse, but that was identifying.

The two white boys had loosed their cats and now came to the fence,

"Who is it, George?" asked Polycarp.

"Go tell ol' Pap, Pa'son Mulry's comin' on his calico pony," directed the black man in a flatted voice.

The younger brother, Augustus, remarked the change in the negro's tone.

"Well, what's the matter with Parson Mulry's coming?"

George appeared annoyed; he thrust out his thick lips.

"Nothin' ee matter. Jess you go tell ol' Pap Pa'son Mulry's comin' on he calico pony."

Augustus ran toward the heavy fort-like house excited by anyone passing along the public road. George continued on the top rail, all his heavy chocolate features involved in a frown. He was thinking with a touch of apprehension!

"Wondah what dat ol' Pa'son Mulry come heah fuh on prexactly dis day. . . . Wondah if dat ol' secon'-sighted Pa'son Mulry foun' out whut I was a gwinter do. . . ."

Here he pressed the outside of the pocket of his homespun trousers and felt the outline of a spoon against his flank. It was a silver spoon. He had just stolen it from the kitchen of the big house with a vague idea of maneuvering himself into a position where he could commit murder or inflict serious injury upon anyone toward whom he felt disposed. His

lethal weapon was this spoon. Now here in the midst of his
preparations came old Parson Mulry, who was a weird.
Either the old man already knew his criminal designs, or
something had sent him to find out. What that something
was George did not inquire. A feeling of fatality suddenly
hung in the bright spring sunshine; it brooded over the
fort-like house and above the red woundings of the hill
where Columbus and Robinet, two older negro men, plowed
for cotton planting. And all this indefinite malevolence had
gathered over George because he had one of old Missus's
silver spoons in his pocket.

Old man Jimmie Vaiden came hallooing out of the big
open hallway that divided his house into halves.

"Hello, Brother Bennie! Light and rest yore saddle,
Brother Bennie! How you feel being jest an Alabamian,
Brother Bennie, with no connection with the dad-blamed
Yankees?"

The old itinerant preacher lifted a hand and answered in
the chanting sing-song he used in his pulpit:

"It was *bound* . . . to come to *that* . . . Brother
Jimmie."

The evangelist tossed his reins to George and dismounted
stiffly from his horse.

"Shore! Shore!" agreed the planter. "It's a load off my
mind, Brother Bennie. I breathe freer. I don't want no
connection whatever with a passel of dad-burned abolitionists!"

"Now, Brother *Jimmie* . . . what does the *B*ible say?
. . . It says *a-s-k* yore brother to repentance . . . nine
and ninety times."

The planter was a powerful old man with a thick neck
and now his face flushed under his white hair.

"Brothers! Thunder an' Aleck, Bennie Mulry, they ain't
no brothers of ours. I believe the lost tribe of the House of
Israel was a symbol of the whole plaguey Yankee nation!
They're agin common sense. They're agin civilization.

They're agin the Bible itself, and Abe Lincoln is their Antichrist!"

"How is *that* . . . Brother *Jimm*ie?" sang the parson.

"Why, if the Almighty hadn't meant for the nigger to be a slave would He have wrote, 'and Ham shall be his servant and dwell in the tents of Japhet forever'? . . . Ain't the nigger Ham?"

Both minister and planter were of one mind on this point but both possessed that legal temperament normal to the South which took the converse of any proposition whatsoever. Now the old parson intoned:

"The nigger is *Ham*, Brother Jimmie, but do *you* claim to be one of the Jews?"

"Why, plague take yore hide, of course I ain't one of the Jews, Bennie Mulry!"

"Who was Japhet the *son* of?"

"Who? Why, Noah, of course! But dad blame it, Bennie Mulry, in writing His Holy Word, God'l Mighty used Japhet as a symbol of the white race! Daggone it, Bennie, the Jew was as clost to a white man as the Lord had made up to that time, so He jest used Japhet as a symbol . . . meaning us."

In their hearts both old gentlemen agreed to this. It explained life to them: the black men reddening the slopes of the hill, the slave quarters, Nigger George standing ready to catch the parson's rein when he tossed it to him. The preacher moved beside his host from gate to porch, combing his thoughts for another anti-slavery argument, when the old planter added a complacent Q.E.D.:

"Yes, it's as plain as the nose on a man's face that the nigger was pre*des*tined to be a slave."

The particular word old man Vaiden used was a red rag to the parson. Immediately he shifted his whole line of battle.

"Looky here, Brother *Jimm*ie . . . I wouldn't say pre*des*tined. . . . I wouldn't use that word, pre*des*tined."

"Yes, and why wouldn't you?" demanded the old planter instantly, equally irritated. "Because you're a daggoned wishy-washy old Methodist preacher, who ain't got the backbone to eat the strong meat of the Word and air goin' to drink milk all yore life with the rest of them logical babies— yore Methodist brethren!"

"But looky here!" sang the preacher earnestly, "Looky what you're gittin' *into*. . . . It's all right to apply predestination to the nigger . . . of course he's pre*dest*ined . . . but don't han'l that term too *loose* . . . you don't want to apply it to the *white* man!"

"As a Hardshell Babtist and a gentleman, that's exactly what I want to do!" cried the planter. "I apply her wherever she hits, white or black, high or low, ministers, laymen, or sinners. They ain't nobody too good for me to apply God's Word to! I'm a meat-eatin' Babtist, not a spin'lin' milk-drinkin' Methodis' like St. Paul tells about."

The two old men moved into the open end of the big hall booming scriptural allusions at each other and filling the sunshine with their theology.

A girl with brown hair and extraordinary eyes came to the entrance of the hallway and stood looking at the old wranglers. Not a word of their debate penetrated her attention. She watched simply for a gap in their quiddities, and presently, catching a pause, asked quickly:

"Pap, can I ride old Joe over to the BeShearses'?"

"Marsh," directed the old man in his outdoor voice, "Go tell yore maw Brother Mulry's come and have Creasy ketch a chicken."

"She's already doing it . . . can't you hear the dawgs? Say, Pap, can I ride old Joe over to the BeShearses'?"

The old planter listened a moment to the shrill cackle of a hen and the baritone shouts of an old negro woman hissing on her dog. The preacher chanted:

"But looky here, Brother Jimmie, how could a loving, all-merciful God create a living soul . . . in his own *image*

. . . with a direct purpose . . . of burnin' it in hell forever?"

"Why, Bennie, that's God's crownin' joy for His elect, to be flyin' around through the sweet airs of heaven and remember that nearly ever'body else has gone to hell."

The two old men passed the girl in the hallway and entered a dark living room where a log smouldered in a great fireplace. The girl at the door interposed once more to ask if she could ride old Joe which her father kept standing saddled and bridled at the gate.

This time old man Jimmie Vaiden heard her and the thought of old Joe being ridden away by his daughter annoyed him.

"No, no, Marsh, I might be called somewhere."

"Who'd call you?"

"How in the thunder do I know? If I knew I'd git on my horse and go there now!"

"I wanted to go to see Ponny BeShears," said the girl in a hopeless tone.

"Ponny BeShears! And a lot of good her silly chatter'll do you! Come in here and set down and listen to me and Brother Bennie and we'll learn you something about the Bible."

"I don't see why I can't have old Joe . . ."

The girl turned, walked across the wide hallway to the company room on the other side. She entered this, an equally dark but cleaner and more formal replica of the living room. She glanced at a tall thin woman sitting with a book at a table. The reader was old enough to have been the girl's mother. Now she laid down her book and stated as a fact, not as a question:

"He wouldn't let you have him."

"He said he might be called off somewhere."

"I fancy somebody calling him away from that preacher," stated the woman ironically.

"Sister Cassandra, you ask Pap to let me have old Joe."

The elder sister clicked her tongue against her teeth.

"*Tchk!* The idea of me going to that trouble so you can visit Ponny BeShears. Ponny's too . . . she's too beefy . . . she makes such a show of herself."

"She can't help it."

"She could . . . corset herself in. She doesn't want to help it! Every time she sees a man she's slapping him and bulbing around him."

Miss Cassandra clicked again, resumed her book, adjusting it to the light from a small delicately curtained high window.

The girl with the gray eyes and the hair and the finely turned lips drew a long breath and walked across the room to the fireplace. The hearth in this room was brick instead of stone, and here too a little fire burned. But the room was chilly and this made the delicate lace curtains look like designs of frost. They were handmade curtains and formed an odd contrast to the heavy, flattened, whitewashed logs that made up the walls of the room.

The girl stood before the smoldering fire in silent rebellion against the monastic silence of the room.

"Oh, sit down, Marcia, and read," snapped Cassandra at last. "Improve your mind . . . you've got a good mind if you weren't so lazy."

With a restlessness bordering on turmoil inside of her, Marcia supposed gloomily that she was lazy, and that her older sister Cassandra, complacently conning the pages of a book, was energetic.

"What are you reading?" asked the girl without interest.

"Paine's *Rights of Man.*"

"Tom Paine?"

"Yes."

"You oughtn't to read that book anyway," said the girl indifferently.

"Paine wrote about politics as well as religion," stated the woman with dignity.

"Oh, did he? Listen, Sister Cassandra . . . I wanted to go to the BeShearses'. Then I wanted to go on over to the Lacefields'. There's going to be a speaking over there to-night and I—I thought I might learn something."

The older woman turned to look at her sister.

"Who's going to speak?"

"The Honorable Emory Crowninshield. He's running for Congressman."

"Yes, I imagine you are interested in what the Honorable Emory will have to say."

"Well, you asked me to read about politics," cried the girl exasperated. "Now when they are really here . . ." She flung out her hands hopelessly to the slow fire.

"I imagine there is something else over there drawing you," hazarded the sister.

"M—m . . . dance, maybe . . . after the speaking."

"I thought so."

"But Sister Cassandra, I'll have to hear the speaking! It'll improve my mind that much."

The improvement of Marcia's mind was not exactly a sore point between the older and the younger sister but it was an uncomfortable one. It was well understood between them that Cassandra's mind was improved and Marcia's un-improved. It was Cassandra's ambition to have her younger sister reach her own high estate, and Marcia was forced into a sort of bored consent that this would be a good thing, but that was as far as they had ever got with the undertaking.

"You'll be cutting your eyes at that young A. Gray Lacefield," stated Miss Cassandra disapprovingly.

"I'll hear the speech," repeated Marcia, sticking to her guns.

Miss Cassandra laid down her *Rights of Man* face up.

"M—m . . . yes . . . much good it'll do you. . . . Well, what are you going to wear?"

"Oh, am I going to get to go!"

"Oh, I suppose you are. The secession of the South will

be almost as historical as the Revolution some day, maybe."

"Why, my silk dress, of course."

"You have two."

Marcia became anxious.

"Well . . . my new one, I suppose." Then she began talking quickly to change the topic. "Sister Cassandra, do you really think our state seceding is as important as the Revolutionary War?"

"Now listen," said Cassandra, "your best dress was not made to wear to frivolous things like dances."

"But Sister Cassandra," cried Marcia in distress, "it's a speaking, too. The Honorable Emory Crowninshield will be there."

"He'll never notice you."

"Of course he won't if I don't have on my good dress!"

"Well, I hope you don't *want* him to notice you!"

This, of course, cut the very earth from under Marcia's feet. A dress must be worn with an eye to meeting the amount of notice she would have received without it. That was modesty. It was logic, and as usual it filled Marcia with exasperation.

"Look here!" she cried. "I'm not a child. It's my dress and I'm going to wear it!"

"Who gave you the dress?"

"You did, but it's mine!"

"All right . . . all right . . . then you can go to Father for yourself and see if you can get old Joe. . . . A dance musses a dress."

"Oh! Oh, me!" Marcia clenched her slim fists and tears brightened her eyes. "To have a new dress and not get to dance in it!"

Miss Cassandra was annoyed by a feeling of sympathy for her sister.

"What do you want to be dressing up to go over to the Lacefields' for!"

"Why, they've got the nicest home in the Reserve!"

"What if they have? They are not intellectual or am-. bitious. If it wasn't for Miltiades that whole Lacefield family wouldn't know their heels from their heads!"

This referred to the fact that Miltiades Vaiden, one of the older set of the Vaiden children, was an overseer on the Lacefield plantation. Miss Cassandra always felt that the Lacefields, taken as a group, were leaning heavily on Miltiades for their existence. Marcia also believed this to be true, but as she was angry with her older sister she said nothing.

"And I don't see what he wants with that little flibberdegibbet, Drusilla," pursued Miss Cassandra adversely. "She's a Lacefield all over—no bottom to her. I hate to see one of my brothers marry a Lacefield . . . or my sister either," she added meaningly after a pause.

This indirect disparagement of Drusilla Lacefield put Marcia into a somewhat better humor, so she said, tacitly agreeing to the second-best dress:

"All right . . . go ask Pap for me."

Miss Cassandra laid aside the *Rights of Man* and arose from her chair when the two sisters heard the loud voices of the two old men coming out of the living room.

"No . . . no, Brother Bennie, there won't be any war. The idyah of there bein' a war because the Southern states seceded from a voluntary union! . . . It was a voluntary union, Brother Bennie . . . we went in because we wanted to and it stands to reason we can get out when we want to."

"Old Abe and his Abolitionists ain't goin' to like it . . . they ain't going to like it, Brother *Jim*mie!"

"What if they don't like it! The aristocratic part of this country don't belong to the Northern riff-raff, I hope!"

"They may come down and try to *make* us come back, Brother *Jim*mie."

"Make us! Thunder an' Aleck, Brother Bennie, they're bound to have more sense than to try to make us! A lot of cobblers and store keepers comin' down to fight anybody or

anything! Thunderation, one gentleman could twist the
tails of a whole regiment of tailors and peddlers and send
'em whooping back up North where they come from!"

The last of this defiance was barely audible to the sisters
because the old men were walking out to the gate again.

A shock of apprehension seized Marcia.

"Oh, Cassandra, stop him! Run stop him! He's going
away on old Joe!"

At the same instant from the cooking quarters in the
rear of the house came the desperate cry of an old negro
woman:

"Hey, Pap . . . stop, Pap . . . dinner's ready. . . .
Miss Cassandra, stop ol' Pap. Dinner's ready!"

A white woman's voice took up the outcry:

"Cassandra, stop your pappy and tell him dinner's
ready!"

Both sisters rushed to the end of the open hallway.

"Pappy! Pappy! Come back, you and Brother Mulry
. . . dinner's ready!"

From under the black oaks in the front yard, Augustus
and Polycarp were relaying the same information in
anxious shouts. The dogs broke into a wailing chorus.

The preacher paused uncertainly but the father of the
family moved inevitably out the big gate and mounted his
horse.

As George handed up the reins he ventured:

"Ol' Pap, Missus say dinnah is ready."

"Don't I know it!" boomed the old man. "I'll be back!"

The two old men turned their horses and moved up the
road toward the blacksmith shop and the gin on some un-
imaginable errand.

The rest of the Vaiden household stood in the yard, in
the front hallway, in the back raised passage between
kitchen and dining room, watching in acute and collective
exasperation the departure of the head of the house.

Old man Jimmie always, always was moved to ride forth

on the eve of the twelve o'clock meal. And always the family must wait till he returned sometime in the afternoon, when the chicken would be stiff, the biscuits cold, the gravy congealed, and nothing would be right down to the salt and pepper.

The family stood a moment longer watching the old planter and the parson ride away. Old Mrs. Vaiden then turned back into the kitchen, shaking her head with the resignation of three decades of living with James Vaiden. She would replace everything in pots and kettles and skillets and keep the dinner warm for an indefinite time as best she and her black women could.

CHAPTER TWO

THE riding away of old man Vaiden was to Marcia not only a vanishing dinner, it was a vanishing dance.

"I vow, Sister Cassandra," she ejaculated, wriggling her slim shoulders in acute disappointment. "You didn't do a thing!"

"Not a thing," agreed Miss Cassandra, in the flat tone of one who is also disgusted.

"I wish something would happen so he would have to come back!"

"Oh, hush!"—then, as an afterthought, "go on upstairs and help Gracie with that wool!"

It was characteristic of the Vaiden family that no member of it ever really heard any other member speak except under aural duress. Marcia pursued her own bitterness!

"Pap's not going off for anything at all . . . he's just going!"

The girl and the woman walked back into the company room. Miss Cassandra resumed her seat and the *Rights of Man*. Marcia went to the hearth and stood before the fire. For several minutes her silent recriminations subconsciously annoyed the elder sister until at last Miss Cassandra discovered what was the cause of the psychic disturbance and snapped out:

"Marcia, do get a book and read!"

The girl looked at the books with distaste. One had a black binding and this one she knew by reputation to be a history of something or other. She inched slowly nearer. The back of another reported itself to be an advanced algebra with which she had nothing at all in common. There were poems by Wordsworth, essays by Voltaire: one of which Marcia considered beneficial, if she had wanted to be benefited, the other she held to be wicked although this particular collection held no reference to the tender subject of religion.

The very way her sister looked at the books was subcutaneously annoying to Miss Cassandra. It was the look of a girl who would not improve a very good natural mind. This non-improvement, one might say, Miss Cassandra could feel going on from moment to moment, and this so annoyed the older sister that she couldn't improve her own mind either.

The droning of a spinning wheel upstairs reminded the spinster that she had told Marcia to do something long ago and had forgotten it. So she rapped out:

"Marcia, go up and help Gracie spin that wool!"

"Well . . . all right," agreed the girl with resignation.

Marcia moved slowly away from the books to the hearth and sank down in a home-made armchair. It was a capacious chair with curving hickory slats at the back, voluptuous with the warmth of the fire. The bottom had long since bagged down and adjusted itself perfectly to human buttocks. The front round of the seat was a little too high and pressed with a slight degree of discomfort against the underpart of the girl's thighs. But by doubling up a leg and sitting on her foot she managed that. Her posture, which would have broken a man in two at the ankle, knee, and hip, yielded the girl a profound comfort.

She looked into the coals and fell into a dreamy enjoyment of fulgent faces and castles and landscapes, all done, not so much in miniature, as far, far away—as far away, perhaps, as the sunset. Single sparks lay gazing at Marcia and dwindled and dwindled, and then, just before they died, they brightened to a point of dazzling brilliance, as if

shooting forth rays like arms for help, then turned abruptly
into undiscernible ash. This suggestion of pathos and death
stirred the girl to a sad and exquisite poetry in the midst
of her flexible and immortal youth.

The elder sister glanced around and exclaimed out of all
patience:

"Marcia, why *don't* you read Wordsworth and improve
your mind?"

"Oh, Cassandra . . ." cadenced the younger sister in a
voice that tacitly agreed that, while her own mental vagaries
were not only vain but downright harmful, the very same
sort of mental processes indulged in by a stodgy old
Englishman decades before she was born contained great
cultural and intellectual benefits.

"Well, if you won't do that, go and help Gracie spin as
I told you to do!"

Marcia glanced around in surprise and annoyance.

"Cassandra, didn't I tell you . . . I . . . would?"

She returned her eyes to the fire with an injured feeling.
It was exasperating to have Cassandra bring up for a third
time a chore which she had disposed of mentally long ago.

In the midst of this conflict between realism and idealism,
the voice of old man Vaiden boomed urgently from the
yard:

"George . . . Polycarp . . . Augustus! You   trifling
boys, come here!"

Both sisters jumped and ran out into the hallway. Marcia
saw George come running from the direction of the plum
thicket below the slave houses.

"What's the mattah, ol' Pap?" hallooed the black youth
excitedly.

"Come here and help me hold him! Brother Bennie's had
a spell! He fell off his mare!"

"Pappy, how come that?" cried Mrs. Vaiden from the
kitchen.

"Lorry, how in the thunderation do I know!" roared her

husband. "He jest had one of his spells. . . . Come on here, George and Carp . . . help me git him in!"

The helpers came a little apprehensively, because old Brother Bennie's spells were not ordinary sickness. There was, in fact, more than a touch of the uncanny about the old minister. As Polycarp came up, the sick man shielded his face from the sunlight with an expression of agony and groaned:

"Oh, my head . . . it's splittin' open. Git me into the house."

"That's where we're gittin' you, Brother Bennie, quick as we can," comforted the old planter, trying to temper his big voice. "Carp," he snapped, "put his arm *over* your shoulder, you awkward mule!"

Polycarp hastily made the shift. His mistake had come about through a fascinated gazing at the scalp under the thin hairs of the suffering man. Polycarp had heard many times that when Brother Mulry had these seizures seams opened in his skull. And these openings admitted to the old man's brain information of distant events.

Polycarp held back his edged curiosity as best he could and gave the old minister his earnest assistance. They got him into the hallway, then into the family room and onto Mr. and Mrs. Vaiden's great four-poster. There he lay groaning with his eyes shut, but evidently the dark interior of the room brought him some relief.

Polycarp backed slowly out of the door, still gazing fixedly at the figure on the bed. He said to Cassandra in a low tone:

"How does it work, Sister Cassandra? What splits his skull open so he can see things?"

"It doesn't work at all," stated Cassandra in a brusque undertone. Then she looked at the groaning old man with a vague apprehension in her heart lest, after all, it might work.

"What is he saying?" asked old Mrs. Vaiden of her husband as she leaned over the bed to place a cold cloth on the preacher's head.

The wife's low question offended the planter.

"Why, nothin', Lorry. What would he want to say anything for when his head hurts? He's groanin'."

"He does say things, Pappy."

"He may say things, but they don't mean anything."

"They do sometimes. He told Salvina Ham what had become of her brooch that she lost two year before."

"Did they find the brooch?" asked the planter in an ironical tone.

"No, but he told her what went with it. He said she dropped it in the creek."

"Whyn't he tell her where it was in the creek?"

"I don't know," murmured the little old woman wonderingly; "he just said she dropped it in the creek."

"Oh, Mother!" shamed Cassandra, who was not superstitious.

"Lorry," flung out old man Vaiden, "you're just as wool gathering as any nigger we've got in the cottonfield."

"He did it in lots of other places, too," whispered the old woman, nodding her head with perfect evenness of temper.

"But Lorry, there ain't any seers and soothsayers now, I tell you. They was once, but the dispensation of Jesus Christ done away with all of them. God'l Mighty don't give out them powers any more."

But the old woman continued closing her eyes and nodding her head slowly as she wrung out and applied the cold cloths.

"Pshaw!" ejaculated old man Jimmie, who had known that serene nodding for many years and with all his blustering had never changed it a barleycorn from any given opinion. He moved to the door as if to go out. At the threshold he hesitated and turned back. He looked hard at the figure on the bed and finally asked in a skeptical tone:

"Ain't he jest groaning? Is he saying anything? What's he saying?"

At this Polycarp, Augustus, and Marcia came closer to the bed and listened intently. The door that led toward the dining room framed the heads of George, the black gargoyle face of old Aunt Creasy, and the oddly regular cream-colored features of Gracie.

Marcia stood next to her mother quite close to the invalid. She looked at him intently, listening with her younger and acuter hearing. Presently she glanced around with wide gray eyes.

"He's saying 'cannons,' " she breathed.

"Cannons!" ejaculated the old planter.

Old Mrs. Vaiden closed her eyes and nodded her head smoothly.

"Cannons, Jimmie," she repeated complacently.

"Well, Thunder and Aleck, what if he is saying cannons!" flung out the old man. "That don't make any sense!"

"That don't, but whatever goes with it I'm sure will make sense——" She broke off her own words to listen intently and everyone in the room listened with her.

The prostrate man was mumbling:

"Firing cannons . . . a house . . . a heavy old house . . . knocking it to pieces. . . ."

To Marcia, leaning over the bed, the room in which she was standing, the house, the plantation around her seemed to dissolve and give her an impression of vast and indeterminate distances. Somewhere in the world a scene of violence registered on her imagination through the words of a cataleptic old preacher. His mumblings became pegs upon which to hang her vision.

The old preacher spoke brokenly and at longer and shorter intervals:

"A fort . . . the men in the fort are firing back . . . ships . . . the ocean . . . smoke . . . the powder smoke hurts my head . . . the explosions . . . Look! Look!

. . ." He lifted the eyebrows of his closed eyes as if he were widening his gaze. "Look . . . the flag is coming down . . . in the smoke!"

"Where in the world do you suppose he's seeing to?" murmured old Mrs. Vaiden, staring at Marcia.

"Why, nowhere, nowhere a tall," scouted the old man in a disgusted undertone. "I declare I've raised a passel of fools right here in my own house!"

"Oh, yes, he's seein' that somewhere," whispered the little old woman, "and it'll have something to do with us, Jimmie."

This passed the limit of the old realist's endurance.

"Do with us! My Lord, Lorry, I hate a fool!"

The old woman looked around solemnly at her husband.

"Jimmie, he never tells anybody anything unless it has something to do with 'em. Why should he?"

"Maybe he's like the prophets?" hazarded Marcia in a hushed voice.

"Prophets!" interrupted her father. "Marsh, God finished his maracles eighteen hun'erd and sixty-four year ago and there hasn't been a prophet sence. He give us a book to go by. He put ever'thing down in black and white and nobody's heard a word from Him sence."

This, of course, was undeniable doctrine. Old Mrs. Vaiden stirred uneasily.

"Anyway . . . it makes me feel queer."

"Well, daggone it, git over your queerness. Don't stand there believin' the ravings of a delirious man. I tell you, ask him something you know about. If we don't settle this one way or the other we'll be disputin' about it till Kingdom Come."

"You'll be disputin'," whispered the old woman calmly.

"I wouldn't dispute if you wouldn't set aroun' thinking such fool things."

Old Mrs. Vaiden cast about in her mind for something closer home than a cannonaded fort.

"Brother Mulry," she began. She reached over and shook

him gently to get his attention by the time she got her question. "Er . . . Brother Mulry, one of my spoons is missing . . . a small silver spoon——" She broke off and listened carefully to a mumbling. "What—what did you say, Brother Mulry?"

"Uh huh. I knowed it—don't know a thing!"

"What . . . plum thicket! A little furnace in the plum thicket!" ejaculated the old wife in amazement. "What in the world is it doing out there?"

"Uh huh, I told you he wouldn't make no sense!"

But Polycarp and Augustus already had started for the plum thicket. Mrs. Vaiden got up from the bed and gave the cloth and pan to Marcia.

"Who in the world put my spoon in a furnace in the plum thicket!"

She was off, out the door, with a level judicial anger against anyone who had outraged one of her silver spoons.

Old Mr. Vaiden followed in complete disgust.

"Of all wild-goose chases . . . sick man out of his head mumbles about spoons and furnaces and off goes Lorry like a jug handle . . . highest-tempered person I ever seen!"

He went out of hearing thus, fuming his disgust for such a powdery woman.

The girl Marcia had no interest in the spoon. She sat by the side of the bed, changing the cold cloths but wrapped in the glamour of distant happenings that had drifted in so strangely upon her.

Suppose she herself could float out of her body and see things afar off. . . . She fancied herself moving, disembodied, over fields and rivers and mountains. And at this vision of herself the words of an old song came to her mind:

I wish I were a little bird.
I'd fly to the top of a tree,
And there I'd find my own true love—
Oh, somebody waits for me. . . .

CHAPTER THREE

I<small>N THE</small> plum thicket, queerly enough, the Vaidens found a little furnace. A blue thread of smoke still winding up from its embers marked its position in the small dense thicket. It had been improvised of a few stones and a piece of a skillet. A bright streak on the rusty iron showed where some metal had been melted and poured.

Old man Vaiden looked at the furnace, then back at the log house which he could barely see through the pale green gauze of the budding plum bushes.

"Thunderation, Lorry!" he burst out. "You kain't tell me that old man Bennie Mulry laid in my bed with a wet rag over his eyes and knowed this was here without seeing it! He didn't do it! He noticed it before somehow. . . . George! Oh, George!"

"What do you want, Pap?" asked Polycarp.

"I want to know if George mentioned this to Bennie Mulry when he hitched his horse. . . . Oh, George, you better come to me, nigger!"

The old planter was disturbed and somehow antagonized by this slight touch of the inexplicable. He wanted to clear it up. He wanted George to have told the old preacher about the furnace to sweep away the possibility that anything unusual had happened on his plantation.

"Why, no, you know he didn't tell Brother Mulry," said Polycarp, very much wanting the preacher's source of information to be the hypothetical crack in his skull.

Old man Vaiden's pink face reddened.

"I don't know any such thing. He found out somehow, didn't he?"

"Why, sure," exclaimed Polycarp with enthusiasm, "the crack in his skull!"

"Crack in your skull, you better say! There you go! Your mammy made over! B'lieve any fool tale you hear!"

Old Mrs. Vaiden stood looking at the little furnace, entirely oblivious to these aspersions cast upon her credulity. She stooped and picked up a broken flint arrowhead that lay on the ground and scratched at the silver streak on the iron.

"Look at this, Jimmie," she said in a level continuation of her anger. "I believe this is silver . . . somebody really melted one of my spoons."

"But Lorry," expostulated the old man, "he's bound somehow or other to have knowed it before. He couldn't 'a' laid there and guessed it!"

"Jimmie, I tell you somebody has melted my spoon!"

"Oh . . . your spoon . . . it's your daggone spoon, *you're* thinkin' about! By the gray goats, Lorry, if Jesus Christ should come down again and change watter to wine, you'd want to know how much wine He'd changed."

To the old woman her husband's fulminating irony was simply another continuous racket that went on around the place like the barking of the dogs and the cackling of the hens. She held the piece of the skillet up to him,

"You can see for yourself this is silver. Now what in the world did that lazy nigger George want to melt one of my spoons for?"

The old planter brought around his sense of logic to bear on this.

"What makes you think George done it?"

"Nobody else has any reason to."

"Well, what reason has George to?"

"That's what puzzles me. I can't think of a reason in

the world why George should melt up one of my solid silver spoons. . . . What made him do it?"

"Lissen to that! Lissen to it!" shouted the old man to the world at large. "You know nobody else done it because they had no reason to, and you know George did do it because he had no reason to either. I declare, Lorry, I might jest as well have married a out-and-out idiot when I took you!"

"Well, what reason do you say he had?" inquired the old woman, who thought her husband was discussing the gist of the matter and not merely its form.

"I'm not sayin' George done it!" thundered the old man. "By the gray goats, I don't skip around like a flea, give one reason one minute for believing a thing and the next breath give the same reason for believing the opposite. I be dad burned if a womern's got any sense a tall!"

"Why, you know Nigger George done it!"

"I don't know any such thing. I haven't got a iota of proof against him!"

"Then let's ask Brother Mulry if George didn't do it?" suggested the old woman at once.

This was waving a red flag at a bull.

"Brother Mulry! Brother Mulry! What in the nation does Bennie Mulry know about this!"

The old woman was amazed.

"Well, he told us where the spoon was, didn't he? I reckon he'd know who put it there!"

"That's jest what you'd think! Well, the facts are jest opposite. It's jest a chance he guessed it was out here a tall. Now, to figger he could make two good guesses hand running and tell who put it here is out of all reason. It's like hoss racin'. If you pick a winner once, you better quit; you're shore to lose next time."

At such silly reasoning the old woman simply turned toward the house.

"You're bound to talk. You know Brother Mulry would

say George done it. But I'll ask him to make sure before I
have him whipped."

Old man Jimmie was exasperated.

"I'll not whop one of my niggers because a wishy-washy
Methodist preacher had a dream about him! That's somethin' I won't do, Lorry Vaiden. Le's call George an' ast
him."

"What's the use? He'd jest say he didn't do it."

"All right, then you've got to prove it before I'll lay a
finger on him!"

The old man followed his wife toward the house, crashing
through the thicket and getting flipped in the face by the
twigs for his hurry.

"George! George!" he trumpeted. "Come here, you
triflin' black rascal!"

As the old gentleman emerged from the thicket he saw a
black figure bending low on the far side of his front-yard
fence, making for the barn up the big road.

The sight of one of his negroes trying to slip away from
him always infuriated the planter. In fact the whole social
system of the South was hinged on the problem of not
allowing negroes to escape. Therefore the sight of a black
man actually slipping away envisaged the whole complexity
at a stroke.

"George! George!" he bellowed. "You low-down black
rascal! I see you! Come here, you triflin'——"

The next moment George broke into a run up the road.

"Polycarp! Augustus!" ol' Pap thundered. "Ketch that
daggone nigger and bring him here! Skin him alive!"

The next instant the two white boys dashed off with the
gusto of youth in a foot race. They sprinted across the
front yard, took the fence in mighty vaults which both were
proud to exhibit before their father. The fox hounds suddenly broke into tongue and went with the boys, flying up
the road after George.

Old man Jimmie Vaiden got to his horse, heaved himself

stiffly up on it, snatched the animal's head up the road, kicked him in the flanks, and was off after the mêlée.

The hare-brained George, hearing the shouts and barking behind him, took to the high ten-rail fence that lined the road side. The top rail rolled when he went over. He was not thrown backwards but he lost time getting across.

By now the dogs had reached him. They were swarming over the fence under the impression that this was the beginning of a glorified rabbit hunt. They did nothing to the negro.

The two white boys were close behind but they had just as much trouble with the fence as George did. While they were negotiating the top rail, they saw George, immediately beneath them, dash away and regain his lead.

This made Polycarp angry.

"George!" he yelled, "you dad-blamed nigger . . . make me run!" He half jumped, half fell from the fence, alighted on his feet and dashed off again.

The fugitive might still have got away, but from his horse the old planter saw his other negroes plowing in his field. Now he began roaring:

"Columbus! Robinet! Ketch that fool nigger and bring him to me or I'll take the hide off both your backs!"

Immediately Columbus and Robinet dropped their plows and deployed over the red freshly plowed earth with their arms spread out.

George began making desperate feints to throw these new men out of direction, but the plowed earth slowed him down. The hounds were now leaping and barking about the black men in everybody's way.

The white boys behind George rapidly overhauled him. Polycarp was so indignant that George should have run away from under his very nose that he made a flying blow at the negro's back, hit and overbalanced him, so that George came down on his all-fours in the soft earth.

The hounds hallelujahed all over George and Carp and

Augustus, licking their faces at every opportunity until Polycarp hit one on the snoot and that sent the whole pack flying in every direction.

George remained on his all-fours blinking at Polycarp.

"You—you hit me, Carp," he panted.

"Yes, I did, and I'll break that kinky head of yours, running from me like that. When I yell at you, you stop!"

George got up and spat.

"You hit me, Carp," he mumbled again.

"Say that over and I'll hit you agin!" snapped Polycarp, pale with anger.

George hushed and walked between the two white boys back to the fence where old man Vaiden waited on his horse.

"Come on down to the barn," cried the old man, shaking his riding crop at George. "I'll learn you how to play the wild-buck nigger with me!"

The trio climbed the fence again, taking plenty of time now. They moved back down the road with George and the boys ahead of the rider. As they went George looked gloomily over his shoulder and mumbled out:

"Ol' Pap . . . Carp hit me."

"What?" cried the old planter.

"Shut up!" whispered Polycarp savagely.

"Ar . . . hi . . . ee," mumbled the negro, still more obscurely on account of Polycarp's threat.

"Speak out! Speak out!" cried the old man angrily. "If you've got anything to say, say it and stop mumbling around."

George merely grunted.

"He is saying Carp hit him," repeated Augustus in the clear, impersonal voice of a younger brother who is willing to let the chips of parental wrath fall where they will so long as they don't fall on him.

"Polycarp," roared the father, "what did you hit George for?"

Polycarp was incensed in his turn.

"Well, you told me to catch him. I had to stop him, didn't I?"

"If you was close enough to hit him you was close enough to grab him! I've told you never to lay a finger on one of these niggers! But you were mad! You lost your temper! I'll teach you how to lose your temper . . . jest march into that barn with George!"

"Well, I be dad blame!" cried Polycarp, outraged at this turn of affairs. "Run my legs off tryin' to ketch him an' then git licked for it!"

At this moment old man Jimmie saw Augustus walking along with his face averted and the wrinkling of a grin on the side of his mouth.

"Gus!" cried the angry old man. "What are you grinning about? You jest walk in there too, with the rest of 'em! I'll teach you to be tattling on your brother! I hate a dad-blame informer of any kind!"

Augustus turned with a face not only sober but in consternation.

"Mammy! Mammy!" he began to yell in a terrific voice.

"Shut up! Shut up!" shouted the planter.

"Mammy!" he bawled. "I haven't done a thing! Mammy, all I done was to tell ol' Pap what George said! Mammy, he's goin' to lick us all because I told him what George said!"

This appeal was addressed apparently to the circumnambient air, but before old man Vaiden could get all the condemned into the barn, old Mrs. Laura materialized hurrying up the road. When she came within feminine talking distance she called out in merely interested tones:

"Pappy, what are you going to whip Augustus for?"

"Mammy, he just asked George——"

"Shut up!" boomed the planter. "For tattling on his brother, Lorry. . . . I hate a tattletale!"

"Just told him what George said."

"What did George say?" inquired Mrs. Vaiden placidly of her son.

"Said Carp hit him," wailed Augustus in his hollow, unnatural voice.

"Why did you hit George, Carp?" inquired the old woman sweetly.

"Why, he lost his temper and hit him!" snorted the old man.

"You don't mean it!" cried the mother sharply. "Polycarp, hasn't Pappy told you time and again you're not to strike any of the servants? And to lose your temper! The idyah of such a thing! Nobody on this place ever loses their temper and you certainly are not going to set a bad example before your father! Come on with me to the house this minute! Both you boys. I'll settle with you!"

Old man Jimmie was disgusted with his wife's laughing at him like this.

"Oh, all right! All right! Go on and spoil 'em! They're as much yores as mine . . . more, more. They're the spittin' image of you! George, you walk into that barn!"

"Pappy," placated the wife, "I wouldn't whip George too hard either . . . after all, he just took a spoon and melted it. I don't know what in the world he wanted to do such a stupid thing for?" She looked at George interrogatively.

"I'm not whipping him for stealing the spoon!" roared the old man. "I've got no proof he stole any spoon. I'm licking him because he run from me when I told him to come to me!"

"George," said the little old woman, shaking her head at the slave, "what makes you run from Pappy? You know he gets madder for that than anything you could possibly do."

And old Mrs. Laura and her two strapping boys went back to the big house together.

CHAPTER FOUR

ALL the members of the Vaiden household were affected in one way or another by George's punishment. For old man Jimmie Vaiden, the flogging of George had pushed into the background the uncanny clairvoyance of the parson; it had somehow reëstablished his complacence and his certitude in the established order of things. The old planter felt relieved and in good spirits again.

The whipping had disturbed Miss Cassandra. She had seen George walk through the yard, still stripped to the waist, with reddish and bluish marks on his chocolate back, holding his shirt and coat in his hand because he could not endure them against his skin. This sight annoyed Miss Cassandra and the image persisted and interfered with her reading when she tried to center her mind on Thomas Paine's *Rights of Man*.

She thought how her father's wrath would rise up explosively against his slaves. He would punish them for nothing, and then let something serious go unpunished. That was no way to handle negroes. Their discipline should be equable and uninterrupted. . . .

Here Marcia entered her door from the minister's sickroom. The girl evoked in her older sister an impression of dewiness and dawn. The sight of her cleared away the vague disturbance George had created in her mind. She said almost absentmindedly:

"Marcia, if you'll ask Father for old Joe you can get him now."

"What makes you think so?"

"He's had his spree. He'll be very obliging to everybody for two or three days."

"Oh . . . all right." Marcia whirled in the doorway.

"Don't run in like that."

"Why?"

"Because he'll think you're sure of getting his horse and won't let you have him."

Marcia slowed down.

"Well, all right." She hesitated in the doorway. "If I do get to go, Sister Cassandra, I know Brother Miltiades will expect me to wear my best dress . . . he's such a dandy."

Cassandra bit off a smile and said dryly:

"After I prompt you it's hardly worth while to try it on me . . . and if Milt doesn't like the way I clothe you he can take over the job."

Marcia was instantly in a temper.

"It seems to me after I stayed in that room bathing Brother Mulry's head when everybody had rushed off to the plum thicket——" She broke off, thinking hotly that if an almost angelic goodness would not bring her everything she wanted she would try other ways and means.

At this moment Gracie came to the company-room door. The quadroon was wiping her eyes on a dainty handkerchief and suppressing her sobs.

"M—Miss Cassandra," she quavered, "can I go help Aunt Creasy with George?"

Miss Cassandra nodded with a faint sense of boredom.

"She always takes on like that when George gets a whipping," observed the older sister.

"George is her half brother," defended Marcia, partly because she was sorry for Gracie and partly because Cassandra had for the second time refused her her best dress.

"I know she is George's half sister, but you are Augustus' and Polycarp's whole sister and I never see you weeping and wailing when the boys catch a whipping. To tell the truth, you rather enjoy it."

"I don't either!" cried Marcia, quite annoyed. "I know I have as much sisterliness as a nigger!" She stared at Cassandra rather indignantly, then after a moment added, "Besides, the boys don't need me . . . Mother takes on over them."

Cassandra bit her lips but did not smile. She was on the verge of saying, "Oh, well, go on and wear your blue-flowered dress," but she did not say it. She felt it was good for Marcia in some mysterious way never quite to get what she wanted. At least, it was the sort of goodness that life bestows on all human creatures in large amounts.

She went back to reading *The Rights of Man.*

Marcia continued in the doorway, looking after Gracie and thinking indignantly that she loved her brothers twice as much as Gracie loved George. Why, of course she did. She tried to think back to some instance of her great affection for them, but all she recalled were continual skirmishes with them: for the horse, for the biggest bowl of strawberries, for the most cream. And really, when they did catch a licking for their endless misdemeanors, the younger sister felt only a complacent self-righteousness clear down to the tips of her slender toes.

Here she stopped thinking how well she loved her brothers and fell to pondering on her dress again. She wondered if she could get the dress through Gracie somehow . . . she had given Gracie the handkerchief with which the quadroon girl dabbed at her eyes.

Now of all persons on the plantation Gracie was the most keenly and bitterly affected by the whipping of George. Her feelings not only were for George, they were for herself, for Aunt Creasy, for Robinet and Columbus, and above all for Solomon.

For George to be seized and flogged thrust all black folk into a deep and unescapable pit. It transformed her from a kind of tentative wife of Solomon into a brood mare; it changed Solomon into a stud; and her child, if she and

Solomon had a child, into a little animal. It cut the whole unstable world of the Vaiden plantation from under her feet and let her go dropping . . . dropping through God knew what despairs.

Here she stumbled up the two steps of the second negro cabin and went inside.

Old Mrs. Vaiden and old Aunt Creasy bent over a corded bed on which George lay face down. The mistress of the plantation and her black woman were daubing melted suet and turpentine over the bright-colored whelps and streaks on George's chocolate skin. Old Mrs. Vaiden attended the black youth with the care she would have given a sick calf, except that her ministrations were tinctured with annoyance that George had got himself into this trouble. When Gracie entered the door weeping the white woman said in a bored tone:

"Oh, hush, Gracie, don't go on so."

Gracie swallowed and tried to hush.

"What made you run from ol' Pap, George?" she gasped.

"It's all right," said Mrs. Vaiden philosophically. "If he hadn't got whipped for that he'd 'a' got whipped for stealing my spoon and melting it up."

The cream-colored girl stared at her dark half brother on the bed.

"George, what in the world did you want to melt a spoon for?"

George said nothing but simply lay in the blank silence of a negro.

The old white woman automatically handed her dish of suet and turpentine to Gracie, who received it and took her mistress's place.

"Whut he got a whuppin' fuh," mumbled old Aunt Creasy, getting up and waddling to one of the cracks in her log hut, "was runnin' f'um ol' Pap. Gawge sho is a fool."

The black woman stated this without derogation, simply as a fact. She took a clay pipe from the crack, waddled with it to the fireplace, put a coal in its bowl and began to smoke.

No one ever saw Aunt Creasy put any tobacco in her pipe . . . a coal, that was all she ever put in . . . then puffed from the stem a thin, whitish, but vindictively stinking smoke of tobacco.

"What you want to run for, George?" blinked Gracie, putting on the balm with a piece of cotton.

"I di'n' want to run," grunted George from where he lay face down. "I jess run. When ol' Pap yell at me lak dat, I's already gone fifty ya'ds fo' I knows whut I's doin'."

"Jest bust out runnin'?" queried Aunt Creasy.

"Sho do."

"Dat's cause you's a fool," observed the old negress impersonally.

"What does you do?"

"Why, I sta'ts right in astin' ol' Pap if he evah got me somethin' or odder. I say, Ol' Pap, have dem lazy niggahs git me dem bean poles, or a battlin' stick?"

"I runs," mumbled George again.

"Yo' heels kain't save yo' back, Gawge . . . got to use yo haid."

Old Mrs. Vaiden, seeing that her servants were at peace again and fallen into the endless philosophizing of their kind, left the negro quarters and went back to her work at the big house.

For a few minutes Gracie rubbed on the liniment in silence, then she turned and peered through the cracks in the hut to make sure the white woman was gone. Thus assured, she asked in a gray tone:

"George, what made you steal that spoon?"

George lifted his face from his crossed arms and looked to see for himself how far old Mrs. Vaiden had got.

"Cause I's tiahed bein' knocked aroun' evah whicherway lak a mule," he said in a gloomy voice.

"So you stole a spoon." Gracie saw no connection at all.

"Sho I stole a spoon. Nen when I see dat conjurin' preacher comin' down de road, I knowed I bettah hurry an' melt it fo' he got hit back frum me."

"But . . . what for?"

Gracie looked at her dark brother blankly.

For answer George reached into his trousers and drew out a shining pellet. Gracie took it and saw it was a brilliant new silver bullet. Aunt Creasy also looked at the bullet, her gargoyle features quite impassive.

"What are you going to do with it?" asked Gracie in bewilderment.

Aunt Creasy made a gurgling draw at her pipe and answered for George:

"Gwi shoot dey picture."

"Gwi fix muhse'f so I kin shoot anybody's picture what I likes," stated George more explicitly.

Then Gracie recalled the whole superstition on the point. If George drew anybody's picture and shot it with a silver bullet, that person would be wounded or killed.

George watched his half sister vindictively.

"When I kills one, I'll dig de bullet out o' de log an' kill somebody else. I keep shootin' evahbody whut knocks me aroun'—aw knock you aroun', Gracie," he added protectively.

The quadroon had stayed in the big house so long she had lost much of the negro beliefs.

"It won't do any good, George."

"Huh . . . want me to put up yo' picture an' shoot at it?"

"Oh, no, no, no . . . of course not."

"Dat's right," nodded Aunt Creasy.

"What you mean, dat's right?"

"Cause a silver bullet'll kill a nigger but hit won't kill white fo'ks."

This irritated George. He sat up gingerly and entered into a defense of his weapon:

"Looky heah, how come dat hoodoo preacher to mesmerize aroun' an' tell where my silvah bullet is if'n it won't wuck? Hit's boun' to wuck aw dat ol' preacher nevah would 'a' come fallin down in a fit tryin' to git hit back."

Aunt Creasy was about half convinced but stuck to her argument.

"Looky heah, Gawge, you know white fo'ks' silvah won't kill white fo'ks. A pusson's own spoon ain't gwi tu'n right aroun' fo' no niggah an' kill they ownehs."

This was becoming too metaphysical for Gracie.

"Look here, George, who you going to shoot with that bullet . . . not ol' Pap's picture?"

"Oh, no . . . no . . . not ol' Pap. He ain't done me no ha'm."

"He whipped you."

"Yeh, but I run f'um him."

"Then who you going to shoot?" pressed Gracie curiously.

"I dunno. I jess walk aroun' wid a silvah bullet 'n' if anybody make me mad enough, I jess fix up his picture, haul out my bullet, an' shoot him in the haid."

" 'Twon't do any good, will it, Aunt Creasy?"

"Not fuh white fo'ks. Silvah spoon jess lak a mammy; hit won't shoot the mouth hit fed. I don' guess hit would do any good aginst you eitheh, Gracie. Hannah, yo mammy, was half white. You is nearly all white, but Gawge there is nearly all black. If Gawge make a mustake an' draw his own picture an' nen shoot hit . . . dat fool niggah jest about kill hese'f."

At this fancy Aunt Creasy took her pipe from her mouth and broke into a high clacking laugh which was remarkable coming from a person whose talking voice was so deep.

Gracie did not follow the humor of George committing suicide with his own silver bullet. She sat looking at her half brother with a feeling of the racial blank back of him— and of herself. They were both like rabbits that sprang from under their feet in the cotton rows, without father or mother, without sons or daughters—both negroes and rabbits simply were.

"Who was George's pappy, Aunt Creasy?" inquired the girl for some tiny hold on her half brother's genealogy.

"His name was Jericho."

"Who was he?"

"Jess a black cotton fiel' niggah."

"What went with him?"

"Sol' down in Floridy somers. Ol' Pap owned Jericho in South Calliny. Yo mammy, Hannah, sho nearly had a fit when ol' Pap sol' off Jericho."

A kind of spasm went through the molded bosom beneath Gracie's coarse dress. What if Solomon—what if some one should sell Sol—— She put the thought out of her mind with a kind of mental writhing.

She asked no question of Aunt Creasy as to her own paternity. It was even vaguer than that of her dark half brother.

CHAPTER FIVE

W HEN Gracie came back to the big house Marcia met her in the hallway. The look on the quadroon's face caused Marcia to comfort her.

"Don't feel so bad, Gracie. Remember boys are a lot tougher than girls. When Carp and Gus get a licking I think how tough they are. . . ." Marcia hesitated a few moments and then added, "A person just has to think these things or she'll weep her eyes out."

Gracie blinked her own dramatic black eyes and tried to straighten her face into a pleasanter mien. This effort at cheerfulness moved Marcia to further comforting.

"Besides that," she added brightly, "Solomon's coming to see you to-night. This is Solomon's night, isn't it?"

Gracie stared gloomily into the yard.

"I don't care if Solomon never comes to see me any more."

"Why, Gracie!" ejaculated the white girl, horrified. "To talk like that about your husband!"

"Well," said Gracie, "he isn't coming to-night, he's coming to-morrow night."

"I'll tell you what I'll do," planned Marcia, in order thoroughly to dry her maid's tears. "If I go to the dance I'll stop by the store and ask Mr. BeShears to let Solomon come to see you to-night and to-morrow night both . . . then you'll be glad George caught a whipping."

"Why, I won't!"

"Oh, of course not, but everything has its consolations."

Here Marcia looked at her maid with such twinkling eyes that both girls began laughing.

Then suddenly a nebulous plan dawned in the white girl's head.

"Oh, Gracie . . . you don't know what I'm about to do!"

"Oh, what are you going to do, little missy?" asked Gracie, becoming excited in her turn.

"You know that pink-flowered dress of mine . . . it really needs cleaning and pressing. If you'll clean it and press it to-morrow you can wear it for Solomon to-night."

At this the quadroon really did forget all about her half brother's catastrophe.

"Oh, missy! . . . Now will you sure get Mr. BeShears to let Solomon off?"

The thought of appearing in such a dress before Solomon filled the cream-colored girl with delight.

"I'll do my best. And I'm going to start right away. You go up and put on the dress this minute!"

"But Solomon won't be here till to-night."

"Gracie, you heard what I said . . . put it on this minute!"

Her manner was peremptory and might have recalled George's tribulation were it not for the esthetic difference between taking a flogging and wearing a pretty frock. The two girls went flying up to Marcia's room to dress Gracie.

This room was a hip-roofed attic lighted by a tiny window in the gable. The roof sloped down on one side to about waist high. In this part of the room Marcia kept a cedar chest and a mighty round-topped trunk. Farther toward the tiny window stood a little washstand with pitcher, bowl, and towel and a fairly large square mirror sitting on it. This mirror reflected darkness until someone stepped in front of it. The bowl and pitcher Marcia never used. She always went to the kitchen and bathed her face sparingly in tepid water.

Now the two girls drew from the trunk ribbons and hose

and shoes, one set of which went with the new blue dress
and the other with the second-best pink-flowered dress.

Gracie began trembling inwardly at the thought of wearing her mistress's second-best dress. She had put it on once
surreptitiously, and the sight of herself in the dark mirror
had been breath taking.

"Looky here, missy," she asked incredulously, "you're sure
you want me to put it on?"

"Make haste, I tell you," hurried Marcia, getting her
own clothes out in a whirlwind.

"What Miss Cassie going to say?" asked the quadroon
doubtfully.

"Why, she'll say there's no harm in your wearing an old
dress that needs cleaning and pressing anyway."

"Do these ribbons and things go with it?"

"Sure, put them all on," directed Marcia generously.

It was Gracie's wont, when costuming Marcia, to go about
her work in a continual chant of adoration for the beauty
she was adorning. Now as the two girls aided each other
Marcia from time to time gave irrepressible ejaculations at
the splendor of her maid in the frilled pink-flowered dress.

"Gracie, that makes your eyes look right swoony! Gracie,
I wish my hair would stay in great big lolly curls like yours!
Oh, what a pity to waste all that on Solomon!"

Gracie's own compliments never ended at all. They held an
ecclesiastical flavor caught from negro preachers. Marcia's
eyes were like the morning stars shining on the New Jeru-
salem; her arms were like the cherubim on each side the
white throne; her lips were the rose of Sharon.

"You've been to too many camp meetings," laughed the
white girl, very well pleased with this particular by-product
of religion.

When they were dressed, the maid and the mistress started
downstairs. Marcia directed Gracie to stand at the head of
the steps and not to come the rest of the way until she

motioned for her. Then Marcia walked down alone in her best blue dress.

Miss Cassandra saw her younger sister through the door of the company room and called out in an astonished tone: "Marcia, what are you doing with that dress on?"

Marcia turned and began in a rather hurried but sympathetic voice:

"Why, Sister Cassandra—why, Sister Cassandra, Gracie was so cut up over George's getting a licking . . . and Solomon's coming over to-night . . . and when I looked at my pink dress it was really dirty and I just told Gracie, to keep her from crying, 'If you'll clean and press my dress to-morrow you can wear it to-night for Solomon,' and—and she said she would . . . that's all."

Marcia came to her last "that's all" with an anxious desire to go on talking interminably and forestall whatever Miss Cassandra was about to say.

Miss Cassandra stared in the utmost amazement.

"You mean to say you promised Gracie she could wear your second-best dress . . ."

"Well, Sister Cassandra, she—she felt so bad about Solomon—I mean George—I mean Solomon——"

"You told me that once!"

"She said she—would wash and press——"

"She said—said . . . Do you have to hire Gracie to press your clothes by letting her wear them?"

"Sister Cassandra!" cried Marcia, stamping her foot. "It cheers her up so!"

"Let her cheer herself up!" retorted Cassandra warmly. "George's whipping is nothing to weep over!"

"But—can't she wear it?" wailed Marcia.

"Certainly not! What's the matter with you? Do you think I'm furnishing ball dresses for the servants?"

Marcia gave a sigh.

"Gracie," she called dolefully upstairs, "Sister Cassandra says you can't wear that dress. Just take it along, Gracie,

and clean and press it . . . I have to go now to the dance."
She moved off toward the gate where old Joe was hitched.

Miss Cassandra looked after her with compressed lips.

"Look here, young lady, you just march yourself back upstairs, take off what you've got on and put on your pink dress as I told you."

Marcia caught her breath.

"Sister Cassandra, I—I can't do that."

"Why can't you?" demanded Cassandra. "Are you paralyzed?"

"No . . . I . . . Oh, Gracie—come down here a minute, please."

"What's Gracie got to do with——"

But the next moment Gracie came shrinking down the stairs, a vivid picture of frightened loveliness.

For a full ten seconds Miss Cassandra simply stared at the chromatic vision on the steps. Then she broke out angrily:

"Gracie! What do you mean putting on that dress!"

"M—Miss Cassandra——" stammered the girl, and then hushed through fear of getting Marcia into further trouble.

"You didn't tell me she already had it on!" cried the older sister, outraged.

"Sister Cassandra," cried Marcia, "you didn't think I'd want her rummaging through my things after I'm gone!"

"You go right back up those steps—both of you," cried Cassandra. "Gracie, you get back into your own duds and stay there! Marcia Vaiden, you put on that pink dress if you expect to leave this place!"

"Cassandra! *Cassandra!*" screamed Marcia. "Put on a dress after a nigger's had it on!"

"I told you you had to wear that dress!"

"Mammy! Oh, Mammy! Come here! O—oh, Mammy!"

"She won't do you a bit of good!"

At this point old Mrs. Vaiden came from the kitchen.

"What's the matter, Marcia?"

"She's got to wear that pink dress."

"But Mammy," shrieked Marcia desperately, "Gracie's got it on! I won't wear it after a nigger! Why, of course I won't wear it after a nigger!"

At this some of the dogs gathered around the end of the hallway and began yelping. Polycarp and Augustus came and suddenly stared at Gracie. Even old Mrs. Vaiden was struck at the sight of the quadroon. After a moment she called out in the turmoil:

"Gracie, what are you doing with Marcia's dress on!"

Marcia began a sobbing explanation all over again:

"I felt sorry for her on account of G-George getting a whipping——"

Polycarp and Augustus began a derisive "Yes, we know how sorry you are to see anybody whipped!"

"Why, you mean, stinking things!" cried Marcia. "Don't you think I hate to see you-all whipped?"

The two boys fell over among their dogs laughing.

"Go on back and put on that pink dress or you don't go at all," repeated Cassandra.

"Cassandra, she's already got the blue dress on now," mollified Mrs. Laura.

"It's not good for her—having her own way, Mother!"

"Well," said the little old woman with a quirk of her lips, "you've had your own way a good deal and you seem to have turned out very well."

"I was an extraordinary child. I think I was really older than you were, Mother, when I was born."

"I never observed anything to the contrary," admitted the old lady, looking wistfully at Marcia and turning back to her own perpetual work in the kitchen.

Miss Cassandra now observed that Polycarp and Augustus were staring at the glorified Gracie, and she ordered the boys on about their business. Then she sent Marcia and Gracie back upstairs.

When everyone had vanished she stood in the emptied hallway, tapping her lips thoughtfully with the pencil with which she had been jotting down notes on *The Rights of Man.*

Marcia and Gracie went slowly back to the white girl's attic room. Marcia was weeping.

"Oh, Gracie," she was saying, "to think I'll have to wear a dress that a nigger has had on! To think of Cassandra making me and—and—Mother permitting it. . . . No—nobody c-cares a—a—thing in the world a-about m-me!"

Gracie took her in her arms, weeping herself. She held Marcia to her full bosom.

"L-little missy," she sobbed, "w-we can j-just pretend you t-tried the dress on me, t-to see how i-it fit. You—you always t-try your dresses on me t-to see how they f-fit."

With a long sigh Marcia released herself from Gracie's arms and set about getting into the contaminated frock.

CHAPTER SIX

Aᴀғᴛᴇʀ Marcia had swallowed the ignominy of the pink dress, the boys exchanged old Joe's saddle for an equally ancient side saddle and she set off for the BeShearses' and the Lacefields'.

The two boys went with her. They also had to maneuver to get their mounts. They went to the same field where an hour before they had captured George, and commandeered Rab and Lou, the two mules Columbus and Robinet were plowing.

Marcia was horrified and the two negro men began a vociferous objection.

"Looky. heah, Mas' Carp," cried Columbus, "you know ol' Pap ain't gon' want us to stop plowin' so's you-all kin go to a dance!"

Polycarp became dignified.

"You know Father wouldn't allow Marcia to go unaccompanied, Columbus."

"But Mas' Carp, we're behin' wid our plowin'."

"Can't help it. I've got to do my duty by my sister."

"Looky heah," put in Robinet. "Sposin' we ast ol' Pap?"

"No . . . no, Robinet, I'm not going to annoy Father with small burdens I can take off of his shoulders."

"Trouble is," grumbled Robinet, "when you take a small bu'den off'n his shouldahs, he puts a la'ge bull whop onto ouahs."

Here Carp stopped one of the plows and took a mule. Augustus took the other one. Everybody protested this—

the two negroes, Carp and Marcia—but Augustus said all
right, he would report the whole matter to ol' Pap if he
didn't get the other mule. So the plows were stopped, the
mules saddled, and the three younger Vaidens set forth.

The fields and woods through which the trio fared were
bluish with distance and greenish and yellowish and reddish
with the gauzes of early spring. Joy was in the air. Polycarp and Augustus, who were cavalierly bound to accom-
pany their sister, hit upon a mule race and disappeared
down the rutty road with a great hallooing and belaboring
of switches.

Their going was like a balm to the girl. She could fall
into a reverie such as the day invited. No Vaiden when in
company with another Vaiden ever permitted himself a day-
dream, but when alone each fell prey to that soft weakness.

The boys were hardly out of hearing distance before
Marcia began thinking of the approaching dance. She
thought of young A. Gray and her brother Miltiades.

Her older brother, Miltiades, was the most wonderful
man Marcia ever knew. He was handsome, strong, he always
looked as if he had stepped out of a bandbox, and he was
rich. The Lacefields paid him a hundred and twenty-five
dollars a month as overseer on their plantation. When he
married Drusilla, half the Lacefield estate would belong
to him. The other half would go to young A. Gray Lacefield. It could quite easily come about that A. Gray's half
would also be her own half. . . .

Here a certain picture came into Marcia's head. She always fancied herself in a long sweeping gown walking up
the grand staircase of the Lacefield manor. One hand she
trailed on the curving balustrade, with the other she caught
up her train, and as she walked up she fancied herself glancing back over her shoulder and smiling at the fashionable
people in the hallway below her . . . she was Marcia
Vaiden Lacefield, young A. Gray's bride.

The actual A. Gray himself hardly entered into this

dream world at all. He had as little to do with it as the husband of the regent of the D.A.R.'s.

So Marcia's fanciful married life consisted mainly of sweeping up stairs, a tall, slender, gray-eyed girl with a shimmering silken train curving after her.

The sound of voices ahead of her drew Marcia out of her imaginings. She rounded a turn in the road and saw Carp and Gus riding alongside an ox wagon. The wagon had a wide-topped bed and bumped forward in a many-keyed creaking.

As Marcia came up from behind she saw the driver wielding a long bull whip over his team. He had the blackest hair the girl had ever seen.

Polycarp evidently had asked the fellow where he came from for he was saying in a deliberate hill twang:

"I come from Lane County . . . where do you come from?"

"Oh, then you don't really live in this nation at all," observed Carp, glancing at Marcia with a wink.

The driver suspected a jest.

"What you mean by not livin' in this nation? I told you I come from up in Tennessee."

"Yes, but you've driven your wagon out of the United States of America into the Confederate States of America, didn't you know that?"

The driver flicked his long whip at the shoulder of his lead ox.

"Yeh, I knew that," he agreed slowly, "I knew Alabama had seceded."

"Well, did you pay any custom duties on whatever you're bringing into this country?" inquired Polycarp gravely.

"No, I didn't," drawled the teamster with equal solemnity. "I crossed the line out here this side of Red Jim Kilgo's cabin, and when I went across I yells out, 'Watch out, Sesesh, I'm a-comin' in!' Nobody didn't say anything, so I just drove on in."

The ox driver's rather well-carved face took on a droll look. Marcia burst into laughter to hear her brother get the worst of the badinage. At her laugh the driver turned quickly and blurted out:

"Oh, excuse me, miss . . . I didn't know you was back there."

"You didn't say anything out of the way," said Marcia, looking at him curiously.

"I said 'sesesh.' "

"And it was the truth," affirmed Marcia. "Alabama has seceded. You really belong to another country from ours." She rode along, regarding him with the oddness of this fact upon her. "Seems funny, doesn't it?"

"M-m . . . yes, I guess it does." His wagon lumbered along a rod or two when he asked curiously, "Ain't you old man Vaiden's girl?"

The homely way he asked this amused Marcia. It denied her any separate existence of her own.

"Yes, I am."

"Are you . . . Miss Marcia Vaiden?"

"Yes," said Marcia, becoming interested. "I never did see you before?"

"No . . . no, you never did."

"Then how did you know me?"

"Well, Sarah Bentley told my sister about seeing you at a picnic at the spring at the Crossroads, and my sister told me."

Marcia felt, in a way, lifted out of her saddle at the precision of this roundabout recognition.

"You knew me by that!"

"Yes, Sarah said you was a tall girl with gray eyes and a—a purty mouth."

Marcia pinkened. Her two brothers began laughing immoderately that anyone should describe anything about Marcia as pretty. They thought that extremely funny. Marcia, however, retained her poise even if she did flush.

"There are lots of girls tall and gray eyed. It was just an accident you picked on me."

"What's your name?" asked Carp.

"M-m . . . I'm jest a Lane County man," said the teamster with the characteristic hill dislike for telling his name.

"Well, you know ours," pointed out Marcia with delicate amusement. "I'm Marcia Vaiden, that's my brother Polycarp, and that's Augustus. I think you might tell us yours."

The youth from Lane County became ill at ease, pondered, and finally said:

"Do you want to know it all?"

"First section for me," said Polycarp.

"Second for me," said Augustus, about to laugh.

"Will you boys please shut up!" snapped Marcia. "Yes— er—Mr.—yes, I'll take it all."

The youth on the wagon reddened, moistened his lips for the embarrassing ordeal, and then said quite rapidly:

"Jeremiah Ezekiel Madison Monroe Thomas Alvarado Catlin."

Marcia almost fell out of her saddle. Her two brothers suddenly sputtered, clung to their pommels, looked away from each other out on the fields they were passing.

Mr. Jerry Catlin himself was exquisitely embarrassed at the sensation he had caused.

"I told you you wouldn't like it," he said unhappily.

"But I do!" cried Marcia in an edged voice. "I—think its a nice name. . . . What have you got in your wagon?"

"Apples."

"Apples!" ejaculated Marcia, as amazed at this as she was at his name.

"Yes, apples," repeated Catlin, who saw nothing unusual in this.

The three Vaidens rode closer and looked in to verify such an extraordinary statement.

"What are you going to do with 'em?" cried Polycarp,

wondering what possible use a person could have for a wagonload of apples.

"Taking them to the still, of course," said Augustus.

"No," said Jerry, still discomfited about his name, "I'm taking 'em to Florence to sell. I figgered they would sell right good early in the spring before any other apples come in, even if they was little and weasley."

This produced another gust of amusement and astonishment in the Vaidens. Nobody ever sold an apple. Folk sold cotton, but apples were given away.

Jerry Catlin had no notion of the stigma attached to selling apples. He thought the Vaidens were still laughing at his name. As his apple cart bumped along he went back to the point and defended it in a rather annoyed tone.

"Pap says Catlin didn't used to be our name. He says folks got it twisted."

Marcia drew a controlled breath.

"What did it used to be?"

"It used to be Kerling or Coerling—something like that."

"Well—does that help much?" asked Carp.

"Of course it does," stated Jerry belligerently; "it means a noble. Over in England our fam'ly was one of the nobility . . . they tell me."

All three of the Vaidens kicked their mounts and Marcia squeezed out past her blocked glottis:

"T—that's very nice. . . . We are late, Mr.—Mr. Catlin. We'll have to hurry on."

The mules and horse trotted away together down the road.

"Say . . . don't you-all want some apples?" called the teamster in an unhappy voice. "I'll give you all you want!"

"No, thank you," yodeled back Marcia, "b-but much obliged just the same."

When they were far enough away they let go laughing, holding to their pommels, their eyes suffused with tears.

"One—of the nobility," gasped Marcia—"peddling apples!"

Augustus became sober before the others.

"Look here," he said, "why didn't we take some o' them apples?"

"Augustus! You can't laugh at a boy and then take his apples!"

Augustus pondered this.

"Well . . . I've quit laughing. I believe I'll go back and git me some apples. I haven't seen a one since last summer."

"Augustus Vaiden!" cried Marcia, scandalized.

"Now why kain't I?"

"Because we've laughed, I told you!"

Augustus rode along with a long face.

"Well, if I'd known that I wouldn't 'a' laughed . . . wasn't nothing to get tickled at anyway."

CHAPTER SEVEN

As MARCIA VAIDEN proceeded with her brothers her amusement at the apple vender gradually changed to a reflection on the fact that Jerry Catlin had recognized her by a third-hand description of her eyes and her lips. The girl rode along in the afternoon sunshine somehow pleased with these particular features of her face.

The hills through which the trio moved were growing smaller as they went along. Presently in the distance Marcia saw the three great sycamores which marked the BeShears spring. Beneath these trees clustered a little group of buildings and right on the side of the road stood a weathered box-like country store. It was spotted with tobacco advertisements and the peeling remains of a circus poster.

This was BeShears Crossroads. The store contained a post office and was the neighborhood loafing place. In the dwelling house back of the store lived Ponny BeShears, a big plump girl in high open favor with Marcia and even higher, but less open, favor with Polycarp.

In fact, as the Vaidens approached the Crossroads, Polycarp sat straighter, kicked old Sue, and said:

"Come ahead, let's trot up!"

Augustus immediately took the opposition and didn't want to trot up.

Marcia said, "Carp wants to ride in and cut a dash."

"I do not want to cut a dash," denied Polycarp at once, and drew down his mule.

Then Augustus shouted, "Oh, well, come on and le's cut a dash!"

And off he went banging old Rab's slats. Old Sue followed suit, as she always did whatever Rab did. So all three made their entrance into BeShears Crossroads with a dash.

There was the usual group of white men around the store playing horseshoes and marbles. What was unusual was a group of negroes, too. Eight negroes—four men, a woman, a girl, and two children—were not playing any games but were simply standing in a group near the big spring at the foot of the sycamores a little back of the store. They watched the white players with the odd expressionless faces of black folk who are restraining themselves.

As the gamesters played a white onlooker talked loudly:

"I tell you what . . . I don't know about this splittin' off from the North . . ."

"Well, I do," said another voice. "I think Abe Lincoln is a knot on the devil's tail, but I give him credit for saying one true thing. He said a country couldn't be half slave and half free, and that's a fact. So by grabs I say let her split. Let them be all free and we'll be all slave."

The speaker had on a pair of new boots. Another man interrupted his discourse by calling out, "Bill, I'll throw you down for your boots!"

"Come on," cried the statesman, "and if I don't send you home barefoot, my name's not Tucker."

Immediately the two wrestlers stood up to each other, breast to breast, and began making passes at each other in a set-to of Indian Hug.

Polycarp looked on excitedly.

"I'll throw the best man," he called from his mule.

"Yeh, Lon Tucker'll mash you like a bedbug," warned a bystander.

"I don't know," said another, "Carp Vaiden is quite a butt of a boy."

At this moment the door of the BeShears residence opened

and a big round-cheeked blue-eyed girl ran out calling, "Hidy, Marcia. Rest your saddles and come in—you and the boys."

Polycarp was torn between the wrestling and the girl. Augustus promptly decided on the wrestling.

"We've got just a little while to stay," explained Marcia from her horse. "We're going over to the Lacefields' to the speaking and the dance."

"Well, I declare! How come you haven't got your blue dress on?"

"Oh, Ponny, please don't mention that . . . Sister Cassandra . . ."

"What a shame!" cried Ponny, instantly sensing the whole tragedy. "I'd like to see a sister of mine boss my clothes!"

"But my clothes aren't mine!" cried Marcia tragically. "I don't belong to myself." She made a gesture toward her dress. "Isn't that awful!"

"Whose are they?"

"Sister Cassandra's. She buys what I wear, and cuts it out and sews it for me. Then after all that she says it's hers."

"That's terrible. . . . How came her to buy your clothes?"

"An uncle in South Calliny left her some money."

"Whyn't he leave some to you?"

"Well, Cassandra was the brightest."

"Then she didn't need it. Dull girls like us really need money."

"Ponny, we aren't dull, we're just unimproved."

Polycarp broke out laughing at the idea that unimprovement was all that was wrong with Marcia.

Ponny walked over to his mule and hit him vigorously.

"Get down, get down," she cried to both of them. "You-all got plenty of time for the dance. I tell you, Marcia, why don't you buy a dress of your own?—then you could wear it when you pleased."

"How could I buy a dress?" inquired Marcia, really interested.

"Just walk in and buy it on a credit, that's how." Ponny made a full-armed gesture toward the store.

Polycarp had got down from his mule.

"Yes," he observed, "Marcia does that and Pap would skin her alive."

For answer Ponny pushed Polycarp. The youth pushed back, and the impact each made upon the other was peculiarly agreeable to the vital bubbling pair.

"You go in right now," proceeded Ponny in a businesslike manner. "Just buy it and don't say anything about the pay. Then when it's cut off you can tell him you want it on a credit. He'll have to let you have it for he can't stick it back on again. . . . Who's going to speak?"

"The Honorable Emory Crowninshield. . . . Say, I wish somebody would just buy me a dress. . . . I don't know about doing it that way."

"Why don't you beg your brother Milt for a dress?"

"He might."

"Polycarp," said Ponny, "don't you wish you were as good looking as your brother Miltiades?"

"Pshaw, no!" cried Carp. "I wouldn't go around as dandified as Miltiades for love or money. . . . Bet I'm stouter than he is!"

"Oh! Oh! Oh!"

And both girls began laughing.

"I am!" cried Polycarp.

"Why, Polycarp!" cried Ponny. "You can't hold my wrist!"

"Huh, I can with one hand!"

"The idyah! . . . Here you are, see if you can!"

Polycarp seized the wrist. At Ponny's first powerful

lunge he almost lost it. He was forced to use both hands. The two bumped together and worked and panted and were filled with a violent delight.

Ponny finally stood still, exhausted. "I give up," she breathed, "you took both hands."

The two stood looking at each other a moment with faces flushed and eyes sparkling. Then the girl erased all this by-play instantly by saying to Marcia:

"Come on, le's go to the store and get it now."

Why Marcia liked Ponny BeShears she did not know. It disgusted Marcia when other girls scuffled with boys, but it was so native to Ponny that Marcia did not even think the catty things about it that prim girls almost invariably think about the unprim. She probably warmed herself at Ponny's vulgar but comfortable fire.

Now she decided to take Ponny's advice about the dress. They started for the store.

Polycarp was shocked at what his sister was about to do. He told her again that her father would skin her alive. Marcia then stated loftily that she wouldn't have the dress charged to her father, she could have it charged to herself, and then she would have Columbus and Robinet do a little extra work outside the family and make the money to pay off her debt.

Polycarp could find no rebuttal for this. Even if Marcia's mind was unimproved, it was at least working fairly well.

The three turned from the BeShears gate and went to the store. The store itself stood on posts and had a high plat-form in front of it, from which barrels of flour could be rolled easily onto wagons. Its interior was quite dark, lighted only by the front door. When one first entered it from the sunshine one could see nothing at all, but smells of coal oil, bacon, cheese, turpentine, and new bolts of calico gave one some notion of its contents. Amongst this olio were odors of sweaty men, whisky and tobacco breaths, and feet, but these were mere accessory stenches and had nothing to do with

Mr. Alexander BeShears' stock in trade. Marcia's straight little nose focused on the mercantile smells.

In the gloom, the storekeeper was represented by a palish blob floating above his counter, and this, if touched, would have proved to be his face.

Marcia, Carp, and Ponny waited till Ponny's father had finished cutting off half a plug of tobacco for a man, then Marcia went over and put her hands on the unseen counter with an odd feeling at her first business venture,

"I'd like to look at your blue-flowered dress goods, Mr. BeShears," she said.

The blob saw Marcia perfectly well.

"Step right this way, Miss Marsh."

Then it floated off down the inside of the counter into a profounder darkness. As it went it said in a casual tone:

"When you first came in, Miss Marsh, I thought maybe your Pap had sent a payment on his account by you."

"No," said Marcia innocently, "he never sent anything."

"M—yes . . . I see."

The merchant paused before some bolts of cloth whose shapes but not whose colors could be distinguished.

"How is yore pappy?" inquired the merchant, standing and looking at his dry goods.

"Why, he's pretty well, Mr. BeShears. . . . How's Mrs. BeShears?"

"By the way, Miss Marsh, are you like Miss Cass, do you want to pay for this yourself?"

"Yes, I do," ejaculated Marcia, pleased at this turn.

The storekeeper looked around at her in surprise.

"Have you been teaching school or something?"

"Oh, no . . . I haven't been teaching," explained Marcia hurriedly.

"Then how did you get yore money?" pursued the tradesman curiously.

"Why-y—I haven't got any," said Marcia, embarrassed and becoming once more dubious about her enterprise.

"Oh . . . I see . . . and how's yore mammy . . . an'
Miss Cass?" he inquired, running his hand idly over the
bolts in his shelves.

"They're very well. . . . Mr. BeShears, what color have
you there?"

"Purple," said the storekeeper, without enthusiasm.

"May I take it to the door and look at it?"

He put it on the counter.

"Oh, yes . . . take it along."

The girl had expected him to carry it to the door for
her, but as he made no movement she took it herself. Her
walk alone, with the bolt of cloth, was embarrassing. When
she emerged out of the darkness, Polycarp saw her plight
and hurried to take the cloth from her hands. Ponny was at
Carp's elbow.

"Pappy ought to 'a' brought that out for you," she said,
annoyed and apologetic.

The three stood in the doorway looking at the purple
figured cloth.

"Now, Marcia," planned Ponny, "you can put a panel in
the skirt and have a flounce. . . ." She began drawing an
imaginary skirt with her short thick forefinger. Ponny
always had good ideas about dresses.

As Marcia stood trying to visualize the flounce in purple,
she saw something that drew her attention from her purchase.

"Why, look yonder!" she ejaculated. "Yonder stands
Solomon down by the spring."

"Yes, Sol and Mamie," agreed Polycarp.

"What's that white man doing to them?" inquired
Marcia.

"Why he—he's pinching their hands," hesitated the
brother, narrowing his eyes to see through the sunshine.

"What's he doing that for?" ejaculated Marcia, looking
at Ponny.

Ponny batted her bright blue eyes in embarrassment.

"Why—uh—Pappy's—uh—selling all the niggers off—to-day," she stammered.

"Selling 'em! Selling Solomon—Gracie's husband!"

Marcia stared in growing horror at Ponny, who could only nod her round, rather pretty face.

The negroes at the spring evidently heard this talk for Solomon called with desperation in his voice:

"Miss Marsh! Ah—Ah thought ol' Pap was gwi buy me."

Marcia turned into the store again with every nerve in her body vibrating.

"Mr. BeShears! Mr. BeShears!" she cried in a rush. "You're not selling Solomon, are you?"

The dim blob said in a flat tone, "Why yes. I'm sellin' off all my niggers. Why?"

Marcia was almost speechless.

"Why! Why! Why, because Solomon's Gracie's husband! You can't sell Gracie's husband! Why, Mr. BeShears, Father was to buy Solomon and have them together!"

"I understood that, too," observed the storekeeper dryly, "but he never has done it."

"But he will!" cried Marcia in the greatest distress. "I'll ride home this minute and tell Pappy; he'll come at once."

"But I've already sold him to Mr. Larribee out there. He was on the ground and ready to pay gold for him."

"Mr. Larribee . . . I never heard of Mr. Larribee. Does he live close enough for Solomon to come to see Gracie on Saturday nights?"

"Why, I don't know where Mr. Larribee lives—I didn't ast him."

"Does anybody know where Mr. Larribee lives?" asked the girl, looking at the idlers.

"Miss Marsh, he's a travelin' nigger buyer," said a man in a flat tone.

A kind of weakness invaded Marcia.

"Oh! Oh!" She stared at the merchant who had come to

the door. "Mr. BeShears, whatever made you sell your niggers?"

The storekeeper reached out and took back the cloth.

"D'you want me to tell you the truth?"

"Of course I do."

"Well, ever'thing's might shaky right now . . . Lincoln's elected and the South seceding. I don't know what's going to happen. I don't know whether niggers is going up or down. So I'm selling and waiting for conditions to settle."

"My goodness!" cried Marcia. "If everybody did like you, there wouldn't be any sense in seceding at all."

A stir and affirmatory grunts came from the front of the store at this speech.

"If everybody followed my example," defended the storekeeper grumpily, "they'd prob'ly use better sense than they are doin'."

Marcia turned and ran out of the store to the big spring where the eight negroes stood immobile.

"Oh, Solomon!" she cried to one of those slender-bodied, large-armed and large-legged black men, "I didn't know Mr. BeShears was even thinking about selling you. . . . Do you know where you're going, Solomon?"

The black man could hardly speak. He drew in his thick carved lips and bit them.

"N-no, li'l missy, that man there ain't say. . . . Ah—ah ast him but he ain't say."

For Solomon to call her little missy, as Gracie did, broke the white girl's heart. It made her feel as if the storekeeper were selling off one of her own family.

She turned to the man.

"Where are you going with him? Can he come back Saturdays?"

"Why, miss," said Mr. Larribee, taking off his hat, "I'm going to Florence this evening, then I'm heading down toward Montgomery."

At this the black girl in the group of slaves dropped on

the mossy side of the spring and began the high weird wailing of her race.

"Oh, Lawdy—I's sol' south! Oh, good Lawd, lemme die! Oh, my Lawd, lemme lay down an' die! Don' sen' me away down south!"

"Hush! Hush, Calline!" plead Marcia, weeping herself. "Don't take on so, Calline. It—won't be so bad. God'll take care of you, Calline."

"Oh, Miss Marsh, pray fuh Calline!" wailed the girl. "Pray fuh po' Calline!"

Marcie looked at the black folk through her tears. "Oh, I don't see how God can allow this!" she quavered through an aching throat. "I don't see how He can!" She caught a breath, swallowed and controlled herself.

"Solomon, what—what must I tell Gracie?"

"Li'l' missy, t-tell Gracie Ah—Ah sends muh lub. Tell huh Ah—Ah loves huh, li'l missy."

Polycarp came and took Marcia's arm.

"Come on, Marsh," he said gently, trying to show no emotion before the onlookers. "Come on and let's get that dress you was looking at."

As Marcia turned away with him Polycarp told Solomon good-bye and the two went back to the store together.

Polycarp shushed his sister under his breath not to cry before everybody. Marcia straightened her face, but all the onlookers knew she had been crying. The men quit their games and stood at a sort of attention.

One of the men said, "Alex BeShears would sell his soul if he thought the price of souls was a-goin' to fall."

"Well, if niggers do fall we'll all wish we'd sold our niggers," opined a third man practically.

Polycarp and Marcia went into the store.

"Marcia will have a dress off the piece you showed her, Mr. BeShears," said the brother, in order to cure his sister's grief.

"How many yards?"

"How many?" asked Polycarp.

"Twelve," said the practical Ponny.

The storekeeper placed his hand on the bolt in the darkness.

"And Polycarp, who did you say was going to pay for this?" he inquired.

"Why, Pap, of course," ejaculated the youth, surprised. "Just put it on Pappy's account."

"I'm sorry," said the merchant dryly, "but your father's account is as large as I can carry it already, Polycarp. I'm having to draw in my credit to meet my bills—that's why I had to sell my niggers."

Instantly Polycarp was intensely angry. Marcia's face burned and she wanted to fly out of the store. Polycarp burst out furiously:

"That ain't so! Your bills ain't pressing you! You just don't want to sell my Pap anything! Do you think we'd steal it! For a dime I'd knock your blubbering old grub-worm head off your shoulders!"

Two or three men came from the front of the store.

"Now, Carp," they pacified, "Mr. BeShears didn't mean no insult."

"Let him do what he wants to," twanged the merchant with a metallic vibration in his voice. "Walk aroun' berating me for sellin' my niggers! By God, I reckon a man can sell what's his'n without the whole damn country jumpin' on him!"

"Sure! Sure he can, Alex," agreed the peacemaker. "I'd be proud to lend you and your sister the money for the dress, Carp——"

"Hell, no," shouted Polycarp. "We're not around taking charity——"

"Naw, nor credit either," snarled the storekeeper.

"Alex BeShears, one more word and I'll knock your snaggly teeth down your throat!"

"Come on, Carp, you and Miss Marsh," mollified the peacemaker.

Sister and brother walked out. Marcia's face was flaming. Ponny moved with them.

"Ponny, you stay here," commanded the storekeeper.

Ponny whirled around.

"You tend to your own business and I'll tend to mine!" she flared, and then went on with her friends.

Augustus was pitching horseshoes and knew nothing of what had been happening.

Ponny hurried along with her guests, trembling with anger and excitement.

"Pappy's the biggest fool! Talkin' like that! Why couldn't he . . . at least he could have acted the gentleman and not blared it out before ever'body!"

The three were walking toward the barn where Augustus had put up their mounts.

"He was mad," said Polycarp in heavy tones, "because we criticized him for selling Solomon."

"Yes, I guess he was mad," admitted Ponny. "Mammy and me had been giving him down the country for selling Calline. . . . I'm a-goin' to haff to help cook."

"There ought to be a law against selling slaves," declared Marcia. "It ought to be like selling your home . . . a man can't sell his home without his wife's consent."

"Well, the niggers never would consent," objected Ponny.

"Then I'm sure I don't know what ought to be done," said Marcia, still in a temper.

"Well, you're not entirely by yourself there," said Polycarp, with a faint glint of amusement.

Marcia waited at the lot gate while Polycarp went after the mule and horse. Ponny was so set on showing every courtesy to her guests that she went in to help the youth. Carp objected but the girl was determined.

When the two had entered the stalls and had closed the rough door, Ponny stood for a moment with the bridle in her white strong hands. Then she touched Polycarp's arm.

"Carp," she said in a queer edged voice, "you're not going to hold that against me, are you? I—I couldn't he'p what Pap did."

The youth saw her usually rosy face was colorless. An unexpected squeezing sensation inside his own chest answered whatever it was that moved the girl.

"Why, no, Ponny, no," he stammered, queerly embarrassed.

"Because I—I want you—and Marsh—to come to see me, Carp—like you always have done."

As she gasped out these words she suddenly caught Polycarp's hand and pressed it to her flowing bosom. Its supple amplitude and warmth traveled through the hobbledehoy with a sort of soft shock. The next moment he was pressing the girl in his own heavy arms. Ponny hugged him with muscles almost as strong as his own. They kissed, the first bewildering kiss of adolescence.

Old Sue stamped in her stall.

Polycarp suddenly loosed Ponny and began bridling the mule as swiftly as he could so they would have spent the proper amount of time in the stalls under the surveillance of Marcia.

CHAPTER EIGHT

THE Vaidens rode on to the Lacefield plantation calling down anathemas on the storekeeper. BeShears' refusal to credit Marcia was much worse than the selling of his negroes.

As the three rode away from the Crossroads they saw Mr. Larribee drive off toward Florence in a three-seated hack with all his black purchases on the seats behind him. It shocked Marcia; not so much the injustice of it as the spiritual impossibility of such a casual ownership. To own negroes, to possess them body and soul, connoted with Marcia a spiritual relation. Negroes were part of one's family. They wrought and shared in the fortunes of their master. When they were ill you nursed them and when you were ill they nursed you. An intimacy wove about the possessor and the possessed. Now for this Larribee suddenly to assume such a position to a hackful of negroes; to be thrust suddenly into the center of their lives without his caring a straw for them, without his even knowing their names . . . it filled Marcia with horror.

To go to the Lacefields', the brothers and sister left the Florence-Waterloo road at the store and took a side road down into the Reserve.

Polycarp rode down this lane lost in a boy's first kiss from a girl. To him the fields and skies breathed of Ponny. He rode somewhat to the rear of Augustus and Marcia because he had a feeling that anyone who looked at him might see Ponny's kiss still on his lips.

Yet, aside from the persistent titillation of the kiss, a grayness permeated the youth. He was sorry he had threatened and bemeaned the storekeeper, and he wondered rather hopelessly how he and Ponny would ever get married. His quarrel with her father was not an auspicious start.

By this time the landscape had undergone another change. The hills were no more. The riders were moving through river-bottom land, level as a surveyor's line and dark as chocolate.

This was the Reserve. When Andrew Jackson thrust the Seminoles out of Alabama into Florida, in the treaty, Doublehead, the Seminole chief, had reserved this flat fat land for a tribal camping place when his people should revisit Alabama.

The three riders could see over enormous distances in the Reserve. All of it was cleared. Field after field stretched away, with here and there a clump of ornamental trees. At wide distances apart great brick manors flanked by white-washed slave quarters dominated the landscape. Over all lay the soft blue-and-lavender haze of spring. Aloft floated the clouds in great scrolls and strata. It seemed to Marcia that the clouds over the Reserve were more magnificent than any-where else.

A faint, almost incorporeal chanting began to grow in the air, as if the scene itself exhaled a haze of music as well as moisture. The black workers were quitting their labors for the day. Far away, Marcia could see them unhitching their mules and leaving their plows sticking in the furrows. They leaped astride their work mules and started home yodeling to the jingling of their trace chains.

In a field on the left Marcia saw a trim broad-shouldered figure on a shining black horse. The girl's heart leaped. She fluttered her handkerchief on high.

" 'Lo, Brother Milt! Hey oh, Brother Milt!"

The horseman in the field waved his hat, turned his steed and came at a canter toward the fence. At about thirty yards' distance he spurred his thoroughbred. It broke into a smooth run and the next moment steed and rider sailed over the fence, looking to Marcia like a descending glory.

"Goodness, Brother Milt, but you're a wonderful rider!" pæaned the girl.

"I ride to the hounds to-night," smiled Miltiades. "Going to be a big fox hunt."

The leap filled Augustus with emulation.

"Look here, I'll bet I can make old Rab jump that fence, too!" He hauled his mule's head about and began to kick it in the flank.

"Augustus!" screamed Marcia. "You'll break your fool neck and the mule's, too!"

"You haven't a running start in the lane, Augustus," pointed out Miltiades tactfully.

"Then I'll lay down a gap, get in the field, and jump out!" cried Augustus.

"Don't do that," begged Polycarp. "Old Rab would jump so high and so far, you wouldn't get back by supper."

Marcia began laughing and Augustus rode on, mumbling that he knew old Rab could jump as high as Brother Milt's horse.

As the riders moved down the lane Marcia recalled the episode of the Crossroads store.

"Brother Milt," she exclaimed indignantly, "what do you think? Alex BeShears wouldn't let me have a dress pattern I picked out!"

"Wouldn't let you have it . . . what do you mean, Marcia?"

"Why, he wouldn't credit her for it," put in Polycarp sharply. "He said he was drawing in his credit."

The elder brother compressed his lips, his delicately cut nostrils expanded.

"I'd like to know when the Vaiden credit went bad!" he snapped.

"And he's sold Solomon," added Marcia accusingly.

This particular charge did not register with Miltiades.

"Solomon belonged to him," he answered absently.

"But he was Gracie's husband!"

"Yes, that's right." The older brother lifted himself in his stirrups and called across the field:

"Blue Gum! Oh, Blue Gum! Come here!"

The very way he called the negro, his control of tone even when carrying long distances, struck Marcia as something fine and aristocratic.

A black man turned his mule out from the jingling procession and rode up to the fence.

"Yes, suh, Mas' Vaiden."

Miltiades ran a hand into his pocket, drew out a purse and produced a gold piece. He tossed this to the slave.

"Go to old man Alex BeShears' store, buy a dress pattern . . . will he know which one?"

"Oh, Brother Milt, you mustn't do any such thing; why, that's ridic—— Yes, he'll know which one."

"And you tell Alex BeShears for me that's he's a damned stingy penny-grabbing old skinflint; that's he's an abolitionist or a secessionist, just whichever way the cat jumps, and that if he had a breath of gentility in him he would never have embarrassed a young lady over a few cents!"

"Oh, you mustn't do that, Brother Milt . . . it was terribly embarrassing . . . and listen, Blue Gum," she called after the negro, "tell him to send fifteen yards instead of twelve. I might just as well have an extra long train, don't you think so, Brother Milt?"

CHAPTER NINE

Before Marcia reached the manor she contrived to drop behind the boys with Miltiades and ask about Drusilla Lacefield, her elder brother's fiancée.

The man became grave.

"Dru is talking about putting the wedding off till June," said Miltiades in a troubled tone.

"June! After she has just been to Washington buying her trousseau!"

"She says June is the bride's month. She is very changeable . . . but of course," he added after a moment, "that is one of her charms."

"I think love ought to be like religion, Brother Milt," said Marcia, looking at her handsome brother adoringly; "it ought to be the surest and solemnest thing in a person's life."

The man reached over and patted his sister's hand on the pommel of her saddle.

"I wonder if there'll ever be anybody good enough for my little sister," he said almost jealously. And Miltiades thought how kind fate would have been if it had endowed Drusilla Lacefield with his sister's qualities of heart and soul. Then his thoughts shifted away from this point and he rode on, glancing over the broad acres with a titillation of proprietorship which the thought of marriage with Drusilla always evoked.

The Lacefield manor sat some distance from the road, half

screened by a grove of silver poplars. Behind the glistening fretwork of these trees glowed the old brick mansion with its white columns and multiplication of tall French windows.

As Marcia and her brother turned into the great stone gate of the manor they heard an outbreak of barking and snarling from the kennels, and the shouts of a negro trying to quell a fight among the strange hounds.

From the manor itself a negro man came running out to hold Marcia's stirrup as she alighted on the mounting block. This negro was part of the whole ensemble which breathed an air of magnificance and luxury to Marcia. Even the horse block had easy steps to walk up and down it. Out on the lawn two heraldic peacocks spread green-blue semicircles and uttered an occasional shriek which sounded to Marcia like blasts from the bugles of Pride.

The door onto a high small iron-grilled balcony set at the second-floor level of the piazza opened and a man and a dark-haired girl came out. When the girl saw Marcia she called in a casual voice:

"Hello, Marcia. I was hoping you would come to the dance." Then she added, "Let me present Mr. Crowninshield, only presenting him so high up is like flinging him at your head."

Marcia began a formal acknowledgment when Mr. Crowninshield laughed and declared if Miss Lacefield hadn't flung him at Marcia's head, he had intended to fling himself at her feet . . . it was a mere choice of ends. Marcia's spirits began to rise.

"I hope it will come to a happy end—like a comedy."

"It will if you'll come up and join us," suggested the guest. "We're on our way to the observatory."

"Marcia has seen the observatory many times," said Drusilla in her soft drawl.

"Yes, but I never can remember how it looks," cried Marcia, and she thought if Dru Lacefield imagined she was

going to have that man all to herself, it was simply another
illusion destined to be shattered.

"We'll wait," called Crowninshield.

Marcia waved a hand at Miltiades, then dashed into the
great hall and up the wide staircase that made a half turn
around the end of the hall. Marcia bent a trifle to kiss
Drusilla but the shorter girl turned her cheek for the kiss,
and Marcia turned hers, so the caress didn't come off.

Crowninshield stooped to kiss Marcia's fingers.

"Mr. Crowninshield is running for Congress," explained
Drusilla, looking up at her statesman. "This evening he's
going to make a speech with a lot of poetry in it."

"I shall quote poetry to the Muses," said the politician.

Marcia was interested. She had met characters who talked
like that in the novels she read. She wondered what he really
thought.

The three went from the upper floor through the attic to
the observatory. This was a platform about twenty feet
square with benches and a hand rail. From all sides of the
observatory one looked out into immensity. Far away to
the south and west lay the enormous loop of the Tennessee
River glinting in the sunset. To the north the remote Tennessee hills stood in purple against the lemon sky. In all the
prolonged reach of the Reserve only two other manors were
visible. Such widespread holdings suggested the space necessary to this patriarchal mode of society.

Immediately around the mansion lay two long rows of
whitewashed slave cabins, forming a kind of street. Then
there were kennels, stables, arbors, a glazed flower house.
Dogs barked. Here and there a negro sang in the melancholy
cadence of his inheritance.

"I declare," mused Crowninshield in a grave voice, "isn't
this wrapped in peace? It doesn't seem possible that anyone
would disturb it . . . would even want to disturb it."

"Do you think we are going to be disturbed?" asked

Marcia, pleased at this genuine mood of the man, which seemed as poetic as his careless gallantries.

"Nobody can be sure just now, Miss Vaiden. States seldom allow themselves to be dismembered without resistance. Of course our Southern states have every legal and political right to secede. The colonies joined themselves together for mutual protection. That certainly implies the power to separate when that protection becomes oppression."

"Looks like the Yankees ought to see that," said Marcia.

"A man's moral judgments always point to his pocketbook," observed Crowninshield, "and of course that would be doubly true with a Yankee."

Drusilla caught hold of Crowninshield's arm.

"You scare me talking so seriously, Emory. But there won't be any war. Who's going to fight us? Why, the North won't fight. Do you know who I met in Washington? A Mr. Breiterman. He was quite wealthy, and guess how he made his money."

"I don't know," said Marcia in a bored tone. She wished Drusilla would not interrupt Mr. Crowninshield.

"By making shoe pegs!" cried Drusilla.

Even Marcia was interested and amazed at this.

"Nobody could make money out of shoe pegs, Dru!"

"Yes, sir, shoe pegs; the sort our nigger shoemakers whittle out with their pocket knives. Breiterman had a *factory* making 'em!"

Both girls burst out laughing at the absurdity of it.

"When I found that out, I simply couldn't be nice to him."

"I am simply charmed with his occupation," declared Crowninshield.

"Why?"

"Because it excluded him from your society."

Drusilla laughed and leaned on the speaker's arm.

"I don't believe you really care who I go with. Let's go down."

When they reached the lower floor again a crowd had gathered from the neighborhood. Drusilla became busy introducing Crowninshield to the newcomers.

A slender youth with narrow face, sandy hair, and merry hazel eyes appeared at Marcia's side.

"How are you, Marsh?" he ejaculated in an eager tone. "Carp told me you were here. I've been looking all over the place for you. Where have you been?"

Marcia told him in the observatory.

"Fine!" cried the youth, catching her arm. "Let's go up and look again!"

"Oh, no, A. Gray. One look upon the face of infinity suffices."

A. Gray stared at her.

"Well, for God's sake . . . where did that come from?"

Marcia began laughing.

"It's a left-over from listening to Mr. Crowninshield."

"Isn't he a talker?"

"Yes. If I'd said that to him he would have said something twice as big back to me."

"I imagine he would," agreed the youth casually.

"A. Gray, why don't you buck up and say a few things now and then?"

"Well, to-night I'm too busy with the dawgs. We're going to have the greatest fox chase. We've got the Bailey hounds and the Ham hounds and two dawgs Sheriff Dalrymple had shipped to him from Virginia . . . and girl, to keep those dawgs from declaring hostilities has taken a whole diplomatic corps of niggers."

Marcia began laughing.

"Come on out and look at 'em," cried the youth.

The girl agreed to this and they went out together.

The Lacefield kennels were divided from the garden by a high stone fence. The two leaned over this fence and looked inside. Marcia, in reality, despised dogs because they were always in her front yard and quite often in her kitchen

snatching the dinner out of pots. The Vaidens had no kennels. In the South no country girl worth less than a hundred
thousand dollars could possibly be expected to like a hound.

A. Gray did not know this. He began pointing out the
Virginia dogs enthusiastically.

"Those dawgs that Sheriff Dalrymple bought," he said,
"run so true that they wouldn't cut across on a fox if it
circled back and brushed their tails as it went by."

"I say they're mighty stupid hounds," said Marcia.

"Why, they're sporting hounds!" cried A. Gray.

"The idyah is to catch the fox, isn't it?"

"No, the idyah is to run true and far and fast."

"If I was a hound I'd not only cut, but I'd study cuts. I'd
make my head save my heels. In fact, I'd find out where
the fox holes were, and I'd go there and get inside and just
lay there with my mouth open."

"Yes, and you'd get marked off the registry books, too."

"Little would I care. On a spring night like this I'd jump
out of the kennel and go off on my own and run a hundred
miles shooting along up hill and down dale, in the fields, in
the woods. I'd run up on a high bluff and jump off and sail
down through the moonlight into the river!"

"Good gracious!" ejaculated A. Gray. "I didn't know you
were so unconventional."

"You make me that way!" declared the girl warmly.

"How do I make you that way?"

"You just do . . . you make me want to burst out and
do something!"

"That's not a compliment," complained A. Gray. "The
way you said that, I can tell it isn't a compliment."

"No, it isn't," admitted Marcia; "it's an uncompliment."

The youth pondered a moment.

"Look here, I don't know of any practical way for you to
run hundreds of miles through the moonlight and leap off
of bluffs into the river, but we can take a horseback ride if

you say so. I might be able to get a horse to fall over a bluff for you . . . I could back him off."

"Oh, pshaw, A. Gray!"

"Look here, Marcia," said A. Gray uneasily, "I'm sort of fizzling out, aren't I?"

"Well, yes, you are."

He placed his hand on Marcia's fingers lying on the stone wall and leaned over and kissed them.

"Marcia, I've asked you to marry me already so many times that's it's beginning to be embarrassing. Marcia, if you refuse me this thousandth-and-first time you'll positively make me suspect that you don't want to marry me."

"Is this your thousandth-and-first declaration?"

"It is."

"Listen, A. Gray, suppose someone described a girl to you as being tall and having gray eyes and a pretty mouth, who would you think that was?"

"Well . . . it wouldn't be you."

"Then you wouldn't be able to pick me out on a public road by that description alone?"

"I certainly would not."

"Why not?"

"Because gray doesn't describe the dark mysterious beauty of your eyes; tall doesn't connote the lissom perfection of your form, nor pretty the dewy petals of your lips. . . . Marcia, for God's sake, do marry me. Marcia!"

"Come on, let's go in. You've been talking to Mr. Crowninshield, too."

And she took him by the finger and led him to the manor.

CHAPTER TEN

To the right of the Lacefield kennels lay a flower garden and a vegetable garden, divided from each other by the long arch of a grape arbor.

As Marcia turned back toward the manor with A. Gray she saw Crowninshield and Drusilla stroll through the gardens and enter this arbor.

Drusilla evidently continued to show her guest over the place, but the way she clung to the politician's arm annoyed Marcia in a peculiar manner. It did not seem in good taste for a girl who was betrothed to her brother to be walking so intimately with another man in the obscurity of the grape arbor. She herself wouldn't do it, she thought.

What made it particularly disagreeable was the sister's feeling that Drusilla did not appreciate Miltiades; to be precise, that Drusilla was not the kind of a wife Miltiades deserved.

The manor, the stables, the kennels and slave quarters of the widespread barony had, in Marcia's estimation, no effect on the marriageability of Drusilla. A girl's worth inhered strictly in her own personal qualities. Precisely what those qualities were Marcia did not analyze, but she could feel them within herself: vague excellencies—a power of romance, idealization, industry in the service of her beloved, loyalty, a selfless tenderness. These particular qualities which Marcia so profoundly desired in a wife for Miltiades, Drusilla Lacefield lacked.

Chimes in the manor and the wooden note of a conch shell

being blown by a negro announced supper. Laughter and chatter broke out in a number of places over the darkened grounds as the scattered guests were enlivened at the approach of food.

As A. Gray and Marcia passed across the piazza into the great hall they saw an old negro man already lighting candles in the parlor for the evening dance.

The entrance of the dining room was the third door on the left of the hall. Marcia and A. Gray entered with a file of guests. The sudden brightness of scores of candles, the white napery, the twinkling silver, the long board and graceful backs of Duncan Phyfe chairs gave Marcia a swift grateful impression of reality.

It always appeared to Marcia, when she entered the Lacefield manor, that here was life, and that her existence at home, or existence for the BeShears or the Hams or the Dalrymples, was somehow but a prologue to this warm fullbodied reality. It gave her a sweet, intimate feeling toward A. Gray who could introduce her into this luxury. And the thought dawned on Marcia, as she went in on his arm, that she loved him.

At the head of the table Mr. Lacefield directed his guests to their seats.

"Mr. Dalrymple, will you sit there by Eliza. Maybe she'll listen to what you have to tell about your Virginian hounds."

"I may not listen," demurred Eliza.

"Somehow I feel you will, Miss Eliza," smiled the master of ceremonies.

He went on around the table placing his guests. Marcia and A. Gray were given chairs well up toward their host.

"At last," concluded the head of the house, "our next Congressman, the Honorable Emory Crowninshield, and my beloved daughter, Drusilla, will sit on my right."

Came a general seating of the diners. Marcia looked up the table at Mr. Lacefield's finely carved face sown with a mesh of delicate wrinkles; this always seemed to the girl the very picture of what a landed proprietor should be. She turned and whispered to her companion:

"A. Gray, if I just knew you would grow into a man like your father . . ."

A. Gray considered her a moment with his light hazel eyes then relayed the information:

"Father, Marcia says if she just knew I would be like you . . ."

"Then what would happen, Marcia?" called Eliza Ham from the foot of the table.

"Yes, tell us what would happen, Marcia," seconded two or three voices.

Marcia's neck and cheeks grew warm. She was not accustomed to badinage among so many persons. She stretched a hand toward her host.

"Mr. Lacefield," she begged, "tell them what would happen."

"Why, you would trade off your dinner partner, of course," suggested the host.

"No, it wasn't that at all," and suddenly Marcia was composed again with a very delicate and pleasant feeling in her heart toward both A. Gray and his father.

The host ended the small talk with a slight gesture and requested his son to bespeak God's blessing on the meal and on their country.

Somehow it moved Marcia to hear A. Gray's light voice asking the Creator of the world to devote their food to their use and their lives to the service of their newly created nation.

Came grave responses of amen . . . amen . . . from around the table; a general lifting of heads and adjusting of napkins. From the kitchen a line of waiters filed in bearing platters.

At the lower end of the table the men began talking hounds. Dalrymple told how his hounds had chased something up into Tennessee and hadn't come back till the afternoon of the third day . . . a deer, he supposed, or possibly a wolf.

Mr. Crowninshield spoke of the probable legislation for the newly formed Confederacy . . . manufactured articles would be entered at Confederate ports duty free, the North would have to take its chances in the open markets of the South.

"Our tariff has been ridiculous in the past," assented Mr. Lacefield warmly. "The South paid a bonus on everything the Yankees manufactured when England could ship a superior article across the ocean for a less price."

"There is no equitable argument against free trade," declared Crowninshield. "It is right economically and morally for any people who can produce a commodity most cheaply to furnish that product to the earth. By this means the blessings that God has bestowed on every land would be enjoyed throughout the world."

Marcia leaned over the table, listening intently. Everything the politician said bore an aura of profundity to the girl.

She asked in a low voice why countries should furnish their cheapest things to the world.

The speaker seemed a little surprised at the girl's intent face.

"Because, if every nation supplied the world with what it could produce the most easily we would all share in those natural benefits—it would save everybody work."

The simplicity with which Crowninshield explained these matters to her surprised and pleased Marcia. She had thought heretofore that it was impossible for her to understand anything about the tariff. She had heard her father discussing the tariff with his cronies and Marcia had decided it was a very obscure question indeed.

In the very middle of this Drusilla began telling Crowninshield about a man she had met in Washington. Marcia felt a wave of honest irritation at the interruption. Drusilla was such a cat. She was jealous even when Marcia was improving her mind. Marcia had enough of Miss Cassandra drummed into her that she considered this the equivalent of the "sin against the Holy Ghost."

Talk fell into desultory channels again with Marcia trying to follow every little thing Crowninshield said.

A. Gray murmured in her ear, "Marcia, it's lovely to have you here. Why can't you just stay here permanently?"

The girl felt a touch of self-reproach that she had been neglecting A. Gray.

"I'm afraid one member of your family would get awfully bored with me, A. Gray—she already is."

"You mean Dru?"

Marcia nodded.

"When there are no strange men around she'll be all right." He hesitated, then added wistfully, "I wish I could feel by Dru as Miltiades feels by you."

Marcia touched her suitor's arm.

"Isn't he a wonderful brother?" She glanced across the table at Miltiades, who was talking dutifully to a stocky brunet girl.

"He's frightfully proud," said A. Gray. "I—I think——"

"What do you think?" inquired Marcia a little defensively.

"I think he would be happier if he wasn't so much that way."

Marcia suspected that this was not what A. Gray had meant to say.

The meal drew gayly to a close. Black servants moved around the table, offering renewed helpings which were supposed to be rejected, but which were not in every instance. At last came nuts and wine.

Mr. Lacefield stood up and proposed a toast to the Confederacy. Marcia did not drink her small glassful. She had the hillman's social intractability of drinking too much or

none. She looked down the table and saw Polycarp making up for what she lacked and decided to tell on him. Then she forgot this when Crowninshield responded to the toast:

"Here's to the Southern Confederacy, the sword of Chivalry, the gauntlet of Honor, the heart of Fidelity: a nation like Mercury, new-lighted on a heaven-kissing hill."

A slight cheer from the lower end of the table where the wine was freest, and a voice called out:

"And here's to the first statesman Lauderdale County will send to the Congress of our country!"

The whole tableful drank this toast with much enthusiasm and clinking of glasses.

Supper was over and Mr. Lacefield took his wife on his arm and led the way to the ballroom. It was gayly lighted and at the end of the room on a dais screened with potted plants, six black musicians tuned their instruments. The negroes, dressed in white stiff shirts and long black coats, achieved a hair line between the grotesque and the formal. They were jolly to look at, with their oily black faces and thick smiling lips. When the music began one negro had two light sticks with which he tapped the strings of the violin when the fiddler played. This produced a gay clucking effect to the rhythm of the dance.

Marcia's first dance went to A. Gray. As the girl was swung through the figures from hand to hand, her attention kept wandering to Crowninshield and Drusilla. Both were very graceful in their bowing and advancing and retreating. When she, in her turn, came to the politician's arms, it seemed as if the quadrille suddenly formulated in that instant, and then became a kind of waiting until Crowninshield came around to her once more.

The third dance after the quadrille was a waltz. Crowninshield asked Marcia for that. The girl was sharply tempted, but at last confessed to her companion that her sister, Cassandra, disapproved of round dances.

The politician seemed amused, but he seemed also to approve of this. He suggested that they stroll out on the lawn during the waltz. Marcia took his arm and they stepped out on the piazza through one of the long windows.

The piazza was dark and beset with negroes looking in on the dance. The lawn lay in a weft of moonlight filtered through the trees. The two walked in silence, looking up at the moon through the poplars.

For some reason Marcia thought of Gracie and Solomon and told Crowninshield how Mr. BeShears had sold Solomon away from his bride.

The politician paused a moment and then said gravely:

"That is the price of our social achievement here in the South, Miss Vaiden. Wherever there is a good, somewhere or other there is a compensating pain."

"Just what is our social achievement?" inquired the girl, with a certainty that her companion could make all things clear.

"Well, we are not a material nation . . . for instance we wouldn't think of going to war to pick pennies out of the pockets of the Yankees."

"Do the negroes make that difference?"

"I think so. When wealth comes without effort, nobody haggles over dimes, but if we were born North we would act exactly as the Northern people do."

"Oh, Mr. Crowninshield!"

The man laughed and patted the hand on his arm.

"I talk like a Vandal, don't I?"

"No, you talk like a person who has thought of a great many things."

"Be careful what you say. You tempt me to go on. There is nothing more demoralizing to a man's modesty than for a pretty girl to suggest that she likes to hear him talk."

Marcia was curiously entertained. The man's grave humor seemed poised on the brink of something intimate and profound. She thought again of "improving her mind" and for once in her life desired it so eagerly that it seemed to move something inside of her.

"Oh, I wish I could ask you questions," she said with a little twitch of her fingers, "but I can't think of a one!"

"You mean about the North and the South?"

"Yes . . . some more differences that make us seem grand and them seem mean and little."

Crowninshield began laughing.

"Miss Marcia, you have a wonderfully clear way of stating what everyone would like to hear. You are the heart of the people."

Marcia didn't like this so well. She began defending herself.

"Well now, you have to do a lot of talking before you can make selling Solomon away from Gracie seem right."

Crowninshield became serious again.

"I see that's on your heart . . . it's on the heart of the better part of the South. It's the price we pay for our spiritual freedom, Miss Marcia. The North is concerned mainly with gaining a livelihood; the South is trying to mold something out of life itself. We try to do a number of things with it. We try to make it beautiful and courteous; we try to live gracefully; we try to talk well. Do you know cultivated conversation has never been practised anywhere in the world except when supported by slavery or its equivalent?"

"What connection have the two?" asked Marcia curiously.

"Because good conversation requires leisure, politeness, impersonality, uncommerciality, and acute observation. To possess slaves gives one those qualifications. Take the North. There are many brilliant minds in the North, but they maintain almost a cult against conversation. They say a man is 'all talk,' as if that were a fault. The few Northerners who might talk do not; they either write books or make orations. That's because they are commercial, they want to make their conversation pay. I have been among intellectual groups in the North and I have seen men break off in the middle of excited conversation to scribble something on their cuffs, and then fall into complete silence."

"What for?" asked Marcia in amazement.

"Because the talk had given them a bright idea, and they were afraid, if they said it aloud, somebody would get to press with it before they did."

Marcia trilled into laughter.

"I should think that would ruin conversation!"

"It turns it into a convocation of Indian adepts—all the speakers are trying to attain the silence."

Marcia pondered this extraordinary state of affairs.

"After all, more people enjoy their ideas when they print them."

"I can't agree with that. It's more like picking green fruit that never comes to maturity. The Greeks wrote well because they were slave owners and talked well. The French, under absolute monarchy, produced a splendid body of conversation and out of it flowered a literature. Conversation follows the law of Christ, 'He that loseth his life shall find it'— he that spendeth his idea shall receive it. Conversation is like roses: you can't save them, but if you get enough of them together you can distill a few drops of attar—and that is literature."

When Crowninshield mentioned Christ's name, Marcia became grave again. She thought once more of the eight negroes being carted off somewhere in Larribee's hack through this moonlit night while she stood enjoying the peculiar poetry of this moment. In her heart she renounced her advantage.

"I wouldn't be willing to be unjust to anybody either for the roses or the attar," she said at last. "I think folks should be considerate, and just."

The politician looked through the screen of moonlit trees at the great manor behind it.

"Do you know the doctrine of original sin, Miss Marcia?"

"My father believes it."

"It holds that even a suckling baby is a sinner and is condemned by its very nature."

"Yes, I know, but I never did believe that, Mr. Crowninshield. Even if I was convinced it was so, I still wouldn't believe it."

"Marcia, you're a breathing delight. But suppose we take the doctrine as an allegory. The only way we can have any feeling whatever for justice and morality is through injustice and immorality—do you see that?"

"No, I don't."

"The only way to see a right course is by comparing it to a wrong. If we didn't have this contrast the human race would pursue the way of virtue with the automatism of the insects. Without vice good would become mere habit, it would drop into a moral non-existence. Every unselfish thought we have, every good deed we do must be painted against a background of cruelty and suffering or it could not be seen at all. A young animal is not innocent because it is entirely amoral, but we feel that a baby is at present innocent because in it we discern a future capability to sin. So you see a baby's innocence is a melancholy question with a tragic answer."

The two were leaning on the stone fence beside the pillar of the Lacefield gate. At this mention of babies and the seeds of sin in their expanding lives the same sort of penetrating restlessness filled Marcia that she had known when she gazed into the fire in Miss Cassandra's room. Only now it seemed to her that some solution of her unease almost fluttered in her grasp. She had a feeling that Crowninshield in his penetration could show her the way to some freer and less smothered air. She drew a long breath. She had a sensitive feeling in her fingers and along her arms as if they were about to be touched.

"If slavery," she said vaguely, "is the original sin of the South, will she ever have to pay for it some day?"

"Retribution, you mean?"

"I—I suppose that's what I mean."

"Let's hope not. The good and bad of slavery are inextricably mixed. Let's hope somehow they will balance each other on the ledger of God. . . . You have beautiful hands, Marcia."

He touched her hand lying on the fence in the moonlight. Instinctively she started to withdraw it, but did not. His comment on her hands and his touch seemed to hold more nearly a solution of her vague restlessness than anything he had said.

"My hands are rough because I have to wash the dishes sometimes," said Marcia, feeling keenly the silken texture of her skin under his fingers.

Crowninshield gave a little laugh.

"I never knew before that dishwashing was a beauty recipe."

A sort of tingle spread up through her arm from where the man touched. She said a little uncertainly:

"I'm afraid you're practising on me, Mr. Crowninshield, to flatter Drusilla."

"I could praise Drusilla's hands," admitted the politician gravely, "but I could never have talked to Drusilla about slavery and sin and retribution as I did to you, Marcia. In fact, I had never thought those things at all until the moment I said them to you. There's a sort of magic about you. Your mere silence fills my mind with great thoughts. I think women and men occupy toward each other a curiously similar rôle. A man gives a woman the beginning of a new physical life, and a woman begets great visions in a man."

A kind of melting suspense filled the girl as he stood with his hand over hers looking away into the moonlight. She waited with lips open for what more he would say, or do. Her expectation of sweetness was painful.

She heard far off down the public road the faint rapid hammering of a horse's hoofs. The horse was running and the clatter grew swiftly upon the air.

Crowninshield held her fingers and looked down the moon-blanched thoroughfare. The shape of a horse and rider glimmered into view. It solidified swiftly and the rider swung his horse toward the gate.

"Are you Mr. Lacefield?" he cried.

"No," said Crowninshield. "Mr. Lacefield is in the house. Will you come in?"

"I've got to get to the Ham plantation! Tell Mr. Lacefield Fort Sumter has fallen . . . just got the telegram at Florence. . . . Fort Sumter has fallen! We've taken the Yankee garrison! Tell him that!"

He spurred his horse and dashed off down the road through the moonlight.

CHAPTER ELEVEN

Aт тне sight of Crowninshield's and Marcia's faces the dancers nearest the French window gave up their rhythmic turning. They asked what had happened and the politician told them.

Ejaculations filled the ballroom. Questions began buzzing among the guests. . . . Where was Fort Sumter? Whom had it belonged to?

The dancers crowded after Crowninshield into the hall toward the Lacefield living room. The ballroom became empty except for the six musicians in their semi-formal and semi-grotesque clothes. These black men slowly gave up their strumming and fiddling and looked at each other with white eyes, listening.

Mr. Lacefield heard the trampling and voices of his guests and met them at his door.

The politician repeated what the messenger had said and added:

"In view of this solemn news I thought perhaps you would feel that further dancing this evening was frivolous."

"Of course we don't want to dance any more," cried two or three girls' voices. Then others began asking again where was Fort Sumter? Who had captured it?

Another voice shouted, "Be quiet, everybody. Listen to Crowninshield!"

The babble quieted and the politician began speaking with his tempo hurried a little by excitement.

"Ladies and Gentlemen, I wish to announce first of all that I hereby withdraw my candidacy for a seat in the Congress of our Southern Confederacy. War has begun. Older men than I can sit in the council of our nation. I draw my sword in defense of my country and I ask for volunteers to form a regiment. Do I hear any response?"

The speaker flung up his arm at the question and a number of voices cried out:

"We're with you, Crowninshield!"

They collected around him to go into the details of the matter. Where would his headquarters be? When would he begin his organization?

Mr. Lacefield at once offered his home as a base of operations. He had plenty of space for a drill ground. Crowninshield could stay at his home and the men could assemble there for their training.

The younger men now began pushing their way through the crowd to assure the politician personally that they would join. Among these volunteers, Marcia saw Polycarp.

"I'll make one of your men, Mr. Crowninshield," he said.

Civilian-like, the two shook hands on it.

Marcia's heart made an extra beat at her brother's action.

"No you won't, Carp," she called promptly. "You're not old enough."

"But Marsh, I've shook hands on it," cried Polycarp in confusion.

But her objection and Carp's defense were lost among many voices:

"How long do you think it'll last?" "Not long, we've captured one of their forts already." "Will we invade the North?" "Will the Yankees fight . . . won't they surrender when they see we're in earnest, just like they did at Fort Sumter?" "Oh, one Southern man can lick six Yankees!" "Seven." "Eight." They placed the ratio at different figures.

Marcia wanted to rush home and tell Cassandra and her

father and mother, but the excited talk and speculation kept her lingering on hour after hour.

War had begun! This knowledge changed the whole atmosphere of the manor and the times. Everything tingled. The young men whom she had known all her life and for whom she had cared nothing at all now took on a subtle nearness toward her. They were going to be soldiers. They were going to accept the hazards of war to protect her and girls like her. A foreshadowing of the heroic entered their commonplace appearance.

At last some of the party began making their adieus and went. Then the necessity of telling her own folk drove Marcia to seek out her host and hostess.

When she found Mr. Lacefield he was quite excited. His delicately meshed face was transfigured by the moment. He pressed her hand in bidding her good-bye.

"Marcia, my child, who is going to see you home?" he inquired.

"Why, the boys, I suppose."

"No, don't take them away until they are ready to go, Marcia," he begged for them. "This is a moment in their lives . . . in all our lives. Let them stay as long as they will. My son A. Gray will escort you home."

The old gentleman called a slave and directed that Marcia's and A. Gray's horses be brought around to the front of the manor.

The girl remained a few minutes talking to the planter and his wife, then A. Gray came up and said their horses were ready. A few minutes later when she rode away from the mansion a distressing change set up in Marcia's mood.

Now that she was away from the crowd, the enthusiasm and certitude of victory began to fade from her mind. In the manor the Confederates were sure to gain rapid and glorious victories, but in the immensity of the night brooding over the Reserve she was not sure.

The moon had set and only a glimmer of starlight made

out the road. On her left moved the dark shape of A. Gray
Lacefield and his horse. At long intervals a spark of fire
blinked beneath the clattering hoofs of the horse.

A. Gray himself rode for a long distance in silence. Presently he leaned forward and took old Joe's rein and slowed
down both animals.

"Why . . . what is it?" asked Marcia surprised.

"Marcia," asked A. Gray in an odd voice, "do you know
why Father arranged for me to ride home with you?"

"So the boys could stay at the manor."

"No. It's because he admires you very much, Marcia."

"Why, A. Gray, what has that got to do with the boys
staying over?"

"Nothing at all. He wanted to put us together in the face
of this tremendous news, Marcia. I am sure that he hopes,
just as I do, that you'll marry me, Marcia."

An odd dismay came over the girl at this grave offer of
marriage so in contrast with A. Gray's usual light-hearted
declarations of love. Bringing the elder Mr. Lacefield into it
gave the proposal a certain moral pressure.

"Why, A. Gray," she said uncertainly, "you know he
didn't mean that."

"Oh, yes, he did . . . I'm sure he did . . . and then you
admire him very much, don't you, Marcia, even if you don't
care a great deal about me?"

"Why, A. Gray, I do care about you!" cried Marcia reproachfully. "I care a lot about you . . . of course I do!"

"Well, I've always loved you, Marcia. I suppose I won't
be home very long now." He moved his horse closer to her
and put an arm about her shoulder. "You don't love anybody else, do you, Marcia?"

"Why, A. Gray," said the girl, a little startled at the
question, "I have never been with anyone but you . . . I
mean—you know—regular—like this."

"There you are," said the youth, with a little more hope

in his desolate tones. "I think we ought to make it even more regular. I think we ought to get married."

This was beginning to be light again. Marcia, and perhaps A. Gray, too, would have been willing to make it quite light and flippant had it not been that the war forbade. It was very pleasant to Marcia to refuse A. Gray's heart and fortune every time she saw him, and to fancy herself accepting both every time she did not see him. But the war, her anxiety about both A. Gray and her brothers, Mr. Lacefield's maneuvering to place her and his son together, A. Gray's arm tentatively about her shoulders—it all conspired to fill Marcia with responsibility and change her pleasure in their courtship into concern.

The youth himself began shivering uncontrollably; he slipped his arm down about her waist and drew her a little toward him as the horses walked along.

"Listen, Marcia . . . l-let's get married to-morrow—or day after—or Sunday."

The feel of his arm around her waist was disappointing to Marcia. They might have been dancing together in the manor.

"Come on, let's trot," she said suddenly.

"Oh no, no—please don't trot—Marcia!"

In the slight conflict, with Marcia spurring her horse onward and A. Gray holding him back, a heavy sound, far away, muttered in the night.

It was enough to stop the little love duel.

"What was that?" asked Marcia, straightening in her saddle away from A. Gray's arm.

The youth, on the other hand, was keenly annoyed.

"I don't know what it was. What difference does it make?"

In answer to this the sound was repeated, evidently a distant heavy explosion.

Genuine curiosity took the place of Marcia's pretense.

"You don't suppose we are hearing cannons somewhere, A. Gray?"

"No, there aren't any cannons. . . . I know what it is."

"What?"

"It's somebody shooting an anvil to celebrate."

"Yes, I suppose it is that."

She started old Joe to trotting again. A. Gray quickened his own horse, but Marcia could feel his disappointment and this reproached her. The way she had just treated him was a sort of betrayal of her long-time suitor. She had refused him the intimacy and sympathy of her caresses just at the dramatic moment of both their lives. Now A. Gray had nobody to whom he could turn. To the romantic girl this seemed a bitter thing for a soldier to go to war without a wife or sweetheart to kiss him and wait for him and pray for him. Marcia herself was quite willing to pray for A. Gray and to wait for him, because when he was absent she felt very romantic toward him, but kisses, unfortunately, are always in the present tense.

Another concussion from the distant anvil switched Marcia's mind from the uncomfortable topic to old Parson Mulry.

"Oh, A. Gray!" she ejaculated in the utmost amazement. "I already knew about that battle . . . I knew about it at dinner time!"

"What battle—Fort Sumter?"

"Why, of course! How stupid I was not to think of that before . . . I ought to have told everybody at the manor!"

"What in the world are you talking about?" cried her suitor, jostled out of his pique at Marcia's manner.

Then she began telling him excitedly what old Parson Mulry had mumbled about cannons and forts.

A. Gray listened dubiously.

"I don't take much stock in anything like that," he said when she had finished. "You know the niggers believe in things of that sort."

"Yes, of course, that's a fact," agreed Marcia, a little dampened.

For negroes to believe in a thing seemed a good reason for white people not believing in it. She became silent and began wondering what Crowninshield would have said to Parson Mulry's clairvoyance. The thought of the talk she had had with the politician at the manor gate returned now to Marcia with a sense of something long past. The fall of Fort Sumter already had cut Marcia's life in two. Everything antecedent to that moment was something definitely in the past, and all things subsequent were a part of her present. In this past, on the very edge of it, lay her talk with Crowninshield, with its abstract intimacy . . . and the pressure of his fingers on her hand.

A closer and louder explosion caused A. Gray to ejaculate, "I declare, Marcia, I believe that's your daddy shooting the anvil in his old blacksmith shop."

They began spurring their horses in good earnest now, and presently, far up the road, they saw a flash of fire followed by a rolling detonation. A. Gray waved his hat and cheered.

When the two came up they found the whole Vaiden household out at the old forge across the road. Men and women, black and white, were celebrating victory in the first battle of the war. But the women, while they celebrated, were already trying to stop the celebration as quickly as they could.

Miss Cassandra was threatening her father with dire physical penalties if he didn't go to bed and quit hammering nails in his own coffin by staying up so late.

The roaring old man ordered Robinet and Columbus to go on with the anvil shooting, but Miss Cassandra and old Mrs. Laura spread such an aura of lateness over the hour that it seemed surely it must be day after to-morrow night instead of the night they were inhabiting, and that old man Jimmie already had lost a week of sleep.

Young A. Gray wanted to stay and watch the blastings with Marcia, but he so obviously meant to renew his caresses and his pleadings that Marcia began helping her mother and sister laten the hour, and presently A. Gray went home.

When Marcia went upstairs to her room she found her maid waiting for her.

"Gracie, you nee'n to have stayed up for me," said Marcia to the cream-colored figure.

"I thought you'd want your hair combed," said Gracie in an anxious tone.

"I could have done it myself to-night, Gracie," offered Marcia generously, since it was established that Gracie would do the combing.

She sat down in a chair and gave her hair into Gracie's hands.

"I'm not a bit tired or sleepy," yawned Marcia. "I declare that man came galloping up the road . . . I could just tell something exciting had happened by the way he galloped!"

"And the Yankees are whipped?" asked Gracie in a wondering voice.

"Well, that much is whipped. They say over at Mr. Lacefield's that it will only be a little while till they're all whipped. Mr. Crowninshield is making up a regiment."

"M . . . uh," said Gracie. "You know he'll whip 'em with a whole regiment."

"Carp wanted to join but I put my foot down on that." Marcia yawned again under the brushing of her hair.

"Uh . . . little missy . . . did you stop by Mr. Be-Shears'?" inquired Gracie in an impersonal tone between strokes.

"Yes, I did, and guess what happened! He refused to sell me a dress pattern on credit—right there before everybody. Why, I could have murdered him!"

"Why, little missy, he let you have it!" cried Gracie excitedly.

"Let me have it . . . what do you mean?"

"There it is, layin' on your bed. Blue Gum brought it

here and give it to me. And Blue Gum was battered up so you wouldn't know him. He sure was bunged up."

Marcia was struck with wonder at such a report about Blue Gum.

"What in the world had happened to him—did he fall off his horse?"

"No. I asked him. What he said didn't make any sense. He said he got bunged up in honor of Mr. Miltiades, and that's all he'd tell me."

Marcia stared and suddenly clapped her hands together.

"Oh . . . the idiot! He told Mr. BeShears what Brother Miltiades told him to tell him! Oh, what a dunce!" And Marcia began laughing till tears rolled down her face.

"What did he tell him to tell?"

"W-Why he told Blue Gum to call old man BeShears all —all sorts of bad names. I—I suppose he did."

Gracie waited soberly until her mistress had finished her laughing.

"Little missy, did—did you think to ask about Solomon?" queried the maid in a small voice.

Marcia's mirth dropped from her suddenly.

"Oh, Gracie!" she gasped, turning and staring at the cream-colored girl with shocked eyes.

Gracie stopped brushing with a startled air.

"What is it, little missy?"

"Gracie! To think—to think it went out of my mind!"

"What went out of your mind, little missy?" asked Gracie in an edged voice.

"Oh, Gracie—Mr. BeShears has—he—he—has——" She broke off, unable to go on.

The quadroon's eyes widened into pools of black.

"Do you mean he's—sold Solomon?" she whispered in a ghastly voice.

Marcia nodded mutely into the widened eyes.

The brunet girl's lips made a movement and Marcia knew she asked, "Where to?"

"To—a trader. All his niggers—Solomon—Calline—he went off with 'em in a hack."

Gracie simply stood with comb in hand looking at Marcia. Tears began running silently down her cheeks in the candlelight.

"I—I thought ol' Pap said——"

Gracie reached out as if for some support in the dim attic and then toppled forward.

Marcia caught her and staggered with her to the bed. She got her half on it.

"Cassandra! Mother!" she shouted. "Bring some water!"

Her call went unheard for at that moment came another heavy detonation of old man Jimmie's anvil in celebration of the defeat of the Yankees at Fort Sumter.

CHAPTER TWELVE

THE FALL of Sumter aroused the South out of its dreamlike idyl with the quick and vivifying pulse of war. The speculations of the Lacefield ballroom were repeated multitudinously all over the country. The Southern people talked of other impending victories. They speculated on how long the North would endure. Newspapers spread everywhere and were bought and read even by the poor whites, whose reading hitherto had been confined to the almanac and the Bible.

The different Southern states suddenly developed personalities of their own. Men speculated on what Kentucky would do, which way Tennessee would lean, on which side Missouri would cast her shield. These doubtful states became like beautiful women and Southern statesmen wooed their favor.

Everywhere were barbecues, picnics, patriotic speeches, and enlistment rolls. Volunteers drilled in every village. Martial technique, which lies dormant in peace, now broke forth, and veterans of the Mexican War taught the manual of arms to youngsters eager for the field of Mars.

In the general exaltation and optimism these youths, marching and countermarching in civilian clothes, appeared to be in no danger at all. It seemed they would march forth bearing charmed lives. The real anxiety among the volunteers was that the war might cease before they reached the front.

On the Lacefield plantation Miltiades Vaiden drilled a

company of volunteers mornings and evenings. A kind of grave exultation filled this eldest of the Vaidens at this change from overseeing negroes to drilling white men.

Miltiades had a room in the office of the Lacefield plantation. It stood on the lawn, detached from the manor. Now on these spring mornings the man awoke with a renewed sense of station and power. He would shave the black beard from his bluish square-cleft chin, then, powdered and manicured, he would look out over the grounds with a spiritual satisfaction. He would feel that this scheme of luxury was upheld, not by his labor as overseer among the negroes, but by his courage and military skill as a soldier.

Already he had ordered two uniforms from his tailor in Florence, a dress uniform and a service uniform; and two pairs of military boots from the cobbler.

From where Miltiades looked out the doorway of the office, the great columns of the manor appeared yellow in the sunshine and bluish in the shadow. The piazza suggested Drusilla, and the man thought when he came back from the war he would not be an overseer, but a high Confederate officer and the husband of Drusilla. He would be the lord of the manor.

At the moment the daughter of the house herself stepped out of the front door, glanced around the piazza, and was about to reënter.

The brown, ivory, and blue-black prettiness of the girl caused Vaiden to call her name and cross the lawn to her. He wished her good-morning and she said she was looking for Major Crowninshield. Miltiades said he had not seen the major, then glanced about the empty sun-shot lawn and leaned down and kissed the girl.

Drusilla turned her face away.

"Don't do that, Milt . . . out in the open like this."

"You mean not now." He pinched the lobe of her ear, which was perforated for a ring but which, at the moment, held none.

"Not anytime," said Drusilla, half in annoyance but still with a lift of her brows and a tilt of her chin.

The instinctive coquetry of the girl always stirred a kind of impatient desire in her lover. He took her smooth forearms and began moving her light graceful figure into the shadow of the hallway.

"I'm going to have a kiss," he whispered, with a kind of soft determination.

Drusilla was filled with the harassed pleasure of a woman resisting a man whom she likes. She pulled back, flung out her hand to the edge of the door to stop herself. Then suddenly she called:

"Major Crowninshield! Major Crowninshield!"

The politician's voice answered from the lawn around the house:

"What is it, Drusilla?"

Miltiades loosed the girl with a kind of annoyed good nature. It had been one of those sharp little moments when he had wanted to feel Drusilla's lips against his own and caress her soft curves.

The girl's dark eyes were full of amusement at his face. She turned to Crowninshield who came up on the piazza.

"I was sent to call you to breakfast."

"Dear me!" said the major. "I thought I was rushing to aid beauty in distress, and here I'm to be fed." A horseman riding up to the gate drew his attention. "Captain, yonder's one of our men come for the drill."

"I'll see him," said Miltiades. "I'll be with you and Drusilla in a moment."

The overseer set out to the gate. He meant to pass the time of day with this first comer. As yet the young men of the neighborhood who gathered to drill in the Lacefield pasture were about half soldiers and half guests.

As Miltiades walked out to speak to this man, Drusilla came running back on the piazza.

"Milt, I want that book," she called. "I let you have it. You'll have to come find it in the office for me."

She started across to the office and the man turned and hurried after her. Inside she pushed the door shut and then stood smiling and lifting her arms and lips to his. She gasped in baby talk in the midst of his pressure:

"After . . . all . . . I woul'na . . . do . . . my sojer boy . . . that way."

"Listen, Drusilla," begged the captain, holding her hard against him, "we can't wait till June . . . June! Heaven knows where I'll be by June!"

The girl put up her fingers to the bluish sandpapery dimple in his square chin. She felt languorous.

"When do you want to marry?"

"This afternoon."

"Oh, Milt . . ."

"To-morrow then."

"Let me see . . ." The girl moved her palm delicately over his chin. It sent a sharp sweet tingling through her arms and down into her body. "I might get ready in a week."

Vaiden picked the girl up off the floor and kissed her again and again.

"In one week you'll be Mrs. Miltiades Vaiden!"

She twisted her lips away and wriggled down out of his arms.

"If I don't change my mind. . . . Let me go. I must eat breakfast with Major Crowninshield now."

"Surely you wouldn't disappoint me again, Dru?"

"Well, I did once . . . I may again. I never know what I'm going to do, Milt. . . . Doing that makes the soles of my feet tickle . . . wonder why? Well, good-bye. I've got to fly to the major and feed him."

And off she went out the door and across the lawn.

Miltiades stood looking after her, moved by her waywardness and odd remark about the soles of her feet.

His heart beat in sympathy with her vagrant sensation. Marriage with her, at the moment, appealed to him with physical voluptuousness. But this voluptuousness was somehow keyed up by the background of the manor, the broad acres, and the silver maples weaving blue morning shadows across the golden lawn. It was a demesne that begged for sons and daughters and lusty children.

Out in the pasture more recruits had gathered for their endless drilling. The captain went in to his breakfast with his major and his fiancée, and an hour later turned out to his work.

Around the pasture there were always onlookers watching the new men turn into soldiers. During an interval of rest, Polycarp and Augustus came out of the string of spectators. Augustus began in his complaining voice:

"Look here, Brother Milt, me and Polycarp want to join up with your company."

The social awkwardness of his hobbledehoy brothers always slightly amused and slighted grated on Miltiades. He had no desire for them to be in his company.

"What would Cassandra say?" he asked, as if he would be very glad to have them.

"Oh, my goodness, we don't have to ask Cassandra! A fellow don't have to ask his sister to go to war."

"No, but you have to ask Father and Mother, and that will simply get back to Cassandra at last, so it is not unreasonable to ask straight off, what would Cassandra say?"

"Dad blame it, Carp, I told you how it would be!" grumbled Augustus.

"Listen," said Miltiades more soberly, "there'll be opportunities for you boys to enlist later."

"The devil there will!" ejaculated Augustus in the keenest impatience. "They tell me our army is about to capture Washington now. As soon as that happens where'll we be? Left! Left down here on the plantation——" He broke off in exasperation.

"Look here, Brother Miltiades," compromised Polycarp, "let us drill with you to-day, then if Sister Cassandra makes us quit, we'll quit."

Miltiades began laughing.

"Polycarp, that's a liberal offer. I'll take it up with President Davis." He drew out his watch, made of new gold and chased with yellow old gold, noted the time, and rode out on the field again. "Company attention!" he called. "Forward march!"

And off went the recruits in their civilian clothes with squirrel rifles and shotguns over their shoulders, training for glory in the midst of their jolly youth.

The two younger brothers were disgusted at the outcome of their attempt. They began criticizing Miltiades adversely.

"If I was going to be a soldier," said Carp, "I'd look like I was going to a battle, not to a dance."

"Me too," echoed Augustus.

"I don't believe Brother Milt will ever go into a battle anyway . . . he'd be afraid of getting his clothes wrinkled."

Augustus laughed, and the two boys remounted their mule and set out on the return home. They had only one mule between them this time. They had got only Lou. The negroes had saved Rab for the field, so they were forced to ride double.

As they returned home the recruits still marched and countermarched in their imagination. They could fancy them on the field of battle with cannons roaring and rifles crashing. The thought of such a spectacle going on with them left at home became unbearable.

"Gus," said Carp tensely, "let's talk Mother into this, and she'll get around Cassandra."

"Cassandra's not our boss anyway," declared Augustus. "The trouble is, Mammy won't stick. She'll say yes, then Cassandra will blab around for an hour or so and Mammy'll say no."

The two brothers enjoyed using scornful words of their

elder sister when out of her presence. They planned ways to circumvent her.

By this time they were approaching the Crossroads and the three great sycamores by the spring. As they drew near the merchant's residence Polycarp saw a pink dress run from the house out into an uncultivated field, in a direction parallel to the course of the road. Involuntarily the older brother kicked up his mount.

Augustus was aggrieved.

"Hey, watch out! Tell me when you're going to make the mule lope like that!"

"I'm riding this mule!"

"Yeh, and if I haul off and hit you, you won't be riding this mule."

"Naw, I'd be riding you."

"Shoo, you would!" scoffed Augustus, who knew Polycarp was much stronger than he, and would certainly be riding him, figuratively speaking, just as he said.

"I'll bet you," said Polycarp, "it would be easy in a cavalry charge to ride up alongside a Yankee, jump over behind him on his horse, stick him in the back, and ride his horse away. . . . What chance would he have?"

"Huh, he might take it into his head to jump on your horse behind you and stick you in the back."

"He couldn't do that because Yankees can't ride very well . . . they live in cities." Here he broke off his ideas on cavalry tactics to shout, "Hello!" draw up old Lou as suddenly as he started her off, and ejaculate in apparent surprise, "Well, if there ain't Ponny out there in the field."

"Well, what if she is?" asked Augustus, who looked at Ponny with the same eyes with which he would look at a sassafras bush.

"Don't you think we better stop and give her the news?" demanded Polycarp, out of patience with his younger brother.

"What news?"

"Why, dad burn it—that—that the Confederate army is marching on Washington."

"She already knows that—ever'body does," said Augustus, kicking old Lou in the flanks to force her on against Polycarp's reins.

"Listen," cried the elder brother, "if you're in such a plagued hurry you can't stop a minute to tell a neighbor the news, let me off a minute, then you ride on slow and I'll run and ketch up with you."

"Now I'm not going to ride very slow very far. It's a fool piece of business anyway, telling a girl something she's bound to know already. Why can't you just holler to her that the Confederates are about to capture Washington? . . . I'll tell her—lemme holler to her——"

"Oh, shut up! Hollering! You have no more politeness than a cat. You don't holler news at a lady!"

"Oh, now—a lady. When did Ponny BeShears get to be a lady? She's no more a lady than Marsh is."

Polycarp ignored his brother and got to the ground. Augustus watched him in astonishment. As he slid over the cantle into the saddle he said:

"I b'lieve you're stuck on Ponny."

"You shut up," warned Polycarp belligerently.

Augustus rode on slowly for fifteen or twenty yards, as he had promised Carp he would, then he began whooping and lambasting old Lou with his hat. He had waited for his brother as long as he could.

Polycarp Vaiden approached the high rail fence acutely conscious that this was the first time that he had ever sought out Ponny as Ponny.

The girl herself, in her print dress, with her round face and china-blue eyes, stood watching him cross the ditch along the road with a warm color in her neck and face.

As Polycarp jumped across and scrambled over the rails he called out that he thought he would come over and tell her the news.

"That's nice of you," said Ponny.

The hobbledehoy could not immediately think of anything more to say. He was somehow bewildered by the girl herself. He had never quite seen this Ponny before. She seemed crystalline, as if a soft light were shining through her. It seemed impossible that he could ever have kissed such a glorious creature. He became very busy climbing the fence, so there would be no need of saying anything for the moment.

When he finally dropped down inside this reprieve expired.

"I—uh—saw you run out of the house as I rode up," he said.

"Oh, was you riding up?"

"Yes, didn't you see me?"

"Well, I thought maybe it was you."

"Is that why you come out here?" inquired Polycarp hopefully.

"Why, no!" cried Ponny. "I wanted to see if there was any strawberries." She held up a quart bucket defensively.

"I'll help hunt," offered Carp at once, and together they began looking under the clumps of sedge for early berries.

There were none. The delicate wild strawberry plants had not even bloomed, but an exquisite sweetness settled over boy and girl as thy wandered aimlessly together looking in the stubble.

A field lark burst out of a clump of grass, with its graceful half-sailing, half-winging flight. Ponny ran to the place.

"Look," she cried, "here are two eggs!"

Polycarp peered into the delicate woven cup.

"Le's eat 'em."

Ponny caught his hands.

"Oh, no . . . ain't they sweet!"

She held away his hands from this natural spoil of boyhood. The anxious little mother was fluttering only a few yards away, making a great show of a crippled wing and a speckled breast.

Polycarp wanted to throw a stone at her. He believed he could kill her, but he did not even mention this.

"Come on and let her get back to her nest," said Ponny, leading him away and watching the bird over her shoulder. "Isn't the sun bright? . . . doesn't everything smell good?" She squeezed his fingers. "Oh, Carp, isn't this a beautiful day? . . . Le's set down. . . . Did you ever hear so many birds singing all at oncet?"

Polycarp sat down with her in the yellow sedge in a kind of haze of happiness. He had had no idea, when he climbed down off the mule, that there could be such a delicate halcyon mood. Their fingers, still lightly linked, seemed to transmit to Polycarp myriad charms he had never observed before. Truly, birds were everywhere. From far and near came the silver lash of the cardinal, the soft repetition of doves, the passing metallic confusion of blackbirds, the loud trill of tiny wrens.

"I was awfully afraid you'd be mad at me for what Daddy said the other day." Ponny held up her face to the sun, recalling the quarrel.

"Oh, the idyah!"

"Well, I didn't want you—and Marcia—and Augustus to be mad at me."

"Ponny," objected Polycarp uncertainly, "was it as much Marcia and Augustus as—as—somebody else?"

Ponny pinkened.

"Why, Polycarp, Marcia and me are the dearest friends!"

"Yes . . . Augustus then," pressed Carp in his demurring tone.

"Gus is just a child."

"Isn't that the truth!" agreed Polycarp with rancorous enthusiasm. "That boy is a wart on the devil's tail. He's about as agreeable as a stone bruise, he's about as polite to the ladies as a dawg is to a fence post."

"Polycarp! Hush!"

"Excuse me," blurted out Polycarp, rather disconcerted himself, "but Augustus makes me so pop-eyed mad!"

"Oh, me!" sighed Ponny. "I'm sure if I had a little brother I'd just worship him." She shivered and drew up her shoulders. "O-o-o—how I would love a brother—or a sister. It's so lonesome to be an only child."

"I've got plenty of brothers and sisters," said Polycarp, "and I feel a lot lonesomer with 'em than I do away from 'em."

"O-o-o, I wouldn't!"

"Yes you would. Brothers and sisters are all just alike. They either try to boss you or they won't do what you tell 'em to do."

"O-o-o, but without them, Carp, I nearly go crazy sometimes being all by myself. I want someone so-o bad!"

"Do you want a brother or a sister now?" inquired Carp jealously.

"Oh, silly, of course not!"

A sort of wave of physical sweetness went through Polycarp to think that he so completely filled the hiatus in Ponny's life. A notion of kissing her again floated through his head and moved tangibly on down into his body. But their initial caress seemed utterly vanished as a precedent for action. The boy sat in the sedge mutely wishing to kiss and to be kissed.

After while Ponny asked with resignation in her voice, "What news was you going to bring me?"

"Oh . . . that. I'm going to join the army."

"You don't mean it!" cried Ponny, her plump fingers catching Polycarp's hand.

The boy was delighted at this turn,

"Yes, ever'body's going. I don't want to be the only man left at home."

"Oh, Carp, I'll pray for you every night."

A tingling went through Carp at the intimate idea of Ponny thinking of him every night in her nightgown.

"Ponny, will you sure 'nuff?"

"Of course I will. I'll pray God to protect you."

"Just you praying will be enough," said Polycarp in a rapture. Neither one of them knew it, but what Polycarp meant was that they could leave God out of the picture and Ponny's prayers in her nightgown would be enough for him.

Ponny moistened her dry lips and squeezed the boy's fingers with both hands.

"And Polycarp . . . these days . . . all the men who are about to go to war . . . they're just a-marrying like ever'-thing. Only day before yestiddy Sue Ham, that's Eliza's cousin, married Heck Northrup. And Daisy Fowler married Newt Thompson, and Sally Dalrymple married somebody who lives close to Waterloo . . . Ooo, they're just marryin' ever'where!"

A sudden idea of asking Ponny to marry him popped into young Mr. Vaiden's head. Where it came from he had no notion. A strange impression came over him that he was sitting on a crystalline hillside which might at any moment break through and let him fall into endless space. At the same moment he was saying:

"Ponny, would—would you marry me—would you mind marrying me?"

The next minute, quite miraculously, he found Ponny in his arms and he in hers. The softness of Ponny's rondures beneath his fingers and against his legs and chest made him drunk. They kissed endlessly in the spring sunshine and the soft air. Her hair and flesh surrounded him with the faint, pleasant odor of a young girl who has not bathed for two or three days and is not disguised with perfume. The passion of the young lovers was utterly satisfied by this tense kissing embrace; they did not even think of the givings of sex. They experienced only one annoyance. Their bodies somehow or other seemed to be in the way. They were kept apart distressingly by their arms, their shoulders, their hips.

"How are we going to get married?" breathed Polycarp, to whom now an unmarried state had become unthinkable.

"I've thought all that out," explained Ponny at once. "I'll go to Florence to see Jenny Millsap. You come up and buy a pair of licenses, Jenny'll call in a preacher for us and she'll be the witness. . . . Jenny don't care what she does—she's that sort of a girl."

"Ponny, d'you suppose I can get a pair of licenses on a credit?" questioned Polycarp in an emotional haze.

These financial preliminaries to marriage were sidetracked by a man's voice rasping out:

"Ponny BeShears! What do you mean? Get on back down to the house! Carp Vaiden, you low-down, dirty scoundrel! Come insulting me in my store, now ruinin' my gal!"

Boy and girl scrambled up.

In the daylight, out of his store, Mr. BeShears was a square bewhiskered man whose eyes looked as if they had been slightly burned by powder.

"He hasn't done nothing wrong!" cried Ponny, angry and crimson. "We're going to get married!"

"Married! You'll not marry that good-for-nothing! . . . Git on home! And you, Carp Vaiden, if I ever ketch you on my land ag'in I'll tan your jacket tull you kain't set down!"

The idea of such a nonentity as the storekeeper whipping anybody filled the planter's son with wrath.

" 'Y God, you'll brush my jacket now!" he cried. "I'm on your land and I'll stan' here! Nobody's afraid of a derned old counter jumper!"

The father snapped off the limb of the nearest sassafras and swung at Polycarp.

"Carp! Carp! Polycarp! Don't hurt him, Pappy!"

The limb bruised Vaiden's back and shoulders. The boy stared at the grotesque clubman with a flickering realization that this was Ponny's father.

"Run! Run, Carp! You can outrun him—I can!"

"Run hell!" shouted the boy. "I won't."

Suddenly Ponny dashed into her father.

"Leave him alone! Quit! Don't you see how brave he is?"

Mr. BeShears flung his daughter aside and gave her a rap with the sassafras.

A tingle of justification rushed through Polycarp. In a split second he lunged into the merchant with the address of a hill fighter. He caught BeShears' throat. He tried to trip him but could not. The storekeeper reached for Polycarp's throat, but had the bad luck to jab his thumb in the boy's mouth. The thumb was crushed in the stout teeth. The next instant boy and man went to the ground in one of those silent, biting, eye-gouging fights of the hills.

Ponny went into hysterics, shrieking, screaming, pulling desperately at one man or the other. She might as well have pulled at bulldogs who had got their teeth set.

Four or five men came running and shouting from the store. When they reached the fighters rolling on the hillside there was a brief argument among them. Some wanted to see which one would lick. After a moment they obeyed Ponny and dragged the fighters apart. The last thing to come loose was the merchant's thumb from Carp's teeth.

On this technicality the men awarded the fight to Carp.

The boy's face was bruised. One of his eyes, which had been gouged, was a red-and-purple circle.

"Go on home, Carp," the men advised in excited but friendly voices. "He's too old a man for you to straddle!"

To BeShears others were saying, "Let him alone Alex, he's nothin' but a boy!"

"Philandering aroun' my gal!" cried the old man, still struggling against the men who held him, and his voice was hoarse with rage.

"My Lord," drawled a peacemaker, "if courtin' a gal is a hangin' offense, we'd all be strung up, includin' yorese'f, Alex."

They took the old man back down to the store, and as they went suggested sugar and turpentine for the thumb.

The others got Carp into the road and headed him for home.

The boy called back to the girl in a defiant voice, "That's all right, Ponny . . . remember!"

He held up a hand and nodded back at her with his bruised and swelling face.

CHAPTER THIRTEEN

THE OPINION Polycarp Vaiden expressed to Ponny, that
the more kinsfolk a man has the lonelier he is, found poign-
ant corroboration when that young man reached home.

He had had to walk. Augustus had been even better than
his word. He had ridden old Lou home so fast that when she
arrived there Columbus promptly discovered that she had
the heaves. When Polycarp reached the mule's sickbed he
found his father and the two negroes burning tobacco stalks
under Lou's nose in a desperate effort to save her life.

To Polycarp's dismay, he found that he was the one who
had undone old Lou. When he came in sight old man Jimmie had boomed out, "What in the thunderation do you
mean, letting this little feather-headed fool ride old Lou by
himself for?"

He had his whip and was evidently going to start on
Augustus, even if Polycarp was wholly to blame, when Mrs.
Laura came down and began talking of the night old man
Jimmie had run his thoroughbred horse to death in a fox
hunt. She said she supposed Augustus, being a Vaiden, it
was born in him to give a mule the thumps.

As soon as the old man had wrathfully admitted there
was an affinity between Vaidens and thumps, and that one
brought the other on inevitably but without guilt, he wanted
to know who in the Sam Hill Polycarp had been fighting and
didn't Polycarp know that he (old man Jimmie) had forbidden him to fight?

As Polycarp said nothing at all, the father whirled on Augustus.

"Who in the thunder has Polycarp been fighting?"

Augustus was too puffed up with anger even to enjoy his brother's peril.

"I do' know," he mumbled. "I left him telling Ponny Be-Shears about the war."

"About the war!" echoed the old man. "What in the blazes does he know about the war that everybody else don't know?"

"That's what I told him," cried Augustus wrathfully, "but instead of listening to me he started me on home by myself, and ol' Lou run away with me and got the thumps, and now I get the blame!" Augustus would have sobbed if sobbing would have crippled anybody.

Polycarp was glad enough for his fight to simmer down to what novel information he had about the war, so he turned away from the stable and the tobacco smoke and took himself to the kitchen to skirmish for something to eat.

Old Mrs. Vaiden had an idea that Polycarp's news from the front which he had imparted to Ponny had some very intimate connection with his bruised face. She went straight to Cassandra with it. She said:

"Cassie, Carp's started going with Ponny BeShears. He's already had one fight about her with somebody. What can we do to break it up?"

The old woman, some decade before, would not have thought it necessary to break it up, but that was before Cassandra's advent. Since then her eldest daughter had advocated the idea that nobody was good enough for a Vaiden and the mother at last had been won over to the opinion. For the last ten or fifteen years now, for a Vaiden to marry anybody at all was to set a pearl in the snout of a swine. It was to mingle the Vaiden blood with that of the "commonality."

When Miss Cassandra thus learned from her mother that Polycarp had stooped from his gens to dally with one of the

commonality she immediately looked out the door, saw Polycarp heading for the kitchen, and walked around through
the family room ahead of him. When he stepped into the kitchen Miss Cassandra looked at his face and ejaculated disapprovingly, but in complete innocence of its cause:

"Polycarp, what in the world have you been doing?"

Polycarp blinked a right eye which was warm and too
large.

"I had a little brush with a fellow," he explained indefinitely. At the moment he hoped to keep Augustus's information and Cassandra's cross-questioning in rumor-tight com-
partments from each other.

"Who did you have the brush with?" demanded the sister, wondering who was Ponny's other beau.

"Why—er—me and Alex BeShears had a little set-to,"
admitted Polycarp grudgingly.

Old Mrs. Vaiden was now in the door of the kitchen and
the two women gasped. They suspected wildly why the fight
had come about. Cassandra said:

"You ought to show more respect for Mr. BeShears than
that."

"When a man jumps on you with as little sense as Alex
BeShears showed, he loses out in respect among his neighbors pretty fast," growled Polycarp, getting angry again.

Old Mrs. Vaiden considered her son in horror.

"Polycarp—what in the world were you and Ponny doing?" she asked in a strained whisper.

"Nothin'! Not a thing in the world!" cried Polycarp.
"We were just sitting there talking!"

"Sitting where?" interpolated Miss Cassandra brittly.

"Out in the pasture and Mr. BeShears come up on
us——"

"How close?"

"Right up on us."

"You didn't see him?"

"I—ee—no, we didn't see him." The parts of the boy's face that could turn red did so.

The two women stood staring at him, thinkng inexpressible things. Finally Miss Cassandra said in a flat voice:

"What were you talking about?"

"Plague take the luck!" cried Polycarp. "I . . . how do I know? It's passed out of my mind."

"Polycarp Vaiden," said his mother, "you know just as well what you-all were talking about as—as anything."

"Maw, I didn't write it down."

"Polycarp, what were you talking about?" said Miss Cassandra.

"Plague take the luck!" cried Polycarp brazenly. "We were talking about getting married, that's what we were talking about."

The two Vaiden women stared at him as if he had taken leave of his senses. This was evidently the truth. The fight had not occurred over what they suspected. But why any fight at all? They would have thought Alex BeShears would have dropped on his knees in gratefulness at the prospect of Ponny marrying a Vaiden.

"You don't mean getting married to Ponny BeShears!" exclaimed Miss Cassandra.

"Well, everybody else is marrying," said Polycarp gloomily.

"You haven't got anything to marry on," objected his mother practically.

"Well, ever'body else is marrying, and a lot of them hasn't got anything."

"Who?"

Polycarp glibly named the couples Ponny had mentioned.

"Those folks are ordinary people," pointed out Miss Cassandra sharply. "They are the sort who get along somehow. And the BeShears . . . what are they? Nobodies. Ponny a great big fat blob of a girl, always bounding around the men." She suddenly raised a finger at her

brother. "I'll bet dollars to doughnuts she proposed to you.
. . . She did! I see she did and you're such a goose as to
accept her!"

"She did not!" yelled Polycarp in the utmost confusion.
"She didn't have a thing in the world to do with it!"

"And you tumbled right into it," pursued Miss Cassandra with great contempt—"you, a Vaiden, permitting yourself to be made love to by that shapeless thing."

"Well, that's exactly what me and old BeShears had a
fight about," cried Polycarp.

"About Ponny's vulgarity?"

"No, about me being a Vaiden. He said he didn't want his
daughter marrying a no-'count Vaiden."

Miss Cassandra's face cleared up at this unexpected ally.

"I certainly hope he sticks to it. And Polycarp, why can't
you maintain some self-respect? Wait till you meet a girl
of your own class. . . . Now *she* won't come up and ask you
to marry her, I can assure you that. She won't be bold or
fat. . . ."

Miss Cassandra continued her description earnestly and
with enthusiasm. She drew the picture of a perfect wife for
Polycarp who was composed completely of negatives. She
did not do this, she was not that, she did not talk so. Every
sentence the elder sister spoke clipped away some undesirable quality, and whatever was left was to be Polycarp's love.
Polycarp was not only to be most lonely when most surrounded by his family; even when he married this perfect
creature of Miss Cassandra's continued subtractions, he
would be, to all intents and purposes, alone.

Polycarp started to his room. As he passed through the
living room his mother asked him in an aside if he wanted
to put anything on his eye. Polycarp told her it didn't hurt.

In the safety of his room the youth looked at his eye in a
small wavery mirror. It looked more battered than he had
expected but he found some solace in the thought that Alex
BeShears' thumb must be much worse.

As he meditated with satisfaction on the mayhem he had committed, there came a tap at his door.

"Well, who is it?" he called in a disagreeable voice which he knew he would have to modify as soon as he found out who had knocked.

"Marcia," said a voice.

"Oh, all right, come in," he said in sullen good will.

Marcia entered. She had something in a saucer and some rags.

"Mother said this would be good for your eye," she stated with detachment.

"What is it?" asked Carp, looking at the saucer.

"Fresh chicken liver. Mother said for me to tie it on your eye."

"Well, all right, tie it on."

Marcia made the liver poultice and tied it on in obvious dissympathy. In the midst of her bandaging she said in a flat tone:

"You kissed Ponny the other day in the stable."

"What in the thunder makes you say that?" began the brother in a blustering denial.

"Because you both looked so silly when you came out."

She finished her surgery and went downstairs again.

Polycarp remained in his room in that loneliness of which he had complained to Ponny: that complete isolation in which a young man finds himself when harbored in the loving bosom of his family.

CHAPTER FOURTEEN

LIFE ON THE Vaiden plantation had its spiritual focus on Miltiades' wedding. The connection between the eldest son and the family was purely one of spirit. The economic bonds which once held the overseer to his people had long since dropped away, as usually happens when the son of a family becomes prosperous. However, on Miltiades' marriage all of the Vaiden family would come into spiritual possession of the Lacefield estate.

Of all the Vaidens, only Miss Cassandra opposed the marriage. Her expressed reason was that Drusilla had manners but no bottom. Her real reason was that to object to the marriage placed the Vaidens on some incalculable height where even a Lacefield was not good enough for one of them.

Of course, as a counterpoise to Miltiades' nuptials was the inexplicable attraction of Ponny BeShears for Polycarp. None of the family rated Polycarp very highly, but as a Vaiden he was entitled to something better than a Be-Shears.

Marcia's concern, thank heaven, was not with all this balancing of social and hereditary values; it was with something far more practical than that. She was asking her sister circumspectly:

"Sister Cassandra, don't you think—uh—you know—the new dress pattern Brother Miltiades bought me—and me begging him not to just as hard as I could, Sister Cassandra . . ."

"I imagine your efforts to stop him were frantic," agreed the older sister dryly.

"I did!" reiterated Marcia, annoyed.

"Well, what about the dress pattern?"

"Don't you think we sort of owe it to Miltiades to make it up and wear it at his wedding?"

"I do not," said Miss Cassandra.

"Well, why don't you?" cried Marcia, instantly vexed.

"Because you have two best dresses now. Make up another one and the styles change, then you have three and all of them out of date."

A physical pang of frustration went through Marcia's diaphragm at this reasoning.

"Then when are we going to make it?" she cried.

"When the styles change."

"Oh, my goodness, the styles may never change! Or if they do change they'll be ugly! And it won't be in time for the wedding! Brother Milt will think I have no appreciation!"

She plumped herself down in the big chair in the sitting room so that she vibrated for a moment or two on the feminine fullness of her hips and buttocks.

"Marcia, you're so silly," observed Miss Cassandra from her book.

"And it's you being unreasonable about my dresses that got Polycarp into that fight over Ponny BeShears, and goodness knows where that'll end. . . . Maybe they'll marry . . . maybe somebody'll get killed . . . you don't know; and every bit of it was because you wouldn't let me wear my blue-flowered dress when I asked you to!"

Miss Cassandra put by her book.

"Marcia, you're worse than silly, you're idiotic." She waited for several moments, but as Marcia made no reply the older sister asked in an annoyed tone, "What do you want to say such a foolish thing for?"

"It's the truth," repeated Marcia doggedly. "When you wouldn't let me wear my blue dress I told Ponny, and she put me up to buying myself a dress. Mr. BeShears wouldn't credit me and that made Pollycarp mad. Then Ponny was afraid Polycarp would hold it against her so she kissed him in the stable. That set Carp off like a banty rooster and he started courting Ponny like a haystack on fire. That made old man Alex madder than ever and they had a fight about it, and every bit of it is because you wouldn't let me wear my blue-flowered dress to the dance."

Miss Cassandra lifted a bored eyebrow from an inexpressibly high point of view.

"So that's what you think about. I've often wondered if you thought at all when you popped yourself down in a chair like that. It's a pleasure to know."

Marcia made no reply. And since her thoughts did not devastate her older sister as she hoped they would, she began thinking of something else. All of her wrath at the tragedy which Miss Cassandra had caused by the undue restraint of her costume vanished; and presently she said in a conciliating voice:

"Sister Cassandra, I've got to go over to the Lacefields' and help Drusilla decorate the house."

"Does she want you?"

"A. Gray sent word for me to come and help plan the decorations."

"Oh, so it was A. Gray who sent word for you to come!"

"Cassandra!" cried Marcia. "He was speaking for Drusilla!"

"M—m . . ." She gave a sigh. "I wish A. Gray had more stability."

"Well, am I going to get to go?"

"Go ask Father for the horse."

"I'd rather you'd yell in there and tell him I'm going."

Miss Cassandra got out of her seat.

"If I yelled in there you were going he'd yell back you were not going, but if I go in there and tell him you're going he won't say anything."

"Sister Cassandra," said Marcia, genuinely impressed, "I wish I had as much sense as you've got."

"I wish you had half as much," said Miss Cassandra, reducing her sister's aspiration to something within reason.

Marcia was the family's accredited representative at the Lacefield manor these days. The rest of the Vaidens had little in common with the approaching festivities, but Marcia breathed the air of a wedding.

An hour later she turned old Joe into the Lacefield gate and the wan and intricate beauty of the silver poplars against the deep blue sky welcomed the girl to reality again. Marcia drew a long restful breath and thought of A. Gray. Something about the silver poplars reminded her of A. Gray. She thought, if he came into her mind like that when she looked upon a lovely thing, then she must be in love with him. And looking up through the myriad of tiny pale leaves, flat against the blue, she decided, that afternoon, when he asked her to marry him again, she would accept him. She made a little vow to herself that she would do it. She silently crossed her heart and body to that effect.

A slender figure in gray uniform near the mounting block caused the heart, thus crossed, to give an extra beat. The sight of her lover actually in his uniform brought a feeling of high romance to the girl. She shook old Joe's rein to bring him quickly to the block when, with a queer little twist in her chest, she saw it was Major Crowninshield.

Immediately the older man's aura of sympathy and understanding came over the girl. There was something pleasant in the mere way he disengaged her foot from her stirrup and took her hand and steadied her as she stepped on the block.

"Marcia, I'm glad you came. You are like a reprieve to a man under sentence."

The girl stood looking down at him with a faint questioning smile.

"What sort of a sentence?"

The major signaled a negro to come and take the horse.

"Let's walk down in the flower garden and talk," he proposed.

"I'm supposed to help Drusilla . . ."

"That's good. It's with her flowers—we'll go down and see what you have to work with."

Marcia saw that for some reason the officer keenly desired a talk with her and she recalled on the evening the horseman had brought the news of Fort Sumter, how much he had left unsaid. The thought that he might want to continue that conversation now, in the flower garden, gave her a sort of titillating anxiety. She wondered if she would better hear what he had to say when at that very instant she had silently plighted her troth to A. Gray. With a little shivery feeling she drew in her breath to say that she thought she ought to go and see Drusilla first, but with a still odder feeling she expanded the breath to say:

"Well . . . I . . . suppose Drusilla can wait."

And she took his arm and moved with him through the atmosphere of the circumnambient wedding into the flower garden.

The negroes had collected great baskets of roses at the mouth of the glazed flower pit. Marcia ran forward, gathered up an armful and buried her face in the damp fragrant petals.

"Aren't roses like weddings?" she asked with a long inhalation.

"Conventional weddings," said the officer, looking at the girl and the flowers.

"But all weddings are conventional, Major Crowninshield."

"The old savage weddings weren't . . . kidnapings and barter."

"Did men used to kidnap women?" ejaculated Marcia in surprise.

"That's what the anthropologists tell us. However, if it was a small man and a large woman, it must have been co-operative."

The major's half-pensive absurdities amused the girl, not enough to make her laugh but to provoke a sort of internal warning toward him. They made all the jokes she heard at her own home sound crude.

"But Major," she said after a moment's thought, "the preachers say God began weddings in the Garden of Eden."

The major considered this gravely and rubbed his jaw.

"Well, I'm sure that's what happened, but after the expulsion men forgot about that and began capturing their wives, then later the preachers read the Bible and started up the ring ceremony and the flowers again."

Marcia had that delicately uncomfortable feeling of not quite knowing whether her companion was serious or not. Still, she supposed he was. Nobody had ever made the Bible seem so reasonable to her as the politician. Then, to show that she herself was not entirely without some learning on the point, she suggested:

"Kidnaping wives may have started four thousand eight hundred and sixty-nine years ago," she surmised.

"Why exactly those figures, Marcia?"

"Because that's when the Tower of Babel was built. And if a woman couldn't understand a man, he'd just have to drag her off home and—and show her."

This last clause rather embarrassed Marcia. It was one of those instances when a person starts a sentence and doesn't really foresee where it is headed.

The politician saw her disconcert and thoughtfully vacated the point.

"How did you get the exact number of years, Marcia?"

"Well, one Sunday afternoon Father and Parson Mulry were figuring out how old the earth was, and they counted up to and then from the building of the Tower of Babel."

"M-m huh. . . . I see."

The major was, beyond question, serious now. They were sitting on a garden bench. Marcia studied her companion's sensitive, understanding face. He reminded her a little bit of Mr. Lacefield. Both of their faces were lovely without being at all handsome.

"Were you troubled about that, Major?" she asked in a low tone. "Is that what you wanted to talk to me about?" And she hoped nervously that he wouldn't say anything that would compromise her determined love and loyalty to A. Gray.

"Yes," he said, "it—it had something to do with that."

"What?"

He drew a long breath.

"I was wondering whether men should be loyal first to men or first to women."

A delicate tickling moved through Marcia's chest once more.

"I—uh—it looks to me like you ought to know, Major Crowninshield . . . you know so awfully much."

"The trouble is, two sets of conventions come into conflict, Marcia. Loyalty to other men, especially to comrades in arms, must be as old as war itself. Loyalty to women must be as old as life. It's a sort of horrible problem, Marcia." He sat looking over the garden with distress in his eyes. "I wanted to talk to you, because—well, you clarify my thoughts. When I am with you life becomes simpler and kindlier, less cruel."

A glamour came over the day for the girl; a delicate pulse set up throbbing at the base of her neck.

"Do you mean," she asked, drawing in her breath, "that you . . . have to give up one or the other?"

"That's it! That's it!" agreed the man eagerly. "I've thought and thought. I'm an officer—my country is at war

. . ." He sat looking at Marcia, asking her help with his eyes.

"How does the—the army have anything to do with it?"

"The faith of comrades; not to wound, not to, perhaps, injure the actual fighting ability of a comrade in arms."

"If you don't," said Marcia, shaken, "perhaps you—you will injure your own fighting ability."

The glimmer of a smile came into the officer's suffering face.

"What a practical feminine way of looking at it. Nobody but a woman——" He broke off, somber again.

A high exquisite pity dawned in Marcia both for Crowninshield and for herself. She had read in novels of such exalted resignation, but she had never fancied it would come to her.

"But there's the woman herself," went on Crowninshield. "A man is inclined to discount her pain because she will bring him such happiness that even to consider her seems utter selfishness in the man. . . . I wish to God I'd never started a speaking campaign!"

"Why Major Crowninshield!" cried the girl, then she said with big solemn eyes, "I think you'd better stand by your comrade!"

The thought that she was losing him through idealism and love of her country filled Marcia with a kind of rapture, a grief that was an ecstasy. She would marry A. Gray and be tender and loyal to him all his life, as women did in novels, and when A. Gray was dead, Major Crowninshield, a beautiful old gray-headed man, would come to her and say, "I have loved you all my life, Marcia."

And she would say, "I know it, Emory."

Tears of grieving happiness filled Marcia's eyes.

The major arose slowly and offered her his uniformed arm. They walked back through the rose garden with hardly a word.

As they passed the kennels, young A. Gray saw them and

came hurrying toward them. He, too, was in uniform. All the uniforms had been rushed up for the military wedding on the following evening.

Major Crowninshield made excuses of drilling the men and left Marcia with the young captain.

A. Gray immediately possessed her, directed her steps toward the grape arbor. The moment they were sheltered from sight he asked her to marry him.

Marcia felt dizzy. She had to put out a hand against the arbor for support. She accepted him.

His kiss and embrace seemed to come to her from a long way off.

He said, "I just knew you'd accept me, Marsh, when you saw me in my new uniform!"

She stood leaning against the trellis with a faint smile on her lips.

"Oh," she murmured, "you have got on your new uniform, haven't you?"

CHAPTER FIFTEEN

At the manor A. Gray announced his engagement, probably as a sort of moral underwriting to insure his marriage would come off.

This produced an unexpected result. His mother, Mrs. Lacefield, was a small, lively, gregarious woman, and she hit on the idea of a double wedding in the family.

Marcia was quite taken aback. In her vaguely sacrificial mood she was willing to be affianced to young A. Gray, but suddenly to be married to him went a deal further than she had allowed for in her emotional dead reckonings.

As a matter of fact, in the sort of fiction after which Marcia was planning this episode in her life, there was always a turn in the plot by which the true sacrificial lover invariably came back and claimed his bride. And Marcia had a feeling that this would happen to her and Major Crowninshield. But Mrs. Lacefield's rushing up of her marriage didn't give the plot a breath to turn in. So Marcia began framing any objection she could concoct. She had no clothes; she had not consulted her mother and her sister Cassandra; and were sudden marriages wise?

Mrs. Lacefield cried down all these objections; they could send a negro for what clothes Marcia had and Drusilla's trousseau could supplement the rest. Drusilla had bought enough frocks in Washington to outfit a dozen brides. As for Cassandra, Marcia could write a note to Cassandra and ask her advice and send the note by the negro who went after

her clothes. In regard to sudden marriages, Marcia and
A. Gray had been sweethearts from a time when the memory
of man ran not to the contrary.

This last was the elder Mr. Lacefield's phrasing, and it
cut away the girl's final objection.

So Marcia hesitantly decided to write the note asking
Cassandra's and her mother's advice as to her marriage with
young A. Gray.

She was convoyed upstairs by Mrs. Lacefield, the ecstatic
A. Gray, and Eliza Ham, who was a kind of permanent
guest on the premises.

The troupe went up laughing and chattering with excitement and lodged Marcia in a boudoir. Then they all got
out of the room so Marcia could compose her note. A. Gray
was the last to go. He seized an unchaperoned moment to
put his arms about Marcia's slender waist, kiss her ear and
whisper:

"Oh, Marcia, do get Cassandra to say yes!" Then he
hurried after the others, trying to appear casual, but they
laughed at his radiant face.

Marcia seated herself at a dainty mahogany desk that
was inset in sandalwood with yellow figures of ladies and
gentlemen. The faint pleasant odor of this wood floated up
to her as she let down the apron of the desk.

Pink paper, a pen with a pearl stock and a gold point
awaited her convenience. She dipped this into a silver ele-
phant inkstand and sat thinking what to write.

Not a sentence entered her head. She looked out the window of her boudoir. It was guarded with a delicate wrought-
iron grille and beyond were the silver poplars on the lawn.
A soft luxurious feeling came over the girl which always
interpreted itself to her as reality. Whatever was sad or
painful or ugly or disagreeable translated itself to Marcia
as unreal, and whatever was happy and sweet and beautiful
seemed real. She was a living triumph of optimism.

She wrote in big sharp angled letters:

"Dear Sister Cassandra . . ."

And then sat for two or three minutes thinking of what Major Crowninshield had said to her in the garden.

Behind her conscious thoughts was a feeling that something would happen before her marriage with young A. Gray and Major Crowninshield would be substituted. In fact, marriage with A. Gray seemed as far away and shadowy, as she sat writing her note for Cassandra's permission, as marriage with the great Khan of China.

Just then she heard Drusilla's light feet pass her door. Marcia suddenly straightened.

"Drusilla! Drusilla!" she called.

Her door opened.

"Got it finished? Mother has Blue Gum ready to dash off with it."

Marcia looked at her blank paper.

"Listen, Drusilla, I know you don't want to give me your wedding clothes . . . that's silly, Drusilla."

"But I do! I do!" cried Drusilla, fluttering her hands and dancing up and down. "I'm gladder than anything!" She caught Marcia's face and kissed her.

Marcia looked fixedly at her friend.

"Are you going to be happy, Drusilla?"

"You know I am!"

For some reason Drusilla's kiss made Marcia's marriage seem right upon her. It perturbed the girl.

"I do hope you will be, Drusilla."

"Hurry up your note and then go down to the sewing room and have some of my frocks altered to fit you."

Marcia went back to her writing, worked briskly for a few minutes, and then the two girls went downstairs.

On the lower floor Mrs. Lacefield was waiting expectantly. She took the note.

"I want to read this, Marcia," she beamed. "We want to put this in the best way to Miss Cassandra. She's such ah . . . such an intellectual woman, you know."

"Certainly," agreed the girl, handing over the note.
Mrs. Lacefield read in an undertone:

" 'DEAR SISTER CASSANDRA, A. Gray wants me to marry
him and have a double wedding with Miltiades and
Drusilla. Have you and Mother any objections?
                                            " 'Marcia.

" 'P.S. If not, send my blue-flowered dress by the
nigger. M.' "

Mrs. Lacefield nodded.
"That's very nice. That's very sweet. But Mr. Lacefield
and I were thinking it over. Do you mind our sending a note
by Blue Gum, too?"
"Of course not," said Marcia.
"Well, we'd thought of this," and Mrs. Lacefield read in
a somewhat louder tone:

" 'Mr. and Mrs. James Vaiden, and Miss Cassandra
    Vaiden,
        Vaiden plantation.
" 'DEAR NEIGHBORS AND FRIENDS:
    " 'A great and long-hoped-for pleasure and honor has
just been bestowed upon this family and particularly
upon our son, A. Gray. Your daughter, and sister, Marcia, has consented to become his bride.
    " 'We trust your family approves of this alliance. And
we would be greatly pleased if the nuptials could be
arranged to take place when our dear daughter Drusilla
is married to your son and brother, Captain Miltiades
Vaiden.
    " 'We feel that the threat of war hanging over our
country makes this expedient as well as beautiful and
romantic.

" 'Trusting that your sentiments coincide with our own, we subscribe ourselves

" 'Very respectfully,
" 'Mr. and Mrs. Caruthers Lacefield.' "

Marcia listened to this with a private sinking of the heart. She knew her own note would have been refused at once, but she foresaw that even Miss Cassandra could not deny any such request as that. It was too suavely bent on affirmation.

And Marcie realized that she had been gambling quite heavily on the chance that her sister Cassandra would absolutely forbid her marriage with A. Gray on the ground that that young man was without bottom.

But the note Mr. Lacefield had drawn up breathed bottom; one might say it was bottom.

It was handed over to Blue Gum and dispatched while Marcia's hopeful request for a snub was lost in the shuffle.

However, in the sewing room, in the midst of refitting Drusilla's frocks, Marcia's qualms vanished.

The rapture of a pale-blue silk before a French mirror effaced her conversation with Major Crowninshield in the rose garden. Then came exquisite moments when her beautiful gown intensified her own tragic position of resigning her lover for her country. After all, great sacrifices should be made in costume.

Within about three hours Blue Gum returned bringing Marcia's blue-flowered dress and a note from Miss Cassandra, twice as formal as the one she had received and saying that she would come over the next day to attend her sister's wedding.

When Marcia read this tears filled her eyes. She felt as if her older sister had deserted her in the midst of her exquisite necessity. If the note had been the reverse, she would have been even more distraught.

Mrs. Lacefield, who was watching her, exclaimed, "Why, darling, what's the matter?"

"I don't know," sighed Marcia, drawing a long breath. "It seems Cassandra is—is sort of—giving me up!"

"Drusilla," snapped Mrs. Lacefield, "send a nigger up for the salts. She's nervous, poor darling." She began patting Marcia's shoulders.

"That's all right, honey. You're not losing Cassandra. You will have two families who will love you now." She turned to her son.

"A. Gray," she directed, "have Prince and Madelon saddled and you two go for a little ride. She's such a horsewoman. She rides like a dryad, the precious."

"Mother, whoever heard of a dryad on horseback!" cried Drusilla. "A dryad never rides. They stay at home like the bark on a tree."

"Well . . . Aurora, then; she's got something to do with horses."

"I think she uses a racing sulky," said A. Gray.

"Anyway, you take Marcia and ride for about an hour, then she shall try on her dress again."

In due time the horses were brought around and Marcia and A. Gray set forth. The mare, Madelon, was a Kentucky horse which Mr. Lacefield had bought in Lexington. To ride her was to sway swiftly through the air in an animated rocking chair.

Madelon possessed that beautiful trait, natural to highly bred horses: she had personality. To ride Madelon was to enter into comradeship with a great soul. No rider ever forgot Madelon between her knees. She was part of the scenery. She was a ballad in action, playing her own accompaniment with the swift and intricate music of her hoofs.

When Marcia and A. Gray set out the pleasure of the thoroughbred absorbed Marcia's mood.

A. Gray rode by her side in an adoring ecstasy.

"Marcia, you do ride like a Valkyrie—that was what Mother was striking at. You're so—so flexible. . . . Say, how would you like Madelon for a wedding gift?"

"Oh, A. Gray, you have the loveliest idyahs!"

"I have to have. It's part of the family tradition. The Lacefield men always marry beautiful girls and have lovely ideas about it."

"Still," pointed out Marcia practically, "there's not much use asking your father to give me Madelon. I'll ride her anyway. We might as well have something else."

A. Gray, who was in high spirits anyway, shouted with laughter.

"I believe we're going to be a wealthy couple one of these days."

"You're wealthy anyway."

"Not as much as everybody thinks. Nobody in the South is as wealthy as everyone thinks."

Marcia wondered how wealthy Crowninshield was. Not so wealthy as the Lacefields, certainly. If Crowninshield were with her now as her future husband, she wondered what he would do and say . . . something beautiful and intimate and uplifting. He would say something that gave her a great sweet vision and at the same time made her breasts melt. She thought to herself:

"I ought to tell A. Gray how I feel toward Major Crowninshield. That's only fair."

She drew in a breath to say this but her voice was nowhere close to her admission. She rode along repeating it in her mind, more and more loudly, "A. Gray, Major Crowninshield loves me and I love him. I can't marry you, A. Gray, I really can't . . ."

The sentence wavered back and forth in her mind, now on the verge of words, now far away, a faint sad echo in the deepest recesses of her heart.

Their gallop had translated them to BeShears Crossroads. A. Gray drew out his watch and pulled Prince down.

Madelon checked her own speed as became a mare of breeding.

Young A. Gray was now talking about the war: how long it would keep him away from home . . . six months . . . possibly a whole year. The interim would be a yearning to come back home to her.

As they sat talking at the juncture of the roads they heard hoofbeats from the direction of Florence.

Youth and girl began looking in that direction with the impatience of disturbed lovers who wait for an intruder to pass.

When the intruders came in sight A. Gray ejaculated, "Why, that's Mr. BeShears and Ponny and—and Sheriff Dalrymple!"

Marcia looked, and sure enough it was. The two sat speculating on why exactly this trio should come down the road from Florence.

A disturbing explanation came to Marcia. She hoped Mr. BeShears was not under arrest. She hoped this because she felt she ought to hope it. Then, remembering that Ponny was her dear friend, she really did hope it for Ponny's sake. She hoped Mr. BeShears would be jailed for his own sake and be saved for Ponny's sake. So no matter what happened Marcia was well on toward being pleased.

As the youth and the girl stood watching this unaccountable cortège, a distant voice hallooed from behind the bend in the road:

" 'Y God, this isn't the only day in the year, Alex BeShears! There's another'n comin' . . . it'll be here to-morr'!"

The loose shout had defiance in it and it threw the father into a rage.

"Dalrymple," he cried, "you've got to arrest that damned kidnaper!"

"Now, Alex," mollified the officer, "I kain't do that. I kain't arrest a boy for ridin' along the road and sayin'

there's another day comin'. . . . I shouldn't be supprised
if they is."

"You know dern well he's after my money!"

Ponny whirled in her saddle.

"Money! Money! That's all you ever think about! Plague
take your money! I don't want it an' he don't want it either!"
and of a sudden she burst out weeping loudly, as Ponny
would weep.

"Be another day comin' an' she'll be here to-morr'!"
boomed out the voice behind them. "You kain't set on Ponny
forever, Alex BeShears!"

And from around the curve came Polycarp swaying back
and forth on old Lou. He was barely able to keep his saddle
and was correspondingly defiant. He snapped his fingers at
the riders ahead with drunken contempt on his face.

A kind of sinking went through Marcia at the sight of
her brother.

"A. Gray!" she gasped, and the next moment spurred
Madelon out into the road.

"Ponny," she cried, "what in the world has happened?"

When the plump girl saw Marcia she began weeping again.

"P-Polycarp an'—an' me w-went to Florence to get
m-married and P-P-Pappy there——Oh, hoo hoo hoo——"
and her sequence was lost in renewed sobbing.

Sheriff Dalrymple was moved to explain.

"You see, Alex here had sort of forecasted what they'd
be up to. So he posted the county court clerk to put 'em
off for a while and send for him, whenever they tried to buy
their licenses."

"Yesh . . . yesh," nodded Polycarp, riding up on his
mule, "interfered with th' workin's of th' law. That—
that's misprision, ol' man Alex BeShears!" He wagged a
finger at the father, then grabbed to stay on his mule.
"You've convicted yo'se'f, out o' yo' own mouth, uv—uv
the crime of m-misprision."

"Oh, Carp!" cried Marcia, disgusted at her brother's

state and fumbling pronunciation. "What on earth made you get drunk—and you out with Ponny!"

" 'Y God, Marsh . . . have yo' sweetheart snatched out of yo' ver' arms by h-her stinkin' ol' hawg of a daddy——"

"What do you see in him, Ponny?" cried the storekeeper, pointing furiously at the suitor—"a drunk, no-'count, ne'er-do-well Vaiden."

"He wouldn't 'a' got drunk if you'd attended to your own business!"

"He might not, but he'd still been a Vaiden!"

Polycarp rode his mule close to the girl.

"Pay no 'tention to the ol' fool, Ponny . . . 'nother day comin' to-morr'." And he reached as far as he could around Ponny's plump waist.

"Dalrymple," howled the storekeeper, "if you don't stop that I will!"

"Kain't have any fightin', Alex," warned the law.

"Dang it, he ain't goin' to hug my gal right under my eyes!"

The merchant turned and spurred his own horse between the lovers and forced them apart.

"Look here, Sheriff," appealed Polycarp, "it's aginst th-the law to ride aginst a man like that. He's guilty of—of collusion—that's what he is—collusion."

"Dad burn it, come on!" cried the sheriff, out of patience at last. "What did we stop here for anyhow? When I get your gal home my job's over with, and I'll be glad of it."

He moved his horse toward the store and residence. The little cavalcade fell in with him. Polycarp resumed his position in the rear. As he did so he began a loose chanting,

"Ponny, me gal, Ponny, me bride, Ponny, me love, some day we'll ride, you an' me, side by side. There'll be another day to-morr' . . ."

A. Gray broke into irrepressible laughter.

"Marcia, you've got the funniest br——"

Then he saw that Marcia was crying.

CHAPTER SIXTEEN

Marcia's humiliation at her brother's drunkenness gradually subsided as she rode back to the Lacefield manor. A. Gray talked lightly and humorously of what he called Polycarp's occultation. It was a condition, he said, into which any disappointed eloper might very well fall. He began quoting or composing some rhymes about the incident.

Marcia rode along for some moments and finally drifted into the vague general subject of poetry.

"Isn't it strange," she said at last, "the feeling poetry gives you? A fine poem seems a sort of world. You feel you might live in such a place if only you could somehow get in. . . . Do you know what I'm talking about, A. Gray?"

"I think I do, Marcia. . . . I hope I can make your life like that."

"And I must make your life lovely, too, A. Gray."

She looked at his slender figure and his light hazel eyes.

"All you have to do is to be with me," he assured her devotedly. "Whenever I'm near you life is in rhyme for me."

"But that's not what I mean—not exactly. Your life doesn't have to be happy. Sometimes a song will make you cry and yet be the loveliest thing you ever heard. Suppose the sad things of life could come to you like that."

"You wouldn't be living in this world at all."

"I don't know . . ." She drew a long sigh and rode on in silence to the silken rhythm of Madelon. She wondered what Major Crowninshield would have said to that. She did not know, but her mood would have taken some new and lovely coloring under what he would have said.

When they reached the manor again they found jollity prevailing. There were all sorts of jollity in and around the brick mansion: the grinning white-toothed jollity of the negroes; the serene and expansive jollity of Mr. Lacefield; the chattering jollity of Eliza Ham and two or three other girl neighbors.

Then there was the poised, rather cryptic jollity of Drusilla, whose springs of happiness arose from the complicated soul of a brunet. Marcia was nervous and questioning, A. Gray rhapsodic. The jollity of Miltiades was heavy and triumphant, as if a determined spirit had pulled itself over innumerable obstacles and had won a high and deserved goal.

Even in the midst of her own permutations, Marcia found moments in which to admire her brother Miltiades. She was amazed that her own wedding should take place within the splendor of his . . . suddenly it seemed a terrible thing to Marcia for her own marriage just to go on smoothly and mechanically like this—the only marriage she would ever know in all her life, marriage that was to fulfill so many vague and twilit dreams in her heart.

Lovey, the colored sempstress, was letting out and leveling the front of the blue silk dress. In the midst of this Marcia said to the colored woman:

"Lovey, had we better do this?"

Mrs. Lacefield asked solicitously, "Why, what's the matter, Marcia?"

"Miss Sarah, I—I don't know whether I'm going to—to get married or not."

Mrs. Lacefield told Lovey to take the gown off of her, that it would do.

"Of course you're going to get married, honey. It—it's very simple—and married life is much happier than single life, Marcia. Besides that, the Lacefield men have always been lovely men, and my son A. Gray is the finest of them all." She pressed her cheek to Marcia's and then said, "Go talk to your brother Miltiades, my dear, he is such a sensible man."

Marcia put off the dress and went out into the office in the yard where Miltiades had his rooms. When she entered the office she found her brother in his uniform working over a ledger.

His gray uniform and the masculine apartment brought Marcia a sudden realization that in just a little while her brother, A. Gray, and Major Crowninshield would all be away fighting in the war. Her own disturbance about her marriage seemed very petty.

Miltiades arose formally with a pleased smile.

"Well, well, you remembered your brother even in the midst of dressmaking. You are wonderfully unselfish for one of our family, Marcia."

She stared at him in amazement.

"Why, Brother Milt, don't you think we're the most unselfish family you ever knew?"

"Well . . . I suppose so."

"You gave me a dress!"

He nodded and pulled around a chair for her.

She sat down and reflected why she had come.

"You know, Brother Milt," she said in an odd voice, "I don't feel like I'm going to be married at all."

"Y why?"

"I . . . don' know."

"Don't you want to be married, Marcia?" he asked protectively.

"I sure don't know," sighed Marcia.

"A. Gray is a mighty fine boy."

He said this in such a matter-of-fact way that Marcia suddenly felt bereft. She had vaguely wanted him to take her in his arms and let her whisper to him all that she felt about Major Crowninshield, and ask him what must she do.

But now she saw that she could never ask him. None of the Vaidens had ever been close enough together to ask and answer such intimate questions; not even she and Miltiades. If she could not go to her brother, then there was nobody in the world to whom she could turn. She never before had realized that she really was utterly alone in the world. She sat very still, looking out the office door with the sunlit manor blurring in her eyes.

"You are going to be the most beautiful bride in the world, Marcia."

"Oh, you mustn't say that to me!"

"I'll say it to Drusilla, too."

"You're going to be an awfully handsome groom," said Marcia with a faint smile, "and you'll look so brave and noble walking under the swords."

"I think I'll like a military wedding," agreed the brother. "There really is something about it . . ."

But now Marcia had drifted too far away from the real question in her mind ever to return to it, so she began telling Miltiades about Polycarp's effort at elopement.

Her brother listened gravely.

"It's a queer thing, the different members of families, Marcia. We take after different kinfolks, I suppose, away back yonder. But those people who are kin to us were not kin to each other. So a family becomes a kind of hit-and-miss collection of all sorts of folks, most of whom have nothing in common with any of the rest. It's extraordinary that they get along at all."

"I never thought of that," said Marcia. "Our kinfolks really weren't kin to each other, were they? I suppose that is why it is so necessary really and truly to love who you are going to marry."

She had a last faint hope that Miltiades would follow up this tiny clue and let her tell him about Major Crownin-shield, but he did not. They wished each other happiness and she went back with a lonely feeling to the manor.

Late that night Mrs. Lacefield and the girls went with Marcia to her bedroom, the same little boudoir where she had written her note to Cassandra. The bed was of mahogany to match the writing desk and an embroidered gown had been laid across the foot of the bed for her use. A candle burned on each side of the dresser.

"You'd better sleep hard to-night, Marcia," laughed Eliza Ham, "you may be wakeful to-morrow night."

"Tut, tut," deprecated Mrs. Lacefield. "Good-night and sleep tight, Marcia. I'll send up a servant to brush your hair."

"No, I'll do it," said the girl, moved by a desire to be alone.

"Very well, and good-night."

They left her to the endless details of a girl's going to bed.

She took off her shoes, which she always wore too tight, and put on house slippers. She had large feet for a Southern girl; she wore threes and was ashamed of their size. But if she had worn ones she would have squeezed her feet just the same. She put away some ordinary brass pins which were valuable. She wound a little watch that Miltiades had given her. At last she loosed the brown corona about her head and began counting silently the hundred strokes. In the mechanical monotony of the count her mind wandered to Major Crowninshield. Somewhere in the building he was making ready for bed. . . . To-morrow night, when she was A. Gray's bride, he would do the same. Later he would go away to war and all she would ever know of him would be the talk they had had at the gate of the manor on the night Fort Sumter had fallen . . . and their morning in the rose garden.

Here she became conscious that she was counting a hundred and seventy-six to the rhythm of the bristles over her hair. She supposed she had brushed enough.

She began doing her hair into a thick plait and walked

slowly to the window. She opened her jalousies a little way and looked out. The faint radiance of the moon in its last quarter shimmered among the poplars.

She stood in the embrasure of the window, thinking how it would seem if A. Gray were her husband. She would be attired, she supposed, as she was now. He would be in this room with her. . . . The spring night breathed through the window and touched her body with cold impalpable fingers. A profound tremor went through the girl.

"I simply can't marry A. Gray," she thought, with a kind of terror coming over her.

But the appalling part was that she knew she would. She knew when morning came, and all the pleasant people were laughing and talking around her once more, this impossible moment would melt away and all the preparations would flow smoothly on to her marriage. To-morrow night . . . how would she live?

A movement among the dark tree boles on the lawn caused Marcia to step backwards with a sudden awareness of her surroundings. She saw a man move among the poplars. His size and figure gave the girl a sudden tremulous shock.

She drew back until she was screened, then bent forward, wrinkling her eyes against the darkness. When she looked straight at the figure she could not see it at all, but by looking a little to one side she could distinguish it plainly.

It was Major Crowninshield and a dozen speculations rushed in upon her. Had he regretted his adherence to the military code? Would he do anything more than stand and watch her window?

She became keenly aware that the grille of her window formed a little balcony to which a rope might be fastened.

Marcia's heart began beating in her breast. Its pulse throbbed in the base of her throat with a full feeling. Weakness invaided her knees so she had to hold to the window frame for support.

Suddenly she knew that if to-morrow night brought her

Major Crowninshield . . . the thought filled her with the shame of the conventions which she had always breathed.

She stood watching and listening. If he had come closer and called her name she would have answered and reached down to him.

Presently, as she clutched the jalousies watching him, he moved toward the piazza through the spectral light and was gone.

His going filled her with a terrible depression. She groped shakenly back to bed, knelt down and tried to pray. She repeated words with less coherence than she had counted the brush strokes of her hair. Her thoughts were not with God.

She stretched herself out prone on top of the bed covers and the shivering coldness of her body was a kind of comfort. It helped take away the figure she had seen on the lawn. But even so, the thought that he might have climbed up to her filled her with a melting desolation like warm milk.

Her plan to be married to young A. Gray on the morrow became not so much repulsive as impossible.

Then her irrepressible instinct to twist some good face onto any situation rose up in the girl and she thought all this sudden yearning that had rushed upon her was a sign from God telling her not to marry A. Gray. Now she knew that the family might laugh and talk and cajole all they would, she would not change. She would wait for love. Somehow it would come to her.

She got under the bed covers and dropped into a dreamless sleep.

She was awakened by a tap at her door and someone calling her name. Marcia lifted her head with a slight start. It was full daylight. The yellow sunshine struck across her room and glorified an old print of a fox hunt which hung over the escritoire. She blinked at the red coats of the hunters and called out:

"Yes—who is it?"

"It's I, Marcia," answered Mrs. Lacefield's brisk pleasant voice.

"Oh, am I late?" But on second thought Marcia knew that her own lateness would not have drawn Mrs. Lacefield to her door. She would have sent a servant. So she added:

"Will you come in, Miss Sarah?"

The door opened and Mrs. Lacefield stood in the aperture.

"Isn't Drusilla in here?" she asked in an expectant voice.

"No," said Marcia, blinking her eyes interrogatively. "Why?"

"I thought she might have come to your room—to spend the night with you."

"Are you hunting for her?"

"She isn't in her room. I suppose she's walked out. Isn't it a lovely morning? 'Wedding day bright, lifelong delight.' "

Marcia drew in her breath to say there would be no wedding day for her, but did not say it.

"What's the matter?" asked her hostess, seeing her unspoken words.

"Nothing. I'll get ready for breakfast."

Mrs. Lacefield withdrew and Marcia began stirring herself, wondering to whom she would first break the news that she was not going to be married.

She began brushing her hair again as she thought it out. There was no end to brushing her hair. It was the serious physical effort of Marcia's life when she had no maid. She passed in review the different persons to whom she could tell her resolution. She scratched off one after another as impossible. Then she perceived that she had entered upon a very embarrassing undertaking. She thought of getting on old Joe and just riding away without a word, but that, of course, was unthinkable.

Her disturbance grew. At last she thought of Mr. Caru-

thers Lacefield and a great easement and gratitude flowed
in upon her. He would understand her and sympathize
with her. He would tell the others in such a way that no one
could feel hurt or maintain any objections to her change of
mind. The elder Mr. Lacefield was such a sweet man . . . if
only A. Gray were like him!

Here another tap came on her door.

Marcia had an intuition that it was A. Gray come for a
kiss on his wedding morning.

"I'm not dressed yet," she called, with a sudden tremor
lest A. Gray himself find out her plans and succeed in talking her out of them.

With that a genuine terror came before her. Suppose Mr.
Caruthers himself should side against her!

But it was not A. Gray. A negro maid's voice asked, "Miss
Marsh, is Miss Dru in there?"

"No," said Marcia. "Haven't you folks found Drusilla
yet?"

The maid replied with a negro's uninforming repetition,
"No'm, we ain't found her yit." And she went away from
the door to hunt further.

Marcia finished dressing and went out into the upper hallway, vaguely looking for Drusilla herself. She leaned over
the balustrade and saw A. Gray come into the front door of
the hall.

"They're not here," he said with a grave face to someone
in the lower hallway.

"What do you mean by 'not here'?" asked Mr. Lacefield's
voice.

"Major Crowninshield's horse has been taken out of the
stables and so has Madelon."

Mr. Lacefield's voice said, "Oh! Oh! Oh!" three times, not
in pain, perhaps not in shock, in something controlled but
even more moving and distressing.

Marcia stood with a hand on the rail, holding her breath
with her mouth open. A cataclysm was rushing upon her.

Then she saw Mrs. Lacefield coming out of Drusilla's room with a note in her fingers. She moved with a sort of swift aimlessness toward the front door.

"Son! A. Gray!" she cried in a desperate voice. "We will —have to get word to the people. We'll have to—make some explanation."

As she came forward she saw Marcia at the head of the steps. She turned toward her.

"Oh, Marcia! Marcia! What must we do? What can we do? You must help me, darling—tell me what to do! You're my only daughter now! Drusilla has run away!"

CHAPTER SEVENTEEN

THE FLIGHT OF Drusilla Lacefield and Major Crownin-shield on the eve of the double wedding threw the manor into the utmost confusion and mortification. Only the flowers banked all over the house maintained for a space their ironic serenity.

As Eliza Ham phrased it to Blue Gum early that morning, "You're going to have to hurry, Blue Gum, to see that all the guests are cordially disinvited."

Mrs. Sarah Lacefield was not only in a delicate position toward her invited guests, but toward Marcia, too. During the morning Lovey, the sempstress, brought Marcia a note from her hostess asking if Marcia desired her own and A. Gray's wedding to proceed as arranged. This meant, of course, that Mrs. Lacefield thought it would be undesirable, and that either A. Gray had concurred or had been talked into it by his mother. Marcia sat down at the little writing desk for the last time and very gratefully wrote a note canceling her own wedding for the time being.

When the note went down it turned out that A. Gray had not concurred, for he came up to Marcia's room in a most disturbed condition. He kissed her hands and asked why their true love should be thwarted by love that was vacillating. He wept. His tears wet her fingers. He wanted her. He said he hadn't slept a wink last night, he had been so happy, and he wouldn't sleep a wink to-night because he would be so miserable. He did not address his pleas to the propriety of the situation, which was Marcia's getting-out place.

148

The girl sat stroking his smooth sandy hair on her knee and presently he became a little boy whom she was comforting as best she could.

"I'm awfully sorry, A. Gray, but you can't think of just us, you must think of the neighbors and what they'll think. It would draw folks's attention to Drusilla's elopement, and your mother doesn't think it best for that reason."

The reasons Marcia gave for her action were very high and self-sacrificing, as are the reasons everyone gives for everything that is done.

"I—I wish to God Drusilla h-had been as considerate of —of everything and ev-everybody. . . . You—you'll never marry me now!"

"A. Gray," protested Marcia feebly, "what makes you talk so?"

A. Gray looked down gloomily at his uniform in which he was to be married.

"Well, I suppose I might as well keep it on. I'll wear it to the war . . . maybe I can get killed in it."

Miltiades Vaiden and Marcia rode home together. Mrs. Lacefield followed Marcia to the mounting block carrying a bundle wrapped in blue tissue paper.

"Marcia," she said as the girl got on old Joe, "won't you take your dress, honey?" and she held up the parcel toward her.

"Miss Sarah," gasped Marcia with a sudden lump in her throat, "I—I can't take that, Miss Sarah."

"But it's yours."

"Yes, I know, but I—I can't take it j-just like I c-can't marry——"

And she began weeping silently. The lovely dress suddenly made her sorry she could not marry A. Gray. If that young man only had thought to bring up the blue silk dress when he was pleading with Marcia to go on with their part of the wedding . . .

As Marcia rode out of the lawn her eyes were so full of tears that she did not see A. Gray waving a spray of bridal roses after her.

The brother and sister rode on silently, side by side, until they were almost a mile from the Lacefield manor. Here Miltiades Vaiden drew up his horse and looked back.

"Well," he said in a monotone, "this ends six years of work and hope, Marcia."

The girl was looking back at the pale distant poplars set against the soft spring sky. Now she glanced around at her brother, startled.

"What do you mean, Brother Milt? Aren't you going back there any more?"

He looked at her with a faint smile quirking the corners of his lips.

"Do you think I would work on a plantation where there was no chance to become master?"

"Why, no—yes—I don't know," stammered the girl. She pondered a moment on the distant scene and then asked simply and sadly, "Didn't you love Drusilla herself, Brother Milt?"

"I wanted her, I wanted the place," said the man with a tremor in his voice. "I wouldn't have glanced at the place without Drusilla. Everything I wanted was back there—beauty, taste, station. She loved me, Marcia, then—just when she was coming to me . . ." He drew a long breath and said in a hard voice, "I won't forget her."

The feeling, the tone of her brother Marcia did not understand at all. She did not know what he meant when he uttered the words, "I will not forget her." But she reflected that he must mean that he would be endlessly faithful to her memory, as she would be faithful to—— Her thoughts ceased, and she simply sat on her horse looking at nothing.

"Marcia," said her brother, "are you going to marry A. Gray?"

"I—don't know, Brother Milt. I don't think I am."

"Do you love him?"

"No."

"Then why did you ever dream of marrying him?"

"I don't know. When I came to your room yesterday I really wanted to ask you must I marry him."

"Then, darling, why didn't you?"

"I—I don't know." And she began weeping again.

Miltiades reached over and put an arm about his sister.

"Why, honey, I wouldn't have you marry for anything but love . . . not—not for the world."

He kissed her, a demonstration among the Vaidens as rare as a falling star. He looked back once more at the barony he had lost. The muscles in his square-cut jaw twitched. The two rode on together back to the lean old Vaiden plantation among the hills.

CHAPTER EIGHTEEN

After six years of the grace and amenities of the Lacefield manor, this return to his old home filled Miltiades Vaiden with a sharp and painful depression. The log house, the black oaks with their crooked fingers clawing the sky, the lean hounds, the bare yard . . . a sort of violence rose up in the man against his hard milieu.

A queer notation flickered in and out of the man's bitterness. During his whole residence at the barony he had never heard an argument on the thesis of religion. The house he was approaching somehow breathed of such wrangles.

In front of the house he pitched his reins to George and then helped Marcia to the ground. The two went silently into the log house together.

It was an odd fact that the return of Miltiades brought to all other members of the Vaiden family a realization of the barrenness of their surroundings. Indeed, the information that Miltiades had given up his work was somehow appalling to the other Vaidens.

When old man Jimmie heard it he gave his opinion in a loud voice:

"I think you've acted the fool, Milt . . . give up a hundred and twenty-five a month for a gal—or the army either, for that matter."

"I couldn't stay on in her old home, Father," said the son gloomily.

"You'd find it a lot easier to stay there with Drusilla married to somebody else than if she was married to you, Son," boomed the old man.

"If I could find another woman like Mother in the world, I'd be fortunate," said Miltiades gallantly.

"That's all right, Son, I'm used to your paw's railings by now. . . . Had you heard about Carp and Ponny Be-Shears?"

The oldest son said he had heard it and at that moment Polycarp entered the room.

The old mother wanted to talk about Polycarp so she asked him to carry some wood into the kitchen.

Polycarp stepped out into the hallway and shouted, "George! Oh, George! Maw says take some wood in the kitchen."

"George and Gracie are milking," said Mrs. Vaiden.

"Where's Gus?" asked Carp.

"You'd make a pretty husband," observed Cassandra. "I don't blame old man BeShears for not wanting you to have Ponny."

Polycarp came in and stood beside a home-made chair.

"Are you still going to be captain of your company, Brother Milt?" he asked.

"Of course. We'll join the main army pretty soon, I hope." His voice was impatient at the days he must spend here waiting for his regiment to be ordered to the front.

"Listen!" cried Carp to the whole group. "I'm going in Brother Milt's company!"

"Polycarp," commanded the old man, "you'll do nothing of the kind! I'll warn Milt right now I won't have it . . . a youngster sixteen years old!"

"Doggone it!" cried Carp desperately. "Me too young! The men all said I licked Alex BeShears the other day, and if it hadn't been for owdacious luck I'd been a married man this minute!"

Even Miltiades smiled and the others laughed, which made the youth angrier than ever.

"As a company commander, Polycarp," said Miltiades, "I have been notified that your father has objections to your entering the army."

Polycarp clicked his tongue and went out.

Miltiades, looking after him, suddenly remembered that he had meant to sow the southwestern fifty acres of the barony in white clover, then he recalled that he had nothing further to do with the barony and the thought vanished.

He became aware that Miss Cassandra was planning to give him the company room. She would sleep with Marcia.

The returned son said anywhere would do for him. He wanted some place to store his things until he returned from the army, or made some other move.

"As good a move as you could make," repeated the old man, "would be to go back and work for Caruthers Lacefield again."

Miltiades made no reply. He had almost forgotten the atmosphere of his early home; the uncomfortable habit they had of eternally nagging at one another's sore points. It seemed to have some connection with their religion—pointing out and correcting the sins of others. Miltiades did not know.

He tried to remember the sort of thing the Lacefields talked about, but although he had just come from a six-year sojourn at the barony, he could recall the pleasantness but not the subject matter of their small talk.

He listened to his own folk again.

"Marcia," Cassandra was saying, "I couldn't very well write out my real objections to the note the Lacefields sent by the nigger."

"Well, that's all over with now," said Marcia pensively.

"And I'm glad of it. And Miltiades, I know you feel hurt and blue right now. I understand that and I can sympathize perfectly. But I must say I'm pleased. I hated to see the most ambitious member of our family marrying into such a

giddy set as the Lacefields'. I don't believe any of that set
ever had a really serious thought in their lives."

Later in the afternoon old man Jimmie got up on his stout
legs and nodded at Miltiades. The son followed his father
rather wonderingly into the kitchen. The evening meal was
singing and bubbling on the fireplace. Old Aunt Creasy was
hovering over the pots, testing their contents with a long
fork. She bobbed with pleasure at the sight of Miltiades
again, saying that he was a mighty fine man after he had
been living with the quality folks so long.

Old man Jimmie opened the cupboard, took out a demi-
john and two small yellow glasses. He poured out the two
glasses neat and handed one to Miltiades. He lifted the other
to the level of his eyes.

"Here's looking at you," he said solemnly.

"And here's to you and to our army in the field," replied
Miltiades.

They drank their stinging whiskies gravely.

The fact that his father had called him into the kitchen
to have a drink before supper gave the returned son an odd
feeling of gratification. He realized that in his father's eyes
he was grown up. Whisky was not for boys, nor indeed for
casual callers, but for guests of honor, such as Sheriff Dalrymple and old Parson Mulry. With such men of worth, old
man Jimmie drank and proposed time-honored toasts, quite
senseless now, if they ever held any meaning at all.

At supper old Mrs. Vaiden did not eat with the men, but
Marcia and Cassandra did. There was a time when the girls
tried to persuade their mother to eat with the rest, but it
was her custom to move about between the pots and the table
until ol' Pap and the children finished their meal, then she
would sit down and old Aunt Creasy and Gracie would wait
on her.

As the family ate, Columbus and Robinet passed through
the bare yard on their way to the negro cabins. Old man

Jimmie called through the door to know if they had finished planting the Three Oaks Field. Robinet said they lacked about two acres.

That was all the planning old Pap ever did: in the morning shouting to his two negroes any direction that came into his head, and in the evening asking them if it had been done. Usually it had not quite been done.

This casualness disturbed Miltiades after his six years at the barony. He wanted a task allotted and its completion insisted upon.

After supper Miltiades talked a while longer and then went into the company room. Here the blaze of a newly made fire awaited him. The bright fire made him think of the barony, because a negro always had a new fire waiting for him in his office on the plantation.

If things only had gone well with him he would have been at the barony now among candles and roses and the magnificence of the wedding supper. The broken promise of his wedding night swept over the ex-overseer with a kind of shiver. . . . Now he was here in this bare company room with its whitewashed logs, its high port-hole windows.

He drew a long breath and tried to throw off the rising anger and sense of utter frustration that he felt. He felt his heavy chest lift beneath his snug uniform. The very sense of his own flesh reminded him somehow of Drusilla. He thought of her bright dark teasing eyes. Now somewhere she was with Crowninshield, giving to the politician a surrender such as he had never known. The man shivered and held out his fingers toward the flames.

None of his people had mentioned Drusilla except Cassandra, and that was to derogate her. None of them would ever speak a word or give a sign of sympathy for the devastation that had swept over him. None but Marcia would even think a sympathetic thought. All the Vaidens were utterly isolated from each other. They went their different ways in

silence. When Marcia had come to him in the office with her
heart breaking she had looked at him in silence and had gone
away. Over all the Vaidens hung the curse of the solitary.

He turned from the hearth and moved absently to the
table where Cassandra carried on her endless reading. He
fingered the books, barely aware of their titles. Only God
knew what motives drove on Miss Cassandra in her endless
pursuit of culture, or why she considered this culture. She
had been reading and studying for years, and not to one
mortal soul had she ever mentioned anything she had
thought or read.

Miltiades wondered what his oldest sister really did think
. . . He would never know.

Here he remembered something Blue Gum should have
done on the barony. Then he thought he would better tell
one of the negroes here on the place to brush and curry his
horse properly before nightfall. But he recalled that none of
his father's livestock ever received a careful currying. Neither Columbus nor Robinet would do the task thoroughly.
He would have to do it himself if it were done.

That was the bane of his father's establishment, indifference and slack doing. That was really why he, Miltiades, was
in spirit not a Vaiden. He was not indifferent. He could not
endure a crust of dirt in the black shining pile of his horse.

On the other hand, he abominated handling the horse himself. Or brushing his own clothes or shaving himself,
for that matter. The doing of these things for himself
irked him as keenly as it irks an ordinary man to make up
his own bed when there is a woman in the house. Still, his
horse must be brushed. He glanced around the room, saw
one of Cassandra's aprons. He took this along to protect his
clothes and started for the barn.

A lemon-green light lay in the west, deepening overhead
into a profound blue. This struck the man with a renewal of
his loss. On not many occasions, a dozen at most within the

six years, he had watched the last of the sunset with Drusilla.
But these were enough to fill this fading day with the girl.
He thought of Crowninshield again.

At this thought he looked into the dying light and with a
quiver of fury prayed God that some day, somehow, he
could pay Drusilla Lacefield off for the injury she had done
him.

Then he thought how absurd, how helpless, it was to pray
for revenge. To whom should one pray for revenge?

No, let life move on, and if chance or his ingenuity ever
brought him opportunity to wound Drusilla Lacefield he
would do it.

The horse in the darkness of his stall either heard or
scented his master, for he gave a brief whinny.

The man tied on the apron, went to the crack between the
logs of the barn where he remembered his father used to
keep the curry combs and brushes. His fingers found them.
The saw teeth of the comb were worn almost smooth, and one
end of the brush was bare.

The ex-overseer spoke to his horse and stepped gingerly
into the perpetual muck of the stalls. The horse, not accustomed to such quarters, stamped restively on the foul footing.

"All right, boy, all right, all right," murmured the master, with a sympathy so complete it was almost droll. "We'll
be out of this soon . . . the war is coming on."

The man's hands were inexpert, but his knowledge of
where dust and mud befouled a horse was exact. He groped
to the fetlocks with his poor brush and comb, then worked
up the slender silky legs.

Above the stench of the stall Miltiades could catch the
pleasant musky odor of his horse. He curried with a sort of
unpractised thoroughness.

The barn was oddly still. An occasional sound from the
stalls of old Lou and Rab told of other animals in the enclosure. The long clean Lacefield stables had been a contin-

ual theater of kicks and stampings, but this unclean place with its foul stock was as quiet as thought.

The man worked in a corresponding silence, when he heard some movement in the loft. He thought it was rats. Presently it was repeated.

This distressed Miltiades. The Lacefield barns were rat proof, and any black man guilty of leaving open a crib door was sure of a flogging. The thought of the wastage caused by rats was disgusting to the overseer.

He looked upward in the darkness, knowing he could see nothing.

Above him, in the loft, he heard another movement and the tremulous intake of a breath.

Miltiades himself stopped breathing to listen intently. He laid brush and comb in the trough and withdrew without sound from the stall. In the hallway he found the wooden rungs leading up to the loft.

The sound above began again, a faint shaken gasping. The man got out of his apron and went silently up the rungs.

When he stepped off onto the hay a voice gasped, "Oh!" and then came a complete silence.

The opening in the side of the loft flooded the hay with a soft indistinct light. On the hay sat a girl staring at Miltiades. After a moment she said:

"Oh . . . is that you, Master Milt?"

"What are you doing here, Gracie?" asked the man in the noncommittal tone he used toward negroes.

"I was just sitting here . . ." She used the same sort of English as Miltiades' sisters, a trifle softer perhaps. But she almost let her sentence end uninformingly as a negro would have ended it. However, she tacked on a white ending ". . . sitting here . . . thinking."

"Thinking?" repeated Miltiades curiously.

"Yes, sir," said the quadroon faintly.

"You were crying?"

"If—if a girl like me thinks, she's—likely to cry."

She used this somewhat involved thought out of a faint vanity, because Miltiades had lived among aristocrats.

"They pet you too much at the house," said the man, not disapprovingly, but in a monotone, stating a fact.

The girl made no reply but moved as if to get up.

"Just what were you crying about?" asked the man, and the question prevented Gracie from getting to her feet until all his questions were finished and a pause should give her leave to go.

She hesitated a long time and finally said, "Solomon."

"Solomon," repeated the man curiously. "Who was Solomon?"

"He belonged to Mr. BeShears."

"And you're crying for him?"

"Mr. BeShears sold him," said Gracie in a low tone. "They took him off in a hack . . . he was my husband."

"I see." Miltiades' voice was again devoid either of sympathy or dissympathy. He stood looking at the girl for a long time, and to Gracie he gradually grew into something portentous, standing there silhouetted against the fading light.

To the man, the girl in the hay brought a kind of fluctuating impression of Drusilla. At moments it might have been Drusilla's dark mysterious eyes in the faintly seen face. Now it was Gracie's; now Drusilla's.

"To-night was to have been my wedding night, Gracie," continued the man at last in his queer tone.

"I—I—know it, Master Milt," whispered the girl.

"And it seems you are sitting here weeping for a husband."

Instantly Gracie began a hurried whispered denial.

"No—no, I'm not weeping for a husband, Mas' Milt."

The man advanced toward her. The quadroon began pushing herself backwards with her hands and feet.

"No, I'm not, Mas' Milt! No, I'm not weepin' for a hus——"

"Stop! *Stop!*" snapped the man with a dry mouth. He was torn by a sudden mixture of desire and scorn for Drusilla. "What difference does it make to you, what sort of husband——"

He caught her shoulder, and at his clutch she cringed from his fingers, chattering in horror.

"Oh, Mas' Milt! Please! 'Fore God don't do——"

"Be still! God damn it, lie still! . . . and what difference does it make to me?"

The quadroon writhed, gave a smothered cry, lifted her chest as she pulled her hips away from the hand groping up her loins.

CHAPTER NINETEEN

THE LIGHT in the west had vanished when Miltiades Vaiden left the barn. The man walked away from his act almost without feeling save for the faint sense of repulsion and weakness that comes from sexual intimacy without tenderness. His rancor and desire, that Crowninshield at that very moment possessed Drusilla, faded to a kind of mordant indifference. He had made of the wedding night he had planned a saturnine jest at Drusilla's expense. It moved him not to mirth, but to emptiness.

He desired no woman at all, neither for her body nor for that tenderness with which a woman in love heals the subtle trauma inflicted by the act of love.

He was still somber. The Lacefield manor would never belong to him.

Miltiades walked down the road toward the big house, when he saw a man's figure standing by one side of the road in a fence corner. He paused and asked in his peremptory voice who it was. After a little space a negro's voice answered that it was George.

"What you doing, backed up in a fence corner like that?" he inquired irritably.

"Gwine down to de lot to feed de pigs."

The white man didn't believe this. George's manner did not suggest it. However, he didn't care what the negro was about so long as he didn't go traipsing off the plantation for an all-night skylarking and come back sleepy and worthless next day.

George already had been to the barn and had fed the pigs. When Miltiades had passed on the negro continued where he was, almost invisible in the fence corner, filled with a bewildered anger and desolation.

He watched the white man until he disappeared in the night, and then he turned in the direction of the barn again. Presently a woman's form appeared, moving slowly along the dim road. George watched his half sister in a sort of horror.

"Gracie!" he said in a strained voice.

The girl came to an apprehensive halt, then asked in a flat tone, "Is that you, George?"

The brown man moved slowly and incredulously toward his cream-colored half sister, staring at her dimly seen face.

"Well—what do you want?" she cried in a harassed voice.

"Nothin'. Ah do' want nothin'. Ah—Ah thought you wuz mighty near lak white folks . . ."

The girl gave a long, desolate moan.

"O-oh . . . go on away . . . like white folks!" She began a rachetty laugh which changed abruptly into a sobbing, then back to laughing again. "Like white folks!"

She put her hands over her face, racked with her hysteria.

"Good Lawd, Gracie—hush—don't take on so."

George caught his sister. She leaned on him, clinging to him, sobbing in swift cadenzas.

The brown man held the girl with a desire to repay her wrong entering his slow brain.

"Gracie! Gracie!" he asked incredulously. "Didn't you *want* to have no doin's wid Mas' Milt?"

The girl jerked loose from him.

"You know—you *know* I didn't!"

And she broke again into her uncontrollable sobbing.

The brown man patted her arm.

"God damn them white folks—God damn 'em to hell! I wush they was all dead an' in hell!"

His vehemence against the world of whites shocked the girl into self-control.

"Hush! Hush, George! He foun' me up there an' he just . . ."

Gracie started on up the road, holding to George's arm and leading him along. About her loins still clung the residual impressions of her ravishing. She squirmed within herself. She wished she could fling away her whole generative organ. It was like a daub on her.

By tacit consent the two entered the yard and went to the slave cabins, not to the big house where Gracie slept.

Old Aunt Creasy sat over her hearth fishing up a coal with her pipe. The old gargoyle was never found in bed. She was always up, and at night she looked as if she had ceased to belong to the human race and had entered some hobgoblin realm. Even the very rags of her clothes partook of the supernatural and the maleficent.

As George and Gracie came in, old Aunt Creasy appeared to gather the whole tragedy without a word.

"Set in that big cheer, Gracie."

George found a chest to sit on.

The girl sat staring into the fire, with brief rushes of silent weeping. Presently in a quiet space she asked:

"Aunt Creasy, what can I do so—nothing will happen?"

"What you wan' do anything fuh?" mumbled the old crone, punching the coal with her finger.

"Oh, hush! You don't know who it was."

The old woman puffed out her whitish acrid smoke and sat looking with wizened eyes at the ivory face of the quadroon.

"You stay in de big house so long, you got fool notions in yo' haid lak white folks, Gracie. He di'n' beat you wid no stick . . . he di'n' twis' yo' arm . . . he di'n' cut yo' breas' wid a knife."

"No . . . but . . . him."

The old creature made a philosophic gesture with her

crooked hand born of experience on a slave ship in her own distant girlhood.

"What dif'funce do hit make who yo' young un's pappy is? Woman has to have he'p to have chillun."

"But Mas' Milt!" cried Gracie in a rush of horror.

"Man lak all othah men . . . niggah woman has take who comes an' go on."

She ceased her mumbling and sat venting at intervals puffs of her invincible smoke.

George and Gracie stared with her into the coals. It seemed to Gracie as if a thin crust had broken under her and had dropped her irretrievably from some high white estate into old Aunt Creasy's smelly cabin.

As she sat, the sensation lingering in her body faded away and left her depressed and anesthetic. Her feeling of intimacy and equal decency with her mistress, Marcia, was gone. She had been dropped down to the level of Aunt Creasy and George and Lovey, the colored sempstress at the Lacefield manor . . . and Hannah, her mother before her.

The brown half brother, George, got up, went out of Aunt Creasy's cabin and into the next hut. He groped his way in the darkness and took down an ancient single-barreled shotgun, almost as long as he was tall. From the hearth he picked up a piece of charred wood. So armed, he went out into the night again.

The project the negro was about to undertake filled him with a sense of power, and at the same time threatened him with danger. The darkness seemed screwed up to a tension. Things suddenly were poised, so if he set something off in one place it would strike at another. His only unsure point was the effect of the original ownership of the silver spoon that went to make the bullet in his pocket. If he fired white folks' silver at white folks' pictures, would it kill them—or him? He could not forecast that demoniacal partisanship which informed all material things.

As the brown man walked along he pondered where to draw the picture of the spoiler of his sister.

Rain and time had whitened the end of Aunt Creasy's cabin and offered a surface for the picture. The negro stopped before the logs and drew two heavy black circles so he could see them: a large one and a smaller one on top. To the large circle he attached marks for arms and legs, on the smaller he made a square for a hat. Two dots and a line made eyes and a mouth.

"Now dat's Mas' Milt!" he whispered in concentration to himself. "I gwi kill you, Mas' Milt."

The black man's heart began to beat a sort of rubbery crescendo. His fingers trembled so he could hardly drop his silver bullet into the muzzle of his gun. The pellet rattled down the long barrel and clinked to a stop.

George backed away three or four steps, then squatted down and directed his gun upward at the target so the silver bullet would not roll out again. Sweat came out on the strip of forehead between his wide flat nose and his tight cap-like wool.

The next moment the archaic weapon vented a prolonged bellow. The report itself was mixed with a wild shriek from inside the cabin.

Terror filled George at his sister's scream. Fear that his voodoo workings had killed Gracie rushed upon him. He ran around into the cabin and stared about the candle-lit interior, expecting to see the quadroon dead. But the girl was standing up staring at him with dark eyes in her pale face.

"Oh, George!" she quavered slowly, sinking into a chair. "Was that you shot?"

"Y-yeh," stammered her brother. "I-is you hit?"

"No . . . but what were you shooting at?"

"A—A owl—a hoo owl settin' on the ridge uv de cabin. If he start hollerin' somebody in dis fambly gwi die."

As he spoke the sepulchral note of an owl really did sound in the yard, filling the night with its melancholy.

"Huh, Gawge, you di'n' kill it. Somebody's gwi die in dis house."

Horror came over George that he had killed his master.

"Ah—Ah wondahs who it is," chattered the brown man in a frightened voice.

"Hit's somebody, hit sho is somebody," declared the old woman, getting to the door of her hut and looking out. Gracie, too, came, and all three negroes stood looking at the big house and listening intently.

To George, the slaying of his master was now an accomplished fact. The silver spoon had, after all, been nonpartisan. He said he would look around, and went out into the night again with the horror of his master's murder hard upon him.

He knew that Miltiades Vaiden lay dead in the company room with the specter of a silver bullet in his heart. Then suddenly he knew why Gracie had screamed. It was because the man who was the father of the child she had just conceived had been shot.

George moved toward the window of the company room, peering at it and listening with his lips open. He paused under the window but could not reach its height. The black man stood there, listening and listening with his acute negro ears.

Nothing breathed, nothing stirred. Of course he could hear nothing of the dead.

It became impossible to wait in this uncertainty. He moved into the open hallway and tiptoed silently to the door of the company room. He tapped almost inaudibly; waited, then tapped again.

"Mas' Milt!" he whispered, with cold sweat standing on his forehead. "Mas' Milt!"

The next moment a profound shock ran through George. The white man's voice said in a weary tone.

"Who is it? What do you want?"

George stood utterly confounded. He wondered if the

dead man spoke. He was on the verge of running when the voice repeated with the peremptoriness of an autocrat:

"Open the door, show yourself, tell me what you want!"

He now knew the white man was alive and would be out after him in a second. He opened the door an inch or two and put his lips to the crack.

"Dis—dis is Gawge, Mas' Milt," he whispered, with his face dripping.

"Well—what do you want?"

George scrambled for some affectionate, unselfish reason.

"Is—is you gwi 'way soldierin', Mas' Milt?"

"Yes. You come here at this time of night to ask me that?"

"Ah—Ah got studyin' 'bout you, Mas' Milt, 'n'en I hea'd a hoo owl hollerin' on de roof, an' you goin' soldierin', too . . . Ah got skeered 'bout you, Mas' Milt."

"I see," said the voice inside, and to his great relief George knew his master was smiling, "and you thought maybe I was already dead?"

"Y-y-yes, suh . . . Ah wanted to be sho you wuzn't."

"Well, I'm all right so far. I thought I heard a gun shoot."

"Dat was me, shootin' at dat owl. Di'n' lak to heah him set hooin' ovah yo' bed."

"George," said the white man, touched at his devotion, "you're a good nigger. When I'm gone to the army I want you to stay here and help take care of ol' Pap and Mother and the girls."

CHAPTER TWENTY

DURING THIS SAME NIGHT, at a point on the rutty Florence road some three miles distant from the Vaiden home, a rider sat on a mule in the middle of the poor highway.

The man sat sidewise in the saddle, dozed, and at intervals swayed and almost fell off his mount. But always he caught the horn of his saddle, roused, and blinked his eyes at the thin and waning moon that lifted out of the east.

The whole dim world flickered up and down on his struggling eyes, vanished for a second in darkness, then became a blue-and-tinsel shimmering again.

During one of these efforts at wakefulness he became aware of a shadow moving along the inside of the fence. Instantly the rider became entirely awake.

"Hey! Hey, nigger! Climb that fence, nigger, an' come here to me!"

The shadow he had glimpsed became solid and slowly climbed the fence.

"Where's your permit?" asked the patrol mechanically.

The black man began a show of searching his pockets.

"Mas' Padero," he beguiled humbly, "I do belebe I los' my pass. . . . I sho God had a pass, Mas' Padero . . . mus' 'a' lef' hit in my udder clo'es."

"Other clothes," repeated the patrol in good-natured irony. "You still got on your winter clo'es. Mr. Mowbray must have give you a pass last summer and you forgot to git it out of yo' pocket when you changed clo'es las' fall."

The black man stood with a rag of torn felt in his hand which represented a hat. He gave a loud clap of mirth at the patrol's irony.

"Nossah, I ain't got no pass." Here he became intently earnest. He came closer to the mule. "Mas' Padero, a niggah come frum fudder up de road, tell us 'bout de Battle uv M'lasses."

Even in this nonsensical phrase the white guard caught the quiver of excitement.

"The battle of what?" he probed.

"M'lasses."

Like all Southern whites, the patrol was accustomed to getting at the foundation of black reports by elaborate cross-questioning and induction.

"Where was this Battle of Molasses?"

The black man became delphic at once. He broke into the sing-song of a negro preacher:

"Oh, Mas' Padero, de Battle uv M'lasses fought 'way ovah yondah in de eas' . . . ovah whah de sun rises when she comes up out o' de eas'. Ouah men f'um de South met de men f'um de Nawth. An' de Lawd fought on de side uv de men f'um de South! Oh, de sojers f'um de Nawth throw down dey ahms an' run to Wash'n'ton. Oh, dey tho' away dey swo'ds an' run to dey fo'ts, cause dey kain't stan' up ag'in de men f'um de South!

"Oh, Mas' Padero, God done spoke His Word ag'in dat stiff-necked an' stubbo'n Nawth!"

The patrol leaned over the horn of his saddle toward the black man.

"How come you haven't got no pass with sich news as that?"

"Oh, Mas' Padero, ol' man Luger's nigger Jim brung de news to ouah cabin a li'l' befo' midnight. My ole man done uhsleep long ago. Jim go back home, but I say, 'Jim, I take yo' news on fo' de good of man. I tell 'em how de men of de

Nawth an' de men of de South has fit an' died in de great
Battle uv M'lasses!"

The patrol had long since given up the idea of marching
the slave back to his proper quarters.

"Look here, nigger," he ordered, vibrating to the black
man's burst of Biblical eloquence, "go on and spread the
news, but make damn shore you're back at old man Mowbray's by sun-up."

"Yassuh, Mas' Padero! Oh, yassuh, Mas' Padero!" He
began bobbing and backing away down the road.

"What else do you know about the Battle of Molasses?"

"Mistuh Sam Sully's nephew what lives ovah clost to Tuscumbia got killed, Mas' Padero. De war has rech out his
han' an' tuk Mistah Sam Sully's nephew what lives ovah
clost to Tuscumbia."

"Well, I declare!" breathed the patrol to himself, looking
after the black oracle vanishing in the spectral light. "Sam
Sully's nephew killed . . . Sam Sully's nephew . . ." The
patrol strove to place Sam Sully of Tuscumbia, Alabama.
He had heard of the Sullys. He wondered how the boy had
come to be in the Confederate army in the East. The guard's
thoughts moved with a sense of personal shock and loss at
the death of the unknown boy.

It was the first casualty report of the Civil War.

Mr. Lump Mowbray, the illicit bearer of this news, was
now well under way down the road, trotting on perfectly
flat-soled feet with the tireless gait of a stoat.

The road, the dim scenery flowed past the protruding
eyes in his Minié-ball head. Presently the dark big house of
the Vaidens' and a dim light in one of the slave cabins came
in sight.

This meant to the peripatetic Lump that old Aunt Creasy
was sitting up by her fire. Later, as he drew closer he somehow knew that Gracie was in the cabin. He was shocked to
see her trim head against the faint light of the fire. It was a

warm, exquisite shock, as if Gabriel suddenly had trumpeted
Lump Mowbray's name to enter into the gates of pearl.

The knotty little negro got to the door in complete silence.

Old Aunt Creasy said from her brooding and without so
much as a side glance, "What is you come noratin' 'bout to-
night, Lump Mowbray?"

Gracie turned and looked at the caller. Only the whites
of his eyes were really visible. The rest of him was shadow
and darkness. His mere appearance spread a sense of calamity. He advanced into the cabin, uplifting a dark hand.

"Oh, Aunt Creasy, Oh, Gracie, de ahmies uv de Nawth is
whupped. De ahmy whut was sont to set us free is a-runnin'
back to de place dey come f'um. Dey daid is on de groun'.
Dey cha'iots uv wah is ruint! God done lif' up his han' agin
de men f'um de Nawth who come to he'p us. We-all gwi stay
slaves fo'ebbah mo'!"

Gracie looked at Lump with a little cry. The old crone
turned on the visitant.

"What mek you talk lak dat, Lump Mowbray?" she
croaked in a harsh voice.

"Caze de news come to Flawnce, Mas' Sam Sully's nephew
is daid. But he died wid de crown uv vict'ry on he haid. De
Lawd smote de ahmy uv de Nawth at de Battle uv M'lasses."

"I don' b'lebe dat!" cried the old woman in a higher register. "A witch woman told me, Lump Mowbray—a hoodoo
woman what got stole alongside o' me acrost de watter—she
say—she say to me, 'Omalotoga, one day you gwi be free,
Omalotoga. You an' yo' kin gwi be set free.'"

"Don't you know, Aunt Creasy," ejaculated Gracie, with
a white woman's contempt for soothsaying, "don't you know
a black woman on a slave ship wouldn't know about this
war? The Yankees are whipped, just like ol' Pap said they
would be! The Yankees have run! Oh, my God, our saviors
are laid down in the dust!"

"Lawd hab mercy!" groaned Lump. "We sta'tin' out

fawty mo' yeahs in de wilduhness . . . fawty mo' yeahs o'
wuck an' whups an' paderos."

Drawn by these combined groans, George and Columbus
and Robinet came into the cabin. Lump Mowbray retold his
tale of the tragedy of the Battle of Molasses. He embroidered his battle. He added guns and axes and wild horses
covered with spikes.

His black hearers began an antiphonal chanting. They
fell into a rhythm of wailing which ceased to be dismay and
turned into a sensuous pulsation of sound. Gracie dismissed
her white blood. She felt as if she were borne high up in the
dark night on the antiphonal moanings of the men. Their
melancholy caressed the girl with incorporeal hands. She
gave herself over to the dark sweetness of the bosom of misery from whose dugs Africa has drawn an unending and un-
realized strength and solace.

In the midst of this voluptuous grieving an irritated voice
snapped, "What in the hell are you niggers kicking up such
a racket about?"

Instantly silence fell in the slave cabin. Gracie was sharply
embarrassed to be found moaning as a negro among negroes.

Lump Mowbray first gathered his presence of mind.

"Mas' Carp!" he cried. "We's celebratin'!"

The white youth in the doorway considered this with the
skepticism habitual with the master toward his slaves,

"What you celebrating?"

That question once more set off Lump Mowbray's eloquence. He fought the Battle of Molasses again, but this
time triumphantly and with great joy. The Southern hosts
swept away the cowardly and iniquitous army from the
North. It was a holocaust, an Armageddon for the righteous
and invincible South.

All the other negroes, except Gracie, chanted their exultation at the victorious South.

Polycarp listened to this in amazement, but with a mounting belief. He knew there must be a basis of fact behind Lump's fantastic account of the Battle of Molasses.

The name was wrong, Polycarp knew—the negroes always twisted names askew—but that somewhere the South had struck out a great and overwhelming victory he was equally certain.

The knowledge brought the youth a sudden odd feeling of power and courage.

"Whyn't you tell everybody, Lump?" he cried in high spirits. "Whyn't you wake the whole family up and spread the good news?"

"Ah thought in de mawnin' be time," mumbled Aunt Creasy.

"The devil, no!" cried Polycarp, leaping out of the cabin and starting for the big house. Some hounds came loping toward him. He drew in a great breath of cold air to shout his news when a thought struck him.

Ol' Pap would not let him go to the army, and unless he enlisted instantly the war would end. He would never reach the smoke and carnage and the panoply of battle. Peace would come and find him sitting here in a heavy old log house in the hills.

Polycarp did not shout. The cabinful of negroes suddenly had become quiet. Their rejoicing at the great Southern victory of Molasses had hushed.

Polycarp entered the big hallway, then tiptoed through his father's and mother's room to get to the stairs that led to his and Augustus' bedchamber in the attic.

Ol' Pap snored with loud raspings. Polycarp was nearly through the room when his mother spoke sotto voce:

"Is that you, Polycarp?"

"Yes, Mother," said the son, and in view of his purpose a queer thrill went through him at the simple words his mother had said.

"What's the matter with the darkies?" asked the old woman in her low voice.

"Oh, they're hullabalooing over something . . . I went out to stop 'em."

"They waked me, too. Well . . . good-night."

At this Polycarp's heart sank. He hesitated in the dark. He wanted to grope his way to the bedside and kiss his mother good-bye. But such a demonstration would astonish her and cause questions. He moved on to the steps again when his mother said with an odd note:

"Polycarp!"

The youth stopped completely still.

"Yes, Mammy," replied the youth, trembling on the verge of going back to her and kissing her.

Came another pause in the darkness, then old Mrs. Laura said in a minor key:

"Nothing."

The son heard her sigh and lower her head on the pillow.

The steps up which Polycarp climbed were very narrow. He tiptoed up the close passage with a sudden realization that he was climbing to his room for the last time. Imminent change had touched the old attic steps with a quality of strangeness. He went up as noiselessly as he could and entered the attic.

With his head bent to avoid the slanting roof, Polycarp stood thinking what things to take with him; how to make a bundle; what he would need as a soldier.

He groped toward a box where he kept the few clothes he possessed, lifted the lid and fumbled in the end among some balls of woolen socks. He took out two pairs and stuffed them in his coat pockets. Then he felt the bulge they made. It would appear ridiculous, he thought, for a soldier to have his pockets stretched with socks. So he put back one pair, separated the other and placed a single sock in each pocket.

He stood for some minutes in the darkness but could think of nothing else to take with him that would not be bundlesome.

Then he drew off his shoes, reached up and set them in

the small square attic window. He listened a moment, then
caught the window ledge and began drawing himself up
silently.

At that moment Augustus' voice whispered with intense
suspicion, "Carp, where you going?"

A stab went through Polycarp at his brother's untimely
awakening. He remained motionless, with his finger on the
ledge, thinking with disgust, "Isn't that like Augustus? At
night a whisper will wake him, but after daylight, when he
ought to get up, you can't arouse him with a cannon!"

But Augustus was not to be lulled back to sleep by this
false silence. Polycarp heard him get out of bed and stride
toward him. Before he had time to move his brother had
grabbed him.

"Uh huh," he breathed, clutching Polycarp's arm, "I
knew you were there. Nee'n' try to fool me. You're goin-
somewhere. . . . I'm goin' with you."

"Naw! Naw!" whispered Polycarp, quite disconcerted.
"Just coming to bed."

"You don't go to bed through the window."

"I was coming in from the window."

Augustus did not even consider this. He stood clutching
Polycarp as if he were afraid his brother would flirt out of
his grasp. Suddenly revelation broke on him.

"I know where you're going—to the army!"

"I am not!" cried Polycarp in a whisper. "I'm going to
bed!"

"You're going to the army and I'm going with you!"

"Listen," whispered Polycarp angrily, "you can't go,
Augustus!"

"I can go if you can go!"

"Dad blame it, Augustus, you're not old enough!"

"Don't like but fourteen months bein' as old as you!"

"For Geemeny's sake, don't whisper so loud!"

Augustus lowered his voice to the faintest aspirate.

"Don't like but fourteen months bein' as old as you are."

"I heard you before," said Polycarp, glumly wondering what to do in the impasse.

"What did you pick out to-night to start for?" whispered Augustus alertly.

Polycarp's news suddenly burst forth.

"There's been a big battle—the South just wore the Yankees out—the war can't last more than a month or two longer—we haven't got a minute to lose!"

"And you were going to slip off and leave me!" whispered Augustus, too loud again.

"No I wasn't—hush—I was going to wake you up when I got packed."

"What you taking?"

"Socks."

"If I turn you loose to get some will you run off?"

"Naw, of course not. . . . Take my socks, I've got an extry pair."

Augustus hesitated.

"You'll want 'em when you come back from the war."

Polycarp put his extra socks in his brother's hands.

"Now these are mine," stipulated Augustus shrewdly. "When we reach the army it won't turn out that I've been lugging your socks for you?"

There was nothing more for Augustus to do except to dress. He made Polycarp wait and let him through the window first, so his older brother couldn't run off and leave him.

It was a tight window, but the boys had used it at times. They could pass through their father's rooms at any time of night going to their attic, but after midnight that route became a one-way thoroughfare.

Augustus squirmed through the window backward, took his boots in his teeth, and climbed down the two stories by thrusting his toes and fingers in the cracks between the logs.

On the ground below, he stood shivering and watched Polycarp make a like descent.

Hounds came nosing around them, curving up their backs and stretching their hind legs.

The brothers pulled on their boots and moved toward the gate in the glimmering moonshine.

Augustus looked at the crooked oaks and at the dogs walking sleepily beside them. The fact that he was leaving home for the army came over him suddenly.

"Carp," he whispered in an uncertain tone, "don't you think we better tell Mammy good-bye?"

Polycarp stood stock still.

"Don't you know that would stop us?"

"Not if we tapped light . . . jest enough to wake her up and tell her good-bye."

"Why wouldn't she stop us?" demanded Carp in a harassed undertone.

"Why, because we waked her up to tell her good-bye," explained Augustus, annoyed in his turn.

"All right, you go tell her good-bye, I'll go on."

He moved on and Augustus fell in with him, quite angry that Polycarp should be so unreasonable.

They climbed the fence in preference to opening the big gate and stood in the faintly seen road.

"Well," said Augustus, "where we going to enlist?"

"In Florence, I suppose," suggested Polycarp gloomily.

"That's exactly where ol' Pap will think we enlisted and to-morr' he'll come and get us out," pointed out Augustus with irresistible logic.

"Then what do you want to do?"

"I say le's walk up in Tennessee and enlist up there somewhere—nobody won't have the least notion where we've gone."

This was really a good idea.

"All right," agreed Polycarp slowly, "er—uh—only le's walk a mile or two down toward Florence and then we'll come back and walk up in Tennessee."

Augustus stared at his brother in amazement.

"What in the thunder do you want to walk a lot of extry miles for?"

"Why-y, I—I wanted to go down by—you know—the Crossroads."

"Just to see Ponny BeShears!"

"I thought I'd tell her good-bye," flung out the older brother in a harsh tone.

"Well, I be doggoned!" cried Augustus, "slippin' off from Mammy without a word and then walking miles out of yore way to say good-bye to an old fat blob that's not a thing in the world to any of us. I'm not going to walk four miles out of my way to say good-bye to any BeShears that ever lived!"

"Well, I am," said Polycarp decidedly.

Augustus thought for a moment.

"Then I'm going on. If you'll walk down there and back fast maybe you'll ketch me in the morning sometime."

"I may just go on down to Florence and enlist there," said Polycarp ill-naturedly.

"You'll be brought back, too. I'm going up in Tennessee, like I said."

And so they parted, like Vaidens, Augustus northbound, following a half-seen rutty trail that looped and turned and lifted among the cold and glimmering hills.

CHAPTER TWENTY-ONE

W HEN MORNING dawned Augustus Vaiden found that the road he had followed all night had dwindled to the pebbly bottom of a creek. It wound its way through narrow cuts, past the exposed roots of trees, and at times into a wide creek bottom. Here and there a skinned sapling or a worn place in the grass showed where the trail had deserted the creek bed and pursued its own way over rocks and roots and sliding clay banks.

When the trail followed the valleys enormous wooded hills stretched upward until they brushed the sky with a distant fringe of trees. When the trail toiled upward to the crests of these elevations, then the scenery far below would be reduced to a gray-green monotone.

After an endless walk Augustus saw a small cleared patch below him with a cabin in it. A string of blue smoke floated upwards until it flattened out in some stratum of the morning mist.

The boy started to shout across the valley with a hope of breakfast when a sound behind him caused him to turn.

A deer with a glory of horns came walking across the ridge. When it scented Augustus it gave a whistle and a lazy bound which swung it over the tops of some huckleberry bushes. With a last flicker of its white tail it went out of sight into the valley.

Augustus forgot his sore feet in the thrill of seeing a buck. He wanted a gun. He was moved to run to the cabin and try

180

to borrow one. He started to do this when a voice of the peculiar nasal drawl of the hills said quite close to him:

"Hey oh, buddy. Travelin' or jest goin' somewhaar?"

Augustus turned and recognized the unshaven type of man who now and then journeyed down from the Tennessee hills into northern Alabama. He had a long muzzle-loading rifle in his hands.

"What road is this, mister?" asked the boy, considering the formidable figure.

"This hyar is the ol' Notchy Trace, buddy. What's yore business in these parts?"

"I've come to join the army," stated Augustus indefinitely.

"Well, buddy, you couldn't 'a' come straighter with a compass," declared the hill man cheerfully. "Come along o' me."

He turned about in the old Natchez Trace and led the way down the steep hillside in the other direction from the clearing.

Augustus followed his lanky guide dubiously. The fellow had a skin cap which exposed some dirty red hair. He took the downward slope with the effortless ease of a goat. Augustus had difficulty in keeping even with him. Presently in the bushes ahead they heard other nasal voices drawling:

"That's my jack." . . . "Naw, you didn't play that kyard, Bill!" "Hell, I didn't! I drawed the wrong kyard frum my han' . . . here's what I thought I was a-drawin'." . . . "That's my jack."

As Augustus and the red-haired man came up the card playing ceased.

The players were bearded and weather beaten and all of them appeared old as hillmen do, although none of them had reached middle age.

The whole group looked curiously at Augustus.

"Who's that you got, Jim?" inquired a swart heavy man, as if Augustus could not possibly answer for himself.

"Make yore own guess," said Jim, "you know as much about him as I do."

"My name's Augustus Vaiden," said Augustus, looking at the quintet with uneasiness.

"What does he want?" asked a little wizened man.

"He wants to join the army," said Jim with a solemn countenance.

"You've come to the right place, Sonny," said the heavy swart man.

All five looked so much like liars that Augustus immediately doubted that they belonged to any army at all.

"What army is this?" he queried.

"What army do you want to join?" asked the small wizened man.

"Well, I—I want to join the—the Confederate army," admitted Augustus uncertainly.

The five men looked at each other. The wizened man cried out, "Buddy, you're a dawg fer luck. S'posin' you'd met a comp'ny of Yankee sojers. Where'd you been? A prisoner 'fore you ever drawed a gun. But you're the very man we want."

This was more reassuring.

"What do you want with me?" asked Augustus.

"Right over the hill there lives the meanest, pisenest, rebel-hatin'est Union man in Lane County, and by the prong on the devil's tail, we're fixin' to l'arn him better manners."

"Who is he?"

"Ol' man Philo Catlin," grunted the leader, "and a more insultin' dirt-spittin' ol' devil you won't find nowheres."

The name Catlin recalled the apple-cart youth to Augustus.

"What are you goin' to do to ol' man Catlin?" he inquired.

"He's got some fat Union stock in his barn that·ort to be changed into Confederate stock," said the wizened man, "an' us fellers was a-settin' here planning to make the change."

"How you planning to do it?" asked Augustus dubiously.

"Looky here, Sonny," probed the swart man cautiously, "are you a true-blue Confederate sympathizer, or a damn copperhead?"

"I'm a Confederate!" cried Augustus. "That's what I said I was!"

"Well, we thought we'd leave some lad to hold our hosses," planned the swart man, "and we'd go over and change that Union stock into Confederate . . . we'll be back right away."

"And you want me to hold the horses?"

"Yes, that was our notion."

Augustus did not see how the rules of war applied just here, but the swart man went on to say that Augustus' first act to support the Southern Confederacy should be to hold the horses of these patriots.

"Well . . . all right," agreed Augustus doubtfully. "Where's your horses?"

"Back on the ridge about a quarter. Reckon we might as well go back to 'em."

"If they're hitched back there, why don't they jest stand hitched?" inquired Augustus.

"Because, Sonny, ol' man Catlin is a man of brains. If he got wind of what we-all was a-tryin' to do, he might cut aroun' in the woods an' steal more of our hosses than we stole of his."

The swart man's tactics seemed to be above criticism, so the circle got on their legs, picked up their rifles, and tramped back down to their horses.

As Augustus moved along through the pale buds of early spring in the hills, he was very doubtful about his position. A thought of declining the office of hostler passed through his head and was discarded. The idea of stealing Mr. Catlin's horses because he was an abolitionist caused Augustus to break into a light sweat.

Already everything about him seemed a little unreal on account of his loss of a night's sleep. The high ridges, the drawling, half-humorous, menacing hillmen, the fact that he was to hold the horses for a band of Confederates to raid a Union man's barns . . . Augustus felt he might very well wake up and find himself back in his own attic bed again.

The stock of the raiders turned out to be more numerous than the men. A large roan horse, two mules, three ordinary hill plugs, and a cow with a rope on her horns made up the tally.

The thieves took a fresh start after their reconnaissance, examined the caps on their guns, settled the coonskin caps on their heads, then posted the little wizened man, whom they called Runt, and Augustus to watch their horses.

Augustus saw the men disappear, Indian file, down the ridge. He had a faint eerie feeling of cerebral compression. The boy looked at the little man who was helping him guard the stock.

"What'll we do with 'em when we git 'em?" he asked in a queer voice.

"Take 'em down in Alabam and sell 'em to the Confeds," drawled his tanned and wrinkled companion.

"Wonder what ol' man Catlin'll do when he sees all his stock's gone and the spring plowing coming on?"

"He'll do like they do over the river," said the Runt.

"How's that?" asked Augustus innocently.

"Do without," flung out the Runt, and burst into a wheezing laugh, wrinkling his little eyes at Augustus in the ill-natured triumph of the hills.

The jest irritated Augustus as it was intended to do. The hobbledehoy grinned mirthlessly to show that he was a man who could give and take a joke and think nothing of it. He tried to think up a "catch" of his own and get the little man with it, but none occurred to him.

Instead of a "catch" he recalled the black-haired Catlin boy who had offered him some apples, and now here he was about to steal the Catlin boy's horses. . . .

The Runt was still laughing disagreeably. Augustus thought he would take the sting out of his joke.

"Look here," he said, "what river was you talking about?"

"What river?"

"Yes, what river is it that the people live over and do without, and what do they do without? What river do you mean?"

"Hell," said the wizened man, "jest any damn river."

"I didn't know," said Augustus. "I walked all night last night, I'm a good mind to lay down and take a nap."

"You talk like you was sound asleep," opined the hill man, "astin' me what river. I never had nobody to ast me such a fool question before."

"How about behind?"

"Huh?"

"Which side do they ask it on?"

"Aw, hell, lay down an' go to sleep. You're too damn sleepy to understand when you've been sold."

Augustus yawned, glanced around, and chose a chestnut whose shadow stretched down the hill. The boy blinked at the early-morning sun cross-barred by the forest, went behind the tree and lay down.

No sooner had the bole and roots concealed him from his companion than Augustus began a queer crablike retrograde movement down the hillside on his belly.

All his nerves were fixed on keeping in line with the tree and the guard. The hillside lengthened slowly upward. The boy's feet touched another tree. He wormed around this with a growing feeling of safety. Just then he heard the wizened man's somewhat distant voice say:

"Buddy, where'bout was you headin' fer when you struck our gang?"

Augustus arose, half stooping, turned about, and began to take long steps down the hill. Behind him he heard the wizened man call:

"Buddy! Hey, buddy, where in the hell have you got to?"
The next instant came a shout with the overtones of fury:
"You little devil, halt thar or I'll . . ."

Augustus was legging it down through the trees at enormous falling body-shaking bounds. He flung a backward
glance in the midst of his airy downward strides. He saw
the wizened man hunched against the sun pointing something. Crashed the long-drawn report of an old-fashioned
rifle and a bullet snipped at a limb above his head and went
whirring off over the valley.

Augustus loped down the steep descent at dizzy strides.
As he plunged on it seemed his legs must break under the
falls, that he must lose his balance and go over headlong.
Two or three hundred yards downhill he realized that he
must be utterly lost. He grabbed a sapling to help stop his
descent. The thin trunk bent double and slewed the boy
around in a wide arc. His hold broke and he came to earth
sitting flat on the hillside. The next instant he was up and
off, trotting at a long angle down the hill toward the clearing.

Augustus' heart pounded at his side. The sloping forest
danced in front of him. He had had no idea that he was
about to create this diversion. He was suddenly in the midst
of it, hot foot to warn the Catlins that their stock was being
stolen.

Ahead of him in the gloom of the woods he saw the increased light of a clearing. He would have shouted, but the
gang who went before might very well see him and pick him
off.

The descent was growing gentle as the foot of the hill
curved into the narrow valley. Then he saw a rail fence,
some last year's cornstalks, and beyond that the cabin of the
Catlins.

A woman in linsey-woolsey stood in the doorway with a
round home-made broom in her hand. She stood looking at
Augustus.

"Mrs. Catlin! Mrs. Catlin!" panted the boy. "They're stealin' your horses! Some men are stealin' your horses!"

The old woman apparently had been drilled in what to do in case of horse thieves. The broom fell from her hand; she disappeared in the dark cabin. Twenty seconds later she reappeared with two rifles and a cow's horn. She handed a rifle to Augustus, then, without a word, put the horn to her lips and sent forth a high, penetrating, lugubrious note. She repeated this with red face and bouffant cheeks three times. Then she directed tersely:

"You go to yon side the barn, you'll find a holler sweet gum with some knot holes in it. Hide in that and shoot through the knot holes at anybody you see at the barn. I'll ten' t'other side."

And Augustus and the formidable old woman parted company.

The boy ran in the direction the old woman had pointed, keeping a sharp lookout for a hollow sweet gum equipped with natural port holes. Unfortunately he saw the barn first and came to a panting halt in the corner of a rail fence and pushed his rifle through a crack in the rails.

Above the throb of blood in his ears he heard the stampeding of hoofs and the brief, urgent voices of the men in the log stables.

Augustus watched the squat building down his gun barrel. Details of the barn developed under his peering; a tongue of hay hanging out the loft window, the wooden latch on the clumsy door. The latch clacked and the door swung open. Something moved into the light. Augustus almost squeezed his trigger on it when he saw it was the twitching rump of a mule. Someone inside the stable was backing the animal out.

A moment later he saw the swarthy man pressing the mule backwards with a halter. Augustus tried for a bead but the man kept jerking and moving. Then, in the middle of a sudden fair shot, the fact that this man had entrusted Augustus to guard his horses caused the boy to hesitate.

At that moment a rifle clapped from the other side of the clearing. The swart man winced, leveled his own rifle for a shot at the old woman. Another of the gang dodged out of the stable door and began running bent over in the direction of the shot.

Fear rushed through Augustus lest the man reach the old woman before she could reload. Panting through open mouth, Augustus beaded the fellow and touched the hair trigger.

A cracking explosion and a volume of smoke shut off sight and sound of the horse thieves. Augustus had come out with no ammunition. He began backing away in the covert of sumac and blackberry bushes when he saw the swart man and the tall red-headed man riding toward him. He was unarmed now. He did not know whether they saw him or not. The swart horseman leveled his gun and flames seemed to leap at Augustus' eyes.

At the same moment a roar broke forth from an old tree just outside the fence from the boy. Then a gaunt man came running up the fence row behind Augustus. At these reinforcements the swart leader roared desperately:

"Open the gate! Open her up!"

Three or four thieves rushed out of the stable to the barn gate. The dark man whirled his mule for the opening. In the midst of this action a girl thirty yards down the fence behind Augustus leveled a rifle and fired. The man straining at the gate dropped his load. The mule, instead of dashing through, struck the heavy shutter and fell backward. Its rider did a queer flyaway through the air over gate, fence, and everything, and landed sprawling outside.

The dark man flung outside ran to the shelter of the woods. His men bolted through the crack in the gate and vanished with him. Guns had fired on them from all directions. How many defenders the stable had they did not know. Neither did Augustus.

The boy stood holding the long rifle from whose muzzle still floated a delicate thread of smoke.

Absolute quiet descended on field and stable. From across the clearing the voice of the old woman called with a penetrating nasal twang:

"Did they hurt that there boy that holp us, Elviry?"

The girl down the fence row looked at Augustus.

"You're not hurt, are you, mister?"

Augustus had never been called mister before.

"No, ma'am, I'm not hurt," he said.

"No, Maw, he ain't hurt," relayed the girl in a voice pleasingly cadenced with youth and health even in the midst of its hill twang.

"I didn't want him to git hurt," said the old woman in a composed tone. "I warned him to hide in that there sweet gum, but when he shot I knowed by the crack of his rifle he hadn't done what I tole him to do."

CHAPTER TWENTY-TWO

Four persons joined Augustus at the fence row: the old woman, old man Philo Catlin, Jerry whom Augustus had seen in the apple cart, and the girl. This girl, Elvira, was taller than her mother and had the same black hair and ringing blue eyes of her brother.

Jerry Catlin himself showed no surprise that Augustus Vaiden should appear in the midst of a raid of horse thieves and lend a hand in driving them away. It was the likely sort of thing. Now he nodded at Augustus and said to his people:

"This is the little one of them Vaiden boys I was telling you-all about."

The old woman ejaculated with the pleased air of the prescient, "I had a idyah maybe it was one of them boys. He talked kinder sprucy."

"Sarah Bentley," said Elvira, looking at Augustus, "said his sister was the purtiest girl she ever saw."

This surprised Augustus and embarrassed him a trifle, too.

"We don't think Marcia's much to look at at home," he said.

"You wouldn't, she's yore sister," said the old woman.

Now that the fight was over, she produced a small cymling container from her skirt pocket, dipped a brush into it, and mopped some snuff on her teeth and gums. This produced a chocolate-colored streak along the closure of her lips. Old Mrs. Catlin licked this streak with such obvious pleasure that Augustus immediately desired a dip of snuff, too.

The group turned back toward the cabin.

"Er—how did you leave your folks?" inquired Jerry in a diffident voice as he fell in beside his guest.

Augustus blinked his eyes.

"Why—uh—out the back window," he said, with a glance toward Elvira.

"Left 'em how?" inquired Mr. Catlin, voicing the astonishment of the whole family.

Augustus had the flat feeling of one whose joke does not take

"I left 'em very well," he said tamely.

"What did you mean by the back window?" asked Elvira curiously.

"I climbed out of the back window last night and slipped off," stated Augustus more lucidly; "that's how I left 'em."

Jerry and Elvira began laughing, and Jerry said:

"That's how he left 'em, Mammy—don't you see?"

"Well, I declaar," ejaculated Mr. Catlin disapprovingly, "that's a nice way fer a young man to leave home! Don't yore folks know whaar ye air?"

"I hope not," said Augustus. "I done all I could to keep 'em from it."

"Paw!" cried the girl, "of course, that's why he climbed out the back window!"

"Didn't even tell yore sister, Miss Marcia, where you was a-going?" queried Jerry incredulously.

"You don't seem to un'erstand, Jerry, that Marshy Vaiden is this boy's sister," said the old woman, holding her mouth a trifle upward and talking with a liquid effect. Then she spat.

"All this sounds mighty funny to me," stated Mr. Philo Catlin gloomily. "What did you come up this dorection fur anyway, young man?"

Augustus perceived that he was not making the hit with Mr. Catlin that he had registered with the younger set. Then he surprised himself by nodding and almost falling asleep as he answered:

"Why I—I ran away from home to—join the army." He stretched his eyes widely at the last phrase.

"What army?"

"Confederate, of course."

Then suddenly he remembered in sleepy consternation that Mr. Philo Catlin was, according to the report of the horse thieves, one of the all-firedest pisen-spittin'est insultin'est Union men in Lane County. Augustus dreaded the reply that was coming to him.

"Well, young man," said Mr. Catlin dryly, "you're a nice un to walk out of a sesesh neighborhood into a honest Union section to jine up with the rebel army. How come you to ack such a fool?"

This answer was so much more polite than Augustus expected that he explained very frankly:

"Because if I joined down close home ol' Pap would come and take me out again."

"You desarve to be tuk out!" stated the old man harshly, "joinin' up to fight to keep human beings in sarvitude . . . chain up men an' womern an' childern in slavery gineration after gineration!"

Augustus blinked his eyes and almost went to sleep again.

"That—that wasn't why ol' Pap was going to take me out," he said, drawing a long breath.

"It's why he ort to have tuk you out!" cried old Mr. Catlin.

"Well, it—it wasn't," declared Augustus with dazed satisfaction. "He wanted to keep me out till—till I got older—an' bigger—an'—an' could fight better—an'—an' keep more niggers slaves."

"Well, that's unchristian—it's the doctrine of the devil."

"Why, Mr. Catlin!" ejaculated Augustus, stretching open his mouth to keep his eyes open. "That's according to the Bible, slavery is; it says—it says, 'Ham . . . Ham . . .' The Bible says, 'Ham . . .'" That was all the Biblical pro-slavery argument Augustus could remember.

"Oh, Pappy, let him alone!" cried the old woman. "Don't you see he's nearly dead for sleep? He told you he walked all night."

"That's right," nodded Augustus gratefully, "then shooting and running this morning . . ."

"Did you have any breakfast?"

"No'm."

"Well, I declare! Elviry, run beat up a ash cake and put it in the fire. An' Philo, you hush plaguin' the boy. He b'lieves about niggers jest what his daddy b'lieved before him—same as you an' all the rest of us."

"Now looky here, Hepzy," defended the head of the family, "I take no man's opinions. I foller reason an' the Word of God!"

"Yes, I know you do, but if you lived forty mile furder South, reason an' the Word of God would tell you to chain up niggers an' work the daylights out of 'em, jest like it done this boy an' his folks."

When they entered the cabin Augustus saw two quarters of a deer hanging from the rafters. An ashen lump was steaming in the coals on the stone hearth. He sat down at an oilcloth-covered table and heard the girl Elvira asking him did he want sweet milk or butter milk. He said sweet and she started to the spring after it.

When she returned she shook him awake and gave him the ash cake. He broke it in two and found a hot steaming center sweeter than the nectar gathered by the Hybla bees from the flowered slopes of Hymettus. She gave him a broiled deer steak, too.

Augustus ate, following the girl's movements with wavering gaze. Her intense black hair, her vividly blue eyes gave him an impression of exquisite and unearthly beauty which was transferred from his sated appetite and set up on the borderland of sleep.

He reached for more ash cake, his hand fell and turned

over a squat gourd of milk, and that was the last thing that
Augustus knew.

When the boy waked again the hills and cabin filled his
ears with a silence as if they were stuffed with cotton wool.
Sunshine lay on the cabin floor in a honey-colored trance.
Old Mrs. Hepzy sat by the hearth turning her hickory-
bark toothbrush in her cymling of snuff. The cymling had a
wooden lid fastened on it so it would shut with a soft, insinuating snap. Augustus wished he possessed that identical
snuff box and a replica of the snuff brush. Presently the old
woman glanced around and saw that her guest was awake.

"Well, you slept a whet," she said, in a tone that somehow
did not interrupt the silence.

"How long have I slept?"

"It's next day," said the old woman.

Augustus sat up. He was on a pallet. He stretched his
eyes,

"Well, if it's next day," he said, "I'm twenty-four hours
behind. I must be gettin' on."

"No rush," counseled the old woman, "the war'll be thaar
when you git thaar . . . an' it may still be thaar when you
air gone."

This suggestion of death held no substantiality in the
dreaming hush of the hills.

"Where can a man go to enlist with the Confederates in
this section of the country?" inquired the boy.

The old woman hesitated.

"My ol' man ain't certain whether he ort to let you go on
and join up with the Confederates or not."

"He sure has got a fat way of helpin' himself," said
Augustus. "My brother Carp, who ain't but fourteen months
older'n I am, licked a man bigger than your old man."

The old woman mopped her teeth pensively and savorily.

"Well, that won't come up," she said at length. "We're
beholden to you for our livestock. If it hadn't a been for you

Bill Leatherwood's gang would 'a' drove 'em off an' we'd had to break up our spring patch with a maddick." The old woman rubbed her teeth again and then added, "A horse critter comes in mighty handy breaking up a corn patch."

"Was that the horse thief's name—Leatherwood?" queried Augustus, quite friendly again since the shadow of hostilities had cleared away.

"Bill Leatherwood," nodded the old woman. "Herebefore he's been stealin' sheep and hawgs, but sence the war broke out he's got a good deal forwarder an' takes horses an' cows. He won't even look at a hawg now."

Augustus thought what to say to this and finally ventured, "Well, I hate to see a man get uppish."

"So do I," said the old woman. "If every hawg thief in this county should fly in an' go to stealin' horses, why, nobody could keep their horses."

"They'd have to be somewhere," said Augustus.

"Yeh, I guess they would," admitted the old woman, and she snapped open her cymling and rolled her brush in it around and around.

"That's a mighty nice snuff box you've got," said Augustus, his mouth watering so that he was forced to swallow.

"Jerry fixed the top on it for me," said the mother with a touch of pride. "He used the spring out o' an ol' watch."

"Well, I declare."

"But I wasn't a bit supprised at what happened yestiddy."

"How come that?" asked Augustus, to whom an onslaught of horse thieves was sufficiently unusual to occasion some surprise.

"Why, because day afore yestiddy the dawgs got after a woodchuck an' it dodged through the door thaar an' hid behind the churn. I got up an' driv out the dawgs an' let the woodchuck go. By that I knowed something was goin' to happen to our keow, an' somebody would come along an' holp us out."

"But it wasn't your cow, it was your mule an' horse."

"Goin' behin' the churn made me think it would be the keow."

"M-m . . . yes," said Augustus, perceiving that if one thought it was going to be anything at all, the churn would certainly make one think it would be the cow.

He got up and stretched himself in the trance of the silent cabin.

"Well, I guess I better be moving," he said in a brisker tone. "You never did say where I could enlist in the Confederate army."

"Why, Savannah," said the old woman, spitting in the ashes, "but don't be snatched."

"Yes, I guess I better go. Stayed here now longer than I intended." He was fully dressed, just as he had been the day before when he had toppled off to sleep. There was nothing for him to put on or to pick up in order to be ready to travel, and he had a vague feeling that he ought to do one of these things. His feet were blistered from his yesterday night's walking. He looked out the door.

"What direction do I take?"

"Well, now, lemme see . . ."

And Mrs. Hepzy began one of those long, interminable, and perfectly hopeless set of directions such as flourish in the hills. Augustus was to follow the ridge road for a couple of miles, take the second left fork, pass a blasted tree, turn to the right, keep on to a watermill, turn to the right again, and keep on till he reached the split cypress . . . on and on went the directions.

In the midst of this Elvira came across the clearing with her face flushed and damp from work. When she found Augustus was about to go, she at once volunteered to set him on his way a piece.

She went to the stable and got out the mule. On it she placed a woman's saddle that was even older and more scrofulous than the one Marcia used on the Vaiden place.

"You can ride in the saddle part of the time, then I'll ride," planned the girl.

Augustus looked dubiously at the saddle built for the modest position of one leg hanging down and the other cocked up at a breakneck angle. If his feet hadn't been so sore he would have tabled the motion for the mule and walked. He told Elvira that she could ride in the saddle permanently and he would hold on behind.

Mrs. Catlin hurried about and did up a lunch for Augustus. Then the lad mounted the fence, Elvira rode up close to him, and Augustus turned loose and fell on the croup of the mule.

Once there he found he had to hold tightly either to the cantle of the saddle or Elvira's waist or he would slide off the sharp sloping rump. Both of these holds were embarrassing. When he clung to the edge of the saddle the hips and buttocks of the girl moulded over his fingers and placed him in keen spiritual discomfort.

Elvira, who was nineteen, directed him to clasp both hands around her waist. As the mule climbed the trail to the ridge road Augustus swung almost his whole weight on Elvira's waist. The intimacy filled him with a tingling and violently distasteful rapture.

The girl perceived his trouble and tried talking as the mule struggled upward. Her conversation naturally was jerky, cut off now and then by a sudden surge of her companion at her stomach.

"Jerry says—uh—he's goin' to join—uh—the Union army and wouldn't it be—uh—quare if you two met in a bat—battle."

When they reached the level ridge road Augustus held on as aloofly as possible. He could manage by merely touching the widespread, almost impersonal hardness of her feminine hip bones. This was a great comfort, but somehow or other Augustus felt vaguely unhappy because the whole ride was not a continuous upward lurching of the mule.

He was a difficult guest to please.

An hour and a half later, when Elvira reached the water-mill, Augustus slid stiffly off the mule with the most deserted feeling in the world. The watermill was the limit of Elvira's assistance. The boy looked up at the woman's jet hair and intensely blue eyes with a feeling that all the comfort of life was being withdrawn from him. He had lost all desire to go to war. He wished he could ride on forever with Elvira. He wanted never to leave her.

She told him good-bye in her hill-country twang and wished him good luck in the army of his choice. Then she turned and rode back down the rude trail over which she had come. As she reached a clump of willows beside the mill race, she turned, waved at Augustus, called a last good-bye, and passed out of sight.

Augustus stared after her with a delicate aching in the back of his throat. Then he sat down by the mill race and ate his lunch.

CHAPTER TWENTY-THREE

As augustus vaiden neared Savannah, Tennessee, the great hills grew smaller and the isolated clearings of the hill people widened into formal farms with slaves working in the fields. In brief, Augustus had trudged through the fifty-odd miles of natural Unionist country that separated Florence, Alabama, from Savannah, Tennessee, and had arrived in a territory geographically secession.

It required Augustus two days to reach Savannah. On the last day, as he plodded onward, two horsemen overtook him: a youth not much older than himself who rode a horse, and a negro man mounted on a mule. The two riders slowed down beside the limping footman and the white youth began with the desultory comment that the weather was good overhead.

This remark bore the implicit observation that the weather was not good underfoot. Because in the South the roads were reckoned as one phase of the weather, and while the weather overhead was often as fair as the heart could wish, the weather underfoot always left much to be desired.

Having arrived at agreement on the upper and lower weathers, the two young men introduced themselves to each other. It turned out that Augustus had met Gillie Dilliehay, a youth quite as merry as his name. He was going to Savannah, he said, to enlist with the secessionists on account of Abraham there; and he nodded at his dark postilion.

Abraham was one of those tall gaunt negroes whose blackness was unevenly distributed over his foolish-looking face. Gillie Dilliehay's own face was not exactly wise looking. His hair was so blond it was white; not an old white but a baby white. His skin was so fair that his pale blue eyes seemed fairly deep in color, and his mouth was big with full lips that curled in a smile in his soberest moments.

Augustus said he did not see how in the world Abraham could cause Mr. Dilliehay to enter the Confederate army.

"Well," explained Gillie, "Dad voted for Abe Lincoln and Granddad before him was a Republican. But about a year ago he had a debt on a man and the man paid him off with Abraham here. So when sesesh come along, Dad thought he'd better secede too, seeing as he owned Abraham."

Augustus was astonished to know that a man would change his political belief through considerations of property. He had supposed that politics was like religion, an infallible revelation handed down from on high.

"I wouldn't change my politics for a debt," declared Augustus stoutly.

"I guess you would if politics was about to take your stuff away from you," cried Gillie, laughing. "That's what law is for, to keep your property."

"Now that's right, too," admitted Augustus.

"And it jest struck me and Dad to take Abraham down and make him fight on the Confederate side and make him defend our property rights in himself."

Everybody, including Abraham, began laughing.

"Yes, suh," said the black man, poking his lips out, "I's gwi he'p Mas' Dilliehay keep me."

"Well, what's he going to do?" inquired Augustus, amused at the idea.

"I's gwi stan' aroun' on de aidge o' de battle, an' if'n Mas' Gillie gits hu't I wade in an' fotch he out."

The two boys burst out laughing again at Abraham's idea of a battle.

"Say, nigger," directed Augustus, "slip back behind the saddle on that mule. You can ride behind just as easy as I can walk. That's your first work for the Confederacy."

"Yes," seconded Mr. Dilliehay heartily, "let Mr. Vaiden ride, Abraham."

The change was made and the two boys rode into Savannah laughing and talking. Two or three times Abraham said jocularly:

"Mas' 'Gustus, dis heah mule sho is skinnin' my behin'.'"

"This'll be good practice for you when the Yankees skin you with their bagnets," said Augustus winking at Gillie.

The blond boy was hilarious in his appreciation of Augustus' humor. This attitude was utterly delightful and novel to Augustus. At the Vaiden home in Alabama when any member attempted a jest the others sat on him either singly, doubly, or *en famille*.

At the courthouse in Savannah, Tennessee, the prospective recruits found a patriotic barbecue in progress. A great crowd was on the square, and on the courthouse steps a man was making a speech. He was a compact man with a handsome square-cut dissipated face and curly black hair.

He shook his head, leaned forward and drummed on a little table before him.

"Tennesseeans, countrymen, defenders of man's inalienable right to life, liberty, and the pursuit of happiness! I come asking you to lift your sword to defend the sacred altar of your country's freedom! Vandals ravish the temple! This time not British greed and lust for power, but a motley crew from Yankeedom whose hearts are as stony as the inhospitable soil that bred them; who make gold their god and a tradesman's duplicity their ritual of worship."

Cheers and shouts interrupted the orator's period. Voices cried out:

"That's right, Bailey! Give 'em hell, Bailey!"

The speaker paused, flung out an eloquent arm.

"I intend to give 'em hell! I'm here to-day asking you to help me give 'em hell!"

A roar of laughter greeted the turn, and a medley yelled:

"We're with you, Bailey! Shore we'll help you! Lead us to the damned Yankees!"

Augustus plucked Gillie's sleeve.

"Who is that man making the speech?" he asked.

Gillie was astonished.

" 'Y, don't know him? That's Joe Magnus Bailey, the silver-tongued boy of Hardin."

"He don't look like a boy."

"Well, no, he don't," conceded Gillie. "I've seen two or three silver-tongued boys and they all look old. However, you're mighty lucky to hear silver-tongued Joe Bailey make a speech."

The orator had tossed off some water during the cheering and now proceeded with his speech.

"Friends, countrymen, if you would fight, you must fight now. The foe withers like dried grass before our invincible arms. Joseph E. Johnston has already strung a rosary of victories from Manassas to Winchester and laid it as an offering at the capitol at Richmond. Shall we allow the bosom of Virginia cavaliers to receive the sword that was thrust at Tennessee?"

Cries of "No! No! We'll go with you, Joe Magnus!" An uproar broke out among the crowd. Men pushed forward from all directions. New voices on the courthouse platform took up the direction of the crowd:

"You'll find the enlistment officers in the county court clerk's office!" cried these guides. "Enlistment papers in the county court clerk's room!"

There was nothing eloquent about this. It was edged with fact and serious fighting. The crowd poured into the courthouse in a sluice. In the midst of this press Gillie Dilliehay and Augustus clung to each other and helped push. As they went into the dark room of the court house a sharp-faced man standing beside the entrance said in their ears:

"Boys, when they ask you how old ye are, be shore and say eighteen."

"All right. All right, sir, we will," nodded both youths, deeply grateful for the hint.

CHAPTER TWENTY-FOUR

WITH the recruits in Savannah, Augustus drilled more gloriously than did the men in his brother Miltiades' company because Augustus had fallen in with the cavalry.

Every morning and afternoon for two weeks Augustus trotted and galloped Abraham's mule up and down the Savannah fair grounds. He caught with boyish quickness the evolutions of the cavalry, squadron column, line to the front, squadron charge . . . and off went the long line of horses and mules, anything the men could find to carry them.

It was the most exciting sport Augustus had ever known. At first the horses were inextricably mixed, but gradually both men and animals began to move with that appearance of order which is the terror of cavalry.

The recruits who came from out of town were quartered in the different homes in the village or on near-by farms as long as the drilling continued. In between drills the men played cards or wrestled or jumped or got up bets on who owned the fastest horse.

Augustus and Gillie were quartered with the Poags. The two boys were quite illuminating to Mrs. Poag. She was a large tanned motherly woman, who had thought that cavalrymen were wild buccaneering fellows. To see her two cavalrymen sitting quiet and rather abashed at the table and to hear them giggling in their room at night was disconcerting to her ideas. They were not fire eaters at all but two boys who she begun to suspect might get hurt. They began to prey on her mind. Her uneasiness about them took the form of food, and every meal she prepared was a feast. She said if she had known they were going to worry her life out of her she never would have taken them in the first place.

And Gillie would say, "Now, Miss Emmy, you know you would!"

And Mrs. Poag would declare roundly, "I would not, Gillie Dilliehay! When you-all are gone I'll never know a night's rest wonderin' what's happenin' to you."

One day she asked if they both wrote home regularly. Augustus' evasive answers led her instantly to suspect that not only did he not write but that he had run away and his mother didn't know where he was. Then "Miss Emmy" was going to write herself. Augustus became very uneasy because long ago he had told "Miss Emmy" about his family and where they lived, how many niggers and dogs they had, and all about himself. After Mrs. Poag's threat to write home about him Augustus would not have been surprised any day to see old man Jimmie ride up and snatch him from the glorious hog-killing time he was having in the cavalry.

However, his three weeks' training was up at last and "Miss Emmy" either had never written, or the information was disregarded from the Alabama end. When the boys were ready to start Mrs. Emmy produced two meal sacks and two big pieces of oilcloth as equipment for her riders. The meal sacks were sewn up at each end and split in the middle to make a kind of rude saddlebag. Mrs. Emmy had put in shirts and socks and enough eatables almost to fill the sacks. The oilcloths were for raincoats or for ground cloths, or they could be propped up with sticks for tents. It turned out later than in fair weather they made very good gaming tables, but at the moment of parting with "Miss Emmy" the boys did not think of that.

The whole village turned out to see the troops away. Women and girls were kissing their brothers and sweethearts and sons farewell.

Mrs. Poag started in to shake hands with Augustus and Gillie but wound up by kissing them and crying over them. She was afraid something was going to happen to them.

But up to the last moment Augustus was not quite sure that "Miss Emmy" would not produce his father and have him miss all the battles and the riding. He left her blinking his eyes to keep back uncavalier tears but greatly relieved to get away unhindered.

The troops crossed the river in ferryboats and then rode toward the west, into Mississippi.

The country they traversed rose and fell in long undulations, with here and there deep ravines cut by the creeks in the loamy soil.

When the troops had ridden three days these undulations had diminished to the vast, almost level plain of the Mississippi Valley. The horizon was visible so far away that the trees were a faint purpling against the remote sky.

They themselves were an oddly equipped cavalry, riding horses and mules and armed with rifles and shotguns. However, in their first engagement with the Yankees they expected to improve their mounts and their armament.

One day news came through Captain Bailey that the company would join Forrest's cavalry at Poplar Springs. Immediately the troops were buzzing with talk of Forrest. He was fighting the Union cavalry under General Sturgess. The Yankees were trying to cut the Baltimore & Ohio Railroad which supplied the Confederate forces at Corinth. Here Albert Sidney Johnston blocked the road of the Union armies which were moving down from Kentucky toward Vicksburg.

All this talk painted the vastness of the military operations which engaged the southern half of a continent.

Augustus was surprised that the Yankees had ever got that far south. He asked McClusky, an older man in the troop, if he thought they would win.

"Sure we'll win," said McClusky. "Jeff Davis has ordered

out another hundred thousand men. Lee's moving up into Pennsylvania. . . ." The older man drew out a greasy deck of cards and a handful of Confederate bills. "How about a little game of seven up?"

Gillie Dilliehay played McClusky. Augustus sat by and watched because he had no money. Presently Gillie had no money either, and he sat with Augustus and watched McClusky play.

The following day, at Poplar Springs, in the early afternoon the recruits joined the salted troopers under Forrest. These seasoned men were lank and brown, their horses worn and thin. Some of the men wore Confederate gray, some had on civilian clothes, and some had captured blue coats and sabers and carbines from the enemy. Here and there rode a rider with a bandaged head or arm or leg.

Augustus' own troops set up a great shouting when they saw Forrest's men. They rode forward in their best order while the veterans receiving them laughed with one another at the enthusiasm of the newcomers.

"We'll see what speed you make when the Yankees salt your tails with a few carbine balls," called out one of the older men.

The newcomers were divided up among the seasoned companies. Gillie and Augustus were put in a mess with three troopers named Risner, Haddock, and Brewer.

That evening, when the quartermaster gave out the bacon and meal, Brewer received the supply for the mess. He gave a slice of bacon apiece to Augustus and Gillie and kept the rest for his two comrades.

Gillie was greatly put out. A few minutes later he got up from the camp fire and nodded Augustus after him. When they were aside he said with a long face:

"Augustus, Brewer has given all the bacon to Risner and Haddock!"

"Yes, I see he has," said Augustus, equally disturbed.

"What'll we say to 'em?"

"Well, we can say to 'em they made a mistake."

Just then they saw the older men were laughing as they held the bacon on their ramrods out over the coals.

"All right, you go say that to 'em," said Gillie.

Since Augustus had suggested it it fell on him to say it. So he went back to the men at the fire.

"Brewer," he said, "haven't you made a little mistake?"

"Mistake how?" asked Brewer, looking up innocently.

"Well, in our share of the meat," Augustus exhibited his translucent strip.

"We eat here," said Brewer, "according to how good a man you are. A good man eats a lot of bacon but a couple of thin spindlin' Tennesseeans nachelly don't require so much."

The other two men were laughing and Augustus became angry.

"I'm from Alabama," he said, "and I eat as much as anybody."

"Why, that's funny," cried Brewer. "I allus heard Alabamians was like frogs, they stayed fat on wind."

At this slur on Alabamians Augustus became furious.

"No, we don't eat wind!" he cried. "We eat wind bags, and I'm goin' to make my supper on you!"

With that he shucked off his coat. Brewer handed his bacon to Risner for safe keeping. The two troopers walked away from the fire with a certain formality and the next moment were pounding and biting, gouging one another in the eyes and at the hinge of the jaw.

Men from other messes came running in and formed a ring about them. They put up bets on the outcome.

"Are they fighting about anything," asked a man in the ring, "or are they just fighting?"

"They're fighting about the bacon I got here on this ramrod," said Risner; "the winner eats it if he's got any teeth left."

Just then some person in the ring, either with intent to make peace or have a diversion, yelled out:

"Hey, you damn fools, Risner is eatin' your bacon! You ain't goin' to have none left!"

Augustus happened to be on top at the moment. He leaped up from the ground and made toward Risner, who had faithfully stewarded the bacon. At the sight of Augustus' face, Risner thrust the meat toward the boy,

"Here you are," he ejaculated, "if you can hold it."

Augustus took the bacon and looked around at Brewer.

"I think I can hold it. If—if Brewer don't think so, we'll continue—the argument," he panted.

Brewer was up, merely standing in the ring of men looking at Augustus.

"That was more bacon than me an' Risner an' Haddock could eat anyway," he said. "We intended to split up with you when we got through laughin' at ye."

"Well, you're through laughin' now. It's time to split up," panted Augustus.

The incident of the bacon was a very good thing for Augustus. The show he had made with Brewer helped his morale. He could now talk about what he was going to do when he met the Yankees, and Brewer at least was in no position to dispute his word.

As the troops rode on day after day a tension arose in Augustus and Gillie to meet the enemy. The old men were not uneasy on this point; they knew they eventually would meet some Yankees. They had met them before and it would happen again.

Villages and plantation houses were passed on their endless march through the Mississippi dust. Augustus had never dreamed there could be such thick dust. Compared to it, Alabama dust was as a haze to a bee smudge. It covered both riders and horses in a uniform brown. The troopers' eyes appeared grotesque batting in the brown masks.

One day as the troops rode on, leaving behind them a

cloud of dust in the air, they saw far off on the horizon
another cloud hanging high. It drifted up from the horizon
in the shape of a mushroom. Involuntarily the whole column
quickened its gait.

Augustus turned to Brewer.

"Are the Yankees kicking up that dust?" he asked excitedly.

Brewer turned dryly to Risner.

"Alabama thinks that's a dust he's seeing yonder."

Augustus didn't like to be called Alabama. Brewer never
used that as his nickname except when he had made some
mistake.

"Well, it is dust!" reiterated Augustus warmly.

"It's smoke," said Risner. "From the color, I judge it's
the damn Yankees burnin' up the Confederate taxes."

Augustus saw that Risner had set in to make fun of him,
too, so he rode on in silence. Gillie Dilliehay, however, braved
a possible "catch" and wanted to know how the Yankees
could be burning up taxes.

"Why, the farmers around here have to pay their taxes
in corn and cotton to the Confederate government. That's
corn burnin' . . . it makes a yellow smoke like that."

The ill-equipped cavalry moved faster and faster toward
the distant pyre.

The fact that the Yankees were burning corn in such vast
quantities stirred Augustus tremendously. If it had been
anything else besides corn he could have borne it better. He
had worked too many hot days in the cornfield to endure the
destruction of corn.

He leaned forward on the mule Gillie unintentionally
had furnished him. He glanced around at the dusty riders
and saw that Brewer was watching him. Brewer was watching to see how Augustus would act when the Yankees were
just ahead. Augustus made a resolve that he would outdo
Brewer.

The squadron increased its pace.

"How many men has Sturgess got?" asked Gillie of Brewer.

"Enough for Augustus, there," nodded Brewer.

"What do you mean by that?" asked Gillie.

"Why, I mean they'll be so blamed thick when Augustus shoots into 'em with his shotgun, I imagine he'll blame near bring down the whole covey."

Risner and Haddock broke out laughing loudly enough to be heard above the horses' hoofs pounding in the dust.

His shotgun was another sore point with Augustus. Now as the squadron galloped toward the smoke, Augustus resolved to come back with a carbine if he could shoot a Yankee or find a dead one.

The smoke was rising out of a town. As the cavalry drew near houses thickened around them. An occasional man or woman would run out of a house to scream with joy at the coming of the Confederates. They would shout at the dusty riders:

"They're down at the railroad!" "They're burnin' up the corn pens!"

At a turn in the village street the riders took to an old field and deployed. Augustus fell in his place in the line as he had been trained. A sudden feeling of invincibility came over him. He waited to cock the barrels of his shotgun.

The first glimpse the hobbledehoy caught of the enemy were the silhouettes of horsemen dashing into line in front of the blazing corn pens that lined the railroad. Two hundred yards down the track the little station was in flames.

The riders about Augustus suddenly broke into yells, kicked, spurred, and dashed forward at top speed. The squadron spread out right and left like something that tautened before the wind as it charged. The labor he had spent in the Savannah fair grounds kept Augustus and his mule equi-distant from Brewer and Gillie. Before the burning corn pens the Federal cavalry hastily formed to receive the onslaught.

Before Augustus' eyes everything quivered with the
vibration of his mule. He yelled and could not distinguish
his own voice in the high shrieking uproar of his men.

A grotesque rattle of guns broke out around him; the
snap of rifles, the boom of shotguns. Flowers of fire suddenly bloomed among the Federal horsemen who were still
chivvying into line. Out of the corner of his eye Augustus
glimpsed one of his own comrades slump out of his saddle.
His foot caught in the stirrup and he was dragged forward
with his head pounding the earth by the frightened horse.

Right up on the Federals, Augustus leveled his long
jiggling shotgun at a blue cavalryman. A blast of powder
smoke shut him off from view. As the boy dashed through
his own smoke he saw the fellow sway. But the Yankee
righted himself and drew a saber. A furious hope of finishing the man with his second barrel seized the youth. As the
horse and the mule dashed together, Augustus leaned forward, thrust out his long gun like a pistol, and fired point
blank at his man. The flame tore a hole in the neck of the
Federal's horse. The next moment something bit the boy's
shoulder and back as he leaned almost flat on his mule's neck.

With the saber cut, that assailant made way for others.
The tiny glimmer of another sword licked at Augustus, he
mashed it down with his shotgun barrel and it flickered into
his mule's shoulder.

At that moment the blue fighters around Augustus
wheeled about and were suddenly flying back toward the
burning corn pens. The mixed character of the Confederate
small arms hastened some and stopped others. Augustus
loaded his shotgun as his mule lunged forward. He rammed
down powder and buckshot. The lunges of his mule grew
shorter and unsteady. Suddenly its front legs collapsed, its
sharp breast plowed the ground, Augustus went over its
neck, fell sprawling but did not lose his gun.

In the whirl around him Augustus saw a man holding a
horse near a burning pen. He rushed at the wounded man

to get the horse. The Yankee had a gun. He leveled it. Augustus bent down, leaped sidewise. As the gun fired he was in the midst of these acrobatics.

His own weapon was loaded. He dashed full tilt at the man before he could load his rifle. At that moment the Yankee's gun fired again. Augustus' side went numb. He braced his legs in a desperate effort to keep from falling. He fired both his own barrels and the man with the rifle dropped to the ground.

At that moment Augustus saw all the Confederate cavalry had turned back. Up from the village came another galloping horde of blue coats.

Augustus tried to get to the horse the dead Federal still held. His legs seemed limber. If he could reach the horse . . . and mount him . . .

At that moment hoofs dashed up behind him. Somebody leaped to the ground, seized him around the waist, and hurled him upward to the saddle. Brewer's voice shouted:

"You Goddamn fool, don't you know enough to run when the rest of us run!"

The blue cavalry down the track let loose with a crackling volley at the two riders on the flying horse.

CHAPTER TWENTY-FIVE

T HE Confederate cavalry had employed the usual Forrest tactics at Okalona, Mississippi, where the main body of
Sturgess cavalry had been concentrated. They had struck
and vanished with equal suddenness.

The ill-furnished gray horsemen went out of Okalona at
full tilt. They dashed out on the road they had entered and
slid down the railroad track for another stab at the Yankees.

As Augustus clung on before Brewer, the dust, the flying
horsemen, the people running out of their houses to shout
at the Confederates all formed a scene painful and vaguely
unreal, as violent action always appears to a wounded man.

In the clatter of flight Brewer growled, "You're bound
for the hospital, damn you! . . . what the hell I ever fooled
with you for?"

Brewer gave the last acrid flavor to Augustus' bad day.

"Where are we headed—camp?"

"Camp hell! We'll camp when we can't see how to ride."

Augustus looked at the red sun through a haze of dust.
One side of him seemed dead, but his back and shoulder
where the saber marked him burned. He didn't know how
far he could ride.

Brewer was bitter against the boy he had picked up.

"What did you run on that Yankee for, him with his gun
on you? Whyn't you shoot him at the start?"

"Hell," groaned Augustus, "his gun ought to 'a' been
empty . . . he shot at me once!"

"Of all damn fools!" flared out Brewer in utter disgust.

"You ain't worth totin' off. Don't you know them Yankees load their guns in the mornin' an shoot 'em all day long?"

"That's a lie," said Augustus. "You're trying to stuff me."

"You're hard to convince," observed Brewer dryly.

Amid the painful jostling of the horse, Augustus wondered if the Yankee could have shot time after time without reloading his gun. He had never heard of a repeating rifle. He thought of the terrible advantage such a weapon would give a man. Here he was with his side numb because he had made a mistake. His frustration and his pain made Augustus sick.

The flying cavalry turned off the road and halted in a grove of cottonwoods. The sergeants began the roll call. When it came to his own company and mess, Gillie Dillliehay was missing. The colonel came around on inspection. He looked at Augustus holding on to Brewer's saddle.

"That man goes to the hospital," directed the officer.

A fear that had been hovering in the back of Augustus' head materialized.

"Isn't that hell," he mumbled to Brewer—"sent to the hospital at my very first battle!"

"You'd fought better if you'd had brains," growled Brewer. "Besides, that wasn't a battle; it wasn't even a skirmish; it was a tiff."

The colonel said, "Your lieutenant tells me you rescued Vaiden under fire, Brewer."

Brewer put his hand to his hat with the awkwardness of a volunteer soldier.

"I'll mention that in my dispatches," said the colonel.

Brewer glanced from side to side to see if any of the men were listening.

Just then the colonel said, "What's wrong with your boot?"

Brewer looked down.

"Nothin' wrong with my boot that I knows of."

"It's full of blood, you're wounded."

Brewer dropped all military formality and began swearing it was nothing but a flesh wound. The colonel dropped all military formality and told him to get off his horse damn quick and let a surgeon put a tourniquet on that leg. Brewer and the colonel argued about this. The colonel threatened Brewer with arrest.

When Brewer got off his horse he couldn't stand on the leg.

"Well, damn such a come-off!" cried Brewer, holding to his saddle.

Brewer and Augustus and twelve other men were put in wagons and started for the hospital. The wagon beds were padded with pine tops and covered with blankets.

CHAPTER TWENTY-SIX

In the hospital at Lauderdale Springs, Mississippi, Brewer lay two cots removed from Augustus. For that much luck Augustus was thankful, but he could have wished the fellow well on the opposite side of the big square frame building. At times he wished Brewer were kicked completely out of the hospital and that he himself was the kicker.

The cause of this mental violence was Brewer's jokes. The trooper was the sort of fellow who keeps telling the same thing over and over. The two of them had been in the hospital barely two hours when Brewer began explaining to the surrounding cots that Augustus was wounded because he had stood waiting for a Yankee to get through shooting at him before he opened fire in return.

Everyone laughed. This embarrassed Augustus, and when he tried to explain that he never before had seen a repeating rifle, the laughter rose to an uproar. One man, to whom laughing was agony, pleaded with Brewer to shut up.

Even the woman nurses had to control their faces, and this took the last remnant of self-assurance from Augustus. After that he lay thinking of the different things he would like to see happen to Brewer: scalding, to be led around by the nose with red-hot pincers, and so forth and so forth.

Brewer would repeat the story of Augustus' wound at least three times a day. He would turn to some cot and ask its occupant if he had heard how Mr. Augustus Vaiden came to be wounded, or how Mr. Vaiden of Alabama came to be wounded. The addressed man would always declare, with great interest, Why no, he hadn't heard it, how did it happen?

Then Brewer would tell it over again with any variation that he had studied up since the last rehearsal. The story grew more and more ridiculous from day to day.

Augustus' wound ached at fairly regular intervals but he suffered acutely only when the surgeon dressed it. Augustus did not like the particular surgeon who attended him. His name was Wright. He was a young doctor who was still in the stage of using long scientific terms before the nurses. Also he had the Napoleon complex and moved about the hospital with lips set very firmly together. He performed any operation indicated without regard to the fact that wounds are the torn ends of agonized nerves. He attended the patients under his care in the spirit of Napoleon destroying the enemy at Austerlitz.

A nurse whom everyone called Miss Mack helped Wright at these dressings. Now it was a point with Augustus never to seem to be suffering. He tried to keep the muscles in his face from twitching, he regretted the perspiration that broke out on his forehead. But with all his resistance, once under an excruciating stab, he gasped out:

"Gad damn it, Doc, can't you be easier?"

Lieutenant Wright was neither easier nor harder. He proceeded without a word, as if Augustus had said and felt nothing at all. Presently he went away and Miss Mack finished the dressing.

Augustus lay very chagrined and angry that he had exhibited pain before Miss Mack. However he made an *ex post facto* show of stoicism by saying:

"Look yonder at Brewer lying there. That's all he does, lies . . . and usually about me."

Augustus had not intended this pun when he started his sentence, it had just worked itself out to his own surprise and pleasure.

Miss Mack broke into pleased laughter.

"You oughtn't to let him tease you. You ought to say that to him and cut him off."

"I'll do that next time," said Augustus, "if I can remember it."

"You stand your dressings better than any man in the ward," added the nurse.

An almost pathetic gratitude flooded Augustus to find an unmocking soul in the midst of a life of endless mockery or inattention. He would have thanked her but he had no words. He said:

"How long have you been here, Miss Mack?"

"My name isn't Mack," said the nurse. "They call me that. My name is Rose McClanahan."

"Oh!" ejaculated Augustus, with a very odd impression, as if the nurse had gone to the trouble of taking off her cap and apron and showing herself a woman in a pretty dress and with bright combs in her black hair. It had accomplished more than any mere telling of a name Augustus had ever heard. Then he added awkwardly, "Much obliged."

Miss Mack simply smiled in response to this. As she bent over him, fluffing his pillow, he could see the closure of her full lips, the tiny darker flecks in the iris of her brown eyes. Her eyebrows were dark and a little rough. One had a tiny curl at the bend of her forehead. Her complexion was smooth, and looking up under her chin he saw a delicate ivory cast blending into her whiter neck.

What her age was, or even that she had an age, never entered Augustus' head. When she finished his pillow she left him for other patients.

That is to say the nurse, Miss Mack, went to the other patients; the astral Miss Rose McClanahan remained by Augustus' cot. When the wounded boy looked out the window at a grove of maples he saw Miss Rose McClanahan there. She looked at him also from the rolling clouds of spring beyond the maples. Breaths of cold and scented air that came in through the window were Rose McClanahan's cool fingers on his face.

Other things amused Augustus through the hospital window. Buzzards sailed across the sky in funereal argosies . . . and the boy wondered where was Gillie Dilliehay? Then two squirrels lived in the maple grove and made Augustus wish he had a gun to shoot them. Bluebottle flies cruised into the unscreened window with metallic whines. They plumped down on Augustus' blankets with an abrupt stoppage of their drone that was like a tiny blow. Now and then Augustus poised his good hand and tried to catch one, but it always launched its note three semitones higher and vanished in a gleaming greenish streak.

Presently Augustus dozed off to sleep. When he awoke two patients were arguing in angry voices about which was the greater general, Joe Johnston or Beauregard. Finally Brewer spoke up and laid a claim for Forrest. It finally wound up in a quarrel and one of the patients climbed out of his bed and wanted to fight, but a doctor ordered him back in his cot.

As a tag to this incident, Miss McClanahan came and sat down by Brewer's cot and began talking to him in low tones. One of the other men had called Brewer a liar and the nurse was soothing him, telling him that the term liar could not be applied to a matter of opinion.

Brewer said when a man called him a liar he took it as meant and didn't try to sneak out of it by the rules of grammar.

Then Augustus could hear Miss McClanahan say soothingly, "A big strong man like you oughn't to pay any attention to . . ."

For some reason Augustus grew acutely depressed and miserable; for Miss McClanahan to be wasting her time on Brewer seemed outrageous. Brewer was not particularly strong or big, and was not the sort of person a woman like Miss McClanahan ought to talk to. Presently he could endure the conversation between them no longer and he called in an uncertain voice:

"Miss McClanahan, my—my bandage is pulling."

A few moments later, when the nurse came to him and asked where the bandage was pulling, Augustus was in much confusion. He pointed out a place and then said rather breathlessly:

"M-Miss Rose, if I was you I wouldn't fool my time away on Brewer."

Miss McClanahan considered this cryptically for a moment.

"You don't like him, do you?"

"It's not that," said Augustus, taking higher grounds. "Him telling you how big and stout he was . . ."

"He didn't tell me that."

"Well you-all were talking about it," complained Augustus. "I heard you."

"I think I said that he was big and strong."

"Well, something like that. He ought to 'a' told you better. Why, I licked him when I first joined the army . . . nearly."

The nurse tried to compose her face.

"Your bandage didn't really hurt, did it?" she asked.

Augustus' face reddened.

"Naw, it's all right," and he looked away from her.

The woman stood smiling faintly at him, revolving in her own thoughts whether to ignore the meaning of the boy's unconscious attitude or to accept it on his own terms and make of his hospital days one of those sweet foolish extravaganzas of adolescence. She decided and said:

"Listen, Augustus, after while when your back and arm are better we'll go out and have tea in the garden at the back of the hospital."

"Tea?" repeated Augustus, who had never heard of taking tea as tea in a garden or anywhere else.

"And sandwiches," included Miss McClanahan by way

of information, and then on an inspiration she added, "Or we might have gingerbread."

Augustus' face lighted up.

"I like gingerbread," he admitted, and then he pondered mentioning pies. He really would like a green-apple pie, and there was something about Miss McClanahan that suggested she made excellent green-apple pies.

From that time on the nurse was never entirely out of Augustus' head. He fancied himself eating gingerbread, or pies, with her in the garden. The tea part had dropped out of the picture. He had no idea why one should choose a garden to eat a snack in. At home Augustus had always made his four o'clock tea on whatever he could find to hand while he moved out of the kitchen as discreetly and as inconspicuously as possible.

At night the nurse haunted him most persistently. At night Augustus left behind him his wound and the hospital and went forth to war again and did mighty things for Miss McClanahan. He would start off his mental adventures by licking Brewer for insulting the nurse. Brewer never had insulted the girl, but each night in Augustus' fantasy he did so and got licked for his pains. After this auspicious start Augustus fared on to other high emprises, such as founding great cattle ranches in Texas and finding gold mines in California, all for Miss McClanahan.

Between the hours of 1 and 3 A.M. Miss McClanahan was indeed a great boon to Augustus, because between those hours, as regularly as the clock struck, the soldier's arm began to ache. Then he lay and watched the stars move through the dark branches of the maples, and he clung to the thought of his nurse against the crescendo of pain. He thought of how beautiful she was, what he would say to her the next morning. He would tell her he loved her and ask her to be his wife.

At three o'clock his arm eased off and he went to sleep. Then the next day, when Miss McClanahan really sat by his cot finishing Dr. Wright's dressing, all he did was to look at her and talk of indifferent things such as what went with Gillie Dilliehay at the battle of Okalona.

But one night at three o'clock the arm did not ease into sleep. It continued an angry throbbing until morning. Ten o'clock brought nurse and surgeon to a nerve-racked boy.

When the two came to the cot Dr. Wright produced a thermometer and stuck it in the patient's mouth. Rose ejaculated with concern:

"Augustus, did you sleep well last night?"

"All right," said Augustus, who never admitted a frailty.

"How does your arm feel?"

"All right."

However, his wound throbbed so that he turned faintly sick when Dr. Wright removed the bandages. A peculiar malodor penetrated Augustus' nostrils. The surgeon looked at the arm and then at the patient with a sort of impersonal annoyance.

"This arm has been exposed," he said, and pressed the flesh until it sent streaks of pain deep into Augustus' shoulder.

Miss McClanahan ejaculated under her breath, "Oh, isn't that——" and caught herself.

The doctor said to the patient, "You must have worked the bandages loose."

Augustus clenched the rail of his cot, caught his breath and asked in a brief strained sentence, "What's the matter with it?"

"Thagedæna gangrenosa," said the surgeon, replacing the bandages. Dr. Wright got as much satisfaction out of the incomprehensible term as Napoleon from some military subtlety. Then he added, "I think I'll go speak to Major Landry about this. You may come with me, Miss Mack."

Something in Dr. Wright's manner penetrated even the boy's suffering.

"What you going to do?" he asked apprehensively.

To this the young doctor made no reply whatever but walked out of the sick bay. As Miss McClanahan followed him she glanced back at her patient with her dark eyes wide and a look of anxiety on her face.

The professional pleasure in Dr. Wright's manner and the distress in Miss McClanahan's face told Augustus what they were going to do.

For a moment he lay perfectly still. His horror was so great that he did not feel the pain ringing up and down his arm like a struck bell. . . . That was what they were going to do! He knew that in a few minutes Dr. Wright and Dr. Landry and the orderlies and Miss McClanahan would be back for him, and then, no matter what he said, no matter how he begged . . .

Two cots from him lay Brewer. Augustus eased over, put his chilly legs out in the aisle. Then, with a flame licking out from his arm into his neck and side, he inched himself up to a sitting posture. The soiled white walls of the hospital seemed to sway. He got to his feet, and bending over, holding to the edge of the cots, he crept along the aisle toward Brewer. The intervening man drawled in amazement:

"For Gawd's sake, what are you doin'?"

At the second cot Augustus shook Brewer's shoulder.

"Brewer! Brewer!" he quavered.

The trooper awoke with a start.

"Is that you, Vaiden?"

"Brewer, they're going to cut my arm off!" said the boy in a ghastly whisper.

Brewer lay staring at Augustus out of slate-colored eyes.

"By God, they'll haff to hold their noses when they do it."

"But I won't have it! God damn it! I don't want my arm off!"

"I'm glad you told me that," said Brewer, "I thought you did."

"Damn it, Brewer," gasped Augustus, about to faint, "I

want a knife—a pistol—something. I tell you they're goin' to cut my arm off!"

Brewer lay blinking at his comrade as if trying to think what the word "pistol" meant. Finally he said:

"My clo'es are under the cot," and turned his back on Augustus and seemed instantly to go to sleep.

Augustus got down, fumbled through the clothes with his good hand, then crawled on his all-fours back to his cot.

The feel of the cold butt of the revolver under his blanket almost eased the beating in the patient's arm. He lay watching the door and panting as if after some enormous exertion. Presently he saw the two doctors, two orderlies, and Miss McClanahan coming up his aisle.

Augustus wriggled his head further up on the pillow to talk.

"Listen," he said to the five with a quavering certainty in his voice, "you're not going to cut my arm off."

All of them came to an involuntary pause except Dr. Wright. Major Landry, the head surgeon, began in a conciliatory tone:

"We may not need to take your arm off, Son."

Dr. Wright was coming up to the cot when the boy lifted the blue cavalry pistol.

"Take another step, Doc, an' I'll shoot you!"

Miss McClanahan cried, "Augustus!"

Even the immutable lieutenant paused.

"Where did you get that revolver?" he asked in a peremptory tone.

The major repeated, "It isn't a certainty we'll want to take your arm off, Augustus."

"Yes it is," chattered Augustus, "and you can't do it. . . . I won't be one armed! I won't go around one armed!"

"If we decide to, it will be purely for your good, Son," argued the major.

"Rather be dead than one armed!" cried Augustus.

"Look here, Vaiden," condescended Wright, "there is

necrotic tissue in your wound. It will create a toxic condition."

"He means you've got proud flesh and it'll poison you unless we take that out," explained the major.

"I don't want my arm cut off—I don't want——"

"All right!" cried the major at last. "We won't cut it off. Let us take you to the operating room."

"You won't cut it off?"

"No, we won't cut it off—put down your pistol."

The only person in whom Augustus had the least confidence was the nurse.

"Miss Rose," he quavered through fear-dry lips, "if I put down my gun you won't let 'em, will you?"

"They won't cut off your arm unless you consent, Augustus."

He dropped the great weight of the pistol and reached for her. The orderlies and the doctors concentrated quickly around him.

In the operating room Augustus was at times conscious of nothing except the stream of agony from his fly-bitten arm. Between spasms he dimly realized he was clutching Miss McClanahan's waist, her hips, her arms as he writhed and dripped with sweat. . . .

The Confederate hospital at Lauderdale Springs had no anesthetics.

CHAPTER TWENTY-SEVEN

CONVALESCENCE flooded Augustus with its voluptuous weakness, of which, naturally, he was ashamed. Miss McClanahan was with him very often even during her rest periods.

When he could walk they did go out into what she called the garden; but there was not a vegetable in it, just flowers and bushes and seats.

Miss McClanahan no longer seemed smiling at him within herself but appeared thinking, pondering. He would surprise her gazing fixedly at him with her dark eyes, and if he asked her of what she was thinking, she would say:

"Of nothing at all. . . . You'll be discharged before long, Augustus."

To Augustus the phrase "before long" sounded millenniums distant. Life had ceased to be anything but a loitering among flower beds with Miss McClanahan. His discharge held the insubstantiality of the fancy of winter in the summer time.

The convalescent neither thought of nor wished anything more than to sit in a chair near Miss McClanahan. She would put off her nurse's cap and her dark hair would glint in the sunshine. That was quite enough for him in his lassitude.

Once she asked, "Why do you look at me all the time, Augustus?"

"Mainly to see you," he said, making his adolescent jest.

"Can't you remember how I look?" she asked with a faint smile.

"Even when I'm looking right at you," said Augustus, dropping his rustic smartness, "somehow you sort of surprise me like I'd never seen you before. Your eyes surprise me. Your hair is done up in shining black ropes."

"What are you going to do when you get out of the hospital?"

"Go back to the army, I suppose."

"You can't, you aren't strong enough."

"Shoo! I can fight," bragged Augustus dreamily.

The mere weak look of Augustus somehow hurt something in Miss McClanahan's chest.

"If they don't take you in the army what will you do?" she inquired.

"I—don't know."

"Go back to your home?"

"No-o," he decided slowly, "I wouldn't go home."

The woman studied him.

"What is your home like, Augustus?" she asked in a softened voice.

Augustus inhaled a long breath.

"We-ell . . . there's nobody to talk to at home."

"Why, haven't you any brothers and sisters?"

"Oh, yes, lots of 'em. But take Cassandra. She tells you what to do. And Marcia, if she's not trying to get something out of you she's not thinking about you at all. And Miltiades, he's always studying about getting rich and what a grand man he is."

"Is he very grand?" smiled Miss McClanahan.

"I . . . guess he is," Augustus admitted rather unwillingly.

"And who else?"

"Polycarp. Me and him started for the army and he walked two miles out of the way to see his girl."

Miss McClanahan sat under some roses. She broke one off.

"I think I like Polycarp next to you, Augustus."

"Polycarp gets nearly everything. He's Mammy's pet."

His life at home seemed something quite gone; a kind of cramped existence which he would never take up again.

He had never in his life held so long a conversation with anyone as this tête-à-tête he was having with Miss Mc-Clanahan. He had never before found anything to talk about because up to this moment nobody had ever been willing to talk about him.

On the third day after tea in the garden the blow descended upon Augustus quite suddenly. The orderly came up the aisle with fresh linen in his arms and told him quite casually that they wanted to see him in the office. And that he might take his things. When Augustus lay in bed his things consisted of his hat and shoes, when he sat up his things was his hat. When he walked outside he had no things.

Now he sat up, put on his shoes, took his hat in his hand, and went down the aisle toward the office.

As he moved away the orderly began stripping the cot, throwing the used sheets and pillow slips on the floor. And Augustus knew that he was leaving the hospital.

He felt a little queer, really walking down the aisle, not to come back anymore. Through the windows he saw a number of ambulances had arrived. The orderlies were hurrying to make room for new casualties.

In the office a group of men were being discharged from the hospital. A clerk was busy asking questions and filling out papers. He asked their name, company, and regiment.

Augustus waited on a bench in a queue of men. The men on the bench were talking about where the new arrivals had come from. They were some of Pat Cleburn's men. General Pat lost men but he gained victories—he ought to have been in control of the defenses of Vicksburg and Corinth.

Augustus asked if the speaker were not an Arkansas man. He was.

At this point Augustus heard his name called. He got up

and walked slowly to the desk. He answered the questions
saying:

"Augustus Vaiden, Company K, Seventh Tennessee
Cavalry, a private."

The clerk handed Augustus a paper.

"You enlisted in Savannah, Tennessee," said the clerk.
"If you can find any supply wagons going in that direction
you can catch a ride."

"Oh, I'm to go back to Savannah," said Augustus.

"Not unless you want to," said the clerk.

"Well, I don't want to."

"That's with you," said the clerk, and he called another
name.

Augustus turned away from the desk with a queer lost
feeling. He didn't belong to the hospital any more. He didn't
even belong to the army any more. He was in Okalona,
Mississippi, about which he knew nothing at all. He moved
toward the reception-room door and out into the sunshine,
paused there, looking about aimlessly on weak legs.

If he had felt strong it wouldn't have been so bad, but
he wanted to sit down at that very moment. He thought of
going and sitting in one of the empty ambulance wagons.
But he really had to start in some direction.

In order not to be without any guidance at all he spat
several times in the palm of his hand, then thumped it with
his forefinger and watched the direction it splashed. Earlier
in life he had found strayed cows by this method of divina-
tion and it might work in pointing out the best general direction in starting one's life. It splashed more or less in the
direction he had meant it to. He started walking weakly in
this direction.

He had gone perhaps fifty yards when he heard steps
running behind him and a voice in distress:

"Augustus! Augustus!"

The boy stopped, turned about slowly, and was amazed to
see Miss McClanahan. He stood looking at her curiously.

"You—you're discharged?" she panted.

"Y-yes," nodded Augustus.

"Well—come on into the garden. Let's talk it over. You can't just walk off like that—without any plans at all."

"Well, I . . ." He started to tell her about thumping spittle in his hand to get a point of departure, but let it go.

She took his arm and they walked around through a side gate into the garden. As he entered the enclosure the colored light of flowers poured upon him, and a seat under the rose arbor invited them, and Augustus had the relaxed feeling of reaching home after a desolate journey.

The two sat down together.

"There's a lot of new casualties come in," explained Miss McClanahan in a distressed voice. "They had to make room for them."

"I understood that," said Augustus.

Her fingers still on his wrist were cold.

"Were you going to leave without—without saying good-bye?" She glanced at him with a kind of sad smile.

"I didn't know what to do," said Augustus with a queer dizzy feeling.

"When I went into your ward and saw your cot made up," said Miss McClanahan in her shaken tone, "I—I didn't know what to do either. I didn't even know how long you had gone or where." Her voice still held overtones of her shock.

"Well, if you'd come out a little later I'd been gone," said Augustus, "and I sure don't know where."

She squeezed his hand tightly.

"Just suppose I had!"

Augustus had a feeling not that he had barely escaped tragedy but that he had barely escaped vacuity. It was just a chance that the warmth and reality of Miss McClanahan had held him back, momentarily, from wandering into nothingness. Of course, in ten or fifteen minutes, or half an hour, he would get up and go away.

"Now—now we've got to make some plans—where you'll go?" said the nurse.

"Well I—I sort of had a plan," said Augustus vaguely.

"Oh, you did," she said in a somewhat dampened tone.

"Yes. I—uh—you know—popped some spit in my hand and it went over in that direction." Augustus looked about, got his orientation in the garden, and pointed. When he looked around at her again, Miss McClanahan was crying. She said: "Oh!" and took her hands from his and placed them determinedly in her own lap.

"Listen," said the woman. "I—I don't know whether to or not—but when you clung to me so, Augustus—you know —when the doctors cleaned your wound—you remember——"

"Y-yes, I remember," said the boy, with her excitement somehow entering his body.

"Well, ever since then . . ." She hesitated, then went on unsteadily, "I don't know . . . when I saw your cot made up, Augustus, I thought I would faint—it was like my heart had suddenly—been torn out."

"The cot—my cot?"

"Yes, your cot." Miss McClanahan was weeping. "If—if you hadn't held to me like you did, I could have stood it; but now . . . you weak and helpless . . . spitting in your hand to see which way to go . . ."

Miss McClanahan sobbed outright. She reached her arms for Augustus, guarding his wounded arm, and the boy found himself amazingly kissing the lips as he had imagined incessantly in his night-long vigils.

"We can either marry, or you can just stay at my father's home as long as you want to. I want you to be happy, Augustus."

Augustus came out of the bewilderment of her softness and perfume to plan on an inspiration:

"I tell you . . . Brewer was discharged, too. Let's find him and have him stand up with us for best man."

CHAPTER TWENTY-EIGHT

Fʀᴏᴍ ᴀʟʟ ᴛʜᴇ countryside around BeShears Crossroads
the men were gone. Only the women were left, the negro
slaves, an occasional boy, and a few oracular graybeards
making phophecies that grew more and more uncertain as to
the probable duration of the war.

The war itself was a kind of swelling rumor that seemed to
be moving closer and closer. The men who had gone to it,
on the contrary, seemed to be moving farther and farther
away.

Those distant soldiers acquired something of a legendary
character. Youths from the Crossroads neighborhood whom
Marcia Vaiden had known and overlooked in their ordinary
state were now soldiers, and took on the dignity and importance of the cause for which they fought.

Lieutenant A. Gray naturally shared this romantic enhancement in Marcia Vaiden's thoughts. He had, in fact,
ridden away with a tacit understanding of marriage with
Marcia on his return. Marcia had been washed into her second engagement to A. Gray on the surf of the war. The
impact of hostilities had brushed away those nameless per-
ceptions which had separated Marcia from the young officer.
On the day A. Gray actually marched away Marcia would
have married him point blank out of an overflowing heart.
His uniform fitted beautifully.

Another to whom his general enhancement would have
spread was Major Crowninshield, except for a puritanical

strain in the girl's thoughts which would not permit even an unacknowledged glamour toward a married man whom once she had loved.

Marcia's knight paladin was, of course, Miltiades. He fitted perfectly with the heroes of the fiction she read. He had flung away his position to serve his country, he had been betrayed by a supposed friend, deceived by his sweetheart. It never occurred to Marcia that the betraying sweetheart and false friend might have had their own inward compulsions.

Naturally, Polycarp and Augustus and such emotional small fry obtained no such hero worship from their sister. The manner in which they had gone to war precluded that. Nor did the boys have their hearts broken, which was a prerequisite for Marcia's heroes. Of course there was Polycarp's escapade with Ponny BeShears, but that was merely absurd.

Augustus touched the nadir of the romantic. Extraordinary rumors were afloat about Augustus. Tales were in circulation that Augustus had gone up into Tennessee and enlisted in the Yankee army, that he had been in a skirmish against a small Confederate force. Marcia got the first inkling of this news from Eliza Ham under the usual irrational promise of secrecy such as obtains among girls. Marcie denied the charge bitterly for Augustus. When she went home from the Ham plantation she asked Gracie about it. She knew that the negroes would have more details about any rumor in the neighborhood than would any white person. These details might be a bit distorted, but there would be more of them.

Gracie looked at Marcia with a doubtful face.

"You really want me to tell you, little missy?"

"Of course I do!" cried Marcia, wondering what in the world Gracie had to tell.

"Well . . . they say he—he went up into Tennessee and . . . joined up with a band of Yankee horse thieves."

Marcia stood staring at Gracie with the strength gone out
of her.

"Why, that isn't so," she said out of white lips.

"No'm, no'm," echoed Gracie earnestly, "that sho' ain't
so, little missy. I told them it wasn't so. You asked me what
they said."

But back of her denials Marcia believed the rumors about
Augustus. He had always been so hare brained . . . she
had never known what Augustus thought about anything
except when he was angry. Now, for him to run away from
home and become a Yankee horse thief . . .

She said, "That's all, Gracie . . . that's the meanest tale
. . ." She caught her breath and held it like a lump compressed against the base of her throat to keep from crying.

Gracie turned and went up to her eternal spinning in the
attic.

Marcia went to the door of the living room on legs that
felt weak. Miss Cassandra looked up at her and then got to
her feet.

"What's the matter, Marcia?" she asked anxiously.

"Sister Cassandra, I went to see Eliza Ham. She asked
about Augustus. The way she asked I knew she had heard
something about him. And then she said . . ."

"What?" cried the older sister, staring at the girl's white
face.

"Augustus is fighting on the Yankee side!"

Cassandra stared ten seconds longer and then broke into a
contemptuous laugh.

"And you believed it?"

"Why, no, I didn't," said Marcia blankly. "I told 'em I
didn't believe it."

"Yes, you told 'em that, but you did believe it—that a
Vaiden would fight against his country. *Tchk!* You're such
a fool, Marcia!"

"Gracie knew about it, too," said Marcia, now beginning

to uphold the idea of Augustus' treason since he had a defender.

"Oh, Gracie . . . Hadn't you noticed something about Gracie?"

"Why, no," said Marcia. "What is there to notice?"

"I think she is about to become a mother," said Miss Cassandra disapprovingly.

"Well, what of that? She's married."

"Oh, I'm not talking about the baby. I mean she's nervous and flighty. What she says doesn't amount to anything. I'll venture you first asked her about Augustus?"

"Yes, I did."

"And I'm sure she told you something different from what Eliza Ham told."

"That's right."

"There you are. Never pay any attention to nigger gossip; it's merely a corruption of white gossip, and the white is bad enough, goodness knows."

Although white gossip was discountenanced and nigger gossip was set aside unconditionally by Miss Cassandra, still the tale lingered in the minds of the Vaiden family. When old man Jimmie Vaiden got wind of it he declared he would give that stinking yellow nigger gal a beating and make her take it back. But Marcia stopped this by declaring that she had to drag the story out of Gracie, and Cassandra pointed out sardonically that if one beat his niggers for tale bearing none would be left alive.

The old war horse had to content himself with wagging his head and grumbling out, "Anyway, she needs a good beating. You-all are ruinin' Gracie, the way you treat her."

Augustus got on old Mrs. Laura's mind, and one morning the old lady told Marcia in the kitchen that the tales about Augustus were going to be cleared up that day.

"How will they be?" asked the girl curiously.

"We're going to get a letter from Augustus," stated the

old woman with the utmost simplicity, "and I imagine it will clear up the tales they're telling."

"Mammy, how do you know we'll get a letter?" inquired the daughter curiously.

"I'm just sure there's a letter in the office from Augustus."

"But that's what I'm trying to get at—how do you feel?"

"Why, you don't *feel* at all. I just know there's one there and that's all there is to it."

The two had been lifting their voices somewhat during this conversation, and now from the living room old man Jimmie thundered:

"Marsh, don't pay no attention to your mammy's superstition! I declare, when I married her I might jest as well have married a cotton-fiel' hand . . . presentiment about a letter! There ain't no such thing as a presentiment, and if there was it wouldn't be about a letter!"

The two women in the kitchen fell into complete silence. Marcia pointed to her chest to ask if her mother knew it emotionally. The old woman pointed to her head to show that it was a purely mental operation.

And this was one of the reasons old man Jimmie became so furious over these matters. No matter how much or how well he reasoned, these irrational beliefs simply sunk below the surface and flowed smoothly on. The old man got up from his chair in the living room and went out to the lot because he could feel the two women looking at each other and motioning about the letter, when any idiot would know there was no way of obtaining information on any point whatsoever, except by a matter-of-fact seeing and hearing and touching.

Some time later that day, when the two women had supposed old man Jimmie had forgotten his irritation, Mrs. Laura suggested that her husband ride down to the Crossroads and buy a spool of No. 60 white, "and," she added casually, "you might ask if we've got any mail."

"Are you in any grand rush about the thread, Lorry?" inquired the old man craftily.

Well, in no particular hurry . . . she was out of 60.

The old man narrowed his eyes and nodded sardonically to himself.

"Send me riding two and a half miles because she's got a feeling she's got a letter at the Crossroads. She ain't a-goin' to do it! I'll be dad blamed if I'll go traipsing around over the country follerin' a cotton-field superstition!"

So he told her he would get the thread the next time he went to the store.

Nevertheless a restlessness began to invade old man Jimmie's bones. At odd moments he would find himself thinking intently what it was that he had to get at BeShears' store, and after a minute or two he would remember it was a spool of 60 white.

So a few minutes before twelve o'clock, just at a time when he knew they did not want him to go, he stalked out to the gate, heaved himself on old Joe, and set off for the Crossroads.

Old man Jimmie Vaiden liked to ride alone. He enjoyed old Joe's sleepy singlefooting, the blue horizon, the red hills, and the yellow sedge.

He abhorred company on such rides until company caught up with him and began gossiping. Then he would not have had the fellow ride on and leave him for anything.

This time it was Sheriff Bill Dalrymple. The sheriff was a leathery man who wore a holster and bore a sort of provisional good will to the world at large which could be revoked without notice for good cause.

Now he rode up beside old man Jimmie and stated with some passion that he be God damned if he believed the Southern Confederacy should be held responsible for a passel of Yankee hoss thieves.

"Why, what's the trouble?" inquired old man Jimmie

with the sharp pleasure of a countryman in the villainies of
the neighborhood.

"Well, a gang of damned Union guerillas stole old man
Candy McPherson's hoss last night and run off up into Tennessee. Now in dealin' with this there's a number of things
to be tuk into consideration."

"Which one of his horses?"

"That ol' stump-suckin' claybank."

"Whyn't they take his saddlin' filly?"

"He was off fox huntin' on her. But Candy says it's a
matter of principle with him. He swears he's jest as mad as
if they'd got a hoss that was some 'count."

"Well, Candy's swearin' a lie," stated old man Jimmie
flatly. "He's human even if he is a Campbellite."

Old man Jimmie hated the Campbellites bitterly because
they believed so nearly the same thing he did there was no
chance of downing one of them in an argument.

"He's honest in it," opined the sheriff generously, "but if
they ralely had tuk his saddlin' filly he'd be surprised how
much deeper down in hell he'd wish they'd sink."

"I agree with you there," conceded old man Jimmie. "It
may be a error of the head and not of the heart. Candy's
heart ain't much, but his Maker knows it's a lot better'n his
head. . . . What time o' day did his claybank git stole?"

"Don't know exactly. Some time before Candy got back
from his fox chase."

"He didn't see nobody?"

"No."

"What makes him think it was Union men? They don't
usually work at night."

"Well I . . ." The sheriff paused, looked intently at his
companion for a moment. "Do you know it wasn't any Union
men?" he asked oddly.

"Why, no," said the ex-blacksmith blankly, "why should
I?"

"I was just askin'," replied the officer vaguely. "It's my duty to make inquiries."

This slight quirk upset the rambling conversation that usually enlivened the ride along the road. Old man Jimmie felt constrained to shake his head once or twice and repeat that he didn't know a thing in the world about it. Thus they came to the Crossroads where Sheriff Dalrymple left him.

Old man Jimmie Vaiden dismounted and climbed the high platform in front of the store with a good deal of effort. The sun was hot and he mopped his face as he stepped into the dark multi-scented house.

"Alex," he called loudly, seeing nothing in the gloom beyond the dim outline of barrels and coffee sacks, "wrap me up a spool of No. 60."

As the noise created by the old man subsided, he heard someone say in a low tone, "There's old man Jimmie now," and nothing more was said.

Mr. Alex BeShears bestirred himself somewhere in the depths of his cavern.

"White or black, Mr. Vaiden?"

"I be dad blamed," boomed the old man in frustration, "I don't any more know whether my ol' woman wants white or black." He stood considering what he should do. "What's it wuth, Alex?"

"Five cents cash, ten cents credit."

"Well, by the gray goats I'm goin' to take one o' both, Alex. After all's said and done, a man ain't got but one wife and he might as well treat her right. She can use the one she wants and lay the other'n by."

"Oh—er—Mr. Vaiden, would you step back here a moment?" invited the storekeeper. The old man walked back into complete darkness in silence.

Talk started up at the front end once more. Some of the customers with finer feelings were faintly shushed by others who wanted to hear what the merchant said to the old man. However, the talker went on:

"The Montgomery *Advertiser* says that Grant has lost three thousand five hun'erd and eighty-nine men at Fort Donelson. Our boys simply butchered 'em."

"Yeh, but they fin'ly tuk the fort."

"Yeh, but Gosh, man, he's bleedin' the Nawth white."

"The papers said it was a Pyrrhic victory," put in another voice.

"What's a Pyrrhic victory?"

"That's one where you get the hot end of the poker after all."

In the back end of the store Mr. BeShears was inquiring whether Mr. Vaiden wanted the thread cash or credit. Disregarding the difference in price, old man Jimmie chose credit.

The storekeeper then explained with morose courtesy that times were uncertain and he had adopted a cash-payment plan.

Old man Jimmie was instantly angry.

"You mean my credit ain't good for two spools of cotton thread!"

"Thread nothin'!" snapped BeShears in irritation. "I'm tellin' you this for future tradin'. Undoubtedly you got a dime in yore pocket!"

"Well, by the gray goats, I wouldn't spend a dime with a derned ol' skinflint who'd sell off his house niggers when his country was goin' to war about that very thing."

"I can buy 'em back to-day for a third what I sold 'em for," snapped BeShears with an edge to his drawl.

"Yes, and you may buy 'em back to-morr' for half what you can to-day!" roared old man Jimmie. "But by the gray goats I say you're robbin' me and ever' other patriotic slave holder in Alabama when you done it."

" 'Y God," flared the merchant, "I'd a lot ruther sell my niggers than to go over to the Yankee lock, stock, an' bar'l!"

"What! What!" shouted the old man, beside himself at

this thrust. "What in the thunderation do you mean, Alex BeShears . . . goin' over to the Yankees?"

"I mean your dad-blamed sprat of a boy, Gus," snarled BeShears, "that's who I mean. He's stealin' with the——"

Old man Vaiden made a flail-like blow in the direction of the voice. He struck nothing. BeShears wheezed out:

"By God, you damned Vaidens——"

The loungers leaped from counters and barrels.

"Alex!" "Mr. Vaiden!" "Don't hit him with that cleaver, Alex!"

"Let him come! Let the damned traitor come!" roared old man Jimmie. "I'll pestle his pants tull his tongue lolls out!"

But the loungers did not permit such a one-sided fight. They got between the two and began their soothing:

"Now, Mr. Vaiden, after all this is Alex's store. What he done may not be patriotic but it was legal."

"Thunderation! A man can be the worst neighbor in the world and still be legal—the legaler a man gets, the worse he is!"

"Yes, but I wouldn't give him Hail Columbia in his own store."

"Are you boys Christians?" demanded the ex-blacksmith angrily.

"We hope we are," said one of the men who was easing the old fire eater out onto the platform.

"Well, don't you know the Bible says to reprove, admonish, and take counsel with your neighbor?"

"Was that what you was tryin' to do?"

"Hell far, of course it was . . . an' you boys draggin' me out!"

However, before he went out of the door he turned and ordered within his unquestioned rights:

"Alex BeShears, my wife Lorry's got a letter in your stinkin' Yankee post office, and by the gray goats you've got to hand her out!"

The storekeeper went to a little square of nine pigeon-holes and handed out the letter.

Old man Jimmie received it with satisfaction. He looked at the postmark and suddenly exclaimed:

"Look where this come from—Corinth, Mississippi. My ol' woman said it was from Augustus! Well, if it's from Augustus, how in the tarnation could he be in this country and writin' letters from Mississip'?"

CHAPTER TWENTY-NINE

W HEN OLD MAN JIMMIE returned from the post office, he found even some of the negroes on the place waiting around the entrance of the big hall to see what Augustus said in his letter.

When ol' Pap came riding up with the letter old Mrs. Laura made no comment on the fact that her presentiment had come true. In fact she never thought of it as a moral victory over her husband. These victories over the old ex-blacksmith's unbending logic occurred with such regularity that they had ceased to attract any attention at all.

The letter itself was addressed in a lamentable handwriting. It's ink was washed out and brownish colored of a sort that cannot be purchased in any store, but of which every well-regulated Southern family possesses about a fourth of a bottle.

The letter was handed to Marcia to read because Miss Cassandra read a personal letter in such a detached fashion it did not seem to be from anybody or to anybody in particular.

Old Mrs. Vaiden, to whom it was addressed, did not read it because in her youth her father had not considered that the art of reading pertained to girls.

"It's from Augustus, sure enough," said Marcia.

"Den he's boun' to be alive," opined Aunt Creasy.

Marcia tore open the letter with the greatest curiosity, ran her eyes down the page, then paused, her mouth dropped open. she looked at the family in utter blankness.

243

"What's the matter?" "What is it?" cried a chorus.

"Why . . . he's married!" gasped Marcia.

"Not married . . . at his age!" cried Miss Cassandra, because, according to Miss Cassandra, no Vaiden ever became old enough to marry, much less Augustus.

"Pappy!" ejaculated Mrs. Laura in dismay. "Imagine . . . our baby, married!"

The old woman's eyes filled with mist at the untimely complication and responsibility that had befallen her baby boy.

"Well," said old man Jimmie philosophically, "it don't make no diff'runce whether a man marries early or late, he always feels like he's been married forever anyway."

"Read the rest of the letter, Marcia," advised Cassandra. Marcia did so. It ran:

"DEAR MOTHER, I joined the army at Savannah. I came to Mississippi. I got wounded but not bad in the Battle of Okalona. I went to a hospital at Lauderdale Springs. I married Miss Rose McClanahan who nursed me. We have moved to Corinth. Your very respectful son, AUGUSTUS VAIDEN."

"A nurse!" snapped Miss Cassandra. "I wonder what sort of family she came from?"

"He doesn't say," said Marcia, looking at the simple letter again.

"She must be a fine patriotic girl," hazarded old Mrs. Vaiden, "to be nursing the wounded soldiers."

"I'll venture," said Miss Cassandra, "she couldn't get married around her home and she went to a Confederate hospital to catch a man while he was weak."

Old man Jimmie stood by with a worried look on his face.

"Which army do you reckon she followed him to?"

Everybody was amazed at this question.

"Why, the Confederate army, of course!"

"He don't say so," observed the old planter gloomily.

"Why, Jeems, it's bound to be the Confederate army. Don't he say he was in the Battle of Okalona?"

"Don't be a fool, Lorry! D'reckon the Confederates got out an' fought that battle all by theirselves? Bound to 'a' been some Yankees thar!"

"Well . . . I s'pose they was," agreed the old woman at this wider view.

"What are you asking for?" inquired Miss Cassandra with a touch of uneasiness.

"Why, by the gray goats," flung out the old man roundly, "I come purty near havin' a fight with Alex BeShears down at the Crossroads while ago. He said Augustus had joined the Yankees."

"How in the world did that rumor ever get out on Augustus?" cried Marcia. "It's so ridiculous—nobody would believe it for a minute."

"Why couldn't he say in his letter which side he was a-fighting on!" boomed old man Jimmie, quite out of patience with Augustus.

"Now, Pappy," put in old Mrs. Laura, "ain't you glad you didn't whip Gracie for telling a lie when she didn't tell one?"

This was news to Gracie, that she had ever been in danger of a flogging, and she looked at her master and mistress with widening eyes.

"She may not 'a' lied," brushed away old man Jimmie, "but you kain't give a nigger a lick they don't deserve."

Gracie stood silent at this. Marcia cast her a glance of passing sympathy. In her heart Marcia excluded Gracie from her father's blanket condemnation, but all other negroes, the girl felt, could be disciplined at any time with good effect.

This diversion about the advisability of whipping negroes removed Augustus' marriage a little out of their minds. Old Mrs. Vaiden said:

"I didn't know they were fighting down in Mississippi?"

"Yes, in Mississippi and Arkansas, too."

"Goodness gracious!" exclaimed the mother. "That sounds like the fighting is coming South. I had an idyah the battles would be more and more toward the North."

"De Battle o' Molasses was two'd de Nawth," mumbled old Aunt Creasy.

"Manassas, Creasy," corrected Miss Cassandra. "You always call it the Battle of Molasses."

"Dat niggah Lump Mowbray come ovah heah an' sta't me off wrong," complained the gargoyle.

"What diff'runce does it make what she calls it?" said the old planter. "Let her call it Sorg'um if she wants to. . . . By the way, Lorry, I didn't get the spool of 60 you ordered. Why in the thunderation didn't you tell me whether you wanted it white or black? . . . but anyway I wouldn't have bought it from Alex BeShears. I'm through with him after his insults about Augustus."

The old wife was disturbed.

"Where you going to trade?"

"Florence, of course."

"Ride sixteen miles after a spool of thread?"

"When I first built this house here there wasn't any Crossroads!" snapped the old man. "We got along then just as good as we do now. No, if Alex BeShears thinks I'm beholden to him, he's wrong. I'm through with him."

"Jeems, you're always bitin' off your nose to spite your face," disparaged the old wife mildly.

"No man can talk about a son of mine like he did an' hol' my trade. He's lost it. I'm through with him!"

If old man Jimmie was really through with the Crossroads storekeeper, the planter received lively and immediate proof that the storekeeper was just starting in with him.

About two days after the near fight in the store, Sheriff Bill Dalrymple came riding up the rutty public road and stopped at the Vaiden gate.

Old man Jimmie came out of his open hallway, calling in a

loud voice for Dalrymple to alight and rest his saddle. The sheriff alighted but did not rest his saddle. He stood with his hand lying loosely on it. Neither was his reply delivered in the same hearty tone of the planter. He asked if he could see the old man a minute.

"Why, shore," cried the ex-blacksmith, a little at sea. "Come right on in."

No, the sheriff wouldn't do that. He had just a minute to stay. He was riding up the road. Candy McPherson had located his claybank up near the state line and he was going up to reclaim him as stolen property.

So old man Jimmie walked out, rather wondering at the sheriff's haste.

"Well, what did you want to see me about, Bill?" he asked.

Dalrymple reached in his saddle pockets and drew out a great bundle of yellow paper with red and blue lines on it. The sheets were covered on both sides with an endless string of items whose price bore a monotonous repetition in the figure column of ten cents, fifteen cents, five cents, twenty cents . . . page after page. At the end of each column the total was added up and carried over to the next page.

It was an itemized account of the purchases of the Vaiden family for a period of more than a quarter of a century. Not once during all that time had the Vaiden account at the Crossroads store been balanced, although at intervals it had approached a balance.

The mere meagerness of the list of a lifetime's purchases was as pathetic in its way as the bare yard and heavy log house where that lifetime had been spent.

"We-ell," said the old man in an odd voice that somehow suddenly had lost its boom and violence, "what—what about this, Bill?"

"It's Alex BeShears' account," explained the officer in a dry, impersonal tone.

"How much does it come to?" asked the old man.

"Well, three hundred an' forty-six dollars an' thirty-five

cents. He put it in my han's an' gimme instructions to c'lect."

Old man Jimmie also put a hand on the sheriff's saddle because his legs felt suddenly weak.

"That's what comes o' truckin' with a low-down snake," he said in a shaking tone; "pretend to be yore friend fer twenty-seven year, then when you begin to trust him a inch, turns an' bites you in the back like a snake in the grass."

The officer said nothing but behind his somber silence old man Jimmie felt sympathy and a tacit agreement that the presentation of this account was a shameful and iniquitous breach of trust.

"Well," said Dalrymple at last, "what are you goin' to do about it, Mr. Vaiden?"

"Bill," said the old man, taking a long breath, "I—I hope you'll—er—give me a little time on this account. I—I can't lay my hand on the whole amount right this minute."

"BeShears' instructions was to c'lect," repeated the sheriff.

"I'm good for ten times that amount," said the old man.

"I know you air, Mr. Vaiden," said the officer grayly, "an' so does Alex BeShears. I'd jest as soon have this account on you as the Bank of England. It's nothin' in the worl' but spite work on the part of Alex BeShears—haulin' you up an' wantin' his account paid off all of a sudden like this—nothin' in the worl' but spite work; but it's legal."

Old man Jimmie stood batting his eyes at the formidable bundle.

"Well," he said finally, "leave it here with me. To-morr' I'll go over it with Lorry an' see if that stinkin' skunk has put anything in here that we didn't git."

CHAPTER THIRTY

Going over the twenty-seven years of accounts was not a gainful task. The storekeeper, from the very first sale, had set down opposite each entry the name of the person who made the purchase. It would be one package of pins *per* Cassandra; half pound of soda *per* Lycurgus; buckles for shoes *per* Miltiades; one barlow knife, *per* Sylvester.

As the auditing proceeded, all of Mrs. Laura's first set of six children came crowding around her again, holding to her skirts, begging her for this and that, desiring once more their outlived and long-forgotten needs and petty extravagances through the pages of an old account.

Most of the things neither the old man nor the old woman could remember at all, but some they could. The barlow knife Sylvester had wanted to skin rabbits—that had cost twenty-five cents. Hair ribbons for her little girl Vivian, who had died of the measles. She would have been older than Miltiades and next to Cassandra, but she had remained in their hearts with clear blue eyes and flaxen hair, unchanged by the saddening changes of time.

So, instead of something to deny, the old account became something the two old persons sat long over trying to remember. It spread before them not a merchant's account but the strange insensible mutations of life which move so slowly that all things seem permanent, unchangeable, and of immense importance, until some day its shifting, casual, and unplanned flow is suddenly and disturbingly reduced to human comprehension in a history or a package of old letters or a storekeeper's account.

The upshot of all their inspection was that, while there was much neither old man Jimmie nor Mrs. Laura could remember, there was nothing they could deny, and most likely the whole long scroll was exact within a sixpence.

At the justice trial preliminary to obtaining a judgment and execution, the account was admitted as far as the Vaidens knew. So in due time Sheriff Dalrymple came around and tacked up two notices of sale copied out in the clear flowing handwriting of the county court clerk.

It gave notice to all men that at the door of the courthouse in Florence, Alabama, the following personal property belonging to James Vaiden, Esq., living and residing in the third civil district of Lauderdale County, would be cried for sale to the highest bidder, viz.:

Three negro men called Columbus, Robinet, and George; two negro women, one black called Creasy, one light yellow called Gracie; two mules, one blind in the left eye called Lou, a horse mule called Rab; one milk cow called Sook; also sundry plows, guns, fox hounds, chickens, a set of blacksmith tools, an anvil; corn, hay, two bedsteads. These articles to be auctioned off both separately and in the lump. All persons take notice.

Oddly enough, it was not the owners of this property who were most utterly dismayed at the impending sale, but one of the chattels themselves. The one described in the circular for the benefit of prospective buyers as one light-yellow negro woman called Gracie.

Gracie was a house servant. She had never worked in the fields. She did not even sleep in the negro quarters but in a walled-off middle attic over the open hallway of the big house. Her bedroom was quite dark all the twenty-four hours but in the daytime fine razor edges of sunshine sliced between the dark clapboards over her bed, and there was a door between her cell and Marcia's room. In the afternoon, when the sun was shining straight into Marcia's small high window, Gracie could see through her open door a sort of ghost of day. The fact that she had never worked, slept, or eaten outside the big house was not so much a point of pride with Gracie as it was a condition of her existence. With a negro's assimilative power she had absorbed the big house. She had a touch of Miss Cassandra; she exaggerated old Mrs. Vaiden's feeling of mysticism; she had molded herself almost into a reproduction of Marcia, whom she loved and admired with the fanatic admiration of a bond maid for the paler beauty of her white mistress.

In the past there had come moments in Gracie's life when she had envisioned the possibility of being sold out of the Vaiden family. But also she had thought of the day when she was going to die. The one was as terrible as the other.

Gracie could read. In fact she could read perfectly. It was impossible for any girl to grow up under Miss Cassandra and not learn to read.

The white bluestocking had carried on quite an elaborate self-deception in teaching Gracie to read. To begin with, it was against the laws of her country to teach a slave to read. But for the strictures of code and ermine no Vaiden, either man or woman, ever had the smallest regard.

As Southerners, the Vaidens believed in states' rights; as Alabamians, they believed in individual determinism on all legal and moral questions; as Primitive Baptists, they believed they were supernaturally foreordained from before the laying of the foundations of the earth to do as they damned pleased on all questions whatsoever—social, moral, legal, and religious.

Therefore one day Miss Cassandra had said to her mother, "I have decided to teach Gracie to read."

"It's against the law," said Mrs. Laura Vaiden, who was not so old then, nor was she born a Vaiden.

"I'm going to teach her to read because I think it will be convenient for her to know how," stated Miss Cassandra.

"The law certainly was not intended to put anyone to any inconvenience."

Mrs. Laura was not sure that laws could be repealed so casually, but she had no argument so she called in Cassandra's father, who could be relied upon to have arguments.

Jimmie Vaiden, he was not old man Jimmie then, went to Cassandra and stormed and thundered that, besides being against the law, there was no sense in teaching a nigger to read. "The law is jest good sense," he said. No woman white or black should be taught to read. That ought to be the law also. Look at Cassandra's own mother; she couldn't read, and what a paragon of a woman she was!

Then Miss Cassandra had said that perhaps some day all of the children would be gone from home and he, her father, would be too old to read; then, when that state of affairs came to pass, Gracie would be useful to read the letters the children would write home.

The father said if the children didn't write with any better sense than they talked, it wouldn't be any great loss if their letters never were read. With that he went back to his forge and set to work and Gracie's education was begun.

Gracie had such a tingling desire to be like her white mistresses that she sucked up instruction as a drowning person gasps at air. But even then, when she made mistakes, Miss Cassandra thumped her shining black curls with her thimble and asked her please to exhibit a little brains even if she was a nigger.

Later Miss Cassandra told her mother that, unless the seams in Gracie's skull hardened pretty quickly and rendered her stupid, after the fashion of all negroes when they gained maturity, Gracie was going to know a whole lot more than Marcia did.

Of course, back of Miss Cassandra's argument about the utility of Gracie's learning to read was merely the bluestocking's fidgety desire to see everyone read and become as nearly like herself as their limited capacity would permit.

Thus it came about, as the usufruct of her study and toil by a candle in her dark room, Gracie was enabled to read, posted on the big gate, "one of light-yellow color, called Gracie, to be sold at public outcry at the courthouse door in Florence, Alabama."

To the quadroon the little white notice stuck on the gate post was the most conspicuous thing in the whole harsh landscape. When she approached the big house it seemed she could see its white gleaming as far off as she could see the house itself.

At times it did not seem possible that the notice included her. She felt that it was possible, even natural, for Columbus and Robinet to be sold, but for her own soul and body to be turned over to some strange man . . . faint chill waves went over the girl's body.

Whether she spun or wove or brushed Marcia's hair, the fact stood before her that she was going to be sold just as Solomon was sold; that she would drop out of existence just as her husband Solomon had dropped out of existence. Some negro trader would load her in a hack and drive away with her to be resold somewhere—to pass from white hand to white hand.

The man who bought her might put her in the field and beat her, or be stingy and give her nothing to eat but fat bacon and corn dodgers such as thousands of her race lived on. Where she lived, what she ate, what she did, what man made use of her—in all of these things her own wishes not only would never be asked, they would never be thought of.

She, who could read the notice of her own sale as readily as the clerk who wrote it, was one with the mules, the cow, and the forge.

Truly, for once Miss Cassandra had been wrong, and the lawmakers of Alabama had been kind, kind men when they forbade the art of reading to slaves.

Marcia was as forlorn as Gracie, but she had hopes. Every night when her maid brushed her hair Marcia would remind

Gracie that ol' Pap was riding the country to borrow money
and pay himself out.

Indeed, every day the old man set forth on old Joe in the
morning and returned in the evening. Each evening he told
his family that he had heard of a man up on Big Cypress or
down in the Reserve with money to loan. He knew he would
get it the next day. These men with money were like will-o'-
the-wisps who floated farther and farther afield as old man
Jimmie advanced.

Old man Vaiden was not the type of man who could
successfully borrow three hundred dollars. None of the
Vaiden family was aware that the borrowing of money is as
much of an art as walking the tight wire and much more
difficult to learn. The very loudness of his voice spoiled his
credit. Money should be borrowed sotto voce . . . or in
complete silence.

One day old man Jimmie rode east to see a man in Waterloo, the next day south, past Florence, to see a farmer near
Tuscumbia. He even traveled as far northwest as Pulaski,
Tennessee. It took him four days. When he got back, George
had to help him from his saddle and to bed.

In the midst of this distress of the white and terror of the
black, Lump Mowbray, one night just before dawn, drifted
into old Aunt Creasy's cabin.

Creasy's cabin was a port of call for Lump. There was
a sort of kinship between the knotty little negro man and
the wizened old crone. The old negress herself, apparently,
never went to bed, and Lump seemed never to spend a night
in a house.

The two of them were tendrils in the vast complicated
grape-vine news service that covered the whole South.

"Where you come from, Lump?" mumbled Aunt Creasy,
preserving her touch of mystery by not looking around to
ascertain who had entered her room.

"Been pas' de McPherson place, crost de line. . . .
Whar's Gracie?"

"You speck Gracie be settin' up evah night. She too much lak hawgs an' white fo'ks . . . sleep all de time. . . . What you been up thah fuh?"

"I heahs a ahmy is comin'," replied Lump with the beginning of his sing song. "I heahs dey's a ahmy ma'chin' in de wrath o' de Lawd."

Aunt Creasy considered this information in the light of what she already knew.

"Whut dey doin'—stealin' hosses?"

"Oh, Lawd! Stealin' an' bu'nin' an' leavin' behin' 'em mo'nin' an' weepin'."

Aunt Creasy became gloomy.

"Is dat triflin' Leathuhwood gang busted loose an' doin' wuss'n evah?"

Lump was incensed at such belittling of his news.

"Leathuhwood nothin'! Dis ahmy don't stop wid no hoss aw cow. Fo'ks kin fight de Leathuhwood gang but dey sho' kain't fight dis ahmy. Feah an' trimlin' goes befo' an' smoke an' 'struction goes behin'. An' niggahs go fol'rin' aftah de ahmy o' de Lawd, 'cause salvation sho' is come!"

The old woman turned and looked at Lump through wrinkled slits of eyes.

"Niggahs fol'rin' aftah?" she probed.

"Some . . . some niggahs," qualified Lump, coming out of his dithyramb.

"An' dey don't tu'n 'em back to whah dey b'long?" queried Aunt Creasy incredulously.

"No, dey march on an' let de niggahs folluh. Guns an' bagnits go befo' an' wagins comes atwixt an' 'mo' guns an' bagnits come behin'. An' dey feet shake de yeth, an' dey bagnits shine acrost de hills . . . Oh, Lawd, yes!"

"An' niggahs fol'rin'?" repeated the old woman.

"Deh folluhs de ahmy o' de Lawd."

The old black woman sat for some minutes gazing into the dying eyes of the coals. Lump finally made a movement.

"Stahs gittin' dim an' I got five mo' miles to go."

"To-morr'," said Aunt Creasy, "is de day befo' we-all niggahs gwi be sol' out."

"To-morr' is de day befo'," repeated Lump mournfully.

"An' de ahmy's headin' dis way . . ."

"Wid guns an' wagins an' bagnits," added Lump.

"Lissen to me, Lump Mowbray," directed the black gargoyle with Delphic solemnity, "fin' out all you kin, an' to-morr' you da'ken de do' o' dis cabin wid de dusk o' night."

"Ah da'ken yo' cabin do' wid de dusk to-morr' night," agreed Lump with equal gravity.

He bestirred himself to go. At the door he probed discreetly:

"Is you thinkin' 'bout makin' some move yo'se'f?"

"Ah dunno whut Ah gwi do," said the old woman. "Ah thought Ah gwi lay my bones to res' in de black folks' en' o' de Vaiden grabeya'd. So come de Jedgment Day, Ah thought Ah rise up fus' an' he'p ol' missy out de groun'. Now Ah guess Ah be somewha' else. Ah guess my ol' bones be flaung in a ditch an' wash away lak dey do de niggahs down South. . . . Ah guess Ah won' be nowha'."

When Lump Mowbray was gone old Aunt Creasy continued in her chair, fumbling her greasy black clawlike fingers at her withered mouth. She thought of her master and mistress, of old Hannah, the mother of Gracie and George, and of Jericho, Hannah's husband.

All this she passed in review with the brooding solemnity of an African headsman deciding the fate of his tribe. She sat on with legs and buttocks numb from her long sitting.

Outside the sea-blue night paled to gray, then, in the east, unfolded the peach bloom of dawn.

In the cabin next to her own, Columbus and Robinet stirred. Sounds came from the big house. Hounds walked about stretching themselves in front of Aunt Creasy's door. From the plum thicket came the noise of a hen flying down from her roost and hitting the ground with a thump.

Aunt Creasy arose painfully, stood on her old legs for a

minute or two, and finally moved. She hobbled out of door
and moved slowly toward the big house. In the kitchen she
heard a rattling. The old woman waited in the bare yard
before the door. Presently Gracie came out with a milk pail.
The quadroon's single outside chore was attending to the
cow.

"Gracie," said the old woman in a significant tone, "Lump
Mowbray wuz heah las' night."

"Oh—Lump!" ejaculated Gracie, who despised the hard,
compact little negro with his bullet head and sooty skin.

The crone fell in beside Gracie.

"Lump is a pusson, same as you is," she said with a touch
of reproof in her mumble. "He gwi come back heah to-
night."

The girl looked at the wizened creature beside her.

"To see the last of us before we're sold and scattered?"

The old woman glanced about the empty yard and
changed her tone.

"Lump tellin' me las' night 'bout de ahmy o' de Lawd,
what's a-ma'chin' dis way rat now."

Gracie looked sharply at the old woman.

"The army of the Lord?"

"Bringin' salvation," intoned the old crone, "niggahs
a-fol'rin' 'um an' dey don't 'low nobody to sen' 'em home. De
padero flies befo' dey might. Dey bagnits shine ovah de hills
an' acrost de valleys, an' salvation comes a-ma'chin' on."

The world to which Gracie had arisen that morning was
gray with grief and fear. Now a sort of questioning horror
dawned upon her at the old woman's words.

"What are you saying that to me for, Aunt Creasy?" she
asked in a shocked tone.

" 'Caze, dat po' white BeShears ain't got no call to come
stribitin' dis fambly to de win's. Dat shurf man ain't got no
call to be nailin' pieces o' paper on ol' Pap's gate pos' 'cause
he owe a li'le sump'n at de sto'. Who would ol' Pap sell me
to? Who would ol' Pap sell me to? Who would he sell Gawge

an' Robinet an' C'lumbus an' you to? Nobody cep'n a call frum de angel ob death . . . you knows dat, Gracie."

The quadroon was beginning to understand the reason back of this visitation. The old mammy's suggestion made her heart beat at once with its danger, it's strangeness, and its equally desolating renunciation of her home.

"B-but maybe ol' Pap'll get money to-day, Aunt Creasy," she stammered. "He's going somewhere or other."

"If he gits hit we-all'll know hit. We'll know hit. But now de ahmy o' de Lawd is sayin' to you, 'Oh yes, Gracie, oh yes, my chile, we's a-comin', we's a-ma'chin' to sabe you frum de han's o' men. No mo' will you haff to lay yo' body down.' Dey say Christ lay his body down fuh de whole worl' an' you don' haff to lay yo' body down no mo', Gracie. . . . God's ahmy comes a-ma'chin' on."

The thought back of Aunt Creasy's chanting had lain like a horror over Gracie. To be used like an animal, by any man . . . and now this army of which Lump Mowbray had caught rumors . . .

"I couldn't ever get there," she trembled in a frightened undertone. "I couldn't possibly get past the first padero."

"Lump Mowbray gwi come heah to-night. He knows evah road, yeh, he know evah hawg path. He kin tell you whah de padero is, what he is doin', an' when he go to sleep. He know whah de padero is when de padero don' know hisse'f. An' Lump'll lead you by de han', Gracie . . . yeh, Lump'll lead you by de han' to de ahmy o' de Lawd."

The old woman turned around and went back into the kitchen.

CHAPTER THIRTY-ONE

To GRACIE the means of her salvation were as repellent and as filled with danger as was the fate of being sold South. Her initial objection was Lump Mowbray. She disliked Lump because he always looked at her. She had for Lump the concentrated despisal which women have for an admirer whom they thoroughly do not admire. Added to that was Gracie's white woman's reactions toward a small ugly black man. Lump could infuriate Gracie by merely turning his head and watching her walk through the yard.

But such an escort to the problematic army was the smallest of her woes. To run away from home was to risk being caught and beaten by old Pap—it was to leave Marcia and never again to lose her heart in the gray eyes of her young mistress, never to brush her hair, never again, in the person of the white girl, to go to white dances and waltz with white men. To every cool love affair Marcia enjoyed, Gracie throbbed with a sympathy more quivering than the original passion. So to leave Marcia was, for Gracie, to fill her life with emptiness. But, on the other hand, if she did not escape she would be sold away from home anyway.

There was only one possibility of escape from one or the other horn of this dilemma—that old man Jimmie might find a money lender.

Late that evening, as the old ex-blacksmith came up the road to the gate, Gracie saw the rider silhouetted against the last umber of the sunset. The droop of the old man's shoulders told her in a picture what she had known all the time, but now that it was set before her like that, Gracie simply stood and looked with a sinking feeling in her chest. She turned and went upstairs to her room. It was quite dark there. She groped to her straw-mattressed bed and sat down. Through her door she could see Marcia smoothing some ribbons under the light of two candles. One of the candles began guttering and her mistress picked up a pair of snuffers and cleared the flame.

The dimly seen white girl came to Gracie like a saint in a niche: Marcia's slender arms, her hair ringed with an aura against the candlelight.

The cream-colored girl began weeping. She wanted to go in and cover Marcia's hands and hair with kisses of farewell. Even her passionate tenderness did not contemplate kissing her mistress's lips.

"Oh, little missy," thought the girl in the black room to the girl under the candlelight, "I wouldn't leave you if I could help it. I'd rather brush your soft hair than to . . ." Her emotion forsook inward words and became a kind of trembling absorption in this last glimpse of her mistress; this white girl who was so far above her, so far better than she, so dear, so lovely, so pure.

But she said nothing at all. To have uttered a word, even to have shown her tear-filled eyes, would have frustrated all her plans. She went silently downstairs, filled with the terror of being caught and the heartbreak of losing Marcia.

In Aunt Creasy's cabin sat Lump Mowbray, a small dark shape with a greasy knot of forehead showing of about the size and convexity of Lump's own fist.

He got up as Gracie entered.

"Well, de Lawd speaks an' de people hears," said Lump oracularly. "You may claim you don' heah, but you do heah. Yo' ears may not heah but yo' hea't heahs."

Gracie did not know what he was talking about—possibly nothing at all. Lump had a habit of venting deep repetitive phrases out of emptiness.

Old Aunt Creasy got laboriously to her feet.

"Ah hopes God dorects you to His ahmy, Gracie. Fare you well. A black woman has a ha'd time in dis life, but a high-yellah gull lak you . . ." She shook her head heavily at Gracie's comeliness. "Well, if'n de Lawd kin make 'em, maybe He kin save 'em . . . I dunno."

"He sont His ahmy," intoned Lump.

"Come on, I'm ready to go," said the girl with a little shiver of repulsion that her farewells were being said to black folk. Somehow, in this tension of parting, they seemed not like persons at all, but like dark silhouettes cut out of the faint illumination of the fireplace.

Suddenly she exclaimed, "Aunt Creasy, why did you arrange all this just for me?"

"Ah promise Hannah when she die Ah look aftah huh light-coloh baby," explained the old negress simply. "Ol' Hannah know what a yellah woman go through if she try to save huh soul. Ah promise Hannah Ah do whut Ah kin, so when Lump tells me 'bout God's ahmy, Ah 'members my word to ol' Hannah."

The thought of Aunt Creasy keeping faith with her dead mother brought the wizened old creature within the range of Gracie's sympathy. She stooped, put her arms about her life-long friend, and kissed her dried cheek.

"Aunt Creasy," she said weeping, "I may never see you again. Before I go . . . who was . . . my father, Aunt Creasy?"

The old black woman came to a kind of pause in the midst of their embrace, then nodded her head silently toward the big house.

The quadroon stared with a catch in her throat.

"You mean . . ."

The old black woman nodded again slowly.

"Yo' mammy Hannah was a mighty purty woman, Gracie."

"O-oh . . ." breathed the girl aghast. "Oh, Lord, help me!"

And she followed Lump Mowbray away from the home of her father and her half brothers and sisters.

Lump Mowbray had a tireless flat-soled gait. He padded noiselessly in front of Gracie at a pace that taxed her powers. She was no sooner in the cotton field than she began having to hurry every few steps to catch up. The effort of keeping within sight and hearing of the glimmering Lump prevented her thoughts from pouring into tragic channels. At times she would lose her guide completely and would have to run forward calling in an undertone:

"Lump! Lump! Where are you?"

And the black man would reappear.

"Rat heah . . . kain't you see me, Gracie?"

Lump, apparently, saw everything and could hardly understand that to Gracie the night was black and impenetrable.

Once he touched her hand and whispered, "Stoop down, Gracie, 'hin' dese blackberry briers. Walk sof'. Yondah's a padero in dat lane!"

She heard the hoofs of the white man's horse and it brought to the girl the realization that she was on an equality with Lump Mowbray. They were two negroes slipping away. She was one of the articles posted up in the sheriff's notice. This body of hers, this intangible something that looked out through her eyes and tiptoed behind briers past patrols, this sentient unique thing that was herself—it was for sale to-morrow at the Florence courthouse, because for twenty-seven years ol' Pap's other children—his white children—had run an open account at BeShears' Crossroads store. They had lived her up.

Hysterical laughter shook Gracie's throat. Lump suddenly whirled and shook her arm.

"Fuh God's sake, woman, whut you laughin' at?"

Gracie drew a long breath, stood still and began weeping.

"Nothing," she said.

Lump stood hushing her and moving his flat feet restlessly.

"Come on out dis fiel'. Jess a li'le way to de woods." He drew at her wrist with the rough hard hands of a cotton laborer.

Gracie quieted and hurried on after the vanishing guide.

At the end of the field Lump helped Gracie over a rail fence and reduced her speed in the comparative safety of the wooded hills. In the inky undergrowth Gracie was forced to hold his shirt to follow the path at all. She could see absolutely nothing. Her heart was beating heavily from her unaccustomed exertion and she breathed audibly.

"When—are we going—to get there—Lump?" she panted at last.

"Tiahed?" asked Lump, with a shiver in his voice.

"No—I'll—go on."

But her legs were like wood that somehow could ache. Twigs of undergrowth hit her in the face. After walking down an endless hill and starting up another, she gasped out:

"Lump—I'll—have to—sit down."

Both stopped. Gracie sat down weakly in the black path just where she was.

In the silence that jellied around her she could hear the *bump-bump-bump* of blood in her ears, and feel her heart like a quick rubber ball bouncing in her breast.

"Oh-o-oh . . ." she sighed.

"Lean on me," invited Lump's voice, and she felt his arm groping around her back.

"No."

"You's mighty tiahed," persuaded Lump.

"I—know I am," she said, with her heart shaking her voice.

"An' . . . we's heah all by ouahse'ves, Gracie," mumbled Lump, with a faintly audible swallow at nothing.

A quiver of alarm and repulsion went through the weary girl.

"Let's go," she said, and got to her feet again.

Lump obeyed mutely. He got to his feet and submitted his shirt to her hand again. He walked much more slowly now.

"Gracie," he mumbled at last, "I been hangin' 'round yo' place a long time on 'count o' you."

"How far is it?" asked the girl, with her fright rising.

"I say to muhse'f, I ruther lay my han' on Gracie than any othah woman in de worl'. You looks lak heben to me, Gracie. You looks like heben walkin' de yeth fo' de sunshine o' man."

"Lump! Lump!" cried Gracie in terror. "Don't talk like that!" The memory of being raped in the barn rushed over her. That was terrible enough, but this small, warped, hideous thing . . .

"Why kain't I talk lak dat," cried Lump, "when I been wantin' you all my life long! Gracie, honey, gimme somethin', honey! Oh, Gracie, you's a flamin' fiah an' I's a can'l fly wantin' to bu'n myse'f up in you . . . Gracie!" He stopped. Gracie felt him turning around on her in the blackness.

"Lump!" screamed the girl. "For God's sake don't touch me! Don't! Don't!"

"Ah ain't techin' you!"

"I know you're not."

"I's axin' to tech you."

"And Lump, I'm asking you not to touch me."

For upward a minute the girl stood in the blackness with her heart pounding in her throat, seeing and hearing nothing.

Then Lump's voice mumbled heavily, "Look like, Gracie, when a man's been wantin' you fuh ten yeahs, an' when he's ca'in' you off fuh always, an' when he's wid you out in de nighty woods takin' you to de ahmy ob de Lawd, to yo' freedom an' happiness, does look like to me, Gracie, you mout lay down wid him wunst."

CHAPTER THIRTY-TWO

Below the two lay encamped the army of God.

Their tents, tiny with distance, lay stretched along the valley, and above the encampment, in a long level line, hung the pale morning mist. This appeared, to the two fugitives looking down upon it, like a supernatural canopy lowered by the God Who sent them to protect His warring hosts.

The serenity, the soft aërial perspective, the great cause behind this armed multitude touched the two watchers with a pentecostal mood. The small knotty man held up preternaturally long arms, his face took on the solemnity of simple negroes,

"Oh, Gracie, Ah brings you at las' to de Promise Lan'. Oh, de Lawd has come, yes, de Lawd has come! He sont His suvants on His holy work; He sont 'em to strack de rope f'um ouah wris'es an 'de whop f'um ouah backs.

"We cry out, 'How long, Oh, Lawd, how long will yo chillun be kep' in Egyp'!' We din' think He was a-comin', but hyar He is. Oh, Gracie, don' nevah say de Lawd don' heah His chillun pray! Don' nevah think His yeah don' heah yo' prayuhs!"

Lump's cadences, the sight spread below her caught Gracie up with a sudden ebullience of strength and mysticism. She forgot her blistered feet, her utter weariness of body; she even forgot Lump's night-long pleadings for the intimacy of her body. She caught the small negro's hand.

"Come on, Lump, let's go down," she gloried.

Lump did not move.

"No, Gracie, I's got to go back."

"You're not going down there with me?" she asked in amazement.

"No, Gracie, I's got to go back an' spread de news ob de glory my eyes has see. I's lak Moses, Gracie. Ah comes to de Promise Lan' an' looks, but Ah tu'ns my back. Dem Ah guides goes in, but Lump tu'ns back. He gwi back to spread de news in Egyp', what his eyes saw an' his yeahs heah."

As he actually turned away, the first quiver of admiration the girl ever felt for him passed through her. For a moment the mantle of Moses covered Lump's shoulders. She had no idea, nor had he, that the real reason of Lump's return was that the flat-footed negro was an irrepressible gossip, and he would rather pad up and down the Crossroads neighborhood with this marvelous tale than be a free man.

When his quick padding steps had removed him from Gracie's sight, a thought passed through the girl that, after all, she might have granted him what all night long he had prayed for and wept for.

Then he passed out of her mind.

Exactly what Gracie expected when she went down alone she did not know. Some great beneficence, some transcendental good. Like all religious expectants, she was unable to define the marvel she dreamed of.

She walked down the wooded hillside, and just when she had decided that she had lost her way a sentry moving back and forth between two trees challenged her. She said she wanted to come inside the lines.

The youth with the musket considered the extraordinary visitor.

"Have you a complaint to make?" he hazarded.

Gracie reflected that she was a piece of property flying from a forced sale and said that she had a complaint to make.

"Well," said the sentry, yielding to the dark eyes in the

pale oval face, "I suppose you've got a right to state your complaint, but I'll tell you now it ain't going to do any good. When a house is burned, it's burned, and that's all there is to it."

"Nobody's been burning any house," said Gracie, utterly at sea.

"Well, all right. I was just telling you that much. Come on with me an' the corporal'll talk to ye."

In a soiled tent which bore not a hint of the fair vision Gracie had seen from the hills drowsed the corporal's guard. Just outside the fly lay a few smoldering faggots on which simmered a coffee pot. A little removed from the fire three muskets were stacked together in the form of a tripod.

The sentry aroused the corporal out of a gray blanket. The noncommissioned officer sat up, looked at Gracie, then rubbed his eyes and looked again.

"She wanted in the lines to make a complaint," explained the sentry, not sure that he was right in bringing her in.

"What's gone?" yawned the corporal—"horse—cow— pigs . . . would you know your horse if you was to see it again?"

"Of course I'd know my horse!" ejaculated Gracie, thinking the soldiers in the army of God asked queer questions indeed.

The corporal rolled his tongue about in his mouth to rid it of the dryness of sleep, then said Gracie would have to remain where she was until the lieutenant waked up and shaved and had breakfast.

"Go to him before he's had his eye-opener," warned the corporal, "and you'd never get your horse back at all."

Gracie almost said she had no horse, but her negro instinct to say nothing and allow as much confusion to gather about her as would kept her quiet.

The sentry returned to his post. The corporal lay down in his blanket, evidently intending to finish his sleep, but his head lifted now and then to look at Gracie. Presently he gave over the idea of sleep, sat up, and asked the girl where she lived.

"Down toward Florence," said Gracie.

"Toad what?" asked the corporal.

"Florence," repeated Gracie.

The noncom considered this for several moments. Finally he pushed another rolled-up blanket with his toe.

"Catlin! Catlin! Wake up," he yawned, "and tell me what these soft-talking Southern beauties mean when they say they live toad flaunts."

Out of the blanket roll lifted the blackest hair and the bluest eyes Gracie had ever met.

"What's the matter?"

Gracie had decided, almost with a feeling of sacrilege, that the corporal in the Lord's army was drunk. She repeated to the youth called Catlin that she lived toward Florence.

The hill youth's ear picked up the lightly touched "r's" which the Northern corporal had not caught. Catlin told the corporal where she lived.

"Where is Florence?"

"About a day's march down in Alabam'."

The corporal became more attentive.

"How in the heck did she lose a horse down in Alabama when we haven't reached there yet?" he inquired of Catlin, in the fashion of a person talking through an interpreter.

Jerry Catlin sat up and blinked at Gracie, then without asking her drew his own deductions.

"I imagine it's that Leatherwood gang. They've been raising the devil all through this section. They claim to be Union men when they steal from secessionists, and claim to be Confederates when they steal from Union men."

"I see," nodded the corporal. "Well, if that's the lay-out, I calculate I'd better take her to the left'nant right now."

He rose up, put on and buttoned his blue coat, looked into a metal mirror and straightened his hair, then told Gracie to follow, and set off some fifty yards to a street of tents. He paused before one and scratched the canvas flap; then called in a voice that was subdued apparently not to awaken the officer inside, but yet it was too persistent to let him sleep:

"Left'nant   Beekman . . . Left'nant   Beekman . . . Left'nant Beekman . . ."

At about the sixth or seventh repetition the flap was jerked aside, a red face with a choppy blond mustache looked out, and a voice brittle with anger snapped:

"O'Malley, how many times have I instructed you——"

"The lady has news of the Leatherwood gang, sir," hastened O'Malley, saluting.

"Wouldn't news of the Leatherwood gang keep till after breakfast?"

"Yes, sir, I'll take her back, sir."

Lieutenant Beekman glanced at the informer on the Leatherwood gang, and his manner changed abruptly.

"Perhaps I might look into the matter. We've been having a number of complaints about those outlaws. Just wait a moment if you don't mind, miss."

The face withdrew and Gracie heard a brisk moving about inside the tent. She and the corporal stood waiting in the gray-lighted street. Presently the lieutenant came out again and looped back the flaps, apparently for the day.

"You may go, Corporal. Now, if you'll be good enough to come in out of the chill, miss?" The lieutenant pulled around a camp chair inside the tent.

Gracie entered with an odd feeling that a white man should call her "miss."

Inside she found herself standing on a rubber ground cloth. In one corner stood a camp trunk; a sword and a holster hung from the tent pole.

Lieutenant Beekman himself was now buttoned up formally. He and everything in the tent looked ready for inspection. He introduced himself and asked Gracie's name.

"My name is Gracie," said the quadroon, then, feeling

the lack of a surname in the first introduction she had ever had in her life, she added uncertainly, "Gracie Vaiden."

Lieutenant Beekman was one of those small, blond incisive men who do not appear small. His lips fitted tightly together. He bit off his words sharply in his friendliest moods. He now said:

"Take that chair, Miss Vaiden. . . . When was your horse stolen?"

"I—Lieutenant Beekman," hesitated the girl, "I—I didn't lose any horse."

"I thought you did."

"N-no, sir."

"No? Then what complaint do you wish to file?"

"Well . . . it wasn't exactly a complaint . . ." Gracie grew more and more uncertain what to do. She saw Beekman had mistaken her for a white woman. She knew she was receiving a consideration based on her supposed whiteness. If she told him the truth she might possibly get sent back home.

"I just heard about this army," she ventured.

"You are not concerned with the Leatherwood gang?"

"Y—n-no, sir, I'm not."

"Didn't you tell O'Malley you were?"

"No, he just—just looked at me and—and supposed it."

The glimmer of a smile went across Lieutenant Beekman's sharp features.

"And what am I to suppose?"

"Well, I—I came up here last night——"

"Where from?"

"From Florence."

The officer reached for a map and looked at it.

"Did you ride all night?"

"N-no-o."

He looked at the condition of her clothing.

"You . . . didn't walk!"

"Y-es . . . I walked," whispered Gracie, not having the slightest notion how this catechism would end.

"Miss Vaiden," inquired the officer, curiously and intently, "will you tell me why you attempted such a difficult march—at night?"

Gracie's heart almost stopped. Her lips grew chilly. She had no idea what would happen to her. Already she had discovered Lump's transcendental notions were incorrect.

"Because I . . . didn't want to be . . . sold," she whispered.

The blue-uniformed lieutenant sat perfectly motionless in body and face.

The quadroon momentarily expect to be asked to get out of the chair, to be reprimanded for her presumption in sitting down to a conversation of equals with a white person.

"Sold," he repeated at last.

Gracie nodded faintly.

"I see," he said, with a faint change in the metallic Northern overtones of his voice.

He sat thinking for several minutes. Gracie watched him anxiously. Finally he said, in the tone of one taking command of actual things and not sentiments:

"You must be very tired and hungry. Your feet must be raw."

"They are," said Gracie, "and I am."

"Well, we can fix that. Just keep your seat a moment, Miss Vaiden. I'll be right back."

He got to his feet with quick movements and hurried out into the street of tents.

His rapidity vaguely alarmed Gracie. She suspected that he might be arranging to have her sent home and get the reward. Why should he be in such a hurry?

However, she had not waited long before he reappeared with another soldier, bearing a basin of water, towels, bandages, and a brown bottle.

He placed them beside her on the ground cloth, told her to bathe her feet and wrap the raw places up in arnica. Then he went out of the tent to let her dress her wounds. He did not go away but stood just outside his quarters. Gracie drew off her stockings with the oddest mingling of gratitude and uncertainty. From the outside of the tent Beekman directed her to pour some arnica into the water. Gracie did so and put her burning, aching feet into the penetrating comfort of a hot foot bath. The sensation spread up her legs and into her weary body, intensifying the gratitude and allaying the suspicion that had just entered her head.

"I'll tell you what I can do with you," said Beekman, in a voice that showed that he had been studying the question.

"Yes, what is it, Mr. Beekman?" asked the girl, in the respectful voice she always used toward white persons.

"You must be acquainted down toward Florence. You must know who are the Union sympathizers and who sympathize with the rebels?"

"Nearly everybody sympathizes with the Confederates," said Gracie.

"Yes, I know that, but that could be a reason why you should come along with the army, don't you see? . . . one of our information staff."

Gracie perceived that he was trying to think up a reason for her going with the army, but she did not know what an information staff was.

After a moment he asked in a less speculative voice, "Don't you need fresh hose?"

"Mine are torn," said Gracie.

Beekman reappeared in the tent while Gracie made an instinctive effort to cover her knees and calves with the towel.

The officer opened the camp trunk in his quick manner and exhibited a surprising collection of spoons, watches, handkerchiefs, hose, and what not. He selected a pair of silk hose and offered them with his slight, rather compressed smile.

"This is the very thing. This holds a kind of poetic justice, of which any sort is rare enough in this world." He hung them over the back of the camp chair.

"Do you know how to bind your feet?" he continued, looking at her feet through the brown arnica-tinted water.

"Oh, yes," said Gracie, suddenly becoming afraid he was going to do it for her.

"Let's see if you do?"

This was an order to the quadroon. She took her foot out, held down her skirt with her elbows as she dried it. It was a well-shaped foot because it had never worn a tight shoe. The girl had no idea at all how to bandage a foot. She passed the cloth around her heel and over the arched top.

Sure enough, Beekman knelt down in front of her, took the bandage, fitted it between her great toe and the next and wound a fan-shaped bandage covering ball and heel and finally tucked in the end without a knot.

"There you are," he said. "Do the other one the same way as this, then roll your stockings and put them on so they won't disturb the cloth. I'm out to get some breakfast."

He got to his feet and disappeared in his usual quick fashion.

After a longer interval he returned with a companion, bearing a tray of steaming pots and platters. A folding camp table came from behind the trunk and the things were spread out on it.

"You won't get cream," said Beekman. "You'll have to take your coffee black."

All these things had been surprising, but for the lieutenant evidently to be about to eat with her was acutely embarrassing to the girl.

She felt very queer indeed. The unknown softness of silk on her calves and knees filled her with extreme luxury. Now

for a white man to sit down and eat with her was incredible.
It was not an honor, it was a nervous shock. As if the man
suddenly had stabbed himself before her eyes. The girl felt
no distaste for it, she simply felt as if such a breakfast
could not go on. Something must happen to stop it. Her
hands trembled so she could hardly lift the thick army cup
to her lips. Her nervousness was so marked that finally
Beekman asked her what was the matter. She said nothing
was the matter, but gave up her effort to sip the coffee.

"Really, what is?" Beekman leaned toward her with sharp
curiosity.

Gracie drew a long breath.

"Must I tell?"

"Certainly."

"Well—I—my master and mistress—never let me—eat
with white folks." Gracie had a faint chill feeling in her
cheeks as the blood dropped out of them.

The blond lieutenant got to his feet, leaned across the
little table and patted the girl's shoulder.

"Oh, well, you were a slave then; you're not now. Go
ahead and finish your breakfast by yourself if you like."

He let his hand remain a few moments on Gracie's shoulder and then stepped away.

Another touch of faint apprehension invaded Gracie at
this touch. It was not a simple friendly pressure. Added to
that, to eat her breakfast alone while a white man waited
was still more anomalous.

She looked at him and felt herself flush. He stood a little
away from her now, smiling faintly at the absurdity of this
reversed position. Presently he said:

"While I was out I spoke for a place for you in the
quartermaster's wagon."

"Did you?"

"He said he'd take you along to-day and dig you up a
tent and blankets from somewhere." He came across and

patted her shoulder again. "That will be very nice, for you to have your own private tent."

At the way he said "private tent," at his renewed touch, Gracie's first faint apprehension was confirmed. She suddenly didn't want her silk hose or her breakfast. The food in her mouth became without taste. For the same sort of thing to spring up again at her first contact with an officer in the army of God! It dawned on Gracie that there was nowhere at all for her to go.

Lieutenant Beekman said, with an effect of his faint mirth, "I'll run along now to the officers' mess, and you can finish your breakfast alone."

CHAPTER THIRTY-THREE

An hour later the camp fell into the stir of departure; tents were struck; blankets rolled up; the mess things were packed; the wagons swallowed them all up. The soldiers marched forward. The encampment unwound itself along the trail and moved deliberately toward the south.

Gracie had been given a place in a baggage wagon. She stretched out among the rolls of canvas tents and rode back in the direction from which she had come.

Behind Gracie's wagon rumbled the rest of the baggage train in a haze of dust.

As Lump Mowbray had reported, a number of camp followers hung onto the regiment; not only runaway negroes but a number of poor whites. This riff-raff carried spoil: things they had picked up for themselves in the spoliated region behind them, or equipment they had stolen from the soldiers.

The teamster who drove Gracie's wagon was a short, square, red-faced man who, at first, had declared he would have no nigger wench riding his cart, but who had changed his morose expression when he saw his guest.

This driver's name was Leeks. He had found a place for Gracie in a space between two rolls of canvas near his seat. He drove three pairs of horses and wielded a maze of reins and a whip. It was a long whip and with it he could pick a horse fly off the ear of any animal in the string before him.

"I understand ye'rre going along with us," called the

ostler, looking around at Gracie once he had his team strung out in the line of march. Gracie said she was.

"W'erre to?" inquired the red-faced man.

"What did you say?" asked Gracie apologetically.

"W'erre to?"

"Oh, I don't know where to."

The fellow jerked a rein without disturbing the others, whistled, drove for some distance with a quizzical expression. Finally he asked:

" 'Ow can they sell a w'ite woman?"

"You mean me?"

"Yes, you."

"I'm not white," said Gracie, with her familiar depression coming over her.

"You look it," nodded the ostler; "if I may say it, you look very w'ite. Not a spavin nor a blemish nor a chafed spot on ye."

"My feet are chafed," said Gracie, smiling faintly.

"I werre speaking figgerative," said the ostler.

"I'm not," said Gracie. "My feet are a sight."

The red-faced man reached over and took hold of her ankle.

"Let's see 'ow bad," he suggested, drawing her leg a little toward him.

Gracie kicked loose in sharp anger.

"Touch me again and I'll——" She searched futilely for a threat, "I'll tell Lieutenant Beekman."

"Ho! . . . yes . . . Beeky Beekman." Leeks wagged his big square head. "Who keers anything about Beekman?"

Gracie pushed herself further toward the rear of the wagon and looked angrily across the hills. A smoke was volleying up beyond the skyline in rolling masses. Leeks drove on for some distance in silence but finally turned about and called back in a rough placating voice:

"Say, I didn't mean nothin' while ago, c'mon back."

As the girl made no reply, he added presently in a

cynical tone, "Un'erstan' the Q.M.'s going to issue you a tent to-night all to yerse'f."

"Is he?" said Gracie resentfully.

"It's what Barney told me." He waited a moment and then added, "I'm a turble timid man, I am," and he touched his leader with his whip.

The silence following this last remark piqued Gracie's curiosity.

"Timid . . . about what?"

"Skeered to sleep by myself at night. Look like a fine-looking gal like you might do something about it." He looked around at her and broke into loud laughter.

Gracie got to her feet.

"I'll get down," she snapped. "I won't ride with such a——"

"Wait! Wait! God'l Mighty, woman, kain't ye take a joke. Set easy in the boat. I won't say another damn word."

Gracie paused on the back of the wagon. She began to see that, no matter to what cart she resorted, it would be the same thing. She and Leeks were almost isolated on their wagon. Winding after them along the crooked road came four or five more wagons. When she turned and looked ahead she saw the infantry, a column of dusty blue winding out of sight over the undulation of the road.

The girl jolted along watching the column of smoke. The fact that the quartermaster had issued her a tent stuck in her mind. To-night she would be in a tent by herself . . . and there was Leeks . . . and Lieutenant Beekman . . .

After an hour or two the quadroon saw still another column of smoke ahead of their line of march. She finally asked the teamster what it was.

The question gave Leeks permission to talk.

"Come sit back herre w'erre you werre," he burred in low-caste Northernese. "Afterr all, if we'rre going to rride togetherr, we needn't yell like this."

Gracie crept along the wagon top and resumed her place.

"Now, therre ye arre," nasalized the ostler comfortably, and with satisfaction. "Now the smoke therre . . . well, they'rre getting theirr dues at last, that's all."

The girl looked from the smoke to the driver.

"Who's getting what dues?"

"Why, the ownerr of that 'ouse, ferr his in'umanity," declared Leeks warmly.

"You mean that smoke's a house . . . burning?" breathed Gracie.

"Surre . . . surre!"

"What did the owner do?" asked the girl blankly.

Mr. Leeks was amazed at his passenger.

"Why, God'l Mighty, gal—you running away to keep frrom being sold, and ast me what he done!"

"What did he do?"

"Why, helping sell you ferr yourr masterr's debt, of courrse."

"He wasn't!" ejaculated the quadroon. "He's not the sheriff!"

"No, but he could 'a' come and bid on ye, couldn't he, if he'd liked to?"

"Of course he could do that."

"Therre ye arre," cried the ostler, reaching over and slapping the girl's knee. "Takes fourr to make a auction: the man that owns th' goods, the man that owns th' debt, the auctioneerr, and the people to buy. . . . We'rre going to clean out all four kinds, miss, ferr theirr merrciless and in'uman trraffic in 'uman flesh! I ferr one am glad to see everr' column of smoke rrise up . . . to 'ell with th' last of 'em, say I!"

Gracie jolted along staring at the smokes. She thought of the hideous things that had been done that deserved this —the selling away of Solomon, her own rape in the barn loft—but whoever lived in the burning houses really had nothing to do with her and Solomon.

The tent wagon drew nearer and nearer to the column of

smoke. As it moved over the hill it came into view of the actual building itself. Then a very strange thing happened to the landscape. Gracie had been moving through an unknown country; now the terrain seemed to gather itself up and mold itself into something solid and known. The cardinal directions suddenly reëstablished themselves with a sort of motionless whirl. Very abruptly Gracie knew where she was. A few miles farther on stood the Vaiden big house. A trembling set up inside the girl that this army would pass ol' Pap's place. She was afraid he would come out, take her off the wagon and whip her. She could not imagine the army itself estopping old man Jimmie from seizing his property.

It seemed to Gracie that she had been gone from home for weeks. Then another fear came to her . . . they might burn down ol' Pap's house!

She reached over and caught the ostler's arm.

"Mr. Leeks, who—who is the boss of all these men?"

"You mean the officer in command?"

"Yes, sir."

"Colonel Higgenbotham . . . but say, Sisterr, don't trry th' colonel. You stick to the damn little left'nant who got ye th' tent."

"But listen," interrupted Gracie, not even understanding what he meant, "five or six miles further down we'll be passing my home!"

"Well, wot'rre ye skeered of . . . they'll ketch ye again? 'Y Gawd, gal, they'll neverr do it!"

"I'm afraid the men'll burn down ol' Pap's house!"

The driver was amazed.

"Hell, don't ye want it burrned?"

"Of course I don't! What would I want my own house burned up for?"

"Because they kept ye a slave all yerr life!" cried Leeks angrily; "because they'rre going to sell ye like a cow! Imagine it! Sell a piece like you to jest any damn man! . . . Gracie! Damn it, Gracie, lemme come to yerr tent to-night!"

He squeezed her soft thigh unconsciously in a spasm of desire.

She shook him loose furiously, then saw a man on horseback, trim looking even in the dust, picking his way down the line of wagons and men. Gracie just had time to compose herself when he came alongside the tent wagon. He lifted a hand to the girl and smiled.

"We're getting into your country," he called up.

"I know we are," replied Gracie, wondering and dreading whatever would happen now.

"There's a man named McPherson lives down yonder where you see that smoke. Do you know whether he's a rebel or a Union man?"

"Mr. Candy McPherson?"

"He may possibly be named Candy," agreed Beekman with his dry smile.

"Why, he—he's a Union man," breathed Gracie, defending Mr. McPherson, whom she liked, by the natural slave method of lying. Then a thought struck her that she had better not say all her neighbors were good Union men or she would not be believed. She would better say some were rebels. She would save ol' Pap and say he was a Union man. Besides, Mr. Candy's house was already on fire. So she caught up her words, swallowed them and gasped out:

"No—I'm wrong about that, Mr. Beekman. Mr. Candy McPherson's got three boys in the Confederate army."

"Have you anything personal against Mr. McPherson?"

"No-o . . . of course I haven't. He's a good man."

The lieutenant was in no hurry. He reined down his horse and rode along looking up at the girl. Even in the dust he enjoyed watching her. Under his eyes Gracie became conscious of the soft jouncing of her bosom at every jolt of the wagon. She wished he would ride on away, and folded an arm across her breast to steady herself.

After riding some little distance, Beekman said, "I succeeded in getting you a tent for to-night."

"Yes," said Gracie.

"Well . . . aren't you pleased to have sleeping quarters?" inquired Beekman lightly.

The quadroon broke away from the topic of sleeping to which, apparently, every soldier in the army of God recurred.

"Mr. Beekman," she said in a disturbed voice, "do you think it's just to burn all the houses in this country just because the people own slaves? Ought their houses to be burned—when us colored folks have to live in them, too?"

The lieutenant looked up at her curiously.

"Do you think this invasion is on account of Southern slavery?"

"Yes—isn't it?" asked the girl, trying to save the last touch of her apocalyptic vision.

The officer gave his thin smile and lifted a dusty blond eyebrow.

"We're invading this country, Gracie, because Southern cotton growers want to buy cheap English goods, duty free, and we want them to buy Northern-made goods with a tariff added to the cost price. Why, after the Battle of Fort Sumter, Lincoln offered to make slavery perpetual down here if the planters would agree to the tariff." He turned off with a shrug. "But that's neither here nor there. . . . I picked up a dress for you at an old log house down the road—a blue-flowered dress. I'll bring it around to you tonight."

CHAPTER THIRTY-FOUR

C ANDY McPHERSON's house was on fire. As the army wagons creaked past, the logs fell in and such a wave of heat rolled out that Gracie held her hands before her face and twisted her shoulders away from the sting.

It seemed fantastic, it seemed impossible to the quadroon, that human beings could march past a burning home, laughing and joking while the family fought the fire and tried to rescue some little part of what they possessed. And she thought with a kind of stunned credulity that all this destruction was being wrought because the people of the North wanted the people of the South to trade with them and not with England.

The explanation Beekman had flung off corroded in her thoughts. So that was the object of the army of God. Beekman's own trunk full of spoons and watches; the immediate attempt of the soldiers to possess her own body—that was the army of God.

The wagons were past the burning buildings now. Beekman was gone. He had ridden back to the head of the column. As Gracie jolted forward the ostler began again talking about coming to Gracie's tent. Her feeling of insult changed to one of simple disgust.

"You can come to my tent and welcome," she said with a shudder, "I won't be in it;" and she turned her legs away from him.

"Wait! Wait, gal!" he cried. "You'rre the purrtiest

283

woman I everr talked to. . . . God damn it, I'll marry yuh rratherr than lose ye! We'll go to the chaplain. . . . Hell firre, wait—ye'rre not climbing down!" When he saw her swing off to the ground with a girl's wobbly lack of precision, he shook his free fist at her and bawled, "Well, go to hell, ye damned ungrrateful nigger bitch!"

He couldn't leave his wagon to detain her. The driver of the next train was roaring with laughter at what he caught of the brief comedy.

Gracie ran to the side of the road and climbed the rail fence, swinging her foot over the top rail and exposing her legs to the passing men with a kind of furious indifference. It was like climbing a fence before animals.

The girl knew exactly where she was. She would cut across field, save three long turns around corners and arrive at the big house quickly.

She hurried ahead in her bandaged feet, peering across the fields, then looking back at the dust that floated high above the army. She did not know what she was going to do but hurried on, moved by some confused motive of protecting her master's home.

Sight of the far-off black oaks in the Vaiden yard gave Gracie's heart a squeeze of recognition. No smoke was coming up from among them, so the big house was not on fire. The girl hurried on, taking long and short steps between the inconvenient widths of the cotton ridges.

As she neared the place she heard a many-tongued howling from the hounds: defiant barkings, yelps of fear, howls of flight. Then she saw a skirmish line of hounds leap over the yard fence, and behind that barrier turn and bark at some intruder in the yard.

The white and black Vaiden family were in the yard talking to some Federal cavalrymen. At one moment all the Vaidens would be trying to say something at the same time, even to the negroes. Then an officer in dust-colored uniform would ask a question. The group was in the midst of one of those fantastic catechisms by the Federal raiders to see if the planter were such a strong rebel that his home deserved to be burned.

"Is there a member of this family in the rebel army?" clapped an officer in his Northern voice.

"No! No!" boomed old man Jimmie with a very red face. "By the eternal, none of my sons are in the rebel army!"

The inquisitor glanced at the negroes.

"No sah, boss." Robinet shook his head with much white eyes showing in his black face.

"Nuh-uh," shook Columbus, "you sho' got dis fambly wrong, Mas' Yankee."

"Aren't you the father of two boys, Polycarp Vaiden and Augustus Vaiden?" inquired the officer.

The old man hesitated, then nodded stiffly.

"Yes, yes, Carp and Gus are my boys."

"Well, I understand they're in the Confederate army?" snapped the officer.

"They are! They are, suh!" boomed old man Jimmie. "But when you say rebel army you're insinuating a damned lie, suh. The South never belonged to the North——"

Here he was interrupted by Marcia who cried out, "We heard Gus was fighting on the Yankee side!"

The old man whirled on his daughter.

"Well, you know it wasn't so, Marsh!" he stormed.

"No, I don't know it wasn't so! You nearly got into a fight about it!"

At this moment the colloquy was interrupted by several soldiers coming out of the house with hands full of plunder. One had the lace curtains from the parlor windows; another the pewter spoons from the kitchen; still another carried two hams which he had found in the smokehouse.

The family stood looking mutely at their tableware and linen being taken away.

Just behind these came three more soldiers pushing a fourth man out the door in front of them.

"Here, Cap'n," called one of the privates. "Here's a fellow we found hiding in the dark middle part of the attic."

"Is that Augustus?" snapped the officer, looking at the prisoner.

"No," cried the old man, "that's a neighbor over to see me."

"Who is it?"

"His name's Dalrymple."

The officer swept away the explanation with a gesture.

"Set fire to the house!" he cried. "It's nothing but a nest of rebels!"

The soldiers went running to the rail fence for kindling, when Gracie hurried through the paling gate that led from the field into the yard.

"No, that isn't Gus or Carp either, Cap'n," she cried; "it's the sheriff who came here to sell all of us colored folks. He's going to take us to Florence and sell us!"

All the Vaidens turned with the utmost astonishment at this sudden reappearance of Gracie.

"What does that nigger wench know about it?" cried old man Jimmie furiously. "Bill Dalrymple's my neighbor."

Just then Gracie recognized the man with the pewter spoons. She ran to him.

"That man came to sell us colored people, Lieutenant Beekman! There's the notice he stuck on our gate!"

"I had nothing to do with it!" cried Dalrymple.

"He's just a neighbor!" boomed the old man.

The officer turned to old Mrs. Laura.

"Who do you say he is, madam?"

"Well," said the old lady in her unruffled voice, "Mr. Dalrymple is certainly our neighbor and has been for many years."

"But is he the sheriff?"

"Well, he was the sheriff—he was elected," admitted old Mrs. Laura reluctantly.

The soldiers broke out laughing. The officer waved the sheriff away, and two soldiers marched off with him.

The particular excitement about the sheriff's capture was forgotten because at that moment the Vaidens saw a column of smoke rising up from the road.

Robinet cried out, "It's the gin! The gin's afire!"

Others took it up. The Vaidens, white and black, cried to one another, "The cotton gin's afire!" "Run for the buckets!"

And off went the white masters and their slaves, making the futile effort to extinguish the houses the soldiers had fired.

Began a great rattling and lowering of the bucket at the well. Columbus and Robinet went running with two pails of water up the road toward the mounting flames. Some of the water spilled on the way. By the time Columbus reached the place a light flame had run all over the film of lint that covered both the gin and the turntable where the mules were worked. The flame danced over the structure from top to bottom, then apparently was gone. Columbus flung his two buckets on the fire the soldiers had built. It died down a trifle, but all the water was spent. He turned and started running back the two hundred yards to the well, when Robinet came hurrying up with two more buckets. Behind him old man Jimmie wobbled with a dishpan.

By this time the van of the marching soldiers was coming into sight. They began shouting and laughing at the familiar spectacle of the rebels trying to save their houses.

"Hurry, old man! Whoop 'em up, old man!" called a dusty stentor.

The old planter paused long enough to wish his tormentors in the pits of hell.

Robinet's buckets almost had the lower fire conquered when little flames, like reddish-yellow banners, began waving in three or four places in the upper works of the gin.

"Git up thar! Mount you, Robinet," roared the old man. "Git watter to them fires!"

Robinet shinned up the central shaft to the great wooden cog wheels above. As the old man pushed up his dishpan half of it spilled over him. A roar of renewed laughter went up from the soldiers. Robinet dashed what was left on the nearer flames. Those in the further cogs made headway.

Marcia came running and sobbing down the road with a quart cup of water. Miss Cassandra hurried out to the well and began urging on Columbus who drew the water.

"Hurry! Hurry, Columbus! They're getting it out!"

Columbus hauled away on the wooden bucket.

"Reckon dey won't set hit afar no mo', Miss Cassie?"

"Don't know . . . pull . . ."

The wooden bucket deep in the well struck the rough stone curbing, clashed from side to side. Miss Cassandra could hear the water spilling from it. Presently there was a *plop*. Columbus staggered backward with a loose line in his hand. The old rope had broken, the bucket was lost.

The negro started hopelessly with the single bucket he had drawn.

The soldiers marching past were now waving at Cassandra and Marcia and laughing at the negroes and the old white man.

One of the marchers stepped out of line, ran in and seized a brand from the gin and flung it into the ancient blacksmith shop.

Old Aunt Creasy screeched, made a queer rush of fluttering rags and waving arms, and got to the brand. It had caught some shavings. The old gargoyle jerked up her skirts, squatted over the tiny flames and watered them out.

Tremendous laughter roared up and down the line of march. A soldier bawled out, "You win, charcoal!" Another hallooed, "That's a rebel fire extinguisher!"

The gin was now wrapped in flames. Presently the particular segment of the column that had seen the old negress's act was out of sight down the road. The men passing saw nothing but another building on fire and another family of blacks and whites standing looking silently at the flames.

When the gin had fallen in and the forge and barns were no longer in danger, old man Jimmie went back to the big house. Marcia had hushed crying and walked silently behind Cassandra. Then came her mother.

"You go on in front, Gracie," said old man Jimmie grimly.

A tingle of apprehension passed over the quadroon. Her sudden shift from the rôle of white girl back to a negro slave again gave her a queer impression. She was a slave once more and old Pap was furious.

By this time the army wagons at the end of the long line of march were rumbling past, but they were nothing; the great wagons, the big horses, the shouting drivers were nothing.

The old man turned on his wife and broke forth:

"Lorry, of all idiots, you're the biggest! Telling Dalrymple was sheriff!"

"He was the sheriff," answered the old woman absently, trying to estimate how many of her things the soldiers had taken.

"Of course he was the sheriff," thundered the old planter, "but he'd never 'a' got away with the niggers! I'd posted Columbus, as soon as he'd levied on 'em, to say who Dalrymple was."

The old woman and the girls stared at the head of the family.

"What's the use o' that, Jimmie?" cried Mrs. Laura in amazement.

"What's the use?—thunderation! If he'd ever levied on 'em I would 'a' got credit for 'em. They'd all got away and I'd 'a' got credit for 'em jest the same. Now my gin's burnt and everything's stole, and they ain't a thing left on the place except the debt. . . . Gracie, you go out thar to Aunt Creasy's house."

At this, apprehension filled both the girls and their mother.

"Pap, what are you fixin' to do?" asked old Mrs. Laura uneasily.

The old man sensed resistance gathering against him in his family. He turned and boomed out with a scarlet face:

"You imagine a yaller wench like her can come disputin' my word before a damned Yankee, gittin' my gin burned, and runnin' away at night and not get the hide skinned off her back?"

Hurried feminine protests broke out against this.

"Why, ol' Pap, she didn't have a thing to do with burning the gin!"

"They were going to burn the house till she come!" cried Marcia.

Such fear filled Gracie that her legs almost gave way under her.

"Ol' Pap! Ol' Pap!" she babbled. "I come back to help, ol' Pap. I—I didn't make 'em burn the gin."

"Shut up, you impudent hussy, contradicting my word!"

"Father," interrupted Cassandra, "you're not going to whip Gracie while you're mad like that."

"Cassandra, mind your own business! No nigger can run off from me an' not get licked."

He caught Gracie's arm and his great bulk bore her toward Aunt Creasy's shack.

The white women were about to try to hold Gracie back. They hurried after her, Marcia weeping. But in the movement they saw the silk hose on Gracie's legs.

Miss Cassandra turned abruptly around.

"Imagine such a thing! Imagine it!" she ejaculated brittly. "One night away from home and trading on herself!"

The white women turned back to the big house.

Old Pap snatched off a peach-tree sprout as he jolted Gracie along toward the cabin.

"Strip off your jacket," trembled the old man. "Take her off! I'm not going to split a good dress to save your yellow hide!"

"O-oh, P-Pap!" begged the girl through blackish-red lips. "I—come back to try to help you—I wanted to help you——Oh! Oh! Pap! Pap! Don't hit me so hard! That hurts! Pap! Oh, God, Pap! I'm going to have a baby!"

CHAPTER THIRTY-FIVE

W HEN the Vaiden family came to take stock of its
losses they found not only was their gin burned and their
home looted, but their livestock had been driven away. Only
one mule remained on the place, old Rab, and this was
because Negro George, on the morning of the Yankee visitation, had, by good luck, turned old Rab out to water. After
the despoilers had gone away the old mule came up again.
Old Aunt Creasy found him at the barn gate waiting to be
turned inside. When the old crone reported this to her
mistress she said:

"If I'd seed the Lawd in his 'cension robe I wouldna felt
no mo' lak shoutin' dan when I seed ol' Rab come back."

Old Mrs. Vaiden told her not to talk of the Lord like that.

To add to their losses, the quadroon girl, Gracie, had
fled on the night of her whipping by old man Jimmie. Her
escape had been the simplest possible matter. The Yankee
detachment had encamped at the Lacefield plantation; their
scouting parties infested the countryside. Under these conditions the regular slave patrol no longer ventured on their
beats. Therefore Gracie simply had walked away during the
night without hindrance. Any of the black folk could have
done the same thing but they stayed on where they were for
several reasons: the plantation was their home, the white
members of the group depended more and more on the black
members. The negroes not only had to plant and tend the
crops, but the black men fell into the most primitive method

of obtaining food. Columbus and Robinet set out rabbit gums and dead falls, while Negro George diverted the hounds from the aristocratic fox chase to trail the unexciting but edible opossum. George ruined the dogs but added sundry platters to the lean table of his master.

Old man Jimmie Vaiden was furious about Gracie's escape. It became certain through rumors that she had found refuge at the Yankee camp. The old planter had ridden down to recover the slave girl.

Old Mrs. Laura advised her husband that he was throwing away his time trying to get Gracie back, that, indeed, he might lose the very mule he rode down there. But the old planter boomed out that he had the law on 'em. He was referring to the Fugitive Slave Act. The old man could quote the text verbatim. So off he went to the Yankee camp, relying with a curious literalism on one of Henry Clay's obsolete compromises.

Exactly what happened to him the family never did find out. Certainly nothing physical. But late in the afternoon old man Jimmie rode back, holding to the pommel of his saddle, barely able to sit his mule, and reviling Lincoln, Garrison, and the Yankee nation. Simple anger had exhausted the ex-blacksmith. When the women and George had run out in alarm and helped him down into the house, they asked him what was the matter. The old man burst out:

"They told me she wasn't there, and me looking straight at her in her tent . . . said she was a white woman visiting her brother who was one of the officers. I yelled at her. I yelled, 'Gracie, you dirty slut, you know that's you! I'll have the law on every damned Yankee here!'

"Everybody was a-laughin' like fools and the surgeon walked up and says, says he, 'Here, here, old man, do you want to drop off with the apoplexy? Come to the dispensary and let me give you a potion.' I said, 'Potion be damned, a Yankee couldn't give me a brush to shoo flies off a dung hill, and you, Gracie,' says I, shaking my finger at her as she

set in her tent, 'May God damn your black disloyal soul to
hell!' "

Ol' Pap was really ill. Mrs. Laura thought he ought to
have some whisky, but naturally the Yankees had taken all
they had.

Miss Cassandra, who was prejudiced against whisky on
account of her brothers drinking, said she thought ammonia
would do.

With patient hopelessness Mrs. Laura replied, "I declare,
Cassie, I don't believe any of you Vaidens will ever find out
anything a tall about each other. Don't you *know* he wouldn't
smell an amony bottle if his life depended on it?"

"It would be the sensible thing for him to do."

"He don't require any better reason than that for not
doing it. Now, you, Marsh, git on the mule and take out
down the road and see if you can get a little whisky somewhere. Git back with it as quick as you can. Your pappy's a
Hardshell Baptist. He believes in water for his soul and
whisky for his body."

So Negro George changed saddles on old Rab and Marcia
set out down the road, apprehensive about her father and
full of disturbed thoughts.

What her mother had just said remained in Marcia's
mind. It did seem that none of the Vaidens understood each
other. Her mother, who was not a Vaiden at all, was the
spiritual center around which the centrifugal Vaidens re-
volved. Without Mrs. Laura the family would fly to pieces
at once because each one would try to insist on some sort of
principle. Cassandra and her father were full of principles
which they applied to other people with a strict morality.

That was the great charm about her mother: old Mrs.
Laura had no principles, she had feelings instead. That
was one of the sweet things about pretty, affectionate
Gracie: she had no principles.

And yet, look what a pitfall into which she had stumbled
—a hanger-on in an army! Marcia could not imagine such a

spiritual cataclysm for the gentle, loving companion who
had grown up with her in her home.

But while one part of Marcia's brain grieved for Gracie,
another sector reflected that, after all, Gracie was a negro,
and negro women were by nature unchaste. They consorted
wantonly with whoever came to hand. They were as the
animals, and so, perhaps, were without sin. That was what
a negro was.

Yet, in all her life, Gracie had never appeared in the
faintest degree like this. . . . Marcia drew a long sigh.

At this point the girl's melancholy logic was distracted
by a dolorous singing and a twanging accompaniment
around the bend in the road. A moment later three blue-clad
soldiers came in sight. One of them had a banjo.

One of the men, with hair so blond as to be almost white,
took the instrument from his companion and said in a hill
accent:

"Dad blame it, Billings, it goes this-a-way." He tucked
the banjo under his forearm, began flapping it with his
finger tips, and in a nasal tenor set up a melancholy yowl-
ing:

> *"Oh, the dangdest luck I ever saw*
> *Was the luck I had in Arkansaw;*
> *I gambled an' drunk like a bold outlaw*
> *But the shurf grabbed me in Arkansaw . . .*
> *Yea Ho!*
> *Dang the luck!"*

Billings received the banjo back, evidently pursuing a
music lesson, but just then he saw Marcia on the mule and
came to a pause.

"Must we ask her, Dilliehay?" he queried of his companion with the blond hair.

The youth with the silver-blond hair shining under his
blue cap looked up and appraised Marcia.

"Might as well."

The three blue uniforms and bright brass buttons looked
to Marcia like three natty demons out of some stylistic hades.
She made up her mind that she would answer nothing they
asked her.

Billings, the short soldier with the banjo, held up a hand
and said in the clipped accent which was so detestable to
Marcia:

"Excuse me, madam, but have you passed some men in
blue uniforms, one of them riding—what was he riding,
Dilliehay?"

"A claybank mare," specified Dilliehay in a voice that
held the nasality of the hills and not the North; "a claybank
mare with stockings on her front feet, blind in her left eye,
and she was a stump sucker to boot."

"If I had," stated Marcia crisply, "I wouldn't tell you."

The soldiers dropped their jaws in amazement.

"Well . . . why . . . wouldn't . . . ye?" drawled
Dilliehay.

"Yes, why wouldn't you?" clipped off Billings.

"Because I wouldn't help you Yankees in any shape,
form, or fashion, that's why!"

The Yankee with the banjo tipped his cap courteously.

"Then, madam, would you pardon us if we run along and
ask somebody else?"

"I won't pardon them if they answer you," bit off the
girl with compressed lips.

There was such anger in her gray eyes that the Northern
youth did not pursue his jest. However, the very blond hillman began to argue:

"Looky here, miss, this is just as much for you-all as it
is for we-uns," he drawled; "more, ain't it, Billings?"

"I consider it much more," stated Billings judicially.

"It don't make any diff'runce to the army," went on the
blond Dilliehay, "if the Leatherwood gang comes aroun'
and steals all your horses an' mules, but the colonel says,

sence we've sorter took charge down here, we orter keep things straight."

"Oh, you're after the Leatherwood gang?"

"Yes, we air, miss."

"What are you going to do to them?"

"Shoot 'em if we ketch 'em, miss. So you see it's in yore own intrust after all."

"Yes, our interest! You Yankees come down here burning and stealing everything you can lay your hands on, then if anybody else starts stealing a little something so you can't get it yourselves, then you want to catch 'em and shoot 'em—in our interest!"

The Northern youth said, "Come on, Dilliehay, this doesn't seem to be our lucky day."

"You're the one who said ask her," grumbled Dilliehay.

"You're a liar, you proposed it yourself," snapped Billings. And the two youths moved on up the road.

Marcia kicked old Rab and proceeded toward BeShears Crossroads. She was incensed at the Yankees. She suspected they had fabricated their question about the Leatherwood gang merely to have something to say to her. She thought how metallic was the man Billings' voice.

She continued these disparaging thoughts, when she heard footsteps running after her mule. She glanced around and saw one of the three soldiers. As he came up her annoyance broke off in surprise as she recognized him even in spite of his spick blue uniform.

"Why—why, Jerry Catlin," she ejaculated, "what are you doing in that uniform?"

"Well I—I joined up," said Jerry, who evidently had expected a more unkind greeting that he received.

"Well, I didn't suppose, when you offered me them apples that day, the next time I saw you you'd be burning our houses when you know all our men folks are gone."

"Miss Marcia, when I joined I didn't know it was going to be like this. I thought we were going to fight."

"Before I'd do what you're doing I'd quit."

"Well, you can't just quit," said Jerry, walking beside her mule; "that's desertin'."

The girl glanced down at him once or twice but vouched no further remarks. His uniform made his shoulders appear much broader and squarer than when she had seen him on the cart. The color of the cloth keyed up his eyes to an almost turquoise intensity of blue. She thought to herself, "If you looked like a prince in blue I wouldn't have anything to do with you."

Jerry was evidently pondering something to say for he brought out:

"Uh . . . what you said to Gillie Dilliehay certainly got him."

"It ought to have got him," said Marcia sharply.

"It did. Gillie joined up with the Confederates before he come here. Now you throwing up to him about burning and stealing, against the very side he used to be fighting for—that got Gillie."

The girl stared at the black-haired youth in amazement. "Do you mean to say he belonged to the Confederates?"

"I—don't suppose I should have mentioned it," hesitated Jerry.

"Then he really is a deserter!" ejaculated the girl. Catlin was troubled.

"I wouldn't exactly call him that, Miss Marcia . . . you see, he really didn't know which side he wanted on."

"What did he expect?" demanded Marcia with gray eyes wide, "a try-out?"

"It's like this," tried to explain Catlin. "His daddy had a nigger named Abraham. So Gillie decided to join up with the rebels and keep Abraham. But when he found out the rebels didn't feed as good as the Yankees, or pay either, he said he'd be blamed if he starved hisself just to save one nigger. Now he tells me the money he'll make in extry pay, if the war lasts two year longer, will pay for Abraham."

"Listen," flashed the girl, "you're not making it a bit
better on that Dilliehay boy telling me this! The idyah!
The idyah! Eating . . . making money . . . no more
principle than a pig! He's exactly where he belongs—slap
dab in the Union army!"

Jerry Catlin took off his blue cap, scratched his head,
and dropped a step to the rear of the mule.

"Sorry I mentioned Dillie," he said in a lowered tone.

The girl returned no answer to this. She considered that
for Jerry to defend Gillie implicated the black-headed boy
in the crime of being a Yankee. The hillman felt this condemnation for he repeated in a flatted tone:

"Wish I hadn't said anything about it now."

And he would doubtless have gone on slowly losing pace
after pace until distance released him from Marcia's baleful
attraction, but in searching about for something to say, he
observed:

"I never could understan' why your brother Augustus
went North to enlist."

If the youth in blue had knocked Marcia from her mule
with a fence rail she could not have been more startled and
dismayed. She stopped old Rab abruptly.

"What do you know about Augustus?"

"Why, nothing, except he come by our house on his way to
enlist," said Jerry blankly.

"Come here!" ordered Marcia with a pale face.

The blue coat came closer with an odd look.

"Where did he join?"

"In Savannah."

"Which—which side?" she almost whispered.

Jerry stared at the girl, as shocked at the idea of Augustus joining the Union army as Marcia would have been
herself.

"Why, the Confederates, of course—he joined with
Gillie."

The blood came back to Marcia's face. She reached an involuntary hand toward the black-haired soldier.

"Oh, Jerry—thank goodness for that! We—we heard he was fighting on the Union side."

The two more or less shook hands on this outcome. That is to say, Jerry had his hand on her saddle and she gratefully pressed it. For a few moments the Federal felt the touch of the girl's slender workless fingers.

"Who in the world started such a lie on him?" cried Jerry, evidently resenting it.

"I think it was the Leatherwood gang. I don't know why they did it, but people believed it—people will believe anything that's bad."

"But what made 'em say he was fighting on the Union side?"

"I don't know at all."

Jerry flung up his hand and caught the girl's pommel.

"I do. Your brother came and warned my mammy when the Leatherwood gang tried to steal our horses. My daddy's a Union man. Augustus was fighting on the Union side then."

"Against horse thieves?"

"Yes."

"Well, I'm proud of that!"

The two went on down the road talking intently. Jerry was telling Marcia all about the fight, how brave Augustus was, how he stood his ground when the whole Leatherwood gang charged him.

All the sisterly pride and affection which Marcia felt for her younger brother in his absence, even if it never took form when he actually was with her, all of this emotion tended to spill over and transfer itself to Jerry Catlin who told her about it.

"Isn't it pitiful," she said at last, looking at the sinewy fingers on her saddle horn, "that he got married?"

"Who got married?"

"Augustus."

"You don't mean he is married!"

"He sure is. Isn't it awful?"

Jerry hesitated, looked at the girl.

"Well, now, I don't know, Miss Marcia," qualified Jerry earnestly. "Marrying isn't such a bad thing if you've got the right person. Nobody's happy till they find somebody they love."

"Oh, well, that's different," said Marcia, "but Augustus——"

She meant by that that marriage might be and perhaps was a proper goal for persons like herself or Jerry, but the idea of her brother falling in love with anybody or anybody falling in love with him was patently absurd.

As Jerry did not follow this logic he said nothing but walked on abreast of the mule in a very pleasant silence indeed.

CHAPTER THIRTY-SIX

WHEN Marcia and Jerry Catlin drew near the Cross-roads store, the girl received a shock. A number of horses were hitched under the sycamores near the spring and blue coats were moving in and out the store.

The girl drew up old Rab abruptly.

"They must be robbing Mr. BeShears. Let's go back—I'm going back. I hope they don't burn his house. Think of poor Ponny!"

She began pulling her mule around hastily when Catlin calmed her fears.

"They're not robbing—they're trading with him."

"Trading! How came them not to——"

"I imagine somebody gave a favorable report about him at headquarters."

Marcia's sympathy changed.

"You mean they found out he was really a copperhead so they won't do anything to him."

"Maybe he wasn't so outspoken as some," minified Jerry tactfully.

"He certainly wasn't," agreed Marcia tartly. "He's as mealy mouthed as a grist mill. Now he gets a big trade for it. That's justice, isn't it? Looks like the Lord wouldn't allow a man to be paid for being a mugwump."

Jerry Catlin pondered what to say to remain a loyal Union soldier and at the same time comfort an indignant rebel.

"The Union army couldn't very well go back on a Union

man, Miss Marcia, even—even if both of 'em was wrong."

"I wish they'd rob him," said Marcia.

Catlin glanced about for some topic more nearly neutral.

"Nice bunch of horses they've got, ain't it?" He nodded at the animals hitched to the fence and the hanging branches of the trees.

"Too good for the use they're put to," said Marcia, who was transferring her irritation from BeShears to her escort.

Jerry perceived this. He wished he had agreed with her in denouncing BeShears. He regretted that he had mentioned the Yankee's horses. As a matter of fact, they were not unusual animals; all sizes and colors champing and pawing against the flies.

He took a last look at them, when one of the horses caught his eyes and sent a little tingle of surprise and the necessity for action through his nerves. He turned to the girl."

"Are you going to the store to buy something?" he asked quickly.

"I'm going to get some whisky for Pappy," said Marcia.

"I'll take your jug in for you."

Marcia looked at him, sensing some sudden change had come over her companion. Her dislike for him vanished.

"Look here, I can tell you're not offering that out of politeness. What's happened?"

"Nothing. I didn't suppose you wanted to go into that crowded store."

"Well, I don't," admitted Marcia, with a nice girl's self-delusion that she did not want to enter a store crowded with strange young men all of about her own age.

She handed her jug to Catlin.

"How much do you want?"

"Well, Pappy feels weak . . . about a gallon, I suppose."

She pulled up her mule. The soldier ran to the store with the jug on his finger. He was hurrying so Marcia would be subjected to the glances of the strange young men no longer than necessary.

Marcia sat her mule with an impassive face, looking straight between the ears of old Rab, but her side glances were fixed on the soldiers going in and out. They, in turn, looked steadfastly at her.

Besides watching the soldiers, Marcia wondered why Jerry Catlin really took her jug. The way he did it showed motive. It annoyed her that she could not fathom him at once as she did Augustus and Polycarp.

While this dissatisfaction moved vaguely through her mind she was also listening very intently to what conversation she could catch in the store, and watching out of the extreme tip of her eye a faint blur of figures in the sector of the BeShears residence.

Inside the store a voice was laughing.

"Hey, Johnny reb, you wouldn't mind an invasion like this every day, would you?"

Another voice answered for the storekeeper:

"This man's a wise man. They tell me he sold his niggers in the nick o' time."

"I hope," said the first voice, "you didn't take shin plasters for 'em, Mr. BeShears."

"Now I'll bet he done that very thing," laughed the second man.

Then she heard BeShears grumble, "Do I look like a fool?"

The two questioners cheerfully took up this topic.

"What do you say, Bill, does Johnny reb look like a fool?"

And the second speaker suggested, "You stand over there by him and I'll see."

Loud laughter filled the store.

Marcia was disgusted at such witticisms. It was as **bad** as Augustus' jokes. At that moment she was interrupted by a girl's voice calling her name. She turned and saw the plump figure of Ponny BeShears at her gate.

Marcia turned her mule and rode toward Ponny, whom she had not seen since the trouble between her father and Mr. BeShears. An inevitable blue soldier was talking to Ponny, and this man now turned and looked with interest at Marcia. He wore a full brown beard and had a rather laughing face with gray eyes. He was not quite so tall as Jerry Catlin but was more compactly built.

Marcia thought with a touch of disgust, "It would be just like Ponny to fall head over heels in love with one of 'em."

Ponny herself was calling in her hearty voice, "Marcia, come over and meet Mr. Maldebranch . . . Miss Vaiden, this is Mr. Maldebranch."

"Er—I'm glad to meet you, Miss Vaiden," said Mr. Maldebranch in a guttural voice that somehow went with his full brown beard.

At this Ponny began to laugh.

"Well, Ponny," cried Marcia, acutely embarrassed, "what's funny about me?" and she tried to look at herself. "Is my face dirty?"

"Miss Vaiden," said the deep voice of Mr. Maldebranch, "I assure you the petals of the rose are not so pink as your cheeks."

"Hush!" cried Ponny, hitting Mr. Maldebranch's arm, and laughing harder.

Marcia was disgusted. Ponny would start a strong-arm flirtation with anything that wore trousers, even a Yankee.

"Do you know her pretty well?" asked Mr. Maldebranch, nodding at Ponny.

"Quite well," said Marcia.

"Will she get over this?"

"She never has," disparaged Marcia.

At this point Jerry Catlin came up with the jug and tied

it to the horn of Marcia's saddle. The subdued excitement which Marcia had felt in him still hurried him. He moved more quickly, explained in less drawling tones that he had to go back to camp, excused himself, and set off down the road.

He had not gone far before he stopped a Yankee cavalryman, swung up behind him, and the two rode off together toward the Lacefield plantation.

Mr. Maldebranch watched the two figures on the horse disappear around the turn in the road.

"That's odd," he commented, "for anybody in the cavalry to give an ordinary soldier a lift."

Here Ponny turned to Marcia.

"Who was your beau?" she asked smiling.

"He's not my beau," stated Marcia tersely, "he's a Yankee."

"He got something for you."

"Ol' Pap ran out of whisky."

"How came that?" asked Mr. Maldebranch in surprise.

Marcia straightened in her saddle.

"You ought to know. You and your regiment stole all he had!"

At this Ponny began laughing again.

"That's right, Marcia, give it to him," she commended. "Tell him what a gang of thieves he belongs to."

This irritated Marcia, for Ponny to speak lightly of all the losses her father had borne while her own father profited by the Yankee invasion.

"I can't condemn them completely," said Marcia, with the faint smile girls wear when they are saying a nasty thing; "they don't seem to steal from everyone alike."

Ponny was not dampened.

"Death and the Yankees," she said, "love a shining mark."

Then Marcia felt ashamed of herself for feeling ill natured toward her friend's prosperity. The two girls began talking about what had happened since they had seen each other. Ponny had Marcia tell all about the loss of the Vaiden stock and the burning of the gin.

As Marcia related her story she became interested herself and began to enjoy the drama of her own misfortunes. She made the flames flicker in the burning gin, be almost extinguished, grow larger before more water could be brought; finally she piled up a great suspense and cried out:

"Just then, Columbus pulled too hard, the well rope broke, we had no water at all. We couldn't do a thing but just stand there and watch the gin burn up!"

Ponny gave a sympathetic scream.

"U-ugh—I know you nearly had a duck fit!"

Here Mr. Maldebranch excused himself. He said he had to go see a man in the store for a moment.

When the Union soldier was gone Marcia's enthusiasm for telling her adventure fell off completely. Ponny herself stopped listening with such eloquent interest. The two immediately began talking of things that could not be mentioned before Mr. Maldebranch.

"Did you hear how old Aunt Creasy put out the fire?" asked Marcia, pulling down her lips.

"Yes . . . wasn't that awful?"

"Imagine such a thing . . . the soldiers nearly killed themselves laughing."

"I was surprised," said Ponny, "to hear about Gracie—doing what she's doing."

"Oh, if a girl's got a drop of nigger blood in her veins," said Marcia philosophically, "she's sure to end up badly."

"I suppose that's so. How do you get your hair brushed now?"

"How do you?" laughed Marcia.

"I do it myself, but I'm used to it, and I haven't got so much."

"Well," said Marcia, rather pleased that Ponny acknowledged that she had the most hair, "I tried to get Aunt Creasy to brush it, but she pulled, then I asked Cassandra would she. She said she had spent years trying to cultivate the inside of my head and had failed, and she had no heart to start on the outside."

Ponny leaned over on the gatepost helpless with laughter. "Marcia, you Vaidens are the funniest family in the world. What you people say about each other is a caution."

Marcia began laughing at the cleverness of her own family.

"Are we really unusual?" she asked, basking modestly in Ponny's description.

"Oh, very. . . . Say, had you heard about Drusilla?"

Marcia's pleasure vanished.

"No—what about her?"

"She's in a family way." Ponny tipped her head to one side with bright-eyed interest.

"Oh . . . is she?" said Marcia, with a complete fall of spirits.

"Oh, Marcia!" ejaculated Ponny, instantly repentant. "I wouldn't have mentioned it if I'd thought of Mr. Milt."

"Oh, well . . . that's all over with," said Marcia, not thinking about Miltiades.

"Really, of all the men I've known, I believe Mr. Milt comes nearest being . . . what you call it?"

"Ideal," supplied Marcia.

"Yes, more like a hero in a book. Just think—after all Drusilla did to him, not a word of reproach. Just went on serving as an officer under Major Crowninshield. I know he still loves her . . . faithful to her memory . . . and to his country . . ." Tears formed in Ponny's blue eyes.

"What gets me," said the sister bitterly, "is that he would ever waste himself on a girl like Drusilla Lacefield."

"There isn't any girl good enough for Mr. Milt, Marcia. You know that. A person can find an ideal man once in a while, but there's no such thing as an ideal girl."

"I suppose that's true," agreed Marcia, with a faint touch of annoyance with Ponny. "I know I am far from one."

These admissions of the imperfections of their sex was interrupted by an extraordinary disturbance far down the road. It looked like a large undefined mass approaching swiftly and leaving a trail of dust in its wake.

Ponny peered through the sunshine, and suddenly ran out and caught Marcia's bridle:

"That's a company of cavalry—isn't that a company of——" The next moment she lifted her voice in a shout:

"Oh, P—— Marcia, what was that man's name?"

"What man's name?"

"That man talking to us!"

"Maldebranch!" prompted Marcia in amazement.

The next moment Ponny dashed out of the gate toward the store screaming, "Maldebranch! Oh, Mr. Maldebranch, the Yankees are coming! Yonder's the Yankees!"

This, of course, was sheer insanity. Marcia sat on her mule, staring after her plump friend in the blankest amazement.

The distant object had developed into horsemen coming up the road at full speed. When within two hundred yards of the store, the horsemen spread out over a wide front and came storming up like a blue cyclone.

Marcia herself became terror struck. She began adding her screams to Ponny's. Just when it seemed that Mr. Maldebranch would be trapped in the store, suddenly out of the dark little house bolted, not one man, but a whole troop of blue coats. They dashed helter skelter toward their horses. The animals were already jerking and pitching with excitement.

From the Union cavalcade there set up a sharp popping of carbines. Splashes of dust flew up about the fugitives from the store. These men leaped at their plunging horses, grabbed them around the necks, and went astride them at a single flying leap. They untied their bridles in a breath, and the next moment were flying up the Florence road, lying flat on their horses' necks and shooting pistols at the troopers.

The air around Marcia was suddenly full of a droning as of bees. Marcia's mule began backing into the BeShears fence. Ponny was flinging up her arms screaming:

"They'll kill him! They'll kill him!"

The Federal cavalry was just sweeping up even with the store. Amid the uproar of their carbines, Marcia could barely keep her seat on her plunging mule. She thought she heard Alex BeShears shouting, "Ponny, lay down, you'll get shot!"

Ponny didn't lie down. She was shrieking:

"Is that him, yonder? Is that his horse!"

Marcia's mule had backed into the yard. The girl saw a chance and jumped to the ground. The whisky jug struck her leg. She fell down but leaped up on her feet.

"Who! Who, Ponny? Who is it?"

"Mr. Maldebranch!" wailed Ponny.

The cavalry was past the store now, spread out over the road in full pursuit of the blue coats from the store. Then Marcia saw two of the horses still tied to the sycamores and two men on the ground twenty or thirty yards distant from the horses. One was feebly pulling himself toward the hitching place.

These were the men Ponny was screaming about.

The fat girl went flying down to the spring with a jelly-like run. Marcia dashed out the gate and went after her without understanding a thing of any of it.

She drew even with Ponny by the time they reached the wounded man. He was not Mr. Maldebranch. He was a small wizened man with a hole in his blue coat where he had been hit.

"What you going to do?" he whispered to Ponny with clay-colored lips.

"Want us to take you in the house?" asked the fat girl, looking in the direction the flying battle had vanished.

"No—no—he'p me on my hoss," he whispered, "I—got to git away!"

Ponny was strong. She put her hand under the wounded man's boot. He clutched the horn of his saddle and the two got him up.

"Can you stay on?" panted the fat girl anxiously.

"Reckon so," gasped the man.

He turned his mount toward the Florence road and kicked it feebly into a slow trot. As he did so the blood leaked out a hole in his boot.

The girls watched him with drumming hearts. When he reached the Florence road he turned west, toward Waterloo, in the direction opposite the course of the fight.

"Ponny, who is he?" gasped Marcia with shaken nerves.

Ponny drew a long breath.

"Haven't the slightest idyah."

"Is he a—a Yankee or—or what?" cried Marcia utterly at sea.

"Marcia, you saw him same as me."

"You mean you were helping men to get away you don't even know?"

Just then Marcia observed that the wounded man was riding a claybank mare with white stockings on the fore feet.

"He was one of the Leatherwood gang!" gasped Marcia.

"Was he?" said Ponny.

CHAPTER THIRTY-SEVEN

As Marcia Vaiden rode home, the assault of the cavalry on the men in the store tingled along her nerves. She had been frightened and excited by the violence of the action. Her heart still beat in her breast at the danger.

She knew now that the fugitives were members of the Leatherwood gang and it annoyed her that she had not guessed it at once. Everything she recalled was informative now: Jerry Catlin's excitement, the clay-colored horse, the villainous looks of the men in the store and Maldebranch; she had felt something odd and villainous about Mr. Maldebranch.

Then she rode along remembering how Ponny had hit Mr. Maldebranch on the arm, and thinking how unmaidenly it was. Subconsciously Marcia listed maidenliness and unmaidenliness as rival forms of attracting and holding the attention of the opposite sex. But unmaidenliness she held not to be quite fair, it was hitting below the belt. And, what was still worse, Marcia believed it eventually lost in the end.

Here she thought of Drusilla Crowninshield who had not lost. She was not very modest and yet Major Crowninshield had loved her and married her. Drusilla could not even understand the major's moods. She, Marcia, understood him and inspired him with great visions; he had said so. Yet he had yielded to the warmly molded and not particularly modest flesh of Drusilla and she was burgeoning with another life.

A sense of vague, impersonal frustration filled Marcia. Of

not many men would she have expected something finer than
the simple use of the flesh, but Major Crowninshield was so
subtle. He could have formulated in words Marcia's quivering feeling that the bodies of men and women were but the
gateways of some divine imminence; that passion was beautiful, but it was only an acolyte in the temple, and not the
high priest . . . he could have formulated it in substance,
too.

Her name hallooed gayly across the hills startled Marcia
out of her reverie. She looked up and saw a horseman galloping toward her. He wore a blue uniform and waved a blue
cap. Three minutes later horse and rider took the fence with
the effect of easy, almost languid strength which the leap of
a powerful horse always produces.

Marcia stared at the rider in amazement.

"Well, Mr. Maldebranch!" she gasped. "So they didn't
kill you?"

"Very poor shots, Miss Vaiden, need target practice."

"Awfully kind of you to provide them with a target,"
observed Marcia crisply, remembering he was a horse thief.

"Oh, it wasn't for that," laughed the horseman in high
spirits. "I thought I'd lead that Yankee beau of yours off
on a wild-goose chase, then circle around and see you home."

Marcia stopped her mule and straightened as stiffly as the
absurd modeling of her side saddle permitted.

"You certainly are not going to see me home, Mr. Maldebranch!"

Mr. Maldebranch was amazed.

"Now, I like that!" he cried. "Here I risk my life to rid
you of a very dull-witted Yankee beau. I lead him away, letting him shoot at the cross in my suspenders, then when I cut
across country and provide you with some really lively and
amusing company, why you don't want it. That's not gratitude, Miss Vaiden."

Marcia remembered once more that the fellow was a horse
thief.

"It may not be gratitude," she said flatly, "but it's decency."

"Decency!" cried Maldebranch in a pained voice. "How have I offended the strictest rules? I was properly introduced to you by a maiden more plump but less fair than yourself——"

"Listen!" cried Marcia in a temper. "You're a horse thief, that's what you are, and that makes it a thousand times worse for you than it does for those poor men who got shot. You're educated, you should know better. I imagine you think it is very romantic, stealing horses. You talk like you do. But you're just a plain ordinary horse thief, and I won't ride a step with you in any direction!"

Mr. Maldebranch began laughing immoderately. He held to his saddle horn and wiped the tears from his eyes. Like all moralists, Marcia was infuriated that her strictures were not received in ashes and sackcloth.

"I hope next time the Yankees see you," she cried, "they hit you instead of that poor innocent man!"

"Marsh Vaiden!" cried Maldebranch in an offended tone.

At this annoyed and intimate use of her name, Marcia stared at Mr. Maldebranch. The eyes and forehead above the brown beard transformed themselves into lines as familiar to her as the reflection in her own mirror. And the annoyed voice was no longer Maldebranch's deep tones, but one she had heard all her life.

"Why, Carp Vaiden!" she screamed. "What in the world?" and she reached for him from the saddle of old Rab.

Polycarp reined his horse over to her. They put their arms about each other, hugged and patted each other on the back. She nearly fell out of her saddle.

"Carp!" she cried incredulously. "What are you doing here?"

"Home on a furlough," laughed the youth, getting her balanced in the saddle again.

"Think of that! But what are you doing running around with a gang of horse thieves?"

"Well, I knew I couldn't stay around home in either civilian clothes or in gray. So when I heard of the Leatherwood outfit rigged out in blue, it gave me an idea, and I got a blue suit myself."

"I hope you're not helping them steal horses so you can wear their color!" cried Marcia with sisterly frankness.

"Well, I say, Marsh—of course not!" He hesitated a moment and then added, "No, I haven't a thing to do with the moral end of their operations."

"What end have you to do with?" inquired Marcia at once.

Polycarp hesitated, stroked his new and highly stylistic brown beard.

"I'm awfully sorry, Marsh, but I'm afraid I can't tell you. I'm not at liberty to tell."

Marcia looked at him sharply, instantly guessed something and became piqued.

"You go to Ponny with it," she exclaimed reproachfully, "tell her all about it, but me, your sister—you're very sorry you're not at liberty to tell."

"Well, Marcia!" cried Polycarp, "I thought you'd be glad to see me when I got home not killed or wounded or anything."

"I am glad, of course," said Marcia resentfully, "but it's silly, you telling Ponny something you can't tell me."

"How do you know I told Ponny?"

"From the way she looked—giggling like a ninny—she knew everything."

"Now, if I had been Miltiades," complained Polycarp, "and I had told you I had a secret, you'd 'a' thought that was grand. You'd 'a' ridden home with me admiring me all the more because I was romantic and had a secret of some sort."

Marcia could not deny this, or, if she did deny it, it wouldn't be believed, so she shifted the subject.

"Say, Carp, listen, would you believe it? Augustus is married!"

"Married!" Polycarp wrinkled his eyes incredulously. "Who in the world would marry him?"

"A nurse!" cried Marcia derogatively. "A Rose McClanahan who nursed him in the hospital. She's a hundred times older than he is, of course."

"Is he at home?"

"No, they live in Corinth, Mississippi. Of course Gus would marry into some outlandish Western family."

"Now, see here, you can't condemn a girl on account of her family. Look at Ponny."

This made Marcia think of the secret again and once more irritated her.

"I am looking at Ponny," she said dryly.

"Now, look here," cried Polycarp, annoyed at last. "You and Cassandra are so uppish about Ponny. She's better natured than both of you put together. And what she says she thinks."

"Why, so do we!" cried Marcia, offended.

"I don't mean you tell stories," explained Polycarp, "but you think other things, too. You go picking everything to pieces in your heads, both of you, especially Sister Cassandra, and you can't help it, neither one of you. Ponny never does that."

"It's because she's dumb!" cried Marcia with warm cheeks; "that's why we don't think she's good enough for you—and she isn't!"

At this point the quarrel was discontinued because they were nearing the house, and the two made it up to continue Polycarp's disguise as Mr. Maldebranch and see if they could fool somebody.

This plan, however, came to nothing because old Mrs. Laura and the hounds recognized the returner at once. Then, after the rejoicing was over, everyone, even down to the last negro, said that they would have known Polycarp.

Since everybody would have recognized Polycarp except Marcia, this caused Miss Cassandra to give her sister a little lecture on using her eyes and wits, and not go about half dreaming, unable to recognize her own brother in the middle of the road.

The phrase "in the middle of the road" seemed to pick out a very reprehensible place for a sister to fail to recognize a brother.

Added to this, the whisky did not please old man Jimmie. In the first place, he wasn't sick and didn't need the whisky. In the second place, he wouldn't have Alex BeShears' whisky as a gracious gift, so Marcia might as well lug it back if it was meant for him. In the third place, he'd order his own whisky when he wanted it.

With these reflections he took the jug, started for the kitchen with it, and nodded Polycarp to follow him.

Naturally, it was not long before Polycarp's blue uniform brought forth comment and demanded an explanation to the Vaiden family. The returned soldier repeated what he had said to Marcia.

Old man Jimmie objected at once.

"That's no way for a Vaiden to act," he announced. "The idyah—sailin' under false colors! I say let a man be what he is!"

"Yes, Pappy," put in old Mrs. Laura, "but if he didn't sail under false colors he wouldn't sail a tall—they'd capture him."

"Thunderation, Lorry, if he gits captured under false colors, do you know what they'll do with him? They'll shoot him, that's what!"

"Just for wearing one of their ugly old uniforms!"

"Why, of course they will, woman!" roared the planter.

The old mother looked apprehensively at her son, think-

ing how she could uphold him against his father. Finally
she said:

"Well, anyway, Pappy, they're not so li'ble to run him
down and capture him dressed in blue as in gray. He won't
be so noticeable."

"Of all dad-blamed fools!" roared the old man. "Lorry,
that's the very thing they'd shoot him for—not being so
noticeable."

"Carp," directed Miss Cassandra in a kind of an aside,
"go into the company room, out of Father's sight. It isn't
good for him to be excited."

"Why, that's not so!" cried the old man, resenting this
accusation of weakness.

"Father, I merely said it wasn't *good* for you," stressed
Miss Cassandra, trying the confusion of logic on her parent.
"I don't say it's bad for you, but what *good* will getting ex-
cited do you?"

"Uh—now, now, that wasn't what you meant, Cassandry,
that wasn't what you meant!"

Cassandra was far too wise to argue with her father. She
turned to Carp again.

"You don't have to wear that blue uniform do you, Polycarp?"

"I'm afraid I do, Cassandra."

"What for? We can post negroes around the place so no
Yankee can slip up on you here in the house."

Polycarp lifted his brow.

"I'll think it over," he said, and walked on into the company room.

The moment he did this Marcia instantly knew that Polycarp was going to tell Cassandra whatever it was that he had
to tell. Jealousy and indignation filled her. To think that
her brother would tell something to Ponny and Cassandra
which he would not tell to her! Tears stung her eyes. She
drew a trembling breath, turned abruptly, and went out of
the house.

In the yard one of the hounds came up behind her and touched her hand with its wet, sympathetic muzzle. Marcia jerked away and rapped the bony head with her fingers. The dog dodged back and walked off in another direction.

The hound itself was one of the foolish younger set of dogs. It had not learned that when a human being came out of the big house wrapped in an aura of tragedy, and also wrapped in skirts, that any proffer of doggish sympathy invited catastrophe.

CHAPTER THIRTY-EIGHT

What the hound could not accomplish, the sunset did. Its smoldering abyss behind the black oaks set forth their hard design with the staccato beauty of a modern etching. The unintentional affront of her brother could not maintain its bitterness against the sad philosophy of the wounded west. Marcia stood leaning against the heavy logs of the big house in that half mood between waning resentment and an evening feeling of loneliness and wistfulness.

Above her head a curtain waved out of the small high window of the company room: a sheer pink-figured substitute for the delicate lace curtains the Yankees had stolen. Well, that made little difference; the new curtains probably would be taken, too. Anything they had to-day might be gone to-morrow. Indeed, everything they had might very well go. Almost every day came the news of the burning of some house in the neighborhood; usually homes of the more violent secessionists.

In the complete stillness of evening Cassandra's and Polycarp's voices became audible through the open window. Marcia could not understand what they were saying but she moved resentfully a little farther away as a moral guarantee against eavesdropping. She moved away four or five steps then stopped and listened intently. She felt within her right to do this because already she had made an effort to avoid overhearing them. To prove to herself that she was not interested in what she heard, she looked at the fence, the barn, the ruins of the gin, until she caught a shocked sentence or two from Miss Cassandra, and then these material objects vanished from her attention.

Polycarp was making an extraordinary disclosure to Cassandra. He had been sent home to observe the Union detachment camped at the Lacefield place. He was to learn its strength, keep track of its movements, report the damage it inflicted on the country, and where it finally went.

"Why, you're a regular spy, Polycarp!" came Cassandra's startled comment.

"I don't have to go inside their lines necessarily," said Polycarp. "I think I might get that information outside."

". . . wear their uniform . . ."

". . . a man in the Leatherwood gang takes my reports . . ."

"Then listen," planned Miss Cassandra in a somewhat louder tone. "Whenever you are on the place we must post niggers up and down the road to give warning when the Yankees are coming."

The voices withdrew and became silent. A little later Marcia heard Cassandra calling George in a high curving voice.

Marcia walked on out to the fence, oddly moved by the romance of Polycarp's mission. She had no very great fear that anything would happen to him. What impressed, what almost irritated her was that such a romantic opportunity should be thrown away on such a person as Polycarp. Now, if it had been Miltiades . . .

Then she thought of Ponny BeShears once more and became irritated again. The idea of Ponny BeShears being the sweetheart of a spy! Big, fat, commonplace Ponny! Now, if it had been she, Marcia . . . Oh, she could see herself standing on the gallows dying to protect Major Crowninshield if he were a spy! She could imagine herself saying, "Shoot! Shoot me. I will never, never reveal his name!"

The intricate rhythm of two horses trotting up the road stopped Marcia's imaginary execution, or at least granted her a reprieve. She peered down the road in the direction of

the Yankee camp, sharing an apprehension felt by every
family in the countryside when they heard horses approaching.

She turned and called in a guarded tone, "Carp, somebody's coming!"

And from the passageway to the kitchen she heard Polycarp's negligent answer:

"Oh, all right, but it won't amount to anything this time
o' day."

This piqued Marcia, that her very first warning should
be set aside as not amounting to much. But there was some
truth to it nevertheless. The Yankees were a methodical set.
The army had hours to go to bed, to get up, to eat, to drill,
to ride forth and steal and burn. If they had been as systematically virtuous as they were systematically devilish, the
whole army would have floated up to heaven, as did Elijah.

So now she put her apprehension away and looked down
the road in simple curiosity.

The confused shape of two horses came into view, and
presently it developed that a man rode one and led the other.

The girl at the fence watched in silence as horses and
man changed into dramatic silhouettes against the somber
coloring of the west. But instead of clattering past as she
had expected, the rider drew up.

"Isn't that you, Miss Marcia?" inquired Jerry Catlin's
voice.

The girl said yes, in a tone bleak with her musings, then
after a moment, with the automatic friendliness of the country, asked where he was going.

"Riding up to see old man Candy McPherson—takin' his
mare back to him."

This was said so simply that only after a moment's
thought did a shock of surprise pass through the girl.

"Taking his mare back!" she cried. "Yankees taking a
person's mare! Is that your idyah, Jerry, or did the Yankees send you with it?"

"A little o' both. When we got the mare Cap'n Sherrill says, 'Send word to McPherson we've got his horse,' and I said I'd lead her up as I'd like to get leave to come up this direction anyway."

This last phrase carried an involuntary unction that caused Marcia to disregard it and change the topic.

"How did you come to get the horse?" she asked curiously.

"Why, we just follered on down the road the direction that wounded man tuk. We found him about a mile and a half from the store."

"Waiting for you!" ejaculated the girl in surprise.

"Why-y, no-o," drawled Jerry slowly. "He was dead an' still holding the mare's reins. We couldn't tell whether he got off and laid down in the road or jest fell off."

"Oh! O-oh . . ." whispered Marcia.

The thought of the wounded horse thief, whom she and Ponny had helped into the saddle, riding on until he toppled off the claybank and died in the dust. It sickened the girl. The help she had given him changed that horse thief into a human being with a claim on her sympathy; his tenacity and endurance of agony until death, brought him some measure of her respect.

She deserted the point.

"It's queer," she said slowly, "that the Yankees would burn Mr. Candy's home and then bring him back his horse."

"I don't know," replied Jerry in a detached voice. "You see, Mr. McPherson reported the loss to Colonel Higgenbotham, so if he relied on the army to get his mare back, naturally the army would turn her over to him when they got her."

"I don't imagine they would," remarked Marcia realistically, "if she'd been anything but an old broken-winded stump sucker."

"That I kain't tell," said Jerry, equally philosophic.

The silence which fell between the youth and Marcia was not only unconstrained, it was unobserved by the girl. The

things he told her, his voice, his presence on the horse became part of the furniture of her thoughts. Presently he
said he was going to have to lead Mr. McPherson's horse
home unless someone would ride it. Then he added that the
McPherson place was only four farms up the road and that
if Marcia rode the horse up there she could ride his horse
back as far as her home and he would walk that distance.

Jerry stumbled through this long rigmarole in a very
uncertain voice. Marcia hesitated about riding with a Yankee, but she reflected that taking a Southern man's horse
back to him was a very good thing to do; furthermore, that
Jerry Catlin was the least Yankeelike of all the blue coats
that she had seen; and finally, that the evening was a very
pleasant time to ride. So she decided she would go.

Jerry maneuvered the old claybank up to the fence; Marcia gave a leap and alighted sidewise on the animal's bare
back. She maintained her seat with the security of riding
many horses to the barn from the pasture. A moment later
the two were trotting up the dim road, with Marcia kicking
her heel into the claybank's ribs to see if she could pace.

The McPherson mare was not a gaited animal. She did
nothing but jog trot. As Marcia rode her up the highway,
the girl talked of a dozen different things, but all the time
kept automatically trying to edge the ancient animal into
some more aristocratic gait. Nothing came of it. However,
the muffled clatter of the hoofs in the dust took on that odd
quality of being a goal within itself, unrelated to mere tran-
sition from one place to another.

Presently, with a touch of apprehension, she discovered
that Jerry was asking her in a troubled fashion about the
man she and Miss BeShears had been talking to at the store.

"What about him?" asked Marcia in an empty, defensive
voice.

"Is—is he a friend of yours or—or Miss Ponny's?" inquired the hillman uncomfortably.

"Oh!" ejaculated Marcia very affably. "Ponny's."

"Well, I didn't know," said Jerry, in obvious relief.

"Yes," said Marcia with detachment, "he's Ponny's beau."

"Then, Miss Ponny goes with a Union soldier, too!" exclaimed Jerry in a brighter tone.

"M-m . . . yes, Ponny seems to—but she's the only one I know who does."

Mr. Catlin was taken aback somewhat.

"Looky here, Miss Marcia," he said argumentatively, "do you think which side a man happens to be fighting on has much to do with the fellow as a man?"

"A good deal would depend on the man himself, I suppose, and quite a good deal on how he fought. Now, if he came out burning down houses and stealing spoons and curtains . . ." Marcia shook her head. "Nobody who would do that could be much."

Jerry came to a halt in his catechism. He rode some distance in the gathering darkness. Finally he said above the mumble of the hoofs:

"Look here, Miss Marcia, I—I don't know what you think of me. I never have stolen a spoon or set fire to anything at all. I wouldn't do such a thing."

"No-o . . . I don't believe you would," agreed Marcia slowly.

"And Miss Marcia, I knew you before I ever heard of an army—ever since Sarah Bentley told Sister Elvira about seeing you at a picnic. She said you were the prettiest girl she ever saw, and I was wishful of seeing you before there was any war."

He had got the two horses together and now touched the claybank's unkempt mane with a short riding switch. "And now that I do see you, Miss Marcia, I—I wish we could just ride and ride and ride like this forever."

A quiver of pity touched the girl. She looked at the switch caressing the mane of her mount.

"Listen," she said, "I want to tell you something."

"Yes?" he queried expectantly.

"The only reason I can ride with you at all, Jerry, is—is because you are a Yankee."

He stared blankly toward her in the darkness.

" 'Y, Miss Marcia—what do you mean by that?"

"I mean I—I'm engaged to a soldier in the Southern army—a captain."

This last bit of information about young A. Gray's rank was a delicate and deadly thrust which Marcia was too feminine to forego.

Jerry took back his switch and allowed the horses to resume their usual distance apart.

"I might have knowed you be engaged to somebody," he said in a monotone. "I might have knowed a girl like you would——" He broke off just at a point where Marcia would have given a good deal to hear the rest of his sentence. A kind of emptiness arose in Marcia, as if something warm and comforting had been withdrawn from her. She rode along thinking of young A. Gray, her Southern captain. He came to her with the vague poetry of resignation. It was the first time he had crossed her mind in weeks.

When the two reached Candy McPherson's plantation, Jerry meant to stay there only long enough to restore the claybank to its owner. They rode up to the gate and saw two stone chimneys and a blackened area where the McPherson home had been burned.

Then Marcia remembered again that Jerry himself was a Yankee.

"I wonder where the family are living?" she asked, with her sympathy for the soldier gone from her voice.

"In one of the nigger cabins, I imagine."

They sat on their horses listening, and presently heard the rise and fall of a negro's voice in some interminable speech.

Jerry drew in a breath and called, "Mr. McPherson! Oh, Mr. Candy McPherson!"

The shout stopped the speech, then a negro's voice answered, "Who is dat wants to see Mas' Candy?"

"Jerry Catlin!"

"Who is Mist' Jerry Catlin?"

"Private in the Union army!"

A low consultation sprang up at this, then a negro's cottony voice inquired:

"Which section ob de McPherson fambly does you desiah to interrogate?"

Jerry and Marcia looked at each other and laughed.

"How many sections has the McPherson family?" inquired Jerry.

"Well, Mist' sojer," said the slave philosophically, "sence you-all bu'nt Mas' Candy out, he fambly has split into fo' sections: one fuh de gu'ls, one fuh de boys, one fuh de ol' folks, an' one fuh de niggahs."

Evidently part of the McPherson slave quarters had been taken over by the whites. This dialogue with the black man probably would have continued indefinitely, going into more and more detail and arriving nowhere, but the voice of the master himself called out in the darkness:

"Here is Candy McPherson in the fourth hut on the right. What do you want, suh?"

The "sir" in this sentence held no courtesy at all but instead the pungent disrespect that a Southerner can inject into the word.

"I've brought back your mare," said Jerry flatly.

"Brought back my mare!" ejaculated the planter in the utmost astonishment.

"We captured her to-day from the Leatherwood gang," explained Jerry briefly. "Captain Sherrill returns her with his compliments."

"Extend my compliments to Captain Sherrill," called back the planter, "and tell him that I never before realized the force of the old adage that there is honor among thieves. And you may turn the mare over to the niggers, Private

Catlin, unless you decide to keep her yourself. Good-night!"
and the door of the fourth cabin on the right slammed shut.

"Well, my goodness," said Jerry, "that's no way to act!"

"I imagine living in nigger quarters puts him out of temper," said Marcia soberly.

In view of old man Candy's insult, she herself felt condemned for riding with a Yankee.

"If you'll exchange horses with me," said Jerry in a disappointed tone, "we'll go back. . . . I'd thought he'd be glad to get his mare again."

"Well, she isn't much of a nag," said Marcia, sliding to the ground before her companion could help her. She was sorry she had come.

Marcia's jump to the ground undoubtedly was another disappointment to Mr. Catlin. He dismounted in silence and walked toward the negro cabins leading the horses.

To Marcia the momentary intimacy she had felt for Jerry during his tacit avowal of love a few minutes past had quite vanished. He simply was another Yankee, one of the detachment sent down to lay waste her country. She moved along very disgusted with herself. Old man Candy's insult unintentionally had hit her.

As the two led the horses down the dark row of cabins the voice of the negro orator once more rose and fell with the hortative cadence of his race.

"Oh, my chillun," he was saying, "de Lawd ain't gwinter be mawked. You may think you is mawkin' de Lawd, but you ain't. You cheat Him when you think His eyes is shet, but His lef' han' will strack you down when you ain't speck'-in' hit.

"So takes you-all wa'nin' f'um Mas' Alex BeShears. He sol' his niggahs away f'um they home. He sol' 'Lumbus away f'um he wife, he sol' Calline away f'um she parents; all fuh money. Now his money is gone an' his feet ah bu'ned an' he kain't walk. Yes, Lawd, he's struck down in he strength an'

now he's in a wuss fix dan de po' niggahs he went an' sol'
south fuh his money!"

At this period the voices of all the negroes arose chanting:

> *"Roll on, Jurdan, roll!*
> *Oh, roll on, Jurdan, roll!*
> *Oh, I lif' my soul to de th'one uv God.*
> *Roll on, Jurdan, roll!"*

CHAPTER THIRTY-NINE

O<small>N THE FOLLOWING DAY</small> the shocked gossip of the neighborhood supplied the details of Lump Mowbray's apocalyptic account of the horror at BeShears Crossroads.

It was, briefly, that the Leatherwood gang had seized the merchant and burned his feet over a slow fire until he told them where his money was buried. Out of this, the negroes, very naturally, had evoked a wrathful God avenging the sale of Solomon and Calline.

Old Mrs. Vaiden was inclined to attribute the merchant's downfall to his attempt to foreclose the Vaiden property. But this irritated old man Jimmie so sharply that his old wife was forced to quit talking about her theory.

Marcia and Miss Cassandra were not interested in the theological aspect of the BeShears torture and robbery. The question the woman and the girl kept silently asking themselves was, "Where was Polycarp on the night of the robbery?"

Marcia had thought he was at home. She had returned from the McPherson place with this questioning assertion in her mind, but when she reached home her brother was not there.

From that night her uneasiness about Polycarp grew more and more disturbing. The suspicion kept moving under the surface of her mind: "What if Polycarp had . . ." and then she would press it down, shove it back somewhere out of her mental foreground. But it would leave the girl with a

330

tremulous feeling, as if some terrible thing, like an enraged bull, had charged her.

Instead of assuming, as she always had done, that her younger brother was fit for any deviltry, Marcia began defending Polycarp in her thoughts. She refused to believe that he would burn an old man's feet over a slow fire for his money. When she was with Polycarp she would study his bold, rather handsome bearded face, thinking how honest and straightforward he appeared. And two or three times she had drawn in her breath to ask:

"Carp, did you help burn Alex BeShears?"

She knew he would have to say no, but she was afraid his face would say yes. Suppose such a truth were writ before her eyes?

So, for the first time in her life, torn by her suspicion and her silent passionate defense, Marcia began to love her brother Polycarp.

It was quite a different sort of love from the adoration she accorded Miltiades. It was an anxiety that made her realize for the first time how isolated she was from her younger brother. She could not mention to him a word about the robbery, she could speak of Ponny only in jest except when she was angry. And to tell Carp a word about her feelings toward Major Crowninshield was beyond the power of her imagination. Indeed, every moment of her life that ever had really moved her was something quite incommunicable to any other member of her family. This seemed a melancholy thing to Marcia. It was like living unseeing and unseen in a house of ghosts.

That Jerry Catlin had anything to do with her realization of her spiritual aloneness, Marcia was unaware. She thought of him often, but that, she supposed, was because she saw him often. She had seen him twice since the evening of the ride.

Once Jerry had come to her father and told him that he believed if old man Jimmie would apply for the mule and horse the Yankees had confiscated, he could get them back.

Whereupon the ex-blacksmith had burst forth:

"Confiscated! Confiscated, you thieving copperhead! You and your accomplices stole my stock and you know it! Before I'd call it confiscated I'd see every damned blue coat frying on the grids of hell!"

On his second trip some days later Jerry told old man Jimmie that Augustus had stayed all night at the Catlin home just before he enlisted in the Confederate army, and he thought perhaps old Mrs. Vaiden would like to hear about her son.

At this the old man must have divined the drift of matters, for he answered with dignity:

"Mr. Catlin, never in my life have I turned from my door a human bein', rich or pore, who comes in frien'ship an' honor." Old man Jimmie paused, drew a long breath, fixed Jerry with his red-rimmed splenetic blue eyes, and continued. "*But* when a man comes to my home one day as a firebug, thief, and robber, and the next day askin' social equality, I regret that I've got to tell him in so many words what he is and where he stan's."

This was probably the most controlled speech the ex-blacksmith ever uttered. The tender-hearted Mrs. Laura remonstrated with him afterwards for being unforgiving to the boy. The old man replied:

"Lorry, I'm willin' to forgive him seven times seventy like the Bible says, but by the gray goats, I don't see any Scripture for colluging with a damn scoundrel after you have once forgive him and got shed of him!"

To Marcia her father's spleen at Jerry seemed somehow anomalous. He seemed to have nothing to do with the Yankee invasion beyond wearing their uniform.

Cassandra said Marcia should never have ridden over to McPhersons' with the Yankee; she might have known he'd come hanging around afterwards.

Marcia laughed and said she didn't see that his hanging

around hurt anything, he got sent away in so many different directions.

"You'd let him come in if it wasn't for Father," accused Cassandra.

"Me!" cried Marcia, astonished. She didn't think she would.

"Yes, me," Miss Cassandra mimicked her sister's bad grammar. "You're like that fat Ponny BeShears—go with anything that wears trousers!"

Marcia felt hurt to be compared to Ponny. She glanced at Polycarp to see how he took it. He seemed faintly amused. He was eating the hind leg of a rabbit, biting the meat from around the bone with his strong white teeth. He seemed to be enjoying the rabbit and amused at his older sister.

"Jerry Catlin is really no more of a Yankee than Gillie Dilliehay," defended Marcia.

"I never heard of Gillie Dilliehay," said Miss Cassandra, in a tone that suggested that she did not want to hear of him.

"He's a boy who went with Augustus to join the Confederates. After he had been with 'em awhile he decided he'd rather belong to the Union army, so he changed."

The whole table stopped eating to stare at Marcia.

"Deserted!" ejaculated Miss Cassandra.

"You don't mean to say one of this gang of Yankees is a deserter from the Confederate army?" propounded Polycarp with sudden gravity.

Suddenly Marcia remembered that her brother was a spy. She became afraid she had let slip something that would hurt Jerry's friend. She began trying to show how innocent he was.

"Well, now, he didn't know which side he wanted to fight on. He lived back up there in the Tennessee hills where the people are divided. He and Jerry talked about which side to join. Gillie decided on the Confederate because his pappy owned a nigger."

"What in the thunderation did he change for?" stormed old man Jimmie.

Marcia flushed as if she were defending herself.

"He said just one nigger wasn't worth going hungry for."

"Marcia Vaiden," cried Miss Cassandra, "of all mercenary reasons!"

"They're his, not mine!" cried Marcia, more embarrassed than ever.

"What's a nigger got to do with it anyway?" demanded Miss Cassandra. "It's the principle of the thing, right or wrong——"

"Cassie," roared old man Jimmie, "you're as big a fool as Marsh. It's obeying the will of God foreordained from before the foundations of the yeth——"

"Oh, my goodness!" cried Marcia. "How did I get into this? I'm not defending the Yankees! I hate 'em! I hate 'em with all my heart. I wish they were all dead and in their graves!"

Suddenly Marcia began weeping. She got up from the table, leaving her piece of rabbit on her plate, and hurried out into the open passageway between the kitchen and dining room.

The group at the table looked blankly at each other.

"Of all things! What's the matter with Marsh?" puzzled Polycarp.

"She's not well," said Mrs. Laura patiently. "A cry won't hurt her."

In the passageway outside Marcia's tears subsided as quickly as they had arisen. She stood as surprised and disgusted at herself as she was at her family in the dining room. She did not understand how she had been maneuvered into defending Gillie Dilliehay, whom she loathed.

What did she care if he deserted a hundred times? She knew why he did it, that was all, and her family had berated her for knowing.

"The less a person knows in a family like mine," thought Marcia bitterly, "the better off she is!"

She thought how her father was continually harassed, flinging out fools and idiots on every hand because no one ever agreed with him; how her mother went her way silently and was never understood. Presently she stood looking across the plum thicket at the fields beyond, her thoughts quite empty of anything except the gray unhappiness that filled her body and mind.

Presently her eyes followed a movement behind the rail fence that divided the field from the road. The thing darted into view and out again behind the blackberry briers in the fence corners. Then she saw it was Negro George running toward the big house. She became interested, stepped off the passageway and walked toward the fence to meet him.

George, she discovered when she reached him, was hurrying in from sentry duty to report that some Yankees were coming.

The arrival of a squad of Yankees was commonplace and did not explain George's excitement. Marcia inquired their number, thinking there must be a whole company on the road.

"Ain't but one," panted George, widening the white eyes in his dark face. "He come snoopin' up all by hisse'f. I look at him. I say to muhse'f, 'Dat man lookin' fuh a niggah posted roun' de big house . . . dat man ketch me he comb de kinks out'n my haid!' "

"So that was why you ran so hard?"

"My 'spicion didn't hol' me back none."

A sudden, rather surprising notion came to Marcia.

"What sort of a man was he?" she asked intently.

"He—he a great *big* man," stressed George nervously. "He could double me up wid one han' an' set on me."

Marcia's flair died down at such a heroic description.

"You go on in and tell Carp some Yankees are coming," directed the girl, "and I'll go down and see who it is."

"Yes'm," nodded George. "H-he come lookin' dis way an' dat cross de cow pasture. I say to muhse'f, 'Dat man see a niggah posted agin' him, he leave jess a greasy spot whah I stood.' "

"You oughtn't to be afraid," counseled Marcia.

"No'm, I ain't now."

Marcia let herself out the big gate and hurried down the road toward the pasture with an odd feeling of relief from some undefined distress.

However, when she saw, standing in the lane, the man she had expected to see her relief vanished. In its place came that sense of strangeness and disillusion which the actual sight of an acquaintance whom one has once met and enjoyed always brings. She paused, thinking with a touch of irony toward herself, "Why should I hurry down like this to talk to Jerry Catlin? What has he done for me except to get me almost insulted by Mr. Candy McPherson?"

She slowed down her quick welcoming steps and looked across the pasture as if seeking some animal, then turned back.

Jerry Catlin came striding up the lane after her with nothing but a hillman's sense of dignity keeping him from running.

"Miss Marcia! Oh, Miss Marcia!" he called in a subdued voice.

Marcia looked around.

"Why, what are you doing here, Mr. Catlin?" she asked, widening her eyes.

"There was a nigger down here," explained the soldier, conveying a sense of hurry and disturbance, "I wanted to send word by him for you to come down here, but he ran off before I could get to him."

"Good gracious!" ejaculated Marcia with the utmost sincerity. "You were fortunate in that. I certainly wouldn't have come if you'd sent word you were down here."

"Why, Miss Marcia, why couldn't you?" pleaded the soldier in a distressed voice. "You know I've done everything I could to see you. I had arranged to get Mr. Vaiden's horse back but he didn't want it, then I thought he would like to hear about Augustus." Jerry came to a pause.

"Well," said Marcia soberly, "I'm here now."

"Yes, you are," said Jerry hopelessly. "I've been thinking about you ever since you rode with me the other night. But you don't like me much."

"I've thought about you once or twice," admitted Marcia.

"You have! Well . . . but Miss Marcia, your family can't stand me. I can't even get to see you except by accident like this."

For some strange reason, Jerry Catlin's privations took away Marcia's own unhappiness. She felt a sense of comfort, poise, and well being.

"Listen, Jerry," she said, feeling very kindly toward the big unhappy fellow, "it's just as well that everything is like it is." Here Marcia suddenly grew sad for him. "Really better, I suppose," she added in a musing tone.

"I don't see how that can be, Miss Marcia, when a fellow has thought about a girl before he ever saw her . . . just thought and thought about her, day and night. I certainly don't see how that can be."

"Because, even if you weren't a Yankee, and my family liked you, and I wasn't engaged to Captain Gray, still we— we couldn't——"

Marcia hesitated at the word because her thoughts really had run on in advance of the situation.

"You mean we couldn't . . . marry?" queried Jerry in an exalted sotto voce.

The girl colored.

"Well—yes—that was what I meant. We couldn't."

"But why, Miss Marcia?" he asked, having hypothetically climbed over all these obstacles and still not being allowed to marry his goddess.

Marcia drew a breath that lifted the yoke of her dress.

"Well, because—because I think you—you really love me," she said in an uncertain voice.

"But Miss Marcia," cried Jerry, "that's a reason for!"

"No—not in this case," said Marcia sadly. "You see, Jerry I—I love somebody else the same way you do me, only —only more so, I'm afraid."

Jerry drew closer.

"Do you, Miss Marcia?" he asked in a stricken tone.

Marcia nodded with a feeling of profound relief that she had touched this thing that lay in the bottom of her heart.

"Do you love the captain like that?" asked Jerry reverently.

"No," said Marcia in a gray tone. "This man—married somebody else. I—I know I ought to quit thinking about him at all—he's a married man——" Marcia pressed her lips together to keep them from trembling.

Jerry's heart seemed to melt at her trouble. He reached out his arms. "Miss Marcia, cry if you want to," he begged, touching her shoulder.

Marcia did not cry but presently she was leaning against him, with his long arms loosely circled about her. Even while she was enjoying the massive comfort of his embrace she was mentally adjudicating the propriety of the situation. What she permitted seemed to be within the bounds of a confidant. If Jerry went beyond the bounds of some undefined dead line this lenten indulgence would be gently called off. Both of them knew this, and Jerry was just as gingerly uneasy about undue familiarity as was Marcia herself.

"I don't see why you couldn't marry me just as easy as you could Captain Lacefield," Jerry was saying in the midst of this probational adjustment.

"Because I think if a person really loves you, you should really love them in return," explained Marcia. "I think love is the most sacred thing in the world. I wouldn't give a person who really loved me less than I got, not for anything in the world—would you?"

"Oh, no!" cried Jerry.

Her speech was a little like religion to the youth. He didn't quite understand it, but it seemed all the more sacred and beautiful on that account.

"What do you think of love?" asked Marcia amid a great contented sadness for Major Crowninshield.

"Well," said Jerry thoughtfully, "I—I don't think so much about love as I do about girls."

"Other girls besides me?" asked Marcia, lifting wide gray eyes with a trace of old man Jimmie Vaiden's intolerance.

"Oh, no, not since Sister Elvira told me about you," assured Jerry at once.

"Well," agreed Marcia, relaxing gently again, "you're a nice boy, Jerry. I hope some day you'll find a girl who loves you as deeply as you do her. I do really." She stroked the back of his hand with her silken, workless palm. A delicate tingle meandered up her arm from it, and behind her words lay the profound feminine belief that he could never love another woman as he loved her; that on her altar must forever burn the candles of his devotion.

Presently she found he was preparing to go. She asked why he was in such a hurry. He said it was nearly night.

"Well, I declare it is!" she murmured, looking at the yellowing afternoon.

The man held her faintly closer.

"Will you . . . kiss me good-bye, Marcia?" he asked without hope.

"Why, Jerry, you know I won't." She stepped gently but decidedly out of his arms. He had gone over the line at last, as both had known he sooner or later must.

If her family found this out, Marcia knew she was in for a wigging.

When he was gone the girl stood where he had left her and continued to think about her family. What a shindy they would kick up for her talking to a Yankee even though she did not care a tuppence about him. Jerry was simply an agreeable person with whom to pass a few minutes of odd time. She remained in the lane looking in the direction Jerry had gone, filled with a purring comfort.

CHAPTER FORTY

Marcia turned toward home with a pleasant premonition of possibly other accidental meetings with Jerry Catlin, when she observed a woman standing in the big road at the mouth of the pasture lane.

A slight disconcert went through the girl at having been seen talking to a Yankee soldier; then she recognized who the woman was and stopped in amazement.

"Why—Gracie!" she ejaculated, almost unable to believe her eyes.

The quarter-bred girl whirled, caught up her skirts with a white woman's movement when about to run.

"What in the world are you doing here?" asked Marcia.

"I—I came back—just to look at the place, little missy," stammered Gracie.

The quadroon stood questioning Marcia with dramatic black eyes, asking what she was going to do; spread the alarm and have her retaken, or let her go?

"You . . . weren't going on up to the big house?" inquired Marcia delicately.

"I—I hadn't intended to," said Gracie nervously.

"Well," said Marcia, disposing of the point of compulsion, "I imagine Mammy and Aunt Creasy and the rest of 'em would be glad to see you."

"I'd be glad to see them, too, but I—I'm afraid I haven't got time to . . ." Her verbal excuse gave out completely and she simply stood looking at Marcia with sad, grateful eyes for her implied promise of safety.

By this time the dress Gracie wore drew the white girl's attention. It was a silk dress made over in such well-tailored lines that Marcia had not observed its costliness or the fact that Gracie was much further advanced toward motherhood.

For the quadroon to have such a dress at all reiterated what Marcia already knew about Gracie's mode of life. Then it dawned on her why she had come here. Her physical condition had made her drab calling impossible. So here she stood in her finery at the end of the pasture lane.

Marcia did not feel the repulsion toward Gracie which she would have felt toward a white prostitute, because Gracie's mode of life was not so much sinful as inevitable. So now she stood speculating about Gracie with a sort of detachment, wondering how such a life was possible; how a girl as sensitive as Gracie could go on with it—but, of course, she was a negro.

"Where are you going, Gracie?" she asked, not unkindly, with a suspicion that the girl had hoped to hide in the slave quarters and let the other negroes feed her.

"Why, back to camp, little missy," said the quadroon, somewhat surprised in her turn.

"Will they . . . they . . . er . . . you in that condition?" ejaculated Marcia incoherently.

Gracie flushed and said in a low tone, "Lieutenant Beekman said it would be over before long."

"You mean . . . you'll be with him afterwards?"

Gracie moistened her carmine lips and said nothing.

"But Gracie," speculated the white girl, disturbed, "Solomon's child . . . it will be so dark . . . he won't have it around."

An odd expression came over Gracie's face.

"It may not be so dark."

"But—you were in a condition before—you left home?"

"Oh, I suppose it will be dark, too," said Gracie hastily.

Marcia stared at her with an intake of breath.

"Why, no," she gasped, "you—you know it won't——Oh!

Oh!" She caught her breath as if at a pang of some strange far-away pain.

"Why, little missy!" cried Gracie, deeply disturbed. "You know it'll be black, little missy, of—of course it'll be black."

She stood gazing with tears of frustration in her eyes at this girl whom she had spent all her life protecting and caressing and serving and loving. Now, at this last moment, to have given her a thread of a clew that her brother had ravished her.

Marcia moved to the fence, leaned against it, and became as colorless as cotton.

"Why—did you come here at all?" she whispered.

"Little missy," trembled the quadroon, "I—wanted to look at the big house and the cabins and the barn again. I'm going away. Lieutenant Beekman said I was going away."

Marcia pulled herself together.

"Where to?"

"Lieutenant Beekman said up in Tennessee, little missy. Savannah, I think he said."

"Just you . . . and him?"

"Oh, no, everybody's going—they're striking camp now."

Marcia straightened.

"You mean the—the whole army?" she asked incredulously.

"Yes'm; everybody; they got orders to march to Savannah."

"Are they going to a battle?" she cried in a breath.

"Why, I don't know, little missy."

"Oh, they are, I know they are! Oh! Oh, Gracie!"

Gracie stared at this amazing turn.

"Are you sick, little missy?" she cried, terrified. "Must I take you to the big house?"

"Oh, no. Go—please go away!"

The quadroon turned, not knowing why, and went hurrying back down the rutty road toward the camp. Marcia

moved with a sick feeling up the big road toward her home.
The rutty clay beneath her feet seemed to sway. She plodded
onward, seeing nothing at all.

That was why he had come: he was going away to-morrow
to a battle. That was why he had waited for her in the pasture—why he had comforted her—why he had asked her to
kiss him a last good-bye.

As Marcia entered the hallway of the big house Miss
Cassandra called out to her to ask what had happened.
Marcia said nothing was the matter.

"I know better," contradicted the older woman. "Where
have you been and what's happened to you?"

Marcia tried to turn her weeping thoughts about and
think of some truthful thing she could use to deceive her
sister. She drew a long breath.

"I—I've just been talking to—to Gracie," she said.

"Where in the world did you see her?"

"Down at the pasture."

"What were you doing down there?"

"George said he saw a Yankee trying to spy on Polycarp
and I wanted to see."

Marcia expected Cassandra to follow this Yankee clue
and catch her, but Gracie was the more interesting topic.

"What in the world was *she* doing down there?"

"She had come to say good-bye," said Marcia with another long breath.

"Who was she going to say good-bye to?"

"Well . . . nobody, I suppose. She had just come to look
good-bye."

"So that's why you come home tuned up ready to cry,"
said Miss Cassandra, half in sympathy and half in contempt.
"You're too soft, Marcia. You look at things too personally."

"I always think, Suppose it was me," said Marcia sadly.

"I," corrected Miss Cassandra. "And that's where you
make your mistake," she went on with the argument. "You

ought to know a nigger girl hasn't got the fine feelings of a white girl. You put too much in their place. You put more than is there."

"She was about to cry," said Marcia.

"Of course, niggers are emotional, but it doesn't last, they haven't got any bottom."

"No-o," agreed Marcia with a long sigh, "I suppose that's true."

This agreement brought this strand of their talk to an end. After a pause Miss Cassandra's sense of logic took her back to the original cord.

"If she was saying good-bye, she must be going somewhere."

"She is—to Savannah."

"What for?"

"Well, you know that—that fellow she's living with. He's going."

"Thought he belonged to the Yankee army."

"He does."

"Is he going to quit the army?"

"No, the army's going too."

Miss Cassandra came to another blank pause; her mouth dropped open. She drew a sharp breath.

"Do you mean the regiment? The regiment is going to leave Alabama?—they are going to Savannah?"

Marcia looked in surprise at her sister's agitation. A fantastic notion flitted through her head that somebody in the Yankee army admired Miss Cassandra, but immediately this explanation vanished as impossible.

"Why, yes, but—what if they are?" asked Marcia blankly.

Miss Cassandra suddenly began planning.

"Listen," she said tensely, "Polycarp must know this."

"Polycarp!"

"Yes—or Red Kilgo!"

"Who is Red Kilgo?" ejaculated Marcia.

"One of the Leatherwood gang." Miss Cassandra stood thinking intently for a moment. "Run get George, Marcia, and bring him to me!"

A glimmer of dramatic understanding flickered through Marcia. She turned and ran toward the negro cabins, calling George as she went. As she crossed the back yard, old Mrs. Vaiden hallooed from the kitchen to know what she wanted with George.

"Cassandra wants him," said Marcia in as commonplace a voice as she could muster.

"You fin' George in he cabin," prompted old Aunt Creasy.

Marcia ran on, and sure enough George was in the second cabin, asleep after an all-night sentry duty guarding his master. Marcia awoke him and took him to Cassandra.

In the meantime Cassandra had written two notes; one she gave to George and directed him to go to the still house over near the Ham plantation, and if he found either Polycarp or Red Kilgo, to deliver the note, if not to bring it back to her.

"And be sure and not let anyone else see it," cautioned Miss Cassandra. "If you get in a tight place, chew it up and swallow it."

"Lawzee!" ejaculated George.

He took the extraordinary note, put it in his rag of a hat, and set forth to whatever end he might come.

The older sister sat at her table, holding the second note and regarding the girl with a grave face.

"Marcia," she said in a low tone, "I'm thinking of sending you with a note down to Ponny BeShears."

"You mean for Polycarp?"

"Yes, certainly. And there may be a little danger—quite a considerable danger—attached to it."

"I see," nodded the girl.

"But it will help—our country and our armies," explained Miss Cassandra in a lowered tone. "The question is, are you willing to run a risk to do this?"

A sudden sacrificial mood swept over Marcia,

"Why, Cassandra, you know I will!" she cried. "I'll do anything—anything in the world to help the South." And back of Marcia's fervor stood Major Crowninshield. It seemed to Marcia if anything should happen to her and Major Crowninshield hear of it, then he would realize . . . She did not frame her thoughts into words, but she could imagine the man she loved and what he would think when he found out that she, too, was a heroine.

As Marcia set out for BeShears Crossroads the sense of possible danger screwed up her nerves to that equivocal line between downright apprehension and a sort of pleasurable brilliance of attention. Her brain danced about thinking up reasons for calling for Mr. Maldebranch. Half a dozen came so quickly that she was afraid in the pinch of action she would forget them all.

Under her stimulation, she forgot all about Jerry Catlin. As she rode along in the deepening dusk the sepulchral note of an owl reminded her of the night Polycarp and Augustus had stolen away from home to join the army. Now here was she being netted in the vast conflict.

A faint brightening of the sky far away to the west, in the direction of Waterloo, caught her attention. She wondered, with a throb of hatred toward the Yankees, whose house they were burning now. Eliza Ham lived in that direction; so did the Treadwells and the Binghams. She studied the illumination, trying to place it in the dark vacuity of the night.

Two dim gleams down the road apprised Marcia that she was nearing the store and residence at the Crossroads. Marcia rode old Rab up to the BeShears gate, tossed her reins over the post, slipped off onto the fence, and thence to the ground.

As she did so a faint start went through her at the guarded click of the BeShears door being opened. After a moment someone came hurrying down the path toward her.

Then the plump form of Ponny BeShears developed against the darkness and came to a stand, staring quite blankly at the visitor.

"Marcia Vaiden!" she ejaculated. "What are you doing here by yourself at this time o' night?"

The two girls embraced and kissed automatically.

"Listen, Ponny—do you know where Carp is?" whispered Marcia.

"Why, no, I don't, Marcia," replied Ponny quickly.

The way she said it told Marcia that she did know, for Ponny was no stickler for those half truths that formed the basis of Marcia's deceptions. Marcia hardly knew how to proceed. A thought flashed through her that Ponny might be inclined toward the Yankee cause.

"Listen, Ponny," said the girl earnestly. "I've got to find Polycarp!"

"What for?"

"Why-y—I want to—tell him good-bye."

Ponny's face took on a different expression.

"Oh, then—you know?"

"Know what?"

Ponny hesitated. The trouble was, both girls had secrets to keep from each other. "Why—where he is," said Ponny; then she ran on whispering quickly, "I was expecting him here. When I heard you stop at the gate I thought it was him and ran out."

Marcia recalled the blobby feel of Ponny during their brief embrace and wondered how her brother could like that.

"Listen, Ponny, I don't know where he is," persuaded Marcia desperately, "and I have something I just must give Polycarp."

"Marcia, if I knew . . ." lied Ponny earnestly.

"Listen," begged the sister, swallowing her anger at Ponny, "even if you don't know, could you give me some idyah about where he usually is? I—don't want to go around inquiring for him."

She could have choked Ponny for keeping back her information.

Ponny was instinctively good natured. She was torn between impulses to keep Polycarp's secret and to reveal it to Marcia. She pressed her friend's finger.

"Listen, Marcia, why—why don't you inquire down about the—the——— Oh, Marcia, I kain't tell you!"

"You've got to! You've got to, Ponny BeShears!"

"Well then," trembled Ponny, at the end of her resistance, "w-why don't you go—down to the Lacefield place and—ask Mr. Lacefield?"

"Does he know?"

"I don't know," said Ponny, resolving to lock her stable, now that the horse was gone.

"Well, all right—I'll ride down."

As Marcia agreed to this, the door of the residence opened again and a slow thumping sounded on the narrow porch. Marcia turned in astonishment and saw a dim heavy figure on crutches leaning and swinging and clumping across the porch onto the graveled path toward the gate.

She whirled to Ponny in amazement.

"Who is that, Ponny?"

Ponny did not glance at the approaching figure.

"Pappy," she said in a sad tone.

"You don't mean———" Marcia gasped into silence. She had heard that the storekeeper had to use crutches but it had not impressed her. Now, to see him swinging along through the darkness was inexpressibly shocking.

"Talk! Talk!" whispered Ponny urgently. "He gits mad if you watch him!"

"As I was saying," began Marcia hurriedly, "he—he—asked me to kiss him, but I———"

"Why didn't you?" rushed Ponny.

"I—wanted to go to Florence and get a new dress———" Marcia bit off the talk about dresses, wondering what in the world made her say that.

The appalling clumping paused at the gate beside them and the incoherent conversation stopped. The cripple peered through the night.

"Who is that you're a-talking to, Ponny?" he asked in a heavy voice.

"It's Marcia, Pappy," stammered the daughter.

"A Vaiden!" ejaculated the storekeeper in a harder voice. "A Vaiden come to look at me, has she?"

"Why, Mr. BeShears!" gasped Marcia, disconcerted, "I—I hope you'll get well soon."

"Get well! Get well when your feet air gone! You hypocritical——" He unlatched the gate with difficulty and swung his heavy body through. He closed it and stood for a moment, panting from his exertion. "What air you doing here anyway, Marsh Vaiden?" he burst out with an increase of anger. "Ain't it enough to beat me out o' my account an' burn my feet an' steal my money——"

"Pappy!" cried Ponny outraged. "You know Marcia didn't have a thing to do——"

"Listen, Ponny," stammered Marcia, utterly confused by this attack, "I must go down to the Lacefields' . . ."

"Don't go on my account," snarled the merchant; "talk here with Ponny all you want to. She loves the Vaidens. She's a Vaiden worshiper!" The crippled man spat, turned painfully, and went clumping and swinging in the direction of his store.

Ponny seized her visitor's hands.

"Oh, Marcia," she plead, "don't hold that against me. I can't he'p it—he's wild about being robbed."

"What does he keep saying 'Vaiden, Vaiden' for like that?" asked Marcia with a painful recurrence of her own suspicions.

"Why-y, I don't know," stammered Ponny. "He—just doesn't like your family."

Marcia pressed Ponny's hand with a question on the verge of utterance: "Ponny, does he think Polycarp . . ."

It was like plunging into a cold, bottomless pool. The sister could not utter it—and then, of course, he did think it.

The fat girl kept on soothingly and apologetically:

"He'll never get over it. I don't mean his feet—of course they won't. I mean the way he hates the Leatherwood gang. He told me he wished he could put all those men in a furnace and—and—— Oh, Marcia, he sits and wishes he could do such horrible things to them!"

Marcia felt sick. In her thoughts she cried out:

"Oh, do you think Polycarp helped burn him? Do you think it, Ponny?"

She asked these question with such silent concentration that Ponny looked at her oddly.

"What's the matter? You—you're not mad at me, are you, Marcia?"

"Oh, Ponny, you know I'm not. Oh, I feel so terrible! Hold old Rab close to the fence so I can climb on."

"Listen, Marcia," advised Ponny earnestly, "if you feel as bad as that don't go down to the Lacefields'."

"Why?"

"It's a sign."

Marcia hesitated.

"I—I don't believe in signs," she answered weakly.

She said this because her sister Cassandra would have said it, but Marcia did believe in signs. A portent filled her with fear as she uttered it.

"Well," said Ponny, "if you don't believe in them, maybe nothing will happen to you. Oh, I hope not!" Suddenly she put her arms around Marcia, hugged the girl to her heavy bosom, kissing her lips.

"If you do see Polycarp," she sobbed, "tell him, I—tell him I love him. Tell him I love him with every drop of my blood—no matter—no matter what——"

And so Marcia's wordless question was answered without words.

CHAPTER FORTY-ONE

So Ponny thought Polycarp was implicated in the attack upon her father, or at least she was not sure that he was not.

And old man Alex BeShears was so bitter and revengeful . . . as he had a right to be. Marcia's sense of justice agreed to that. And yet he had brought it all down on his own head. What calamities had followed in the wake of Alex BeShears' money hunger. He had tried to foreclose and had caused Gracie to be beaten and driven away from home to a life of prostitution in the army. He had sold his negroes and buried his money and invited torture and robbery on himself, and, as far as Marcia knew, he had turned her brother into an outlaw.

No human wisdom could have foreseen such consequences.

And it came to Marcia, as she rode along toward the Lacefield manor, that love and kindness and generosity were a sort of ready-made foresight, a kind of simple wisdom which anyone might use if only he had the heart to do so.

This idea came to the girl with the newness of a revelation. Not once in all the religious arguments that had frothed in her home had she ever heard such a notion advanced. It lighted up her thoughts on this war-filled night with a kind of beauty as she rode on toward the Yankee encampment.

An illumination glowing on the horizon in the direction she was traveling drew Marcia's attention. The girl gazed ahead, kicked the patient ribs of her mule and urged the animal into a stiff trot. As she drew nearer along the soft dark road, the far-away crests of the silver poplars stood painted in red against the blackness of the night.

A stab of apprehension went through Marcia's heart. She saw the manor was burning. She gasped aloud, "Oh, my Lord, it's the manor!"

She shook the reins and kicked the mule into a longer trot, staring fascinated at the distant fire. Presently she could see an occasional tongue of flame or a gush of sparks lick the sky. A faint movement among the trees told her that the silver poplars were swaying and bending in the storm of the heat. The girl pushed on her mule with a feeling of horror. After the Yankees had used the plantation and made their headquarters in the manor, then, on their final night, they had burned it.

Three quarters of a mile farther on the girl rode into an illuminated area and saw scores of tiny silhouettes running to and fro against the flames. They were the Lacefield negroes fighting the fire. On Marcia's right hand, spread over the Lacefield pastures, lay the tents of the Yankees, looking a dim red in the doleful light of the fire.

Soldiers were everywhere idly watching the black men fight the flames. Stationed at regular intervals along the edge of the fields were sentinels with guns. These continued marching slowly up and down their post looking at the flames. Their inertia amazed and angered Marcia. She directed her mule toward one of the sentinels.

"Why don't you soldiers help?" she shouted, pointing wrathfully at the flames.

"We set it afire," said the man in a matter-of-fact Yankee voice.

His Northern brogue completely stripped away any feeling of tragedy or drama that gave beauty to the scene. It was a prosaic burning of enemy material.

When she rode still closer Marcia saw that the actual flames arose from the negro shacks, but that a great smoke was coming out of the doors and windows of the manor itself. She rode between the stone pillars of the gate into the grove of disturbed red-lit poplars.

All the Lacefield slaves, men and women, swarmed in and out of the manor with buckets. High up on top of the building, on the observatory, were posted more negroes with buckets to combat the sparks from the cabins. Marcia wondered what would happen to these negroes if the fire below got out of control.

The girl looked about and saw Mr. Lacefield on the great piazza directing his slaves. He did not appear excited but she could hear his voice sharpened by the exigency calling, "Blue Gum, string your men up the stairs! Henry, keep your men on the second floor. . . . How are the niggers on the roof getting on?"

Inside the smoking building the questions were relayed: "How de niggahs on de roof? Need any mo' niggahs on de roof?"

As Marcia. watched, she suddenly found her heart full of her old love and affection for Mr. Lacefield. And she thought with a clutch in her bosom, If only A. Gray had been like his father!

Marcia had followed the driveway. Now she glanced around and with a faint start of surprise saw Drusilla standing quite close to her on the horse block. The moment Marcia saw her she thought of her not as Drusilla Lacefield, but as Drusilla Crowninshield. The young woman wore a loose dress and the way it hung about her revealed the heavy shape of approaching motherhood. This notation was swept away by Marcia in sympathy for the destruction around her. She directed her mule a little nearer the young wife.

"Drusilla, isn't this terrible!" she called above the shouts and roar of the negro huts. "I'm so sorry for you, honey."

The wife looked around and required a moment to realize who was there.

"We didn't expect this, Marcia," she said, with her lips

pressed close and her face quite colorless, except for the darkened circles of pregnancy about her eyes.

"You might have expected it from Yankees!"

"Colonel Higgenbotham had his headquarters in our parlor. We—we tried to—treat him as a—a guest."

It was evident that Drusilla was about to weep with bitterness over her wrongs.

Marcia compressed her lips.

"Whyn't you poison him!"

Drusilla gave a dry sob.

"How did we know he—he was going to do this when—when he left!"

Marcia sat in her saddle, vibrant to such a double outrage.

"Anybody that would trust a Yankee with—anything——" The impossibility of compressing her contempt into words balked her.

"I didn't know what, but I knew some terrible thing was going to happen by the water buckets," said Drusilla.

"Water buckets?"

"Yes—everywhere."

"Whose water buckets?"

"Papa got them from Colonel Higgenbotham and put them around everywhere."

Marcia stared at this amazing news. She supposed that Mr. Lacefield had foreseen this catastrophe and had borrowed the Yankee's own water buckets—he had so many.

"Well, I'm glad he understood what snakes they were. . . . Oh, listen, Drusilla, can I speak to your father?"

Drusilla looked from the flames to Marcia in astonishment.

"You want to speak to Father now?"

Marcia nodded earnestly.

"Is it that important?" asked Drusilla, lowering her tone at Marcia's manner.

"I don't know how important it is," said Marcia, glancing about to see that no one overheard her.

"We-ell," agreed Drusilla. She began watching the nearer negroes with buckets and presently called out:

"Oh, Lovey—come here a moment."

The mulatto sempstress who had made over Marcia's wedding gown detached herself from the water bearers and came clay colored and panting to her mistress.

"Lovey, go tell Papa that Miss Marcia Vaiden is here and wants to see him as soon as she can."

Lovey curtsied and hurried into the swarm again. Within a few minutes she returned with the message:

"Mas' Caruthers say he hope Miss Marcia will excuse him for a few minutes till he can make his house safe."

The white girl assured the mulatto she could wait, then before Marcia really expected him Mr. Lacefield came out to the mounting block. Drusilla made some excuse for going away and her father helped her carefully to the ground. She moved away with the swaying step of a gravid woman.

Mr. Lacefield came up gravely to his caller.

"Marcia, my girl, I am sorry to receive you like this. You find me at the ebb tide of fortune." He glanced toward his house to see how his negroes were getting along.

"Ought you to go back?" asked Marcia uneasily.

"Not till I know how I can assist you, Marcia." He put his hand on old Rab's neck and looked at her with grave, protective eyes.

The mere presence and manner of the aristocrat lifted Marcia's mood into something elevated above the mere brute violence and reprisals of the neighborhood.

She bent down and pressed the hand on the neck of the mule.

"Listen, Mr. Lacefield—I have a message for Polycarp."

"Polycarp!"

"My brother. He goes by the name of Maldebranch."

"And where do you think he is?" asked the aristocrat intently.

"Ponny said to ask you, I might find him at your place."

"Did she say at my place?"

Marcia tried to think back.

"She might have said near your place."

"Marcia," said the planter in an undertone, "what—what color uniform did you expect to find him wearing?"

"Uh—uh—blue," stammered Marcia.

"Then Ponny may have been trying to give you a hint that your brother is . . ." The aristocrat nodded slightly toward the Union lines.

Marcia caught her breath.

"You mean as a regular——" Marcia moistened her lips. She could not say the word "spy." It was too detestable.

She sat staring at the tents.

"How will I ever get to him to tell him what I know?" she whispered.

"Marcia, my dear girl, I wouldn't think of letting you attempt such a thing."

"But listen, Mr. Lacefield," pressed the girl with growing excitement, "this is important to our armies. Why, Mr. Lacefield, if I could somehow tell him——"

"No! No!" cried the aristocrat revulsively. "Dear Marcia, I wouldn't dream of letting you run such a terrible risk!"

"But I am no better than A. Gray and Miltiades and Polycarp himself!"

"Marcia, dearest," cried the planter in a rush of tenderness, "you're a woman. You are the reason why my son and your brothers and all the countless men of the South are in uniform to-night. You are the saint on the altar, Marcia, before whom they all lay down their lives."

Of a sudden Marcia despised herself for ever thinking of Jerry Catlin. A sharp devotion to A. Gray Lacefield rushed upon her. She pressed the father's hand against the flat bony part of her chest above her breasts.

"Help me think of some reason for going inside," she whispered in an uplifted voice. "I am going on as far as . . . I live to go."

CHAPTER FORTY-TWO

Although Mr. Lacefield dissuaded Marcia Vaiden from her undertaking with every entreaty he could lay tongue to, it was his misfortune that his mere presence, his courtliness, and the admiration for her which shone through his anxiety urged the girl on in her enterprise. Where Polycarp or Augustus could have turned her from her purpose with a breath of home-made ridicule, the aristocrat cemented her. Both she and Mr. Lacefield supposed she was acting from pure love of country. Neither was aware that her audience had anything to do with it.

Marcia had to ransack her brains to hit upon a motive for entering the Union lines, and finally she fell upon the recovery of old Joe. The Yankees had been returning a few horses and cows to the milder secessionist families in the neighborhood, so Marcia had a precedent.

As the girl remounted her mule she said to Mr. Lacefield that it seemed almost providential the Yankees had ever taken old Joe. Whereupon the planter returned grimly that it was always best to decide what was providential and what was not after the fact and not before. At the moment, Marcia supposed the observation to be humor.

A few minutes later, when she actually was riding from the Lacefield gate toward the sentinels pacing back and forth with their muskets, any quality of humor that the planter may have intended disappeared for Marcia.

The Yankee encampment spread darkly away as far as her eyes could penetrate. Marcia did not ride up to the first sentry. She moved along the road counting the guards, wondering what number it would be the luckiest to approach. She finally decided on the twelfth because there were twelve Apostles and also because it was a large number and would allow her to ride some distance before she had to turn in. At last, however, even eleven sentries were passed, and with a chill going over her skin Marcia turned out of the road and approached the twelfth.

When the man halted her Marcia said she was a friend without the countersign. When he asked what she wanted, Marcia began her complaint about old Joe. They had taken her father's horse.

Why hadn't she come for it during the day?

Marcia had just heard the Yankees were going to leave the country.

Why hadn't she come for it long ago?

She had intended to as soon as she found out they were giving back livestock, but she had kept putting if off day after day.

"And I suppose you put it off till to-night for the same reason," opined the Yankee. "You certainly are Southern."

Marcia sat a little straighter in her saddle.

"And you Yankees stole old Joe the very first day you got here," she retorted. "You certainly are Northern."

There was a pause, then the sentry said with an edge of amusement in his voice:

"We don't seem to have much trouble with each other's geography."

Then he asked her name and called the corporal of the guard.

As Marcia waited uneasiness came over her again. She realized now she could easily miss Polycarp even if he were in the camp. She had had no idea that there were so many tents. She had come a long way from the Lacefields' and still there were tents. She looked back and saw the coals of the burned slave houses gleaming in red patches among the trees. Unless luck were on her side she could very well never find Polycarp at all.

A corporal came and asked Marcia to follow him.

As he led the way a discomforting thought came to the girl. Never before had she had men in opposition to her. Always men had been anxious to serve her and please her. Now this heavy man whom she followed moved along without any of that solicitousness which she had always received.

She rode on up a dim canvas street to a tent with a light glowing through its sides. The corporal paused here, opened the flaps and saluted.

"This is the girl, sir," he reported, and brought his hand stiffly down across his front. He allowed Marcia to slide down from the mule herself.

In the tent at a table sat four officers. The oldest man Marcia supposed was Colonel Higgenbotham. He had the thin closed lips, clipped beard, and level dictatorial eyes of West Point.

A smaller man sat by the colonel's side watching Marcia. He had a choppy blond mustache and the blue, slightly puffed and glazed eyes of a man who has indulged too much and too recently in women. A third officer put out a camp chair for the girl.

The younger man asked what sort of claim Marcia wanted to file. The girl began an uncertain explanation that she hoped to recover her father's horse.

"Who is your father?" asked the small blond man.

"James Vaiden."

The blond officer became more attentive.

"And you are . . ."

"Marcia Vaiden."

"Your father is certainly no Union sympathizer, Miss Vaiden."

"No-o, he isn't."

"Did he send you here to try to recover his horse?"

"No, I just came myself."

"Why did you come at this hour?"

"I heard the army was going away and I thought I'd try to get the horse."

"How did you hear the detachment was going away?"

"Why, everybody knows it," said Marcia. "The men are packing up their things."

"That's true," agreed the blond man incisively, "but some one must have told you. Who did?"

The girl drew in a breath.

"We were talking about it over at the fire a moment ago."

"But you came down here from your home to get the horse, didn't you?"

"Yes, of course."

"Then you must have heard we were going before you reached the fire?"

"Y-yes, I did," agreed the girl vaguely.

"Then who told you?"

" 'Y—it must have been one of our niggers," said Marcia, clinging to a literal truth. "They tell us almost everything we hear."

The blond officer frowned and stirred in his camp chair.

"Why can't you say negroes? They possess at least a proper racial name."

Marcia was astonished at such a question.

"I said niggers," she repeated, faintly offended at his manner.

The elder officer spoke up.

"That is of no importance in this inquiry, Captain Beekman."

Captain Beekman paused, tapped the camp table with his pencil, and scrutinized Marcia out of his glazed eyes.

"We would like to know, Miss Vaiden, have you any further information than the mere fact that the detachment will decamp in the morning?"

Marcia wondered how she would get out of that question without telling an outright falsehood.

"I—I just know you're going"; and then added hastily, "Of course I know lots of other things besides that."

"Do you happen to know where we are going?" inquired Beekman incisively.

Marcia became silent. Her fingers twitched on the handkerchief that held her note in its knot.

"I don't know where you are going." She faintly stressed the word "know," meaning that Gracie's information might be false and she did not *know* that the Union army was going to Savannah.

Beekman scrutinized the trepidant girl with her fantastic clinging to a verbal truthfulness.

"You didn't come here to-night hoping to see someone, did you?"

A faint shiver went over Marcia again.

"Yes . . . I did."

"Who?"

"Colonel Higgenbotham about ol' Joe."

"And that's all?"

"Well, if I got ol' Joe I might inquire about ol' Lou," said Marcia with a faint smile.

The gray-bearded officer interrupted this empty questioning:

"Young woman, we were expecting you to come here tonight. However, our informant could easily have been some disgruntled neighbor of yours. I am going to send you back to your home under escort, and I want you to remain there."

Marcia drew a breath of relief.

"And I—don't get the horse?" she asked automatically.

"No, you don't get the horse," said Colonel Higgenbotham dryly.

The gray man arose with an appearance of relief. Beekman seemed irritated. He too, got up with a slight frown on his acute features. He moved toward the girl, looking her up and down, then reached out quite unexpectedly.

"You have a pretty handkerchief," he said.

He took it out of her hands and looked at it.

"Here's a knot in the corner of it."

"Come! Come!" snapped Colonel Higgenbotham. "We have no time to waste."

Beekman swiftly undid the knot.

"And there seems to be paper in the knot."

"Damn it, Beekman," growled Higgenbotham in an undertone, "what officer here hasn't seen that God-damned knot!"

Nevertheless, the knot had been untied before the court, and the message on it presently was read:

"Higgenbotham's regiment on march to Savannah, Tennessee. Federal concentration at that point."

The senior officer's face went as gray as his beard.

"Girl," he said brittly, "you seem to have more information than I have myself . . . a Federal concentration at Savannah."

In her fright Marcia knew that her sister Cassandra had guessed at the concentration. It was like her to put down her guesses as absolute fact and forward them to the Confederate headquarters.

"Do you know the penalty of espionage, young woman?" inquired the colonel.

Marcia stood gripping the camp table, stricken with this sudden reversal of her fortune. She framed the best defence possible:

"Colonel Higgenbotham, this—this isn't espionage," she stammered.

"Why in the hell isn't it?" demanded the officer, furious that he had to deal with a pretty girl.

"B-because," chattered Marcia, "espionage is t-to take information out of a c-camp. I—I'm b-bringing it in."

Such a ridiculous plea accentuated Marcia's helplessness as she stood looking frightened at the men.

"I swear," growled the colonel, "if every Southerner is a sophist like this no wonder they based their slave holding on the Declaration of Independence and the Constitution of the United States."

Captain Beekman did not go off into moralizings on the matter.

"If you will tell us who you meant to give this information to, Miss Vaiden," he offered, "we'll let you go home anyway."

Marcia remained silent.

The court martial spent another five minutes threatening and persuading her to tell where she got the information and to whom she meant to deliver it, but the girl remained silent.

Eventually they turned her over to the corporal again to be taken to the guard house.

The guard house in which Marcia found herself at last was a small frame room lighted by a lantern. In the door sat a man with a musket and a bayonet on the end of the musket. Its only window was a small square hole cut up near the roof for ventilation. Through this hole Marcia could see the faint shaking light of a star.

Every detail of the guard house seemed unbelievable to the girl—the vile bunk with its stench of urine and drunkard's vomitings, the man who sat motionless with his gun. It seemed unbelievable that if she should start to walk out into the night he would force her back into this horrible guard house.

She sat on the foot of the bunk, the least stained spot she could find. She sat with her hands on her lap and seemed to herself to be thinking intently. But she was thinking about nothing. Bits of thought arose and vanished from the surface of her mind: the note in the handkerchief . . . her sister Cassandra who had gone to bed by now . . . the group of officers around the table which she had not recognized as a court martial. They were in sitting, waiting to try her, waiting for her to come. Someone had informed them that she was coming, and she thought of Ponny.

Marcia sat with her hands in her lap, her sick breath coming and going in long sighs. She wondered what her father and mother would say when they heard that she had been shot. She thought of her poor little mother and began to weep.

No notion of A. Gray or Jerry Catlin or Major Crowninshield entered her mind under the threat of imminent death.

Men would kill her. Men, who had served her and wooed her favor all her life had now turned their strength against her because she had brought a tiny scrap of paper—a little sentence knotted in a handkerchief——

Just then a voice in Marcia's ear said, "Alex BeShears told the officers you were coming." It sounded as clearly as if the voice came from some other person, but it was deep inside her head and Marcia knew it was something within herself.

"Yes, that's true," said Marcia to the voice: "he is the only one who would have told—Ponny wouldn't."

"What will he think when he hears you are shot?" asked the voice.

"I don't know," said Marcia sadly. "What difference will it make?"

"He will be glad and bitterer than ever," said the voice, "more hopelessly in hell."

This frightened Marcia. She hushed answering the voice in her head and sat where she was, unconscious that anything strange or abnormal had happened within her.

At sometime during the night the watch changed. The guard she first saw went away and a blond-haired soldier came to take his place.

The almost white hair of the youth finally caught the girl's attention. She kept looking at him, recalling him vaguely, but the main thing that his presence impressed upon her was that the night was half gone.

The last night she would ever know was half gone.

She begged some information of this new guard.

"Gillie," she said in a faint voice, "when will—they shoot me?"

"Miss Marcia," returned Gillie, "I—I don't think they're —going to shoot you, Miss Marcia."

"Not shoot me?"

"Not *shoot* you," stressed Gillie unhappily.

The girl stared at him, coming completely back to the guard house, the stench, and the bunk.

"Gillie," she breathed in horror, "they're not going to— to———" She paused, staring, terrified, at this change in mode of her death. To be stood on a scaffold before endless ranks of soldiers . . . to have her neck bent hideously . . .

"Gillie, I'm afraid I'll twist and struggle—before everybody."

"Miss Marcia," said Gillie unsteadily, "I—I'll pray God not to let you. I'll stand as clost as I can an' pray God not to let you."

Marcia drew a great breath that lifted her small bosom.

"Oh, Gillie, what made you ever desert our army? What made you ever want to come to a place like this?"

"Miss Marcia," choked Gillie, "I wush to God I was out of it! I'd ruther go hongry a year———" He broke off, unable to finish his sentence, if it had an end.

Marcia sat staring at her guard.

"I wonder what God will think of me—being hanged?"

"I don't know, Miss Marcia."

Marcia fell to thinking of God—her father's God—a terrible bloodthirsty creature who burned his creatures forever because he had created them to sin and be burned. To others he was merciful, and there was no reason for that either. He was just like the war and the Yankees.

She heard but did not heed a thump and a muffled bumping on the floor. She was lost in the contemplation of that senseless amoral force that had created the world and was personified by the old Baptist God.

Someone clutched her arm,

"Get up! Damn it, Marcia, get up and get out of here quick!"

The girl stared into the peremptory brown-bearded face of Mr. Maldebranch.

"Carp!" she gasped, rising with a sudden nervous strength rushing into her weak body.

"Step outside, out of the light. Wait a minute while I finish killing this damned deserter." He strode toward the prostrate form of Dilliehay.

She grabbed his arm.

"Let him alone! He's sorry! You're not God!"

And she pushed him ahead of her out into the night.

CHAPTER FORTY-THREE

On the following morning, sun-up found Polycarp Vaiden riding through the hills that lie between Alabama and Tennessee. When he thought of his sister Marcia at all it was with sharp irritation that she should have entered the Union camp with a message for him. She had told him, it is true, that the Yankee detachment had been ordered to Savannah, but he would have found that out for himself— or at least he probably would. And suppose she had found him instead of him finding her; she would have got both of them hanged.

Although Marcia had told him the very thing Polycarp had been ordered to find out, an endless derogation of the sister went on in the head of the brother.

However, these detractions occupied no great portion of Polycarp Vaiden's thoughts. He kept reflecting how loyal Ponny BeShears had shown herself in keeping his secret. Ponny had reported to him everything she had overheard from the soldiers in the store. That, as it happened, never turned out to be of any major military importance, but anyway it gave Polycarp a thrill of romance, admiration, and gratitude to feel that Ponny had shared his danger with him. As he rode along he murmured to himself:

"My brave darling Ponny! My heroine!"

Here his rhapsody was interrupted by the sight of an old hill woman coming out of a cabin wrapped against the faint chill of morning in a heavy blue army overcoat.

Polycarp drew up, surprised at the odd garment, when the old woman ejaculated:

"Did ye git left behin', young man?"

Polycarp asked left behind what.

"Why, the airmy, in course," cried the yellowed old woman. "It passaged my cabin fer three days."

"What army was it?" asked the youth in amazement.

"Why, some of 'em said hit was the Yankee airmy, an' some of 'em said hit was Gin'ral Buell's airmy, an' I'll be tuckered if I jest rightly know who it b'longed to. But hit was the dad-blamedest airmy I ever seen. They went by th'owin' away their coats an' blankets an' ever'thing. . . . Sairey! Oh, Sairey! Bring me some of them thar blankets an' coats, this gen'leman might want to buy some."

At her call a younger, yellowish, bony woman came to the door of the cabin with her long sinewy arms full of blue coats and gray army blankets.

"This is jest a part of 'em, mister," said the younger woman. "I reckon we picked up enough jest about to outfit the whole neighborhood."

The two hill women were overflowing with satisfaction at their salvage.

"Where was this army going?" questioned Polycarp.

"They was a-travelin' the Savannah end o' the road."

"What were they throwing away their things for?"

"Why, they 'peared to be in a kind of a rush, didn't they, Sairey?"

"When they stopped here to fill up their little tin jugs with watter," said Sairey, "they 'lowed hit was too hot for overcoats. Two of 'em jest give us theirn right off'n their backs."

"Was this army in retreat?" asked Polycarp.

"They was in a hurry, mister."

"Were they running away from a fight?" pressed the spy.

"Oh, no," stated the old woman at once. "When a man's a humpin' it to a fight he throws away his coat; when he's

humpin' it away from a fight, he throws away his gun; but
nary a gun did these fellers throw away, did they, Sairey?"

"Nary a one," said Sairey, "an' right glad Mam Kilgo
and me air that it was coats and not guns they was
a-sheddin'."

The name Kilgo struck Polycarp. He asked if they knew
Red Jim Kilgo.

The old woman said:

"Not very well. I'm jest his mammy an' Sairey there
ain't nothin' but his wife." And at this both women broke
out laughing.

Polycarp was full of news of Red Jim, and the wife and
mother must have him in the cabin to give him his breakfast.

In the cabin Polycarp bolted down the multifarious breakfast such as the hill folk set forth: fried squirrel, cold greens,
cold fried pumpkin, cold chicken slick 'ums, and the leavings
of all the previous meals. It was all heaped forth in honor of
their guest. Some of the crockery was the heavy earthenware
characteristic of the hills; some of it delicate china which
Red Jim had brought home as his part of the spoils of the
Leatherwood gang. None of it matched. The very cup and
saucer out of which Polycarp drank wartime burnt molasses
coffee were of different designs. The two women knew that
this was wrong and old Mrs. Kilgo apologized for the mis-
mated ware.

"Men ain't got no taste about sich things," she drawled,
taking the wet cloth top off the crock of butter which she
had brought from the spring. "Red Jim and his bunch jest
divide up ever'thing they git, lickety split, usin' no jedgment a tall. I tell him if him an' Bill Leatherwood would
bring ever'thing they captured to me, we'd all be better off.
But you might as well talk to the bulls o' Bayshan as men."

Polycarp held up and looked at his cup in the dark cabin.

"He gets this stuff from Union and Confederate families
alike, doesn't he?" inquired the spy.

"I can explain that," said the old woman amiably, and

taking no offense at all. "I ast Red Jim 'bout that very thing. Says I, 'Red Jim,' says I, 'how come that?' Says he, 'Maw, we rob the Yankee sympathizers becaze we're agin' 'em; an' we rob the Confederit sympathizers to keep the damn Yankees from gittin' it an' usin' it against the South.'"

Polycarp drew out his handkerchief and wiped his mouth.

"I guess he's right," he said.

"Yeh, Red Jim thinks up a good moral reason for ever'thing he does," commended the old woman heartily. "Well, I trained him right, from a baby. Even if I do say it as oughtn't, me bein' his maw, I will say Red Jim Kilgo, take him by an' large, is one of the most conscientious men I ever knowed."

When Polycarp finished his breakfast and was ready to take his leave he asked his hostess how much he owed, for such is the hill formula of courteous leavetaking. Old Mrs. Kilgo was just as urbane.

"Now, don't make me mad by offerin' no pay. I wusht I could give ever'thing I got in this cabin to he'p the Southern sojers."

So when Polycarp took his leave, the women were in a blaze of patriotic fervor.

The Federal overcoats and blankets which the Kilgo women had picked up hurried the Confederate on his journey to Corinth. The haste of Buell's army suggested a major strategic movement to the scout. By following the route Higgenbotham's detachment would take he had stumbled upon the line of a forced march made by one of the national grand armies.

Common sense told Polycarp that this major maneuver must be well known to the Confederate generals in Corinth. So he did not follow out his instructions to report on exactly Colonel Higgenbotham's regiment. But like all American civilian subordinates, he issued new orders to

himself to fit the situation. He decided he would go to
Corinth by way of Savannah, see just how many Yankees
were there, and then report everything when he reached
Corinth. He had an idea that he would probably be promoted
to a corporalcy—not that he cared anything about that.

The road he followed was cut to pieces. The tread of
thousands of infantry had made the dust ankle deep in
places while artillery and wagons had churned up the perpetual mud holes of Southern roads into loblollies. Along the
way were strewn not only coats and blankets, but cartridge
boxes, old newspapers, cups, bent bayonets that had been
used as pokers for camp fires. This wastage described to
Polycarp the careless roistering columns that had just
marched through the country to the concentration at
Savannah. It was like following the path of a cyclone.

From the time Polycarp struck the trail of the Federals,
he forecast a battle. As he hurried forward, he became terribly afraid he would be late. He listened subconsciously for
signals of the coming storm.

The afternoon was very hot and a remote thunder filled
him with apprehension that the battle had begun. At about
an hour by sun he had reached the outskirts of Savannah.
He emerged from the hills and overlooked a wide stretch of
Tennessee river-bottom land. Above the horizon arose a pall
of light-colored smoke, and broken bellowings rumbled continually from the river itself. Then above the trees the spire
of a church and the bright-colored flag of the Federals came
into view. As he rode nearer he saw innumerable tents, and
then companies of blue coats drilling in empty fields. They
marched up and down in the irregular lines of raw recruits.

Polycarp had no difficulty in entering the village. Nel-
son's army was there. Buell's army had just arrived. The
streets of the little town were full of soldiers so new they did
not know how to find their own encampment, much less

detect a Confederate secret-service man who was equally raw.

Young Vaiden stopped and watched a captain drilling his troops. He would call out, "Now, gentlemen, give me your attention." He was a lawyer out of an Indiana town and had just learned the manual of arms. He knew nothing of the practice of war. He simply had heard that by following these evolutions groups of men would be enabled to slaughter other groups of men more expeditiously.

The Federal concentration at Savannah was far too huge and complicated for any intelligent summation by Polycarp. Five armies were encamped within a radius of twelve miles. The smoke he had seen afar off was from Commodore Foote's flotilla at the river landing. There were so many steamboats and they moved about with such confusion that they might have been sixty or seventy. Their whistles of arrival or departure kept the air full of organ tones.

As Polycarp stood on the high bluff at Savannah overlooking the landing and the flotilla, a great cheering broke out among the soldiers down at the landing below. He asked a soldier near him the cause of the shouting. The man pointed to several officers walking to one of the steamers. They were grouped about a heavily made bearded man limping along on crutches. He wore a loose plain uniform and a slouch hat.

"Why, it's General Grant and his staff!" exclaimed the soldier excitedly.

"Which one is the general?" cried Polycarp.

"Good God'l Mighty!" flung out the soldier, and went running down the steep bank to join the cheering throng.

Polycarp followed pell mell, caught up in the excitement. The general and his staff went aboard a steamer. Polycarp saw the name "Tyler" in huge black letters across the engine room.

Each transport had three gangways laid to the shore, amidship, bow, and stern. Polycarp mixed himself in the crowd and drifted aboard the *Tyler* on the stern gangplank while the staff entered at the bow. His idea was that if he embarked and could fall into conversation with some of the higher officers on General Grant's staff, he might pick up information that would be of service to the Confederate armies in Corinth.

CHAPTER FORTY-FOUR

At Corinth, Mississippi, in the regimental headquarters of the Thirty-first Alabama Infantry, Captain Miltiades Vaiden sat poring over a military map. He worked laboriously, being forced to keep a forefinger on the spot he was inspecting while he turned to the legend at the bottom of the chart for an explanation of the symbols.

Only one other officer was in the tent, Captain Bloodgood, a Kentuckian. He sat in the entrance gazing out at the innumerable soldiers laboring with pick and shovel at earthworks to protect the eastern flank of Corinth.

The next higher officers were away on duty. A Major Spearman was supervising the fortifications, while Crowninshield, now a colonel, had been ordered to report to a council of war then being held in general headquarters, some three quarters of a mile west of the Thirty-first encampment.

If the truth be told, it was this amenity extended to his superior officer that tempered in a peculiar way Captain Vaiden's dogged persistence at the map. The subordinate wanted to feel that he knew more of the country between Savannah, Tennessee, and Corinth, Mississippi, than did the man whom Brigadier General Trabue had ordered to report to the council. He wanted to feel himself the abler man, he wanted to know in his heart that when Drusilla had chosen Colonel Crowninshield she had chosen certainly a less efficient man. . . . His thoughts moved glumly along

375

this path under the illusion that efficiency had something to do with it.

There came a step at the front of the tent and Captain Bloodgood moved his legs to allow the entrance of an orderly with dispatches. The Kentuckian declined the bundle himself and indicated Vaiden's table. The subordinate took the papers to that table.

"Some personal letter for Colonel Crowninshield, sir," said the orderly on delivery of the parcel.

"Very good, Dalrymple. They stay here till the Major arrives."

The message carrier went out.

Bloodgood arose and stretched his long legs.

"You knew that boy, didn't you, Captain Vaiden?" he asked negligently.

"He's a nephew of the sheriff of my county."

Bloodgood pulled down his lips in a dry, characteristic smile.

"Captain, you really ought to be in the Yankee army."

Vaiden had little regard for Bloodgood. The Kentuckian was a dawdler, and therefore Vaiden, as an ambitious man, had a contempt for him. But the Kentuckian was also a philosopher and therefore had an amused indifference toward Miltiades.

Now Captain Vaiden asked without humor, "Why should I be in the Yankee army?"

"A Yankee officer would be that formal with a neighbor boy."

"Yankees get results," said Miltiades, taking a thrust at his fellow officer.

"Men who get results usually are results," observed Bloodgood in a vague generalizing tone which Miltiades especially disliked.

"I don't see the objection to being a result," stated Miltiades concretely.

"No objections are possible," stressed Bloodgood remotely. "You can neither approve of nor object to a natural law. What I am trying to point out is that if a man once sees he is a result, that perception tends to free him from that limitation. Thought is liberating. That is why even the stupidest persons are inclined, at times, to think."

Here Bloodgood got himself up from his chair and strolled out into the camp street.

Miltiades felt indefinitely affronted. He would have called Bloodgood back and flatly insulted him if he had not suspected the Kentuckian would go off in another verbal fog just as uncomfortable as the one he had been through. The annoying thing about Bloodgood's remarks were that they invariably sounded as if they almost meant something, and they were always vaguely supercilious.

Here Miltiades turned impatiently back to his work. He untied the bundle, sorted out the requisitions, dispatches, and reports, and laid Colonel Crowninshield's personal letters to one side. On two of the envelopes he recognized the smooth, delicate handwriting of Drusilla Crowninshield. When he came to them they exhaled a faint perfume.

It was a familiar fragrance, and after the manner of remembered odors it reconstructed the girl, the manor, the silver poplars, the wide level black acres, and with this was repeated Miltiades' sense of profound loss and equally deepseated resentment. He hoped within his soul he could reach some illustrious height. If he could make Drusilla realize . . .

He returned to his study of the maps of Savannah and Purdy and Crumps, Pittsburg Landing and Shiloh.

Here someone entered his tent. Without moving his head, Miltiades turned his eyes toward the newcomer, when the sight of a man in a blue Federal uniform caused him to straighten abruptly.

The blue-clad man broke into laughter.

"You were scared, Brother Milt, you nee'n' to deny it." He came forward and shook Captain Vaiden's hand vigorously.

Miltiades stared blankly at the stranger's bearded face then blurted out incredulously:

"That isn't . . . Polycarp?"

"What's left of him."

Polycarp's beard gave an odd twinge to Miltiades. To be an elder brother to a man like that. . . For the first time it struck Miltiades that he had an age; that a certain proportion of his life had passed.

"Where did you come from?" he asked in amazement.

"Just got in from home."

"How's the home folks?—how's Marcia?"

"All right," said Polycarp casually, forgetting his sister's brush in the Federal guard house. "The Yankees burnt our cotton gin."

"Cassandra wrote me that. Are the niggers staying at home and working all right?"

"Gracie ran off . . ." and Polycarp went on to give the details of Gracie's flight.

"Well, she's just one nigger gone," said Miltiades, who had got in the way of thinking of negroes by the hundreds on the Lacefield plantation.

"She's one more than ol' Pap could afford to lose," observed Polycarp dryly.

"Of course, that's true," agreed Miltiades. Polycarp's words conjured up for him the bleak picture of the Vaiden log house.

The two remained for a moment in the silence of slightly uncongenial brothers. Polycarp chose a humorous quirk to reëstablish their talk.

"Columbus and Robinet have about ruined the fox hounds chasing 'possums with them."

"The devil they did!" ejaculated Miltiades. "Now that's just like niggers—take a trained fox hound for an opossum dog!"

"Well, ol' Pap and Mammy and the girls have been eating the 'possums," consoled Polycarp philosophically.

Miltiades felt vaguely annoyed at this easy philosophy which would ruin a fox hound for a mess of opossum meat.

The truth of the situation was that, no matter what topic was started between the two brothers, a fundamental difference of temperament soon brought them to an unexpressed disagreement. Then each one made a logical skip to something entirely unrelated, hunting for a congenial topic. In one of these gaps Miltiades asked Polycarp what route he had taken to reach Corinth.

"I came through Savannah," replied the younger brother casually. "I rode on a transport with General Grant up as far as Pittsburg Landing and came the rest of the way on wagons."

Miltiades stared at him.

"You've been to Savannah! My God, Carp! Here, come here and look at this map. Here's Pittsburg Landing. How many Yankees have they got there?"

"I passed through Wallace's corps and Prentiss' corps——"

Miltiades became excited.

"What luck!" He paused, thinking intently. "I believe you ought to give those details to the council, Polycarp."

"What council?"

Miltiades explained the general war council then in session. As he did so it struck the older brother that it might not be bad publicity to take Polycarp around to general headquarters and introduce him as his brother.

He suggested this to Polycarp and the two set out from the tent to a wooden structure which they could see across the circumvallation of the earthworks.

As the two started across the field of Mars, among tents and improvised oilcloth shelters and uniformed soldiers, a cheering broke out from the men in the direction of the headquarters building.

This cheering spread like waves on a lake. It circled off to regiments who knew nothing of why they hallooed. The two

brothers hurried forward. Polycarp incongruously waved his
blue Yankee cap and hurrahed with the street around him.
Miltiades remained emotionless, but walked on looking up
the camp street. Presently he pointed out four men in the
gold bars and stars of generals in full dress. They came riding back to their brigades.

"It's over with," called Miltiades, stopping where he was.

"Who's the man on the bay horse?" cried Polycarp excitedly.

"General Trabue," said Miltiades in a commonplace tone.

"And who is that tall thin man shaking his finger at the
man next to him?"

"That's Forrest, he's talking to General Beauregard."

Polycarp turned to the captain.

"Brother Milt," he cried, "couple o' days ago I saw General Grant at Savannah landing, hobbling on crutches.
There's no comparison at all. Our generals look like soldiers!"

In the uproar of cheering about them Colonel Crowninshield rode up. He returned Miltiades' salute and called out:

"We have orders to get the Thirty-first into readiness for
instant marching, Captain Vaiden. You will report to headquarters at once."

The first wave of enthusiasm went through Miltiades.

"Very well, sir." He saluted and immediately turned about
for his own quarters again.

He now understood the excitement that was spreading in
every direction. It was not only the sight of the generals, the
army was ordered to march. They were going out to meet
the enemy. That was why the hurrahs of one brigade answered those of another and still another until the cheering
traveled for miles along the western flank of Corinth.

When Miltiades reached his own headquarters again he
encountered Captain Bloodgood. He came out of the regimental headquarters with a down-drawn smile on his lips. He
stopped Miltiades.

"Do you know why the celebration?" he asked.

"Because the army marches to-morrow!"

"You may think that, but our colonel has just received a letter from his wife, and he knows this uproar is over the birth of his new daughter, little Alberta Sydna Crownin-shield. They named her for General Johnston."

And Bloodgood went off laughing.

CHAPTER FORTY-FIVE

THE ARMY OF THE MISSISSIPPI marched out of Corinth.
Endless ranks of gray infantry moved east with a frieze of
bayonets glittering in the sun; cavalry pranced by with an
interminable clanking of sabers and snub-nosed carbines;
field guns rumbled onward with hooded snouts and rattling
swabs and buckets.

To Miltiades Vaiden, as he stood hour after hour at the
head of his company awaiting his turn to enter the line of
march, this endless duplication of buckets and swabs on the
gun carriages produced a queer smack of the domestic and
the businesslike amid the high pageantry of war. The clanking buckets, the dust, the sweating faces of the marching
men formed a dry, realistic comment on the pulse of drums,
the shriek of fife, and the flaunt of Confederate flags.

The civilians of Corinth had turned out to see the depart-
ing hosts. The citizenry cheered as thousands and thousands
of young men marched away to the glorious and multitudinous slaughter of war.

As Captain Vaiden watched, the first regiment of his own
brigade, the Fifth Kentucky, fell into line; then the Third
Kentucky, the Sixth Kentucky, the Fourth Alabama; presently the head of his own regiment started into motion. The
movement of men flowed back to him, then he and his own
company went forward as part of the endless lines of marching gray.

As the captain rode along, keeping his column dressed, he
thought he distinguished a voice shouting his name in the

tremendous cheering. Miltiades scanned the endless faces along the line of march. A man's voice hallooed his name in overtones of amazement and urgency: "Miltiades! Miltiades Vaiden!"

But the captain could distinguish no acquaintance in the roadside full of waving arms. The voice fell to the rear and was lost. Miltiades peered backward as long as there was a possibility of seeing the man. He believed it must be Augustus. He had heard through a letter that Augustus was in Corinth. He had meant to look him up but he never did. Now, at the urgent affection in the faintly heard shout, self-reproach seized Miltiades.

"I'll be sure and look Augustus up when I get back from this campaign," he told himself.

Two roads led from Corinth across the gently rolling edge of the Mississippi Valley into the hills of Tennessee. Captain Vaiden's study of the map told him that his corps under General Breckenridge was following the river road through Monterey toward Hamburg on the Tennessee River. The road itself was pulverized by the regiments ahead of the Thirty-first Alabama.

The men were exuberant and marched forward cheering and singing during the morning. In the afternoon they went on more soberly but in good spirits. As his own company trudged along, an unaccustomed feeling of protectiveness toward them welled up in Miltiades.

None of these men had ever exhibited any friendliness toward him in Corinth, but now as he rode at their side they would glance at him with smiling, friendly expressions on their dusty faces.

For some reason a thought of Drusilla went through his mind. Something of the same spirit was stirred in him by the cheerful reliance of these men as would have been, he imagined, if Drusilla had trusted her life in his keeping. It was an odd emotion for Miltiades to feel toward any human being, much less for a company of men.

In the late afternoon Trabue's brigade entered the wooded hills of Tennessee. From the hill tops Miltiades caught, on the right, an occasional glimpse of the Tennessee River and the tree-crowned bluffs on the opposite shore. The creeks which lay across the line of march were marshy and spanned by rickety wooden bridges. At intervals the distant blowing of the steamers of the enemy sounded up the winding channel of the river.

At about a half an hour till sundown orders came for the men to be quiet. Later the column was halted on the road. The Thirty-first Alabama marched off at right angles and formed a line in the forest. Here Major Spearman sent orders to Captain Vaiden for absolute silence.

Miltiades moved his horse among the trees and saplings along the front of his company, enforcing silence in flatted, cautionary tones.

"Now men, keep quiet, no singing, no talking."

The excited men quieted. The river steamers filled the evening with melancholy reverberations. The gray line in the dense woods raked together piles of last year's leaves; the men sat down, opened their haversacks, and began eating after their long march.

As they ate, somewhere in the woods ahead of them came the notes of mess call blown on a bugle. This was repeated at greater and greater distances until it was barely audible.

One of the men mumbling his hard tack said he thought orders had been given for silence. A comrade said, "Them buglers don't take their orders from General Johnston today but they will to-morrow."

Night came with abruptness in the deep wood. There were no lights. The orderly hitched Captain Vaiden's horse to a sapling, raked his commanding officer a bed of leaves and spread a blanket over them. Such a bit of military routine always gratified something in Captain Vaiden. It was something to have another man rake up the leaves and spread the blanket.

Late that night music of a military band filled the forest. In the Federal encampment some regimental band was playing.

Captain Vaiden slept badly. It was his habit at about two o'clock every night to wake up. Then the details of his betrothal to and loss of Drusilla would move through his mind. He would tell himself that if she preferred any other man he did not want her. Then he would think over all the little incidents of their courtship, and what he might have done to keep her. He tried not to do this. He would repeat to himself an adage which he had heard his mother use years ago. He would say, "That which is without remedy should be without regard." But no sooner had he thought this than he would go back to replanning his courtship with Drusilla. . . . If he had devoted more time to her . . . if he had gone with some other girl to make her jealous . . . They were always simple thoughts which did not touch his spiritual loss of his betrothed. To-night the news that Drusilla Crowninshield had become the mother of a baby girl gave his reverie a strange and melancholy turn.

This tiny girl baby seemed somehow to reach back into his and Drusilla's past and inevitably to keep them apart from the first moment of their attraction for each other. The baby somehow obliterated any other path their lives could have taken. It deprived the captain even of his gray qualifying "if's." There were no "if's." His happiness, ironically, was lost from the day he saw its first promise in Drusilla Lacefield's eyes.

And this reminded him of the predestinarianism of his father's God; that brutal amoral focusing of omnipotence upon amoral ends; a spiritual mechanism destroying much and saving little; a symbol of simple materialism.

At half-past three o'clock in the morning a kind of faint milkiness formed in the tops of the trees. It was not light, but neither was it the blackness that still filled the undergrowth. A chill came into the air. From some barnyard a cock hallelujahed for the promise of another day.

The sleeping battle line stirred. It became light enough for Captain Vaiden to see the men nearest him sit up and take drinks from their canteens. One soldier looked up at the gray sky and asked what time it was. The men began stretching, standing up, taking out of their haversacks.

At half-past four the line began moving through the woods.

Miltiades Vaiden left his horse in the dense growth and dressed his company as best he could by walking ahead and in the open spaces, indicating the alignment with his sword. Each time he did so the men scrambled hurriedly into place, holding their muskets this way and that to get through the undergrowth.

A tension gradually keyed up the line. As it pushed forward through the dark-green obscurity, men would turn aside here and there to urinate out of nervousness. Suddenly a soldier near Miltiades jerked up his musket, pushed away some twigs. As he sighted, he jerked out, "Yonder's a damn Yankee," and fired.

The gun cracked loudly in the damp morning air. Came a silence, then the men heard three or four picket shots just ahead of them, and the bullets made a brief skittering through the leaves overhead.

The line moved more rapidly. Miltiades pushed out of some undergrowth and saw a picket post just ahead of him. The sentinels held their guns at attention and seemed about to challenge the oncomers when the whole battle line moved out of the brush. They discharged their pieces helter skelter, leaped behind bushes and were gone.

Some of the Confederates laughed. A few men started after the fugitives. Miltiades gesticulated with his sword and forced them back into line, with his attention fixed anxiously on keeping his company in formation.

The greatest confusion broke out in the woods ahead of

the advancing army. A ghostly glint of tents appeared in the gray light. Men came running out of them half dressed. Drums burst into the long roll. Bugles brayed. The Federals, half asleep, pulled open their eyes to the sudden horror of long steady lines of gray slaughterers upon them.

Miltiades swung up his sword.

"Make ready! Aim! Fire!" he shouted.

The endless row of muskets gave a prolonged crash. Some of the half-garbed figures crumpled up; others went flying and limping in any direction. Officers barked to whip their surprised men into some sort of order. From the flying bluecoats came an occasional shot.

The Confederates charged ahead, loading and firing into the unresisting enemy. As they passed through the Federal tents numbers of the men broke ranks to dash inside for loot. Miltiades shouted and cursed and beat them back into line with the flat of his sword.

"Go on! Go on!" he yelled. "These tents are ours already!"

The men broke into a prolonged cheering. The wounded and dead Federals scattered about everywhere, the rabble that had fled before them filled the Confederates with the high ecstasy of multitudinous and organized homicide. Every man was a demigod who swept away resistance at a wave of his sword.

Whether the slight opposing fire had hurt any of his own men, Miltiades Vaiden did not know. He was shouting now to slow down the advance and keep his men in line with the general formation advancing through the woods. His own company ceased firing except for a snap shot at some wounded Yankee making a last effort to escape. To right and left sounded volleys of firing, now near, now remote on a two-and-a-half-mile front. The Thirty-first Alabama moved slowly into the woods again. Ahead of them innumerable bugles sounded a rally. Their confusion of sound sang and echoed in the dense forest.

A voice called in Miltiades' ear: "I think they are arranging a little reception committee for us out there, Captain."

Vaiden looked around and saw the long dark face of Captain Bloodgood filled with a new light.

"We've got 'em between the creek and the river," called Miltiades; "they can't cross either. They'll have to surrender."

The Kentuckian nodded.

"But the harder we press them the solider they'll get."

Miltiades suddenly broke out laughing.

"And the more we'll hit."

Bloodgood turned his head to listen to the growing confusion.

"Hear that—a battery of six-pounders turned loose."

"Are they our guns?"

"Just getting into action. We're warming up, Vaiden."

The use of his name by Bloodgood without his title filled Miltiades with pleasure. Such familiarity was usual among the other officers of the regiment, but up to that moment they had remained formal with Miltiades.

The line had halted now in an open glade. In front of them Miltiades could hear a persistent rifle fire, from the right hand came a fainter receding fusillade. By the time the sun was up this fainter firing seemed to come from behind a wooded acclivity which Miltiades could see toward the right.

Bloodgood nodded toward the nearer small arms.

"Whatever that is, it's holding up our center," he cried. "Our right flank is getting around . . ." He listened. "Can you tell what our left's doing?"

Miltiades paid attention in this new direction. In the persistent cannonading he could detect no movement.

"That's because a battery doesn't have to move often," explained Bloodgood nervously; "to pursue, they simply elevate their guns."

The Kentuckian's nervousness translated itself to Miltiades in a desire to act.

"I wish we'd get a chance at that center," he snapped; "they're holding up our whole advance."

They waited in growing impatience for upward of half an hour when Colonel Crowninshield came riding up the line through the open trees.

"Men!" he called out, "we're to move forward and stand ready to charge the enemy." He pointed his sword. "Clear that out and we'll drive the Yankees into the river!"

The men began shouting. Bloodgood turned back to the head of his company. A few minutes later the column moved forward again, flanking the sunlit hill. From their new position they would launch themselves against the obstinate center.

The line had advanced toward the rifle fire not more than a hundred yards when Miltiades saw horses and field guns dash up on the high wooded ground on the right. They were so far away that they looked like toy artillery among toy trees. The horses whirled the guns into place. Miltiades directed his attention to his own work.

As his line went forward the surrounding woods became more and more open. The rifle fire in front of his men developed into a sound like a continuous terrific tearing of cloth. The uproar tingled through Miltiades' nerves. He even heard distant cheers.

A queer sensation went over Miltiades, as if the whole line of his company were somehow a part of his own body. He felt an impulse to fling this extended self against the tearing gunfire ahead. Involuntarily he set the pace at the head of his column, increasing its tempo into a quick step.

Just then Colonel Crowninshield reappeared, barking an order at his subordinates.

Miltiades almost relayed the command into Forward Charge. The fire seemed just beyond a curtain of trees. Then he saw Crowninshield was making repressive gestures with his blade. He was halting the advance. Here was the position from which they must wait in reserve to strike. Captain Vaiden was in a quiver to go on. The whole Yankee thrust into middle Tennessee was there to be stopped and bagged. He wanted to sweep this resistance out of the way.

The enormous chessboard of war had concentrated itself on this one sharp salient of Federal resistance. Belmont, Paducah, Nashville, Fort Donelson—they were like wounds in the South and all could be cured by wiping out this salient and exterminating the enemy.

The Thirty-first Alabama had halted in a fairly open ground curtained by a heavy wood in front but commanded by the heights on the right.

As Captain Vaiden alternately stared at the skirt of woods and looked to his commander for the order to charge, he saw movement among the toy horses on the distant hill. The gunners worked with mechanical swiftness. A thought came to Miltiades that a Confederate battery was about to be trained on the resistant center. The next moment came a series of far-away flashes and puffs of smoke. Ten seconds later the sunlight overhead was filled with the whir of shells; blazes, smoke, and crashes shook the air. After the exploding shells had shaken into silence, Miltiades heard the heavy rumble of the guns on the distant elevation.

The crashing above the men's heads spread a feeling of indefinite destruction throughout the line. The first salvo had hurt no one, but all the men began watching the distant artillerists. More flashes broke forth; again sounded the crashing about the line and later the grumbling thunder of the cannon.

A fury against the distant cannoneers rose up in the captain. They were so safe, so utterly out of reach of his rifle fire; and to be working like miniature devils pouring thunder on his position!

A private shouted out, "Hell, Cap', le's charge them guns!"

The officer made no reply.

The cannon fire focused itself on the reserves. An exploion tore a hole in the ground not fifty feet from Miltiades. The next instant a dozen men were bowled over by dirt and débris. They struggled to their feet, some laughing, some frightened. Three men were wounded.

Presently the shells were dropping with a certain regularity. Every far-away flash became the signal for a tense motionless waiting; then a crash in air or earth and an occasional smashing of the line.

As Vaiden waited he cursed the withdrawn gunners. He wished furiously that his regiment stood under the foot of the distant hill.

Bloodgood came up to him again.

"This damn pounding will take a lot of fight out of our regiment." He stopped amid a renewed crashing.

At that moment the line about them burst into huzzahs. Vaiden looked and saw a line of antlike men charging the distant hill against the tiny battery. He could hear no reports of the far-away rifles, but he saw a string of smoke along the front of the hill and the sparkle of distant bayonets.

The Lilliputian cannoneers worked furiously at their guns. As the line of gray men crept up they were still loading their weapons. The gray line moved among the pieces. Then there were no gunners. They had fallen under the bayonets.

The fury of Captain Vaiden was suddenly appeased with the slaughter of the cannoneers. The shell fire stopped and his nerves were suddenly eased from an intense strain. They were all parts of a vastly complicated maze. The gray men on the hill died to relieve his own line. His own men in turn were about to advance toward some vast impersonal objective. . . .

A courier came dashing up from General Albert Sidney Johnstone ordering the reserve corps to attack. A few minutes later the Thirty-first Alabama in Trabue's brigade moved into action.

The screen of woods also had been shelled by the guns on
the hill. A mist of acrid smoke hung among the trees. As
Captain Vaiden's company entered it, men appeared in the
mist running or staggering or crawling toward them. Behind these wounded stragglers, still in line, retired the remnants of a brigade. Their numbers increased as Miltiades led
his troops forward. It was like drawing near a swarm of
bees.

Two hundred yards farther on, dimly discernible amid the
pungent smoke, Miltiades saw the center of the lazar cluster.
There was a pond among the trees. It was a red pond. Into
it the wounded men waded to wash their wounds and fill their
canteens. Soldiers who were whole carried water to the
maimed who could not reach the bloody pond.

If the wounded groaned they could not be heard in the
tearing musketry beyond the copse, but all walked or sat or
lay in a kind of ghastly pantomime about the scarlet pond.

The advancing brigade moved in line through the trees
and found themselves looking up a long gentle slope covered
with dead men. At the top of the slope was a heavy tangle of
undergrowth, trees and saplings. This was the obstacle that
lay between the retreating Federals and annihilation.

The brigade formed its line just inside the copse. Miltiades heard the order to charge. He himself shouted:

"Come on, men, we'll take this hill!"

The whole line dashed out of the woods and up the slope.
Their hob-nailed shoes ran over the faces and mouths and
eyes of wounded and dying men. A prolonged tearing set up
on the rim of the hill. An enduring blaze burned there composed of momentary flashes. The air was filled with a multitudinous whining. Men reeled, pitched forward, slumped out
of line, and helped resow the planted slope. Halfway up, the
brigade fired into the abatis. The crashing string of fire
burned on. Their second dash hesitated. Vaiden looked about
for his colonel. He heard Bloodgood shouting through the

din and smoke that Vaiden commanded the regiment. Miltiades leaned forward as if against an enormous gale.

"Come on—to the top! Charge to the top!"

The thinned line surged forward, hesitated, broke, and went scattering, running and staggering back down the slope of dead men.

Miltiades followed his flying men who dropped as they fled. He cursed them and the enemy. He himself was not touched, but as he went back down the great glacis he felt shattered. It was as if his company had been his own body. He had no feeling of sorrow for losing the men he had scattered up and down the hill, but a feeling of shock as if something of himself had been shot away.

In the edge of the copse he reformed his remnants. He suddenly understood what Bloodgood had shouted. He was the senior surviving officer.

He aligned the regiment as best he could and sent his wounded for what relief they could find at the ghastly pond.

Within about an hour a fresh brigade repeated the futile charge. Miltiades formed his men in this new line. The commanding officer asked who he was. He said:

"I am Captain Vaiden, acting colonel of the Thirty-first Alabama! That slope, sir, cannot be taken by a frontal attack! Come on, we'll help you take it!"

At three o'clock that afternoon the massed batteries of the entire Confederate army concentrated their fire on Prentiss' corps. A line of cannons a quarter of a mile long poured iron upon the acclivity of the Hornet's Nest.

From where he still held his battered line in the copse, Miltiades saw the dense abatis crowning the slope melt, explode into the air, catch fire. The storm of shells fired the leaves along the slope and their flames ran along among the wounded and the dead on the long natural glacis. Suddenly, amid the smoke and crash of the shells, a rout of blue coats leaped out of their untenable stronghold and dashed for the river. They were trying to cut through to the main body of

Grant's retreating army. Captain Vaiden, with the remnants of half-a-dozen regiments charged up the hill at the exposed men. The Federals fled over the hill, but presently came huddling back. They were surrounded. From all sides rushed the gray lines. The Yankees who had covered the field with dead now withered among the men they had slain.

Suddenly Miltiades saw the stars and bars on top of the acclivity. The rifle fire slackened and finally hushed. An enormous cheering broke forth. It equaled the continuing thunder of the artillery. Presently the field guns also became silent; the enormous uproar of cheering armies persisted. Miltiades' own men added to the shouts and huzzahs; they dashed unresisted up the deadly glacis.

The Yankees had surrendered. The Confederates had captured the whole army corps. The battered gray lines dashed forward jubilating, brandishing muskets, flinging their caps in air. Every man thought complete victory had been won. They did not know that the Confederate enveloping movement had pinched out only a piece and had stopped. They did not know that two armies of reinforcements were even then double-quicking to the aid of the hard-pressed Grant.

In the midst of the rejoicing, news came that General Albert Sidney Johnston had been killed.

As Miltiades hurried toward the top of the slope, he glanced about where four hours before his regiment had been halted. Among the forms motionless on the ground he saw, here and there, a man he knew. Then, with a kind of stab, he recognized the cottony face of Emory Crowninshield. He ran to his commander and dropped beside him.

"Colonel! Colonel, we've taken the hill! We've captured Prentiss' army!"

The weak hand pulled at Miltiades, feebly drew his ear down to the bloodless lips.

"Captain Vaiden . . ." gasped the fading man . . . "won't you . . . take care of . . . Drusilla . . . and my little . . . baby . . . girl . . ."

CHAPTER FORTY-SIX

During a brief period of peace in the year 1864, A.D., after their final and utter defeat in the field of battle, the planters of the South set about the odd and delicate problem of transforming what heretofore had been so much livestock on their plantations into hired and voluntary labor.

It was almost impossible for men who had owned negroes all their lives really to regard them as free. For example, when Polycarp Vaiden came home after the surrender, when he saw a black man sauntering along the rutty road in front of the big house he would ask Marcia, "Whose nigger is that?"

And Marcia would say automatically, "That's one of the Ham niggers," or one of the Wyndham niggers, as the case might be.

Previous ownership still hung about the black folk as a sort of possessive aura and was felt by both ex-master and ex-slave. To the whites the negroes were now a sort of near-property which must be controlled by the use of some tact and some force, instead of, as heretofore, through simple force. To the negro, freedom had come as to a child who reaches twenty-one under the parental roof. It is free to come and go as it will, but it stays on at home and nearly all the old relations are maintained with certain mental reservations.

Polycarp had made a trade with Columbus and Robinet to cultivate a share crop. Old Aunt Creasy was too aged for any change whatever to be made in her actual station. She, long ago, had received a virtual freedom through age and wisdom and she issued quite as many orders as she received. Now in her age her white masters must take care of her and her legal freedom had nothing to do with that obligation.

Aunt Creasy's chief pleasure now was her age. Her white owners estimated her to be somewhere in the eighties, but Aunt Creasy claimed to be a hundred and one. For two or three years she had been announcing herself as a hundred and one. It was apparently a perfect number which Aunt Creasy declined to surrender to the flow of time.

When she was informed that she was free, she exclaimed in her cracked voice, "Bress God, dat hoo-doo woman on de ship was rat. I lib to see all my race set free." She was referring to a prophecy made to her on the slave ship which brought her from Africa to America.

Also, on the day of her emancipation Aunt Creasy prepared a great dinner. She wrought in the kitchen and set before her white folks a mighty feast. But it was not at all for her masters who ate it. It was for the celebration of her own freedom—at the second table.

The change perhaps brought more to Negro George than to any other member of the Vaiden household. When he was informed of his liberty he departed from the big house, not in any sense seeking a new location, but to assure himself that he actually could walk away, go where he pleased and return when he wanted to. He was gone about four days, staying at the cabins of other manumitted souls in their amazing and newly found freedom. There were no more passes, no more patrols, no more time limits in which to return.

But when George showed an inclination to linger indefinitely at the cabin of the Dalrymple negroes through the attraction of a black girl named Susie, Susie's mother conveyed word to George through Susie's father that unless George got a cabin somewhere and lived with Susie, then they wouldn't have George around. Susie's father explained this as delicately as he could to George, but the matter ended in a fight just the same.

After that George dropped in at the big house now and then, and at such times as he was discovered there the white folks put him to work intermittently with Columbus and Robinet.

Once Robinet asked George what he expected to come to with his continual loafing and philandering.

George was astonished.

"Whah I 'specks to come to . . . huh, niggah, look whah I is at!"

He hung about the big house on no very certain footing until one day he drew old man Jimmie's wrath down on his head and got himself ordered off the place.

This disconcerted George to an extraordinary degree. To walk away in independence was one thing, to be told to go was quite another. After that George was forced to slip in and out of the Vaiden cabins for an occasional meal and bed until one day ol' Pap caught George red handed, eating in the kitchen. George was on the verge of leaping up, grabbing his hat, and bolting out the kitchen door, which, as a free man, he had a right to do, but his old master said nothing to the culprit, which showed George that his expulsion was a closed incident. Thereupon he resumed his former irresponsible standing at the big house.

This period of simple adjustment, this period of peace in the South, did not last long.

Robinet and Columbus were good workers. One day old man Jimmie directed Robinet to thin some sprouting corn. That evening it turned out that Robinet had not thinned the corn but had gone to the barn and altered three boar shoats.

Old Mr. Vaiden was so surprised that for the moment he forgot to storm.

"Robinet," he questioned in his loud voice, "why in the nation didn't you thin that corn like I told ye?"

Robinet stammered and said he forgot to.

"What in the thunder did you go cut them young boars for without being told to?"

Robinet said sheepishly that he knowed they had to be cut so he just went and done it.

"Had to be cut!" boomed the old man, recovering his sharp temper. "Of all fool niggers! I was going to save that little black boar to breed to. I b'lieve he'd made a hundred-and-fifty-pound hawg."

As a matter of fact, old man Jimmie had had no such intentions at all. He never saved males for breeding purposes, he simply turned his females out into the woods and they came home and eventually reproduced. But he continued shaking his head and saying, "Wouldn't 'a' had that happen for a five-dollar greenback . . . what you ever took it into your woolly head for . . ." He went on and on.

A few days later Robinet chopped up some of the top fence rails for kitchen wood. Old man Jimmie's idea was to thrash Robinet but Polycarp said do nothing to him, that a lot of negroes were giving their employers trouble.

"By the gray goats!" cried the old planter, "other men can treat their niggers like they want to, but I'm going to beat some sense into mine!"

"Yes, and they'll have you up before the courts."

"What for?"

"Assaulting a nigger."

"Why thunderation, Polycarp, you know good and well whopping a nigger couldn't be considered an assault even by a dad-blamed prejudiced Yankee judge!"

"Now, Father," put in Miss Cassandra, "Polycarp has good ideas about things. The war helped him a great deal. Besides, Miltiades will reach home some time this week. I'd let everything alone till he comes. He knows how to handle niggers."

"Yes, an' by that time I'll lose all my breeding boars."

"You never have a breeding boar till he's cut," stated Miss Cassandra incisively.

Two or three nights later the secret of Robinet's persistent forgetfulness was cleared up. Polycarp came home late
in the evening from a visit to Ponny BeShears. He heard a
rise and fall of chanting in Robinet's cabin. Polycarp did
not shout for one of the negroes to come put up his horse.
Instead of that he dismounted, approached the cabin, and
looked in.

Lump Mowbray stood in front of the hearth asking, "How
is you free, Brothah C'lumbus? How is you free, Brothah
Robinet, when you-all still plows an' sweats an' does what
Polycarp Vaiden says?"

"Lawzee!" ejaculated Columbus at this use of Polycarp's
name without a title, "jess call him Polycarp like dat?"

"Yes, suh, I speaks plain. I call him Polycarp, jess like
dat. We-all stan' on de same plane now. Abraham Lincoln
done lif' God's chillun up."

"Yeh, but he ain't gwi 'sport nobody aftuh he lif' 'em
up," said Columbus gloomily.

"Oh, Brothahs, oh, Sistahs, what do de Bible say?"
chanted Lump. "Hit say, take no heed of to-marr'; sufficient
unto de day is de ebil dar of."

"Yeh, but ebil ain't grub," complained Columbus. "You
can 'pend on there bein' plenty ob ebil eber day, but how
'bout de grub?"

"No, dat's a fack, de Bible don' say grub, but Gen'l Beekman say somp'n ve'y diff'unt."

"What do he say?" inquired Columbus skeptically.

"Why, he say, if de guv'ment free you, is hit gwi let you
sta've? If'n men lay down dey lives to set you free f'um
chains, won't they lay down dey bread to set you free f'um
honger? No, my brothahs, you knows they will. You gwi git
fo'ty acres ob good bottom lan' to wuck, an' a great big guv'-
ment mule to wuck hit wid. Yes, suh, you wuck fo' yo'se'f.
You don' haff to stan' uhroun' fuh Polycarp Vaiden an' ol'
man Jimmie, naw nobody else——"

At this point Polycarp entered the cabin. Lump made a

leap for the door, got caught by the neck and the ankles, and his buttocks were used as a battering ram against the facing of the solid log doorway.

"Oh, Mas' Carp! . . . [*boom*] . . . Fo' Gawd, Mas' Carp! . . . [*boom*] . . . Ah di'n' mean you! . . . Meant somebody else. . . . Oh, Lawd, Mas' Carp . . . you bus' me wide open."

And Polycarp tossed the little negro outside and let him go. The agitator vanished into the night.

The white man turned on Columbus and Robinet.

"So, Robinet, that's why you go around cutting shoats and burning up fence rails."

"M-Mas' Carp, th-that di'n' have nothin' to do wid me," assured Robinet nervously.

"I haven't done nothin', Mas' Carp," defended Columbus.

Polycarp stood looking at his two black men.

"Both of you know you are free to leave this place any-time you want to," he said with angry gravity. "You don't have to commit little offenses like that to make me or ol' Pap run you off. If you want to go, go like men and I'll get some-body else in your places."

"Ah di'n' do nothin'," repeated Columbus.

"Ah di'n' make a slip-up on dem shoats on pu'pose, Mas' Carp. Ah di'n' know ol' Pap gwi save out a boah."

"Well, he wasn't," agreed Polycarp, "but you certainly know fence rails are not to burn!"

"Well, Mas' Carp, Ah jess burned de top ones what was so high de stock couldn't jump ovah hit noway."

Polycarp walked out of the cabin. As he entered the big house he thought of Lump Mowbray's big talk, and then his begging and pleading while he was being bumped. It was so ridiculous his anger cleared away and he began to laugh.

CHAPTER FORTY-SEVEN

ON THE SECOND DAY after Miltiades Vaiden came home, Polycarp sat in the open hallway telling his elder brother about the thumping of Lump Mowbray. As a bit of humor, however, the anecdote was not a success. To the ex-overseer of the Lacefield estate, Lump Mowbray was not sufficiently human to inject any drollery into the story of his boasting impudence and his swift downfall.

"I hear men are getting into trouble for correcting negroes these days," he observed gravely.

"I wasn't correcting him," said Polycarp, feeling a little flat. "I was simply stopping a nigger's insolence on my own place."

"Yes, certainly . . . I suppose a man would be allowed to do that."

The elder brother had just been mustered out of the Confederate service and still wore the uniform of a colonel. His rank had been made permanent after he had served as acting colonel through the Chattanooga and Atlanta campaigns. To Polycarp his brother's rank seemed an incongruous and silently boastful thing. He himself had come out a private just as he had entered—not that he cared anything about a rank.

The two continued talking of the circumstances around them.

"I was just thinking how easy it would be for the South to fall into the condition of Ireland," said the older brother, "with our Northern military control, our appointed governors and judges—then we have the niggers as an added complication."

Polycarp thought ironically how typical it was of Miltiades to be talking of the national situation when Robinet was getting unreliable and George had turned into a gadabout and Columbus could not possibly do all the work on the place.

"I don't suppose you have heard from Augustus lately?" queried Polycarp.

"No, why?"

"Wonder what he's doing. Wonder if he couldn't come up and help on the place if the worst comes to the worst."

"The worst coming to the worst" meant that Polycarp feared he and his brothers would have to cultivate their own fields.

"As my regiment marched out of Corinth," recalled Miltiades, "I heard someone shouting my name. I tried to see who it was in the crowd, but never could. I imagined it was Augustus."

Miss Cassandra called from the company room, "Miltiades, do you mean to say you didn't look Augustus up when you were stationed in Corinth?"

"I can see how he wouldn't," said Polycarp in an explanatory tone but with a satirical double meaning in his thoughts.

"Well, he ought to be ashamed," condemned Miss Cassandra. "It looks like he would at least want to see what sort of a woman Augustus married, and the sort of family she came from."

"I don't know that her family makes much difference, Sister Cassandra," observed Polycarp, "if she came far enough from them."

"That," said Miss Cassandra dryly, "is something a girl can't do. If her family is the sort she needs to come a long way from, she never can do it. That's a point you might remember, Mr. Polycarp."

Polycarp thought his older sister was a very poor person to make a joke to; she always managed to give it an uncomfortable personal twist.

Marcia, who was helping in the kitchen since Gracie had gone, kept appearing and disappearing in the kitchen door, half hearing what her returned brothers were saying. Now she called out:

"Sister Cassandra, let Polycarp and Ponny alone. When you love somebody you just do and that's all."

"Really, Marcia, in the most important step in life a person ought to show some judgment," called Cassandra.

"I don't know whether they ought or not—nobody ever does."

"It isn't intended," called old Mrs. Vaiden from the interior of the kitchen.

At this the big house was filled with the unspoken and half-suppressed musings of the different members of the family. To each one the presence of the others made all love affairs whatsoever seem faintly absurd. The family gathering was like a scornful gesture which not only halted the wistfulness and passion of life but obliterated it altogether.

In the midst of this nuance a large gingerbread-colored negro rode up to the big gate on a rather dirty roan filly. Negro George hurried out to meet him. George had been hanging around, petting the hounds, in the back yard, in honor of Mr. Miltiades' homecoming. Once George had attempted to kill Miltiades with a silver bullet, but now the white man's return warmed the ventricles of the negro's irresponsible heart. However, when the brown man rode up, Miltiades' presence had its drawback for George. The black idler wanted to go out and meet the brown man with great honor and respect but he could not do this before Mr. Miltiades as the ex-overseer saw to it that one nigger should treat another nigger as a nigger.

When George was close enough not to be overhead from the big house he said in a guarded voice:

"Howdy, Mistah Trine, how's de organization comin' on?"

"All right," said Trine, "they're tacking up notices everywhere about the race men."

"What sawt o' notices?" asked George eagerly.

"Why, the notices say that in the coming election all the race people can vote," explained Trine.

"Vote!" gasped George, staring at Trine.

"Yes, it says ever'body who hasn't taken part in the late rebellion can vote, and that just about cuts out everybody but the race people."

Trine was a full-faced brown man with a curved shining black mustache. He was General Beekman's political whip. Trine never used the word "negroes," they were always "race men." And once Polycarp had observed that the blacker they were the racier they got with Trine.

George was excited about the prospect of suffrage.

"Looky heah," he ejaculated in an undertone, walling his eyes around toward the big house, "if jest us niggahs is gwi vote, Mistuh Trine, who gwi run fuh de offices?"

"Well . . . General Beekman will run for governor," said Trine.

"Yes, in co'se," nodded George.

"And then," said Trine, "we'll need a lot more officials; we'll need legislators to make the laws. We need bright men who know enough to vote like the governor says."

"Sho'! Sho'!" agreed George. "If'n evahbody don' vote jess lak de guvnah says, what's de use habin' a guvnah?"

"And did it ever strike you, George, that the general's wife—you might call her the general's wife—was your half sister?"

"Well, fo' Gawd," gasped George, "would you call Gracie de Gin'l's wife?"

"Of course," snapped Trine, annoyed, "she's his common-law wife! Isn't she as good as any woman anywhere? She's got some of the best white blood in her veins!"

"Yeh, but aftuh all, she's a—a———"

"One of the finest of the race women," finished Trine sharply. "Now listen, I dropped by to tell you that you might be put up for something yourself. Gracie told General Beekman if somebody didn't give you some sort of office you'd starve to death." The whip looked at George with amusement.

The black man accepted this without any offense whatever.

"Me! Gwi run a niggah lak me———"

"Look here," corrected Trine, "you must change your attitude, Mr. Vaiden, if you are going to enter politics."

"Mistuh Vaiden!" repeated George, blinking.

"Certainly, you'll need a name to go on the poll lists. Nearly every voter is taking the name of the family he was born in—that's natural."

"So my name gwi be Vaiden?"

"If you like that—you can pick out any name you like."

"Oh, dat's all rat—sho', Vaiden's all rat . . . Mistuh Gawge Vaiden . . ." and here George fell into loud laughter.

Trine dismounted, hung his bridle over the post.

"Whut office is I gwi run fuh?" inquired George.

"The legislature—you will then be the Honorable George Vaiden."

"Oh, my Gawd . . . de Honahble Gawge Vaiden . . ." and George hung to the hitching post to laugh.

Trine walked on through the yard to the big house. When he came within speaking distance he took off his hat, placed it under his arm, bowed, and said:

"I have been sent here to find Mr. Polycarp Vaiden."

The two brothers looked at the humble brown man.

"Well, what do you want, Trine?"

"I have a note for Mr. Polycarp," said the brown man submissively, "if I may deliver it."

"Why, certainly," said Polycarp, with a faint frown.

Trine handed over the note. It was a warrant for the arrest of Polycarp Vaiden for assault and battery on the person of Lumpago Mowbray, a colored man living and residing in the county of Lauderdale, state of Alabama, etc., etc. . . .

Trine was acting sheriff of the county.

In the trial that followed Polycarp Vaiden's arrest, Polycarp himself was reduced to a mere symbol. The question was: Could any negro enter any white man's premises, speak with disrespect of the owner, and stand protected by the law in his insolence? Of course, the reverse of this proposition, whether a white man could enter a negro's property and abuse him, was unequivocal. It admitted of but one answer.

Details of the assault, changed to taste by the different tellers, went everywhere. According to some white reports, Polycarp merely pushed Lump out the cabin door and told him to go home. According to black reports, Polycarp stabbed Lump three times with a butcher knife, twice near the heart, once in the thigh, and once in the gizzard, and had flung him out in the road to die.

But no matter what the charge or what the defense, the real question at issue was: Could a negro arraign a white man for assault? Since that time when the memory of man ran not to the contrary, no person of colored blood could enter the courts of Alabama for redress of any kind whatsoever. The mere suggestion that such a thing could be loosed all sorts of rejoicing among the blacks, and all sorts of dire speculations among the whites.

For a black man to indict a white man was undemocratic, it was anarchic, it violated the principles of the Declaration of Independence which declared that all men were entitled to the "pursuit of happiness." Under this caption certainly fell the flogging of insolent negroes. If such suits were allowed there would be no living in the same county with the niggers.

The trial came up before a Federal judge in Florence who was appointed by the President. This particular judge was a Maine jurist—Judge G. Y. Britton of Mannegetuck, Maine.

On the morning of the trial, Miltiades Vaiden naturally was going to see his brother in court. He did not believe that Polycarp had enough poise to get out of this trouble by himself. However, Miltiades had no desire to ride sixteen miles with his brother and so hatched up some reason or other for starting later than Polycarp. As soon as Polycarp caught this hint he immediately thought of urgent matters which required his early departure to Florence. But the almost unconscious efforts of the brothers to avoid sixteen miles of each other's company were frustrated by Miss Cassandra, who assumed that they must want to ride together and went to each separately, attacked and defeated their objections, and appointed a common hour for their departure.

Later she told Marcia that if she didn't plan what those boys did they'd never get anything properly done.

So the two brothers rode away together, making an occasional remark and each pursuing his own thoughts under the vaguely irritating presence of the other.

Polycarp stopped for a few moments at BeShears Crossroads and called Ponny to the gate.

The plump girl came as something of a surprise to Miltiades Vaiden. She had ripened into the obvious comeliness of a large fair girl. She had a fleshy woman's animation and vented great indignation at Polycarp's arrest.

"The idyah of arresting anybody because he slapped over a sassy nigger! What was the charge?"

"Assault and battery."

"The idyah—slapping over a nigger being assault and battery! You know they can't do anything about it!"

"No telling how a lawsuit's going to turn out," said Polycarp, making an effort to sound experienced in such things before his sweetheart.

"I'll bet the courthouse is crowded. Nearly ever' nigger

in the Waterloo end of the county has been passing here going to the trial."

"What will the niggers do if Polycarp really is fined?"
put in Miltiades gravely.

"Well, Colonel Milt," ejaculated Ponny in the voice of a
girl who is pleased and honored to speak to a distinguished
man, "there's no tellin' to what extent they'll go. Goodness,
what will the white people do, if a nigger can sass you and
then sue you if you slap 'em over for it!"

From where Colonel Vaiden sat Ponny and Polycarp were
rather obviously pressing each other's hand on the off side
of Carp's horse. The older brother could see only Ponny's
exquisite complexion, her animated blue eyes, and the smooth
white curve of her neck with a faint dimple at its base.

Presently ex-Sheriff Dalrymple rode up on his way to
Florence. After greeting the group he said if a white man
couldn't kick a damned impident nigger out of his own
house in Lauderdale County, then he'd move out lock, stock,
and barrel and go North where the damned Yankees et and
slept and fraternized with the damned niggers and have
done with it. "It's all one," he said. "What's the diff'rence!"

"That's exactly the way I feel," said Ponny, who liked the
sheriff for the way he once had treated her and Polycarp.

"If I was still sheriff," said Dalrymple hotly, "instid of
bedevilin' a gentleman for defendin' his home from insult
I'd try to ketch the dirty hounds that murdered Sam Sloane
last night."

"Who done that?" cried Ponny.

"Don' know. Somebody called him to his door last night
and shot him."

"A man that would do such a thing," said Miltiades, "is
a cowardly scoundrel."

"Can you imagine that nigger sheriff, Trine, going after
a gang of murderers?" Dalrymple's face took on a look of
contempt.

"You haven't got any idyah who did it?" pressed Ponny.

"Why," said the ex-sheriff, "of course I have an idyah. If I was in office now I'd round up that Leatherwood gang. I understan' Sloane had a little money hid out some'er's."

At this moment Alex BeShears came hobbling out of the dark hole of his store, climbed painfully down the six steps, and came toward the gate, swinging himself along on his burned feet with crutches. The men stopped talking of the Leatherwood gang as the storekeeper came up. There were too many in the group to pick up a new topic without awkwardness, so they simply stood in silence.

The crippled man paused at the gate and said in a harsh voice, "Well, has my looks struck you-all dumb?"

"We was jest talkin' about the Leatherwood gang, Alex," explained the sheriff self-consciously; "they killed Sam Sloane las' night."

"How did they kill him?"

"Why, they called him to the door and shot him—robbed him too, I guess."

"Well, they treated him better'n they treated me, didn't they, Polycarp Vaiden?" and the tradesman suddenly burst into a rachetty laugh.

"Why, Mr. BeShears, it's better to be alive than dead," said Polycarp.

"You think so? If me an' Sam Sloane could trade places, I wonder would he trade?"

The storekeeper had aged shockingly during the period of the war. His hair was a disagreeable dirty gray. He had shrunken and somewhat blackened, as if the fire applied to his feet had colored and dessicated his whole body. A feeling of shame went through Polycarp to think that he had ever fought the old man.

"It's sacrilegious to talk about the dead," said the ex-sheriff, "but I'm shore Sam Sloane would trade places with you mighty quick, Alex. I mean no disrespeck, but I will say there ain't no jestice in the hereafter onless Sam Sloane's a-burnin' in hell this minute."

The storekeeper burst into his rack of laughter.

"I think about hell a lot. You burn an' fry an' yore hide busts open, an' by God, you never quit a tall, jest go on f'rever an' ever."

"Pap, hush!" cried Ponny in an aspirate.

"I don't see how it lasts," went on BeShears, puzzled. "I can't see how that could last through etarnity."

"I imagine that's figurative," said Miltiades.

"Figgerative! Figgerative!" repeated the storekeeper gloomily. He went into the yard and clumped into the house.

At his departure the group at the gate broke up. Ponny followed her father to the house. The three men rode on toward Florence.

The ex-sheriff swung his head approvingly.

"A fine butt of a gal, Carp. I reckon you-all are shore goin' to marry now sence you're both of age."

"We sure are," said Polycarp. "Me and Ponny plan to step off together in about a month and a half."

"Well, you are doin' well by yorese'f. Both of ye are doin' well by yorese'ves."

"And she's as loyal as she's pretty," said Polycarp.

The next moment he regretted this sentence for fear that Miltiades would think it a thrust at Drusilla's elopement.

CHAPTER FORTY-EIGHT

JUDGE G. Y. BRITTON of Mannegetuck, Maine, sat in court at Florence, Alabama. He was a smallish man with the characteristic marks of the North upon him; the folds of his eyelids were somewhat flattened as if they had been ironed. His nostrils were cut high and showed more of the septum of his prominent nose than was usual in the South. And then, of course, there was the obvious metallic resonance of his voice which held the qualities of a Hawaiian guitar, compared to the piano-like voices of the Southern whites and the marimba timbre of the Southern blacks.

Judge Britton felt a settled inward superiority to everybody and everything around him, as if he had left a country tuned up to high G and had been stationed in one sounding B flat. The more elaborate manners of the Southern men Judge Britton set down to a national unstraightforwardness and the habit of making three words do the duty of one.

Among other features of Judge Britton's mind, he believed that justice was something actually comprehended in the logic of Blackstone. In his youth he had contributed articles to Garrison's *Liberator*. He played a sound game of chess with an admiration for positional chess and a contempt for the minor strategies.

Judge Britton sat on the dais in the courtroom. Inside the chancel rails, at separate tables, were the plaintiff and the defendant with their attorneys and advisors. At Lump Mowbray's table sat General Beekman as attorney for the black man. The whole audience, black and white, was watching

Beekman, speculating on him. It was clear that Beekman
had taken the case for the impression he would make on the
black voters of the county. He was prosecuting Lump's case
against a white man when no other white lawyer would.

Lump himself looked around continually to nod and wink
at the black folk in the audience.

Judge Britton asked the plaintiff if he were ready. Beekman arose and asked permission of the judge to represent
the state of Alabama in the impending suit.

Immediately Polycarp's lawyer, a Mr. Ashton, asked if
General Beekman were a licensed attorney.

The general replied that no licensed attorney would represent Lump Mowbray and that he had taken the labor upon
himself as best friend of the plaintiff.

"May I inquire, your honor," said Ashton, "if the in-
trepid general who never saw a field of battle would take
upon himself the duties of defending a nigger in a trivial
assault-and-battery case if he were not running for the governorship of Alabama on a nigger ticket?"

"Since I am making the race," returned Beekman with his
wintry smile, "I naturally hope to be supported by the colored citizens of Alabama, since in this year of grace they are
the only qualified voters in our commonwealth."

Loud laughter broke out among the black half of the
audience.

Judge Beekman tapped this down and ruled gravely that
the motive of General Beekman in appearing as best friend
to the plaintiff could not be inquired into by the court.

"It strikes me," said Ashton sharply, "that the commandant of the troops, who, supposedly, are stationed here to
preserve peace and order in our county, could better employ
his time in arresting the murderers who shot Sam Sloane in
his own home last night than in prosecuting a man who
merely protected his home from insult."

There was some handclapping here from the white section.

"Your honor," stated Beekman, "Sam Sloane was in the

Confederate army. At the time of his death he had never surrendered or taken the oath of allegiance to the Constitution. Does the court hold it reasonable that the American government will run down the slayer of her embattled foes?"

"I suppose it is equally unreasonable," snapped Ashton, "to suggest that the commanding general of the troops stationed in Florence, Alabama, should return to their owners the silver, silks, cotton, jewelry, and objects of art which he stole during the recent war, and at least enter a court of justice with clean hands!"

Here Judge Britton warned the attorney that he would be barred from the courtroom unless he abandoned the use of personalities.

Miltiades sat in the defendant's box with Polycarp. He remained there mainly through a feeling that Cassandra expected it of him. He really loathed being seen in a box opposite a negro in the courtroom. He leaned across and said to Ashton, because he would not have wasted a mot on Polycarp:

"In the army we thought we were fighting to keep our slaves; we were really struggling to keep our civilization!"

Ashton nodded quickly.

"With your permission, Colonel, I'll use that in my speech, but that damned Yankee there perched on the judicial bench, like a vulture battening on the corpses of heroes, wouldn't know what in the hell I was talking about."

The actual questioning of the witnesses and the establishment of the facts were very brief. Lump Mowbray described with sufficient drollery how he had been saying "Polycarp Vaiden" and "old Jimmie Vaiden" when Polycarp suddenly entered, bumped him against the door facing, and threw him out.

"Did you expect Polycarp Vaiden to attack you for merely calling his name without a title?" asked Beekman.

"No suh, I din' *speck* no 'tack, I *knowed* hit was a-comin' quick as he could lay a fingah on me."

"What did you do?"

"Ah jump for de do'."

"And what happened?"

"Ah hit de do' facin' 'bout fawty times, den Ah fly out."

"Do all that by yourself?"

"No, suh, Mistah Carp he holp me considuhble."

"You mean he beat you bodily against the door facing?"

"He sho' beat me bodaceously agin' dat do' facin'."

Everyone was laughing by now at Lump's thrashing.

"And he did all this because you spoke his name without using the title 'mister'?"

"Yes, suh," nodded Lump, "Ah'll admit I was talkin' a little big."

"What do you mean by 'talking a little big'?"

"I mean talkin' a little biggah dan what I actually wuz."

"Talking bigger than you actually were?"

"Yes, suh, a good deal biggah."

By this time the courthouse was in an uproar and Judge Britton had to threaten some of the immoderate laughers with expulsion. When the witness could be heard again, Beekman asked:

"Were you speaking to Mr. Vaiden in person when you called him Polycarp Vaiden?"

"Gin'l Beekman," reproached Lump, "does I look lak a niggah widout no jedgment a tall?"

"Then you didn't know he was in hearing?"

"Good Lawd, c'ose I di'n' know he was in hearin'. Thought he was in de big house."

"Where were you?"

"In Robinet's cabin."

"Robinet is a negro laborer on the plantation?"

"Yes, suh, he wucks on de shares."

"A share cropper?"

"Yes, suh, dey 'vides what dey gits. Robinet takes de wuck and Mistah Polycarp takes de crop."

Here Judge Britton was forced to rap again for order.

General Beekman dismissed Lump and called Robinet, who corroborated Lump's testimony. He then rested his case.

Ashton introduced Polycarp for the defense. Polycarp was forced to admit that what Lump said was true, but he dwelt on the insolence of the negro. However, here in the courtroom, in the face of Lump's disarming humor, it seemed that no great affront had been offered the white man.

When Polycarp concluded General Beekman spoke briefly. He said there was no law forcing one man to give another the title of "mister"; that discourtesy was not illegality. Moreover, Lump had not been discourteous either in the presence or in the house of the defendant. He was in the cabin of another negro and had merely spoken of Polycarp Vaiden without any title—merely called his name, that was all. For that offense Polycarp Vaiden had entered on premises that were not his own and——

Ashton interrupted to contest that point. Beekman insisted that the cabin of a tenant belonged to the tenant and not to the proprietor. The point was affirmed by the judge.

"And for this offense," went on the general, "the plaintiff was seized, beaten, and maltreated to his great bodily pain and mental suffering." He continued on this line for some moments and finally concluded:

"The real onus of this case, your honor, rests on the fact that Polycarp Vaiden, after four years on the field of battle, after the Emancipation Proclamation and an amendment to the Constitution of the United States, cannot and will not believe that a man with a black skin is a genuine human being whom a white man's law will deign protect. Polycarp Vaiden believes there should be a law forcing negroes to say 'mister' and there should be another law permitting a white man to enter the privacy of a negro's home and bump him against his own doorpost if he neglects that formality.

"But suppose the negro entered the white man's home— could he bump any white man who failed to call him 'mister'? That is a silly question, your honor. Mr. Polycarp Vaiden means for his law to work only in one direction.

"May it please your honor, the subject of my race for the governorship of Alabama was touched upon by the opposing attorney. I would like to say that I am making that race on the Republican ticket to do what I can to correct the enormous inequality between the two classes of our citizens. For four long and bloody years, your honor, I fought to liberate the bruised and manacled bodies of these black men. Now, as their governor, I will fight to liberate their souls. Justice and equality to all are the foundation stones of the government I drew my sword to defend. If they be wrong and allow our social structure to collapse, I for one am willing to immolate myself in its ruins."

The commandant of the army of occupation sat down. The courthouse remained silent except for the solitary applause of Trine, the acting sheriff. Then other negroes took up the cheering uncertainly because they did not understand what the general had said.

Until Beekman's speech the audience had been in the jolliest of humor. Both negroes and whites had laughed at Lump's account of his own bumping. Now all laughter and smiles ceased. The group of ex-slaves and ex-slaveholders were drawn apart and armed mentally against one another in a manner seldom brought about by slavery itself.

Ashton arose white lipped and considered the Northern man sitting on the bench.

"Your honor," he said, "I do not believe and cannot hope that it will behoove me or my client to suggest to this court that human advancement and spiritual worth are the children of class distinction and a perpetual insistence upon the formalities due from one class to another.

"These formalities, sir, are not a superficial matter of word or gesture; they look to the most intimate mental processes of the actors. Upon them have depended in the past, and will depend in the future, that dignity of port, that purity of breed, that aristocracy of thought which have, until the fatal hour of Sumter, made the South the directress of this nation.

"It is impossible, your honor, for the Northern people, in a section of our country where only one class obtains, to realize in the remotest degree the supreme necessity of maintaining the minutiæ of the difference in rank and race. This instinct is not a reasoned part of the Southern mind, it supersedes and conditions that reasoning. Some sort of caste system has been the condition of every great civilization under the sun, and only the Northern states of America, where historic chance has by accident grafted only one caste, could dream that human worth and culture could spring from any other shoot.

"The Northern people, in their short-sightedness, in their lack of spiritual penetration, have by force of arms broken into the temple and flung its doors open to the mob. But the chrism upon the altar their vandal hands cannot desecrate. It lies in the customs, the beliefs, the inheritances, and the religion of this people, far beyond reach of shot or sword.

"If it be the desire of this court to tax the Southern people for maintaining their traditions, that tax will be paid until it can be repealed.

"Such is my answer to the eloquence of a carpetbag candidate running for the governorship of Alabama upon a miscegenation platform!"

When the shouts and hurrahs among the white part of the audience had been thumped down by the judge's gavel, Judge Britton placed a fine of twenty-five dollars on Polycarp for assaulting Lump Mowbray, and he placed another fine of twenty-five dollars on Mr. Ashton for contempt of court.

CHAPTER FORTY-NINE

THE ACTUAL IMPOSITION of a fine on a white man for
whipping a negro filled both the white people and the black
people of Florence, Alabama, with intense excitement.

To the black folk it brought a moral liberation. It made
more solid and real the rather nebulous equality which their
Northern redeemers had spread upon them. They could be
very offhand in their address to their former masters and
the Yankee regiment and the Northern judge would uphold
them.

No longer on the streets of Florence did they have to step
off the sidewalk and remove their hats when a white man
passed. They, theoretically, did not have to get out of a
white man's way any more than the white man had to get out
of their way.

The result was that on the very day after the trial a number of collisions took place on Florentine streets. In several
of these collisions the negroes fought back, but they gained
little as every white man in reach took a hand in the affray,
whereas the other negroes looked on these painful testings
of Judge Britton's decision with long faces and protruding
lips and moved away.

The whites were even more wrought up about the decision
than the blacks.

In the courthouse, in an anteroom reserved for the delib-
erations of juries, six men had locked themselves in. They
were Ashton the lawyer, Polycarp and Colonel Miltiades

Vaiden, Captain A. Gray Lacefield, ex-Sheriff Dalrymple, and a Lieutenant Crosby, an ex-Confederate officer who lived in Giles County, Tennessee, and who happened, on the day of the trial, to be in Florence, Alabama.

Young Captain Lacefield had known Crosby in the service and when he saw him in the courthouse he had seized upon his former comrade.

"Of all indecent, humiliating trials," began Crosby furiously; "it's the Goddamnedest mistake ever to let it get into court!"

"How in the hell could we keep it from getting into court?" demanded A. Gray, who was just as angry over the situation as Crosby.

"Listen, Lacefield," Crosby tapped the worn shoulder bars of his friend's gray uniform, "introduce me to some more gentlemen down here."

A. Gray acted immediately and got together the group in the anteroom.

The jury room was a very high narrow room with a single dirty window looking down on the street. Polycarp Vaiden, who had just been fined twenty-five dollars, stood looking down through the window on the black crowd milling below. He muttered in a concentrated tone, "Black baboons."

Lieutenant Crosby amputated a chew of tobacco sharply with a pearl-handled knife, thrust it into his mouth, and then exclaimed in a voice a little dulled by his quid:

"This has been an unnecessary shame," he declared.

"How could it have been prevented?" asked the lawyer.

"That nigger should not have been allowed to appear in court."

"How would you have kept him away?"

"Skeer him!"

"Scare him?" ejaculated Ashton curiously.

"Yes. In Pulaski we've got up an organization . . ." Crosby began laughing and spat into a sand box. "We call ourselves the Ku Klux Klan."

At these odd syllables Polycarp turned from the window. All five of his auditors looked at Crosby.

"What does it mean?" asked Miltiades.

"Nothing, not a thing in the world . . . that is, it means nothing down here now, but start it up and it'll mean something. By God, the niggers in Giles County would rather meet the devil at daybreak than a Ku Klux at high noon."

Here the lieutenant was so amused at the memory of the doings of the organization that he had to spit his quid into the sand box.

The men were attracted by this mirth to whatever the Ku Klux Klan was. They asked questions and found it was a secret organization that went about at night masked in white, frightening unruly and disrespectful negroes into submission and setting straight any recalcitrant white man who had strayed from social or political respectability. The lieutenant told examples of what the Giles County Klan had accomplished.

Attorney Ashton looked out the courthouse window.

"How does your Klan know that the suspects actually have committed what they're accused of?" he asked.

"Oh, we're particular about that," explained Crosby. "We hold their trial right there in our own Klan Kon Klave before we correct anyone at all."

"How do you hear his witnesses?"

"Well, we punish only well-known offenders."

Attorney Ashton shook his head.

"As a member of the Alabama bar," he said slowly, "I don't believe I could ally myself with an extra-legal system of jurisprudence."

Immediately the whole group of men were on him. These were no ordinary times. Jurisprudence had been taken away from the people and given over to foreigners while the actual suffrage of the South had been placed solely in the hands of the ignorant, illiterate, revengeful black men. The very civilization of the South was falling to pieces, hacked at by Yankees from above and gnawed at by the negro vote at the bottom.

All these urgings and vehemencies were flung at the attorney by the other five men but Ashton stood looking out the courthouse window at the unruly street and shook his head slowly.

"No," he repeated, "I'm a lawyer . . . I'm a lawyer. I'm not afraid to meet this situation by recognized legal methods. There is no way for an illiterate subordinate race to be thrust into any actual power over the Southern people. The Yankee usurpers of our government can try it but they can't do it."

"The reason they can't," retorted Crosby hotly, "is because when the damn Yankees seize the appearance of power, the real power will slip through their fingers in some such form as the Klan."

"That's nothing more than the war continued," frowned Ashton.

"Who in the hell ever thought the war had stopped?" cried Crosby.

The lawyer gave his head a final shake.

"I'm a member of the bar. I have taken an oath to uphold the written law of Alabama and its judgments."

Young Captain A. Gray Lacefield's attitude on the Klan depended, he said, upon his father. He asked Colonel Vaiden to ride by his home and talk his father into the idea.

"I'm his son," explained A. Gray, "and any father falls naturally into the opposition on any proposition advanced by his son. You, now, have supervised his business for years. He has confidence in your judgment. If you tell him you're for it, he'll not only sanction my joining, he'll go into it himself."

Miltiades suggested they ride back together but A. Gray was staying overnight in Florence; he was trying to rent a house, and was having trouble finding one that would do. This gave Miltiades a reason for starting home earlier than

Polycarp, and the younger brother immediately found a
reason why he should stay on in Florence an hour or two
longer. So Miltiades rode home alone.

On his way past the Crossroads store he saw Ponny Be-
Shears out in her garden gathering peas. She was the sort of
woman who looked her best at a distance in the out of
doors. Her hair made an aura around her head and her bare
arms looked very shapely reaching among the green pea
vines. She held up her bucket and called gayly to Miltiades
in a voice from which the hill twang almost had disappeared.

The colonel turned off the Florence-Waterloo road for
the Lacefield plantation.

It was the first time he had been over the side road since
he had ridden out of it four years ago with his sister Marcia.
Briers and sumac were rank in the fence corners. Small
trees had grown up along the way in fields that had lain
fallow. The road itself was grass grown with an occasional
mud hole here and there, almost as bad as the public road.

A little later he came within sight of the manor itself. Its
silver poplars were thinned to raggedness. The white rows
of slave cabins were gone, and in their stead were only a few
irregular shanghai huts without any whitewash. The barn
was gone. Rails of the cross fences had fallen into decay.
Three or four lean work mules grazed in the meadows where
Prince and Madelon and Brown Hal once played. From the
road he could see that the glazed flower pit in the garden
was a ruin. The office in the front yard where he had slept
had been burned and honeysuckles had shrouded the scar.
The old manor itself, which once had gleamed whitely
through the trees, was weathered to a wasp's-nest gray.

Miltiades rode up in his worn Confederate uniform and
dismounted at the horse block, which was overgrown with
cherokee roses. He walked up on the piazza and pulled the
tarnished lion-claw doorbell.

Mr. Lacefield himself came out, saw who it was, and
greeted his caller with both hands outstretched.

"Miltiades! Colonel Vaiden, I should say! How glad I am; I thought you had deserted us!"

"Not at all. I've been getting things at home straightened out. It's a difficult task."

The younger man was talking more or less at random. He was shocked at Mr. Lacefield's appearance. The planter was deeply and intricately wrinkled and his hair was as white as that of Miltiades' father.

"A difficult task," agreed the planter in a voice a little thinned, like his face. "We are going to have to devise new modes of existence here in the South, Milt——" He broke off. "But let me call Mrs. Lacefield and Drusilla; they'll want to see you."

"Before you do it," interposed Miltiades, "let me tell you the business part of my visit." And he related as fully and as invitingly as he could Lieutenant Crosby's idea of the Klan.

The planter listened carefully with an occasional "hum" or nod. Then he asked a number of questions. Miltiades had begun his explanation with detachment but as he went into the idea and met his companion's objections he became more and more convinced by his own advocacy.

Mr. Lacefield founded his objections mainly on the attitude of General Lee at the evacuation of Richmond. One of the Confederate generals had suggested to Lee that the Confederates escape through Grant's lines, concentrate at certain chosen points, and set up an unrestricted guerilla warfare. General Lee had opposed that plan. He said it would bring endless conflict, endless misery and physical and moral destruction to the South.

"And Colonel Vaiden," said the worn aristocrat solemnly, "your idea is too nearly allied to guerilla warfare for me to indorse it in the face of the sentiments of our commander-in-chief."

"Would you object to A. Gray's joining the organization?" asked the caller.

"He is a man and a Confederate officer. I wouldn't object, but if he should ask me I would advise him against such an affiliation."

"If you did that," said Miltiades, "he wouldn't join."

"He probably would not," agreed the father.

Miltiades was acutely disappointed. He drew a long breath. "Well, that's what I came for . . ." and he was about to go.

"Wait! Wait!" protested the planter with outraged geniality. "You can't ride off without seeing the family. I think Drusilla made some blackberry wine. It's rather ridiculous to offer a guest, but its bouquet is as good as its reputation is bad."

He was ringing for a servant and a very young negro boy entered the room.

"Tell your mistress Mr. Vaiden is here, Abraham," he directed, "and tell Drusilla to bring some of her wine if she can find any glasses left after the deluge."

As the child ran away, the planter added, "I named that boy Abraham after Lincoln. I wanted the little nigger to appear grateful, no matter what damage the Republican party finally inflicts on his race."

CHAPTER FIFTY

WHEN Drusilla Crowninshield first entered the library of the old manor, Miltiades was oddly moved at the changes motherhood had wrought in the girl. She had become a woman. He had known her piquancy and provocativeness as a girl; in its stead had come a grave beauty that suggested neither youth nor age. She produced, at this moment of her life, that impression of timelessness which painting or sculpture conveys. It was impossible, looking at her, to feel that she would ever change again.

Even her voice and complexion had shared in the subtle change; yet she had addressed to Miltiades no more than a dozen sentences before the completeness of what she was usurped the memories of her former self, and it seemed that she had been always thus, poised, gravely sweet, and beautiful.

Her father and mother had left them together in the library.

"We have decided to move to Florence to live," Drusilla was saying. "It would take so much money to put this place in repair. It will seem strange to live in a town. Everything will be cramped and dull. Nowhere to receive company or ride or raise flowers. No horses except two for the carriage, nobody to wait on you except a servant or two, no stables, no kennels, no garden, no smoke house. I understand if town people ever decide to eat they go down and buy a little paper sack full of something and bring it home and cook it."

She had evidently brooded over the coming misfortune and now rehearsed her humorous catalogue of woes.

"Of course, the serious part is," she concluded, "instead of having a governess we'll have to put little Sydna in a public school with a lot of children whose parents I don't even know, much less approve of." She looked up at the colonel with the greatest concern in her dark eyes.

"You'll never get to be like town people, Drusilla," comforted Miltiades, "you are too alive. You would have to ride and have house parties, and go on trips."

"I don't know, I'm afraid I'll get just like them."

The two were now moving through the front part of the manor looking at the damage the Yankee occupation had wrought. The stairway had been slightly burned and so the mahogany spiral had had to be painted to conceal the blackening. The change from dark wood to paint flatted the whole hall. Drusilla began telling Miltiades about the disfiguration.

"Colonel Higgenbotham made his headquarters here, and just before he marched away he lent Father hundreds of canvas army buckets and told him to put them full of water all over the place. Then when the regiment was ready to go they set fire to everything we had and marched away."

"Well, I be damned!" ejaculated Miltiades.

"Yes, the gift of the buckets," Father says, "was the perfect flowering of Yankee courtesy." Drusilla's soft lips trembled. "Now we are completely ruined and have to move to Florence."

A sort of constriction went through Miltiades' chest. They were standing in the great hallway looking at the painted staircase. He took her hand, then put an arm about her shoulders and drew her to him.

"Drusilla, doesn't the whole war, all that has happened, seem terrible, unbelievable?"

"Sometimes when I wake up in the morning," said the

woman in a low tone, "I think we must be back like we were."

They stood holding to each other in the face of the vast physical and social wreckage that had swept over the seceding states. The burned and dingy manor with its mahogany overlaid by paint was the very symbol of the reconstruction swirling and rioting throughout the South.

Their physical loss stressed the spiritual largesse each held for the other. Their embrace formed a lovely inner world untouched by the cataclysm around them.

Drusilla gave a long sigh and lifted her lips to Miltiades. Her wet eyes were so close to his that they were magnified into great glimmering pools of darkness. Her left breast beneath the tip of his fingers was softer than he had ever known. A faint perfume hung about her. It recalled to Miltiades the two letters he had laid aside for Colonel Crowninshield in Corinth on the eve of the Battle of Shiloh.

When Colonel Vaiden left the manor for his home, his thoughts and mood, the very nerves in his body were suffused by the feminine aura of Drusilla Crowninshield. To have been with her, to have had her in his arms filled him with the prescience of a coming happiness. These impressions had a soft vaporous quality about them, as if he saw himself and Drusilla through a sort of mist. What separated itself from these pastel sensations was the little girl.

The child had come up on them unaware while the mother sat on a settee inside of Vaiden's arm.

"This is Sydna, Miltiades," the woman had said, drawing the little daughter around her knee before her lover. Miltiades instantly fell into the rôle of a relation. "Give your uncle Miltiades your hand—your right hand, Precious."

The little thing placed a tiny rose-petal hand in his fingers.

"Who are you named for, Beautiful?"

"Gen'l Alberta Sydna Johns'n."

Drusilla bent down to kiss the little creature but Sydna

slipped aside without taking her eyes off of Colonel Vaiden's face.

And that was what Miltiades most clearly recalled, the great brown eyes and flaxen hair of the baby as she stood staring solemnly at him beside her mother's knee.

When Miltiades entered the main highway at the Crossroads Ponny BeShears came running out of her home holding up her hand to the colonel in obvious excitement.

"Oh, Mr. Milt," she called—"I mean Colonel——"

"I'm just Milt to you, Ponny, if you don't mind," suggested Miltiades.

She opened the gate and came up to his horse, evidently excited.

"Polycarp has just ridden past," she breathed. "I'm so glad you came!" she caught his hand nervously in her strong, moist hands.

"Well, what about him going past?" inquired Miltiades apprehensively.

"He was—sick."

"Sick! How long has he gone by? Whyn't you take him in?"

"Why, you know—" Ponny flushed—"sick like he was when we tried to run away and marry."

He looked at the girl and suddenly understood.

"Oh, you mean he's . . . taken too much?"

"And he had a fight with somebody. His clothes are all torn. Oh, Mr. Milt, I would have taken him in till he got sober, but Pappy hates—— Oh, he hates everybody."

"Well," said the colonel excusingly, "he and Carp have had trouble. And he's had enough besides that to make him bitter. How far is Carp ahead?"

"He passed about ten minutes ago. He wasn't riding fast. He just could stay on."

"I'll catch him. Good-bye."

He pressed her shapely, capable hand. From his seat on his horse he could see beneath her yoke the beginning curves of her ample bosom. And he thought with a touch of impatience, "Drunk and upsetting a fine girl like Ponny. Somebody ought to pull his ear."

He spurred his horse and set out down the road at a gallop. As the colonel rode along he was sharply annoyed that his brother had chosen this inopportune moment to become drunk. He had wanted to talk over with Polycarp how they might overcome the Opposition of the older and more conservative men of the neighborhood to the Klan. Not that Miltiades attached much importance to his brother's ideas, but Polycarp knew the personnel of the community better than he.

What Miltiades wanted was detail: how to maneuver every conservative into their group. His talk with Crosby had convinced him that the only way to elect a Southern white man in the coming elections was to prevent the negroes from voting, and the single way to accomplish that was to keep them away from the polls.

From this point he went on, imaginatively, to amplify the uses of the Klan. The black folk could be coerced into steady labor and not be allowed to drop their hoes at any hour of the day and pole off to the Crossroads store or to a neighbor's cabin. The Klan ought to be a cure for such evils as Negro George.

And if the negroes could be set to work again the Lacefields might continue their old luxurious life in the country and not be forced to the privations of a permanent residence in a town.

Sight of a horseman down the road ahead of him clinging to the neck of his mount told Miltiades that he had overtaken his brother. Colonel Vaiden drew his own animal down and for a space rode along twenty or thirty yards behind Polycarp.

The younger brother had his arm hooked about the horn of his saddle and his horse walked along with the steadiness of an animal that had had experience in delivering his

master to his home. There was something fantastic in the
sobriety of the horse and the drunkenness of the rider.

Presently Polycarp aroused himself, reached back for
his quirt, and, still hooking the pommel with his elbow, began
a loose beating of the horse's flanks crying out:

"Whoa! Damn ye, whoa! Settle down, buckin' an' jumpin'
like this!"

This became too contradictory for equine intelligence and
the horse began dancing with its hind legs. Miltiades rode
up and pulled away the quirt.

"Stop that, Carp, let your horse alone," he directed in
the flattened voice of one who finds a situation untimely but
not otherwise objectionable.

Polycarp moved his face over on the right-hand side of
the horse's mane so he could see what voice had addressed
him out of the air.

"Well, I've got to break this horse, Milt," he complained
thickly. "S'pose Ponny got on him an' he got to buckin' and
jumpin' like this . . . th-throw 'er off an' kill 'er."

The bucking and jumping was the movement of the
horse's shoulder blade and the slight swing of his neck under
Polycarp's torso.

"Well, you can beat that out of him later. Let's get on
home now."

"Well, it's not so com—com—com'tble for me either."

Miltiades dropped the point through a genuine surprise
at his brother's appearance.

"Well—who in the devil have you been fighting?"

"H—haven't been fightin' n-nobody. This damn stallion
r-run away with me while ago—drug me. I—'m goin' t' beat
hell out o' this hoss, if he ever s-sobers up 'nuff to know
wh-what it's aw about."

"Ponny told me you had been fighting."

"Di' she?"

"She did."

Polycarp lay along the mane, looking sidewise at his brother thoughtfully.

"Well, Milt," he decided at last, "sh' ought t' know. I'm goin' t' marry th' gal nex' month . . . intimate relation, Milt . . . ve'y intimate . . . she ought t' know whether I've been fightin' aw not."

Miltiades passed over the confused absurdity of this remark without any feeling of amusement. He said, more to himself than to Polycarp, "The niggers in Florence might very easily have attacked you on the street—or along the road somewhere."

Polycarp struggled to sit upright. He waved an arm at Milt.

"Now, by God, you're my brother. You b'lieve I've had a fight, too. Evidence against me, Milt—p-p-pre—pon—derance uv evidence. You-all mus' be right—mus' 'a' been a fight stead uv a runaway."

He tried to wipe his face, which was sweating profusely.

The two brothers now came in sight of their home. What caught Miltiades' attention was a dust-covered two-seated hack with its shafts propped up at an angle with a stick. It stood just outside the yard fence. Some family had come for an all-day visit to the big house. After the fashion of countrymen, Miltiades began scrutinizing the hack, trying to identify the owners, but he had never seen the vehicle before. It did not belong in the neighborhood.

As the two riders moved toward the log house under the hard glistening leaves of the black oaks, a man somewhat oddly dressed stepped out of the mouth of the lane and stood silent but smiling recognition at the riders.

Miltiades looked at the browned smiling man in the sunshine with a nascent recognition that tantalized him.

Polycarp, who had got himself upright in his saddle, blinked his eyes, studied the figure, and finally blurted out:

"Well, 'y God! I caught up wi' you at las', Augustus . . . where'n hell did you go to las' night?"

CHAPTER FIFTY-ONE

IT WAS characteristic of Colonel Miltiades Vaiden that he utilized for the advancement of the Klan the advent of Augustus and the uncertainty of Polycarp as to what had happened to him on the road from Florence.

He dispatched at once an identical letter to Ashton, the attorney, Mr. Lacefield, Erastus Ham, Candy McPherson, and a number of other conservatives in the neighborhood. It contained such expressions as these:

> "The time is upon us when we must decide whether our crippled people will reassume the management of their own affairs or sink a prey to the cupidity of the Yankees and the stupidity of the negroes.
>
> "Now that the Northern attack upon our civilization has been shifted from the battles of soldiers to the intrigue, confiscatory taxation, and misappropriations of thieves and demagogues, it is our duty to checkmate the villainy of Yankee rule and the obscenity of negro suffrage by the veiled power of the Klan."

He then went on to tell how his brother Polycarp had been beset and beaten by negroes while on the road from his trial in Florence, and how his brother Augustus had lost his home and plantation through ruinous taxes imposed upon the white planters of Mississippi by a carpetbag governor and a negro legislature.

In conclusion he added:

"We can forestall such a fate for Alabama by seizing the negro first. Our only salvation is the Klan.
      "Miltiades Vaiden,
              Colonel Thirty-first Alabama Infantry
              of the Confederate Army."

He dispatched these letters by Columbus, Robinet, and George, and these in turn relayed them by any negro going in the right direction. All the notes reached their proper destination with promptness.

The actual organization of the Klan also was very simple. All the regalia required was a sheet thrown over the whole body of the wearer, with two holes cut for his eyes. These costumes, at night, changed the Klan into a troupe of ghostly horsemen.

Miltiades Vaiden was a humorless sort of man, and after the Klan had once got under way, his movements through the night at the head of a sheeted column were to him not droll. It gave him something of the same feeling of strange and occult power as it did the negroes they visited.

To Polycarp it was all a riotous joke. He devised a way of pushing up his sheet with a pole and extending himself into a monstrous specter. He thought of the idea of painting skeletons in phosphorus on the white sheets. Polycarp's élan was irresistible. He really had some talent for dramatics. When he came home from the nightly visitations of the Klan he gave spirited descriptions of how the negroes ran or knelt and prayed. A number of times negro political meetings were surrounded by horses ridden by fiery skeletons and expansible specters. The very horses themselves had eyes of fire. The black men's meetings were broken up without any parliamentary motion to adjourn.

One of the first objectives aimed at by Miltiades was the negroes on the Lacefield estate. Once news came to him that a negro by the name of Livus was moving out of his cabin at the manor, to go to Florence. Half-a-dozen ghosts called Livus out of his hut and warned him to stay where he was and not to go to the polls on election day. If he did not do this the cyclops would visit him again.

Livus stayed where he was and so did all the rest of the Lacefield laborers.

Restless negroes all over the countryside were visited. If they were accused of theft or insolence or extreme laziness, they were whipped.

The meeting place of the riders was always at some appointed spot in the woods, but often two or three would foregather at the Vaiden home and go from there to the "Kon Klave," as the organization chose to spell their meetings.

Once Marcia said to Mr. Erastus Ham that the Klan ought not to whip a negro for being lazy, that the negroes couldn't help that.

"Why, Miss Marsh, we got to," declared the planter roundly. "Since these niggers have been set free they're gettin' so dawg lazy us white folks are about to starve to death."

"It's a necessary discipline for them," interposed Miltiades, who set aside Ham's quip with dryness. "If you let a negro loaf he'll get into mischief, and if you let him vote he'll bankrupt the country."

That statement stopped the laughter, as Miltiades meant it should. He could not endure for anyone to smile at the ghostliness or grave importance of the Klan.

The personnel of the Ku Klux was shrouded in profound secrecy. It was a widely disseminated secret, as every man, woman and child in the neighborhood knew exactly who were the Ku Klux. This, however, served to make the secret all the more impenetrable as, where everyone knew, no one was left to ferret out the mystery.

Marcia Vaiden was continually amused at this pretense of the mysterious and the uncanny. The habitual amusement and condescending tolerance which every woman feels for the juvenilities of masculine secret societies were accentuated in Marcia. She had three brothers and a sweetheart in it.

She saw young A. Gray now almost every day. He came to the Vaiden home to consult Miltiades on some phase of "the work." To call what they did "work" always was a point of high mirth with Marcia.

"But look here, Marcia," A. Gray would protest, "the niggers are staying on our place now—and everybody else's places too."

"Yes, but prancing around in a sheet isn't work."

"Isn't a preacher's sermons work?"

"Who for, the preacher or the congregation?"

"Now, Marcia, don't get sacrilegious. I consider the work of the Klan just as divinely inspired as the work of the ministry. Look, it started out as a joke with some young men in Pulaski, and it has suddenly spread out to save the civilization in the South. Don't you believe that was intended?"

By the word "intended" A. Gray meant a direct interposition of the hand of God in the affairs of men. Any unusual occurrence in the South was always suspected of being "intended" if it upheld the predilections of the speaker. God's miracles always worked in favor of the man who observed them, otherwise they did not originate with God. Which was quite natural.

It always disturbed Marcia to ring in the "intention" of God into an argument, especially when talking about the monkeyshines A. Gray and her brothers were cutting among the negroes. So she changed the subject.

"Have you-all decided whether you're going to move to Florence or not?" she asked by way of diversion.

"If the niggers stay on like they've been doing, Father

and the folks will try to patch things up and stay where they are."

"What are you going to do?" inquired Marcia, opening her eyes.

"Well, I—I don't know," said the captain a little uncertainly.

"Why, you do know!" cried Marcia in surprise. "What have you got in your head, A. Gray?"

"What would *you* think of living in Florence, Marcia?" queried the captain diplomatically.

"What in the world are you going to do in Florence by yourself?"

"I won't be by myself."

"Well, I mean us," corrected Marcia. "What will we do in Florence?"

"M-m—something in the building trade," suggested A. Gray quizzically.

"What sort of building trade?"

"Well, we might add a new wing to the House of Lacefield."

Marcia didn't like a jest about her possible children.

"Just what are you going to do in Florence?"

But the notion of marriage went more or less to Captain Lacefield's head. He began trying to move her gently by the arm toward the company room.

"Come on, Marcia, a moment," he said in a lower tone. "Let's see how you're getting on with your tatting?"

With the couple, "to see Marcia's tatting" was a locution for giving and receiving a kiss. It had begun when Captain A. Gray had returned from the army. Marcia had piloted her lover into the company room "to see her tatting." There they had rapturously embraced, clinging to each other, Marcia weeping, Captain Lacefield blinking his own eyes and kissing away his betrothed's tears. Amid the recoil from all the apprehension Marcia had felt for him they were wondrously and amazingly happy.

The two had never remotely approached that moment again. It was as if in that instant of ecstasy Marcia had used up all her underlying apprehensions and griefs. Her sorrows were buried, and along with them, as so often happens, her joys.

Now she told A. Gray that Cassandra was in the room. A. Gray went and looked. The room was empty. So Marcia went in and kissed him.

"Now, what are we going to do in Florence?" she asked with a feeling that she had paid for the information.

"Why, Marcia, I—I thought I'd be a—er—newspaper man," said the captain diffidently.

"Run a newspaper!" ejaculated the girl unbelievingly.

"Yes, they're easy to start. I can get a Washington hand press for three hundred and fifty dollars or a roller press for six hundred and eighty-four, plus the freight from Cincinnati. Which would you get, Marcia?"

A. Gray thought if he could get her absorbed in the details, the general idea would pass muster by itself.

"Why, the three-fifty one, of course. . . . A. Gray, what do you want with a paper?"

"Marcia, I—I wouldn't admit this to a soul in the world but you."

Something in his manner, a tinge of the absurd, made her want to smile, but she saw how earnest he was and remained serious.

"All right—admit."

"Oh, I can't if you take it like that."

"I don't take it like that," comforted the girl. She kissed her finger and put it to his lips. "You know I'm not making fun of you if you're serious."

"Well . . ." He appeared to be about to plunge into cold water. "I want to write."

"Write!"

He nodded mutely.

"A. Gray, of all things!"

"I've always wanted to write."

"Isn't that funny!" she cried incredulously.

"And if you want to write you've got to publish it to get it read—and to make it pay. So the only thing to do is to start a newspaper."

This last was not unusual. In almost every Southern village there was a weekly newspaper, not because anyone believed there was money in it, but because somebody wanted to write. As the rather trite focus of this creative urge, the South wanted to express broadcast what they thought of the Yankees, the lamentable condition of the roads, the neglect of religion, and such public nuisances.

Marcia was not only surprised, she was delighted at this unexpected ambition in her fiancé.

"Why, honey," she cried, "you should have told me long ago! I could have helped you."

This phrase did not mean that she would have assisted in his actual writing, which, by the way, he had thus far never attempted. She meant that her conscious love and sympathy with his desire to write would in some mysterious way imbue him with the power of creating thoughts and setting them down on paper. It was a mystical left-over from the days of chivalry.

In the delicate embarrassment of admitting he wanted to write, Captain A. Gray had reached into his pocket and was twiddling a ten-dollar gold piece.

Now, to be seen with a gold piece in the day of shin plasters and depreciated currency was as unprecedented as to be seen abroad wearing the English crown jewels as a scarf pin.

When Marcia caught a glimpse of it, she cried, "A. Gray, isn't that a gold piece?"

"Yes," said A. Gray, quickly putting it back in his pocket.

"How much is it?"

"Ten dollars."

"It—is it yours?"

"No."

"Then whose is it, pray?"

"Well—I have three—they belong to the order."

"Imagine it!" cried Marcia, opening her gray eyes and becoming amused again. "I didn't know the Klan was worth thirty dollars."

"Marcia," said A. Gray solemnly, "the Klan is worth just exactly the combined capital of all its members."

"I hope you don't tote the combined capital of all its members around with you?"

"You oughtn't to talk that way, Marcia, about men who have sworn to protect you."

"No, I suppose I oughtn't."

"You laugh at us but you'd get along rather badly without us. The Yankees and the niggers would take everything."

Marcia skipped to a phase of the subject in which she was interested.

"What are you going to do with that money?" she asked curiously.

"M—m, I can't tell you."

"Another secret?"

"Yes."

Marcia began laughing.

"Then I may expect to hear all about it by night."

"No, you'll never learn about this secret till day after tomorrow," declared the captain lightly.

He began laughing too, kissed her again, and went away.

CHAPTER FIFTY-TWO

THE GOLD COINS which Marcia had seen in Captain Lacefield's possession were Miltiades' idea. It was a dramatic idea and on the day of its execution Colonel Vaiden was in such obviously good spirits that Cassandra called him aside for a little private talk, as she always did when she meant to be critical. She began flat footed, as she always did when putting one of her own family to rights.

"Look here, Milt, you're fixing to go down and see Drusilla Crowninshield again."

"Why, I am not—and what if I were?"

Miss Cassandra was surprised that he was not going at that particular moment, but since she had started she kept on with her objection.

"Because I can't bear to see you trotting back like a little puppy the moment she whistles at you. You know what she did once . . . invitations out, preacher engaged, house full of flowers, then making you the talk of the neighborhood by eloping on the night before the wedding!"

Cassandra's face paled at the remembered insult done her brother.

"And now, just to say, 'Come back, Miltiades' "—Miss Cassandra mimicked Drusilla's soft drawl—"And here you trot back again. It makes me ashamed to be a Vaiden!"

Miltiades, after all, was a Vaiden. His strain had come down through Indian fighters and Baptist predestinarians, and neither they nor their God ever forgave anybody anything. So the brother was a little put to it to hatch up some reason for his action.

"Drusilla was little more than a girl then, Cassandra," he said uncomfortably.

"A girl—you mean a flirt. You weren't good enough for her then. But now that she's a woman with a brat on her hands and no income to speak of, why, you'll do. Everybody knows you'll make a success. You always do what you started out to do. By the time you're as old as Drusilla's father you'll own twice as much as he ever had in his life."

This rather vicious compliment had its effect on the colonel.

"No," he said after a pause, "I'm not going to see Drusilla to-day."

"Well, that's all right," nodded Miss Cassandra, who was not interested in anything else he was going to do, "but if you're not going now you will be pretty soon. I've been wanting to say my say ever since you first went down there." She paused a moment and then added, "If I thought you were fixing to pay her back in her own coin, I wouldn't have mentioned it, but I don't think you are."

This talk with Cassandra Miltiades dismissed with the philosophic indifference any brother feels for the advice of any sister, but it did serve to remove some of the rainbows from the coup Colonel Vaiden had planned with the thirty dollars in gold.

A camp meeting was in progress in the upper part of the county near the Tennessee line, and it was Miltiades' inspiration for his Klan to march into the church in ghostly attire, place the offering in a silver platter on the altar, and march out again in complete silence.

It would be awe inspiring; it would be reverent; the money would be an amazing windfall for the congregation; it would be the biggest advertisement the Klan had ever had.

Now Cassandra's talk struck at his enthusiasm in a very odd and roundabout fashion.

Even if the gold offering worked out at the top of its bent,
he, Miltiades Vaiden, would receive no particular glory out
of the affair. He might be more powerful in the Klan, but
the Klan itself would not last long. It was a makeshift organization to tide the South over a crisis. Colonel Vaiden did not
believe the negroes had either the brain or energy to hold
the reins of government which the carpetbaggers were pre-
tending to thrust into their hands. When the Klan had finished its work where would he, personally, be?

If he married Drusilla Lacefield and succeeded in holding
the negro labor on the Lacefield estate, he would be just
fairly well off. He did not believe the Lacefield estate would
ever again be the barony it once was. Miltiades was not subtle enough really to analyze what had happened in the South,
but he was uneasily aware of a profound dislocation. It was
therefore with a feeling of the temporariness and inconse-
quence to himself of what he and his neighbors were doing
that he rode out alone to the secluded woodland rendezvous.

There was an iron-clad rule of the order that no two members should ride together to the meeting places. That was
because several horsemen seen together might arouse suspicion in the public that a meeting of the Klan was about to
take place.

This rule was so well known that no single rider could
pass along the road but what the neighbors would look out
and call to each other in guarded voices, "Come quick! Look!
Yonder goes a Klansman!"

Then they would watch the long-accustomed neighbor until he rode out of sight.

The meeting places of the Klan were always in the woods
and usually near some fox's den. The reason for this was
that the Klansmen, in the main, had been fox hunters before the war. They knew every fox den from Decatur
County in Alabama to Lane and Hardin counties in Tennessee. They not only knew where the dens were, but they knew
the very foxes that lived in these holes. This one had a toe

gone; that one had a silvery brush; another had a broken ear, and so on and on, throughout the fox population of Lauderdale.

And by the same token, the foxes were acquainted with the Klansmen. A coursing fox paid no more attention to a group of men sitting silently on their horses than it did to the surrounding trees.

Near sundown on this particular afternoon the Klan met at the Johnson Bluff Hole; so called because the farm nearest the den, about four miles distant, belonged to a man by the name of Johnson.

When Miltiades reached the spot he saw a horse hitched and knew that a man named Raspberry had preceded him. After a moment Raspberry stepped out of the bushes, pulling his suspenders over his shoulders.

"Hey oh, Colonel, did you forgit where the Johnson Bluff Hole was located at?"

"No, of course I didn't—here I am."

"Yeh, I see you are here, but didn't you ride on a mile or two an' haff to turn back?"

"No, I came straight here—why?"

"Why, I was follerin' a horse's track that went up the road past here. I thought it was yo' hoss. I thought I knowed yo' hoss's tracks."

"No, I just got here."

"Whose tracks d'ye reckon they was?"

"Don't know."

"Noticed 'em, didn't ye?"

"No, I didn't."

"I be dern!" ejaculated Raspberry. "Well, that shows the result of bein' a big business man, Colonel—got your mind on business and don't notice fresh hoss tracks smack in the road you're ridin' over."

That Miltiades was a big business man was a hangover from his overseer days and this was exaggerated by the important manner in which Miltiades did and said everything.

He always appeared to be conning over the details of some great business combination—and usually he was.

Other members gathered in. Their talk was of crops, of certain negroes in the neighborhood who needed a little working on; but behind their small talk was the underlying excitement of marching into a meeting house in their sheets.

Raspberry said he knew it would skeer the filling out of the congregation and he believed it would out of him, too.

"Well, for God's sake don't show it," cautioned Miltiades, "that would ruin everything."

Raspberry said he wouldn't show it.

Anxiety came over Miltiades. He thought what if one of the ghostly procession should be so struck with stage fright that he couldn't walk. Such a mishap might very well ruin the whole influence of the Klan in northern Alabama. If once people ever laughed at the Klan it would be lost.

So he began instructing the men not to glance at the audience, but for each one to look straight at the man in front of him.

"A lot depends on that," he impressed on them. "We don't want to waste our thirty dollars."

By this time the sun had sunk. An abyss of greenish blue and crimson loomed behind the trees and crags of Johnson's Bluff Hole. Bullbats curved through the night on teetering wings and sounded their raucous note.

The men got out their sheets from inside the folds of their saddle blankets. When they had the white cloth over their heads and bodies the appearance of the others gave each one a sensation of the macabre. What would happen during the night before them they would laugh at heartily when they were in their ordinary clothes again, but nothing would appear droll as long as they saw each other in these ghostly habits.

One of the maskers spoke to another in the unnatural voice that was obligatory upon them while wearing the sheets.

"Is that the sunset?" he groaned.

The whole group looked and a squeaking falsetto answered: "No, that isn't even in the west."

"Well, what is it then?" asked the groan.

"That's in the direction of Amos Johnson's house . . . d'reckon his cabin's on fire?"

"Le's ride over there and see," suggested a hollow baritone.

The squeak said, "If he has burnt out, how about giving him the thirty dollars?"

"No, don't do that," counseled Miltiades.

The horsemen set out toward the distant light, whose position and wavering intensity proclaimed it with certainty to be the Johnson cabin. When Miltiades came within sight of the actual flames it reminded him, oddly enough, of the burning of his father's gin which he had never seen.

The shrouded horsemen had ridden hard. Now as they came up they saw the small dark figures of a woman and some children running to and from a spring under a hillside trying to save their barn. The burning cabin was at its greatest heat. The logs had just fallen in, opening the heart of the fire. The eaves of the barn were smoking.

As the horsemen dashed up the children screamed, threw down their buckets, and vanished into the surrounding woods. The old woman halted in her fight, then without a word hurried on with her one bucket of water to the stable.

Miltiades called in his assumed voice:

"Pick up what buckets you can find—use your hats—get water to this stable!"

Instantly the whole corps were off their horses. One ghost held the bridles, the others fell into a continuous marching and remarching from spring to stable and back, like a human telpherage.

The number of men, the method and swiftness with which they worked decided the fate of the stable. The old woman gave over her fight to her startling helpers and stood staring at her burning cabin. When the intensity of the flames had abated and the barn was no longer threatened, Miltiades went to the woman and said in his sepulchral tone:

"Hepzy Johnson, where is your husband?"

The woman stared at the sheeted form a moment and then said in her hill twang, "You-uns ort to know."

"We . . . don't know . . . Hepzy Johnson."

The woman caught her breath.

"He's in hell, I reckon—you-uns sent him thar."

"What do you mean?" asked Miltiades sharply, losing much of his heavy tone.

"Mean!" screamed the woman suddenly. "You-uns know what I mean. Ye sneaked up an' far'd our cabin, then when Amos went out to see what was the matter, you-uns shot him down."

"Where was he shot?"

"On the doorstep. I guess he's burnt up now."

The ghosts collected about the woman now turned and approached the fire. Their robes protected them from the bite of the heat. In the red lights they made out a form near the edge of the coals. It lay face down. The hair and back of the clothes were burned off. It did not suggest a human being except the legs. As the men neared the fire they caught the stench of burned flesh.

The woman remained implacable where she was, evidently convinced that the men who had helped put out the fire had first kindled it and shot her husband.

"When was he killed?" asked Miltiades.

"When the far started, I told je."

"About an hour ago?" hazarded one of the men.

Colonel Vaiden called his men around him.

"An hour's start won't carry a man very far when he doesn't know anybody's after him," he planned sharply. "We ought to reach Bill Leatherwood's cabin almost as quick as he does."

At such a plan the hill woman looked at the riders.

"Didn't you-uns do this?" she asked in a different tone.

"Hepzy Johnson," said Miltiades, remembering his solemn voice, "you see before you the defenders of freedom—the dragon guarding the wounded South."

At this the woman turned toward the woods and called, in a strained tone, "Chillern, these-uns ain't the ones that shot yore pappy."

She gave a single indrawn sob, then stood in silence looking at the blackened trunk and legs in the edge of the fire.

When the ghostly cortège rode away, they directed their course not directly toward the camp meeting, but veered to the left, following the hill trail that led to the Leatherwood cabin.

CHAPTER FIFTY-THREE

THE TACIT EXPANSION of the Klan's authority to include white men as well as black gratified something fundamental in Miltiades Vaiden. He rode ahead, thinking of himself as arbiter of the community, as ruling with a stern but equitable justice. It seemed to Miltiades that his feeling for and adherence to a strict justice was keener than that of most men, and that, he told himself, was why he was not popular. It was a strange thing that, while he was always chosen for a leading position in anything he undertook, still he had never been what men call popular. The simple geniality which men scattered everywhere among themselves somehow never came to him. It was, he supposed, because there was in him something of the isolation of the arbiter. And he thought of Drusilla Crowninshield sharing this aloofness.

One of the shrouded men moved his horse up to Miltiades' side and asked in a queer voice, "Hadn't we better pull off our sheets so Bill Leatherwood can't see us so plainly in the dark?"

Colonel Vaiden's thoughts came back to the present. The Klan had reached their objective. Ahead of them a faint light marked the location of one of those small log fortresses which were the conventional homes among the hills.

Colonel Vaiden said, "No, I don't believe I ever heard of a soldier pulling off his uniform to go into battle."

The man was disconcerted.

"Well—of course—I thought I'd ask——" and he moved his horse a little away from his leader.

A sound arrested the attention of the sheeted horsemen, a melancholy rising and falling of a voice in the cabin. Amid the clatter of the horses' hoofs the men could not distinguish the words, but the sound of the voice was filled with the outcry of a great grief. The horsemen involuntarily drew rein to listen and speak to each other.

"What in the hell is that?" inquired a voice in wonderment.

Miltiades listened to the wailings in the cabin. The outlaw was crying aloud to the night that he was a thief and a murderer; he was a house burner and a ruiner of women; he was not fit to live—and on and on in astonishing self-accusation.

The riders listened in increased amazement.

"What do you suppose that can mean?" asked one.

"Listen," put in another. "I've heard that Amos Johnson used to run with the Leatherwood gang. Bill must have paid off some old grudge he had against the fellow."

The speaker turned to Miltiades.

"I can tell you what happened," said the colonel crisply. "Leatherwood got drunk, remembered his grudge, rode down and paid it off. Now he's come back, sobering up, and he's sorry he's got himself into trouble."

"Oh, my God," came the voice from the cabin, "airy dawg is better'n I am!"

A man near Miltiades gave a sort of laugh.

"That's the first time I ever heard a man size himself up exactly right," he said in a low tone.

Miltiades directed his men to form a cordon around the cabin, as was their custom in these visitations.

"Six of you hold your guns on the back door," he directed briefly, "so if he comes out shooting you'll stop him before he hurts anybody."

The men saluted, rode around from both sides, and part of their number faded in the darkness.

Miltiades sat a moment longer listening to the wild self-denunciations in the cabin, then he took out his army pistol, cocked it, and shouted Leatherwood's name. At his call utter silence fell in the cabin. Then the whole mountainside was breathlessly quiet except for the stamp or snort of a horse. Miltiades called again in the ominous silence. He expected a shot from the dark interior of the hut.

Instead of that a woman's nasal voice called out, "Who air you-all?"

"We're the Klan," snapped Miltiades. "We've come for Bill Leatherwood."

Another silence followed, then the woman's voice inside repeated, as if she were afraid the man had not heard:

"Bill, it's the Klan—come fer ye."

Another silence, then a cracked man's voice said, "Wall, Bill, thar's ye sign."

And Leatherwood's heavy bass replied, "But what does hit mean?"

And the cracked voice said, "Hit's jest a sign frum God, Bill—they ain't no tellin' whut hit means."

Miltiades called sharply, "Are you men coming out, or are we going to have to come in and get you?"

"We're comin' out," called Leatherwood. "I don't want you-uns shootin' in the cabin where Marth and the young uns is."

"Come out with your hands up," directed the colonel.

Another interval, then movement in the cabin. Hill voices said, "Good-bye Marth. Good-bye Bill—an' you too, Dry."

Children's voices were saying, "Air they gwinter kill Pappy? Whyn't you kill them, Pappy?"

Then the voice of a very small child, not quite the final stoic of the hills, began to cry.

The masked figures around the hut breathed more easily when they became assured that Leatherwood really was coming out with his hands up. Their grip on their own pistols became firmer. They could direct their fire more accurately.

Two dim figures emerged from the cabin door, a large one and a small one.

"Halt!" commanded Miltiades.

The men stopped. Leatherwood said:

"What have you-uns come after us fur?"

"Murder and house burning," said Miltiades in a sepulchral tone.

"Well," said the outlaw, "we shore have done it."

"What air ye goin' to do to us?" asked the cracked voice.

"Walk down the road ahead of our horses," directed Miltiades; "don't try to run. You wouldn't make it anyway."

The two dim figures with their arms still uplifted walked away from the cabin in which a hill woman intermittently hushed the sobs of her smallest child.

The shrouded riders marched the two outlaws on down the road until they came to two white oaks. They stood them up with their backs to the trees in the queer formality of executions. . . .

When it was over Miltiades struck a lucifer and looked at his watch. It was midnight. He was a church member but he never attended the services and so asked a companion if he supposed the meeting was still going on.

"Yes," said a fellow goblin, "that camp meetin' is in a weavin' way now. They'll keep whoopin' it up till mornin'."

"All right," said Miltiades. "Now men, all of you listen. We'll march in in double column, and I don't want anybody getting afraid or nervous. Keep a grip on yourselves. If anybody gets scared up there before all the people—well, imagine what they would think!"

"I ain't goin' to look at anybody but the man in front of me," said Raspberry, putting his pistol back in its holster. "I know damn well I'd flicker."

"Now, when I put the plate on the altar," went on Miltiades, "I'll put my palms together like this for about half a minute. All of you do the same thing. Let every man count sixty to himself, then take his hands down, right about, and march out."

"That's easy to remember," repeated a voice; "fold your hands, count sixty, and march out."

In the church house on upper Shoal Creek there was singing and shouting as the white-robed Ku Klux entered. The religious uproar died abruptly in the back of the church. The preachers and the workers who were facing the door stood stone still in the attitudes in which the entering ghosts had surprised them. Then silence wrapped the whole hot, smelly congregation.

In the midst of it a woman, already hysterical, screamed, "Oh, Jesus an' His angels!" and fainted.

A hillman caught her and held her up without taking his eyes from the veiled processional.

The silver plate with the gold pieces on it was laid on the table. The marchers folded their palms. A woman on an aisle seat heard one of the figures whispering:

"One . . . two . . . three . . . four . . ."

Presently all the ghosts turned and marched out again.

As they hurried to their horses the figure of the parson came running out the church door. Miltiades knew that he wanted to thank him and his men for their astonishing gift. When the preacher came up he stammered in a breathless voice:

"Did—did any of you gentlemen see Bill Leatherwood?"

The Ku Klux sat on their horses as astounded as the congregation had been.

"Why?" asked Miltiades in a sepulchral tone.

" 'Y—'Y," stammered the parson, "he come to the mourner's bench at the afternoon service. I told him to go home, confess his sins and wrastle with God for forgiveness. . . . I was expectin' him back here to-night."

CHAPTER FIFTY-FOUR

Over the county there was naturally a great deal of talk about the Leatherwood execution. Pro-Klan men pointed out that the horse thief and guerilla richly deserved death and that any public-spirited group of men executing Bill Leatherwood could not go wrong.

As Erastus Ham expressed it, "If we had to make a mistake like that, we picked the right man to make it on. The Klan, like the Pope, is infallible."

However the anti-Klan men said the whole affair reflected very little honor on the Ku Klux. There was even some talk of Judge Britton having the matter investigated at the next grand jury, but that was impossible because no one knew the personnel of the Klan.

Besides these simple phases of the matter, the countryside theologians went off into esoteric speculations on the tragedy. The Campbellites thought Bill had gone to hell because he had repented but had not been baptized. Old man Jimmie Vaiden considered that Bill was in heaven because, according to the Baptist creed, repentance alone could send a man to heaven, but it required both repentance and baptism to achieve the bliss of being a Hardshell Baptist. "I'll venture," said old man Jimmie, "he's the only angel in heaven that wasn't a Baptist here on earth, although," he added with a philosopher's circumspection, "a few others may have seeped in the same way he did."

Parson Mulry, who was a Methodist, said it all depended on whether Bill had come through or not. Bill was on the

mourner's bench but he never had shouted any and under
those conditions the Methodist Church declined to place itself on record as saying just where Bill had gone.

Somewhat later in the year a Presbyterian revivalist in
Florence referred to Bill Leatherwood as an extraordinary
example of eleventh-hour salvation.

Mr. Erastus Ham cleared the situation considerably when
he pointed out that it was all a matter of jurisdiction, and
that since Bill Leatherwood was attending a Baptist meeting
at the time of his death, then he was settling up his accounts
with God on Baptist terms, and those terms let him into
heaven. So that was the way the matter was finally disposed
of.

But be the religious conundrum Bill Leatherwood's death
propounded what it may, its moral effect on the negroes of
the neighborhood was tremendous and happy. The black
folk quite rightly reasoned that if the ghosts would shoot
two white men what would they do to a negro?

As a result, the colored population of Lauderdale stayed
on the plantations where they worked more closely even than
in the palmy days of slavery. They did not so much as visit a
neighboring plantation at night for fear of meeting a
ghostly procession.

Under the improved conditions the Lacefields decided to
stay in their country place and build more cabins to replace
their burned slave quarters. The elder Mr. Lacefield had re-
established his line of credit with J. Handback & Son, General Merchandise, the leading retail store in Florence.

The patrician admitted heartily to Miltiades that the
Klan had saved him. He said one day to the colonel in his
study:

"Any man would be proud to call you son, Miltiades,"
which meant whatever it might mean.

Mr. Caruthers Lacefield could say this to Miltiades only
by a squeak. The younger man might possibly have been the

older man's son. However, Mr. Lacefield's pure white hair lent the compliment grace.

"I hope you may have that dubious honor," said Miltiades with a faint smile.

"So do I," said the aristocrat, and he offered his hand impulsively and frankly.

For the first time the two talked about the delicate situation.

"As a matter of fact, I always have been silently a Vaiden man," admitted Mr. Lacefield. "Of course, I said nothing at all. I was looking at it from the standpoint of—well —of life as it has to be lived. A woman, of course, looks at marriage from a higher point than that, the immaterial, the poetical . . . perhaps I should say the spiritual."

"I suppose that is true," agreed the ex-overseer with a faint unhappy questioning if Colonel Crowninshield really exceeded him in such qualities.

"They don't realize," went on the aristocrat—"at least not at first—that spiritual qualities can thrive most naturally in the midst of material abundance. 'When poverty comes in the door, love flies out the window.' " The planter liked an old saw now and then.

Miltiades nodded.

"But on the other hand," conceded Mr. Lacefield, "when riches come in the door, love very often uses the same exit. If you two should ever see fit to unite your lives, Miltiades, I would have more concern for what wealth would do to you than for what poverty would do. I am convinced you have the elements of success in you, Miltiades."

"I certainly hope I fulfill your suggestion and your expectation," said Miltiades, thinking if Drusilla had just a touch more of her father in her what a marvelously charming woman she would be.

The two talked on for several minutes when Miltiades said, "Mr. Lacefield, I have an announcement—a rather important announcement—to make to you."

"Yes?" inquired the older man curiously.

"With your permission, your name will head the Democratic ticket as candidate for the governorship of Alabama."

The planter was surprised and moved.

"Colonel Vaiden, I am not the one to lead the fight for a white man's government in Alabama. I am neither a lawyer nor an orator."

"We discussed all that in a meeting of the Klan," agreed Miltiades. "You see, all your niggers have liked you. We picked on you as a man who might possibly get a part of the black vote; that is if the niggers really get to the polls."

"M—m . . . not likely." The planter shook his head. "A nigger's gratitude is mainly vocal, Miltiades. . . . I might possibly get a few."

"And you would be sure of all the white vote."

"But there isn't any white vote, all the white men are disfranchised."

"Only those who bore arms against the Union."

"But that takes in all the Southern white men, Miltiades!"

"Oh, no, it doesn't. Some of the older men never went to the front, a few invalids, then there were the shirkers, men who ran off in the woods and enlisted under General Green."

"There's not enough of them to elect a constable, much less a governor."

Miltiades smiled.

"On the contrary, nobody but just those white men are going to vote in the coming election. No nigger will appear at the polls; the Klan will see to that."

Mr. Lacefield pondered a moment, his meshed and finely carved face took on a satiric expression.

"Wouldn't that be the very barb of irony if Southern civilization, which was lost through the swords of heroes, should be restored by the votes of the infirm, the aged, the cowards, and the skulkers?" He laughed. "That is a true comment, my dear Vaiden, on the workings of a democracy. Of all mad doctrines, the equality of man is the most insane, and for a black animal to cast a vote because it can balance itself on two legs is political suicide. Look what the outcome is! Black riff-raff egged on by Northern thieves voting against white riff-raff bolstered up by a secret society of terrorists; and between the two hangs the destiny of a nation of disfranchised gentlemen—it's a nightmare out of some political hell!"

"Well," philosophized Miltiades, who held no objections to secret societies, "we must fight back with whatever we can lay hands on. You can't pick your weapon when a robber's on you."

"No, no, I don't disapprove your tactics, although I loathe their necessity."

"Then I can say you have accepted the nomination?"

"Miltiades, I haven't the means to finance such a campaign," said the planter simply. "I can hardly approach John Handback and ask him for credit for such a purpose."

The Grand Dragon of the Ku Klux held up a hand and stopped him.

"You needn't travel a mile or make a speech. The Klan works unseen and our candidate may use the same method. You will poll just as strong a vote as if you had campaigned Alabama from Florence to Mobile."

Colonel Vaiden was thoroughly pleased at the outcome of his mission. If the planters' candidate were successful, it would give him an intimate connection with Alabama politics and legislation. Such a post of power appealed strongly to Miltiades. He fancied himself and Drusilla in the official circles in the state capitol. He could look after the Klan interests in the government. He suddenly wanted to talk over these matters with Drusilla. The planter said she was probably upstairs in her room.

Miltiades walked out of the planter's study, through the painted great hall, and ran upstairs. He tapped at Drusilla's door to know if he could enter.

Drusilla's voice asked him to wait a moment. After a brief interval she opened the door. She wore a house dress with enough red in it to point the depth of her eyes, the darkness of her hair, and the soft crimson curves of her lips. She looked at him in surprise.

"I didn't know you were on the place!"

He put the door shut then took her in his arms and kissed her.

"You can't guess what I'm here for."

"To kiss me, of course." She lifted herself to him again and pressed her lips to his repeatedly.

Her fragrance, the pressure of her mouth on his own swung the man's thoughts a little away from his remarkable news. He came back to it after a moment.

"Your father has consented to run for the governorship of Alabama!"

Drusilla caught her breath.

"Miltiades, you don't mean it! Did you engineer that?" She held her torso away from him and scrutinized his face with a great gladness.

"Well . . . I wasn't exactly an obstacle," he laughed.

Drusilla's delight translated itself into a diffused passion for her lover. She put her hands to the sides of his face and kissed him again.

"Honey, you are wonderful! You just wave your hand and the niggers stay on our plantation . . . then Father's running for governor . . ."

She drew him to a settee and they sat on it with their arms about each other.

"How did you ever get Father's name before the Klan, Milt?" she asked eagerly.

Miltiades gave one of his rare laughs.

"I talked to the men separately about him. I would pick

out his strong points, be dubious about them, and get the other man to defend him."

The woman gave him a hug.

"Milt, you are clever!" She drew his arm more snugly around her waist and patted his hand in content. "Suppose I get to be the governor's daughter . . ."

The smile vanished from the colonel's face. He sat looking out the second-story window at the untrimmed poplars.

"I wonder what would happen?" he mused soberly.

Drusilla looked at him intently. She divined what he had in mind and a feeling of tension went through her breast.

"Listen, dear," she said with an odd edge to her voice, "don't think—what—what you are thinking. Quit it—don't think it!"

The man held her in lax arms and looked at her.

"Suppose I did get you and Mr. Lacefield to Montgomery . . ."

She knew that he was thinking of the men she would meet —handsome men, clever men, distinguished men—and a certain new fixity of admiration and desire for Miltiades himself made her cry out:

"But darling, can't you feel I am different to—to what I ever was?"

"Drusilla, I don't know. . . . Do you know," he broke off oddly, "I have had a feeling that your beauty as a girl was dangerous—well, of course it was——"

"But I'm—not any more?" asked the woman equivocally.

"Oh, good Lord," ejaculated the man hopelessly, "you are double—treble—any man who saw you—it would tear out his heart——"

"But listen," begged the girl nervously, "if I am nicer to —to look at, Milt, I—I'm nicer in every way—really." The girl's breathing pressed her torso against her red blouse; she looked at Miltiades out of wistful half-closed eyes.

"You listen yourself," said Miltiades, with a kind of clumsy surface playfulness covering the shake of his pulse in his neck. "I wouldn't go through with what I did, not for an entrance into heaven, Drusilla—to want you as I did—to wake up every night for months, for years, and have your face and form before my eyes and your place beside me empty. It was a kind of hell, a kind of cold gray hell."

The woman gave a sort of nervous laugh.

"Well—that isn't all in the past, is it—Milt?" She drew his arm more tightly around her waist.

"You don't want it to be?"

"Of course not," she breathed. She gave his hand a little convulsive pressure. His fingers touched the full margin of her bosom. With a shiver she drew up his palm and cupped it hard over her left breast.

At the feeling of his fingers sinking into the soft mound a kind of voluptuous melting filled Drusilla. The sweet, tantalizing hunger of women who have known and need men swept over her. They were quite near the window out of which, four years before, she had eloped with Crowninshield. The difference in the quality of her two passions flickered for a moment in Drusilla's thought. She suddenly drew the man's face down into her neck.

"Honey," she shivered, "if—if it hadn't been for—for the other—I—I couldn't possibly love you like this."

"Then you do love me—me?" he stressed in torture.

"Oh, yes—yes. It—makes me weak—I—I feel ill," she gasped.

"Drusilla, listen. When are we going to be married?"

"Oh—I don't know—why?"

"To-morrow."

She pushed her torso up towards his, flattening her full breasts against his chest.

"We—can't go through with—with the ceremony—that soon." She began shivering uncontrollably.

"The ceremony?"

"Not—not the ceremony."

The man pressed his mouth to hers. Their hearts became

suffocating. And they drifted for a few moments outside of time and space. . . .

At some time later they sat almost without words in the midst of a profound peace and lassitude: that peace and lassitude which run like far-off heralds before their great lord, Death. They sat holding each other laxly by the hand. The woman was lost now in a vague questioning mood. She was thinking of the ceremony which had not been said; as though that had anything to do with it—as though there were some exquisitely subtle connection between her bestowal and abrupt loss of her swooning passion and the altar of a church.

The door opened and little Sydna entered. The mother looked at Miltiades with a faint smile and held out her hand to her little daughter.

"Come kiss Miltiades, Sydna," she directed. "He is going to be your father."

"Are you going to marry Miltiades, Mamma?" asked the little thing.

"Yes, Beautiful."

The child came and touched her cool moist mouth to the hot dry lips of the man.

CHAPTER FIFTY-FIVE

MARCIA SAW Polycarp mounting his horse at the big gate and walked quickly out to him. There was something pleasing about Polycarp, as there is about most men who are of the temperament occasionally to become intoxicated. The sister had never thought out the connection between charm, conviviality, and drunkenness. If she had, the pleasant combination of Polycarp's military shoulders and careless posture on his horse would not have pleased her. A thought of Gracie's baby flickered through her mind but was instantly suppressed, then her brother appeared as manly and smiling as if her former maid had never stumbled into her half confession.

"All right, Marsh," he called, waiting for her to come up. "What's the password now?"

Since he had joined the Klan, Carp's talk had taken on clannish allusions.

"Where you going, Carp?"

"Over to the Amos Johnson place."

"What for?"

"M—m . . . well, for one reason, the road leads by Ponny's home."

"And the other?"

"I'm taking Hepzy Johnson a pair of quilts—but that's a graveyard secret."

"Well, of all things, how came that?"

"Klan charity, my dear girl. I'm an elf. Wherever there are goblins there are bound to be elves. The elves are as good

462

as the goblins are bad. I'm to slip these quilts in the barn. Hepzy and her children are living in the barn now, I understand. They sleep in the hay. I'm to leave the quilts unbeknownst, together with a note saying, 'From the Invisible Empire' . . . you mustn't tell that."

Marcia smiled sympathetically.

"The note won't do much good. She can't read, I'm sure."

"No, but she'll take it to somebody and get it read. It will be a bigger send-off for the Klan than if she could read it herself—you see that, don't you?"

"That's a fact . . . you didn't think of that, Carp."

"No, Milt thought of that."

"You know," said Marcia, nodding and wrinkling up her nose, "Milt is pretty bright."

"I couldn't go as far as that," said Polycarp, "but I will say I've seen dumber members of our family."

"Yes, so have all the rest of us," snapped Marcia.

Polycarp laughed.

"Oh, well, it isn't my brains that are going to get me through, it's my goodness, so I'm off like a regular old Haroun-al-Raschid."

Marcia's mind came back to the original notion which had brought her out.

"Carp," she asked, with a touch of self-consciousness, "when are you and Ponny going to be married?"

"No indeed, I go last. When are you and A. Gray going to step off?"

Marcia flushed.

"That—that's what I wanted to talk to you about. Sister Cassandra is nearly dead for all of us to—to—well, all be married at the same time."

Polycarp pulled down a smile.

"Yes, Sister Cassandra is bitterly opposed to any of us marrying anybody."

"I know that, but if we must marry she wants us married in a group."

Polycarp began laughing.

"I see. She wants a Vaiden majority in the combined cere-monies. She will overwhelm the enemy in detail, so to speak."

"It's a sort of effort to hold the family together," said Marcia pleadingly. "She cares so much more about that than we do."

"She's the only one who gives a rap about it," agreed the brother.

"I do," protested Marcia, not willing for any virtue to pass her by.

"Yes you do! You know you don't want to stand up with me and Miltiades and all be married together. Milt won't want to either."

"He was going to once," hesitated Marcia with a wince at the recollection.

"Well, he's ten times as top heavy now as he was then."

"He's reserved," softened Marcia, "but I think it's dis-tinguished to be reserved."

Polycarp began laughing and put Marcia out of patience with him.

"You ask him, Polycarp," she insisted.

"I'll do nothing of the sort. Let Cassandra ask him. She's the one who wants it. I don't want it. If me and Ponny stum-ble into Miltiades' ceremony, when we come out nobody will ever know whether we were married or not."

"But you'll do it."

"Oh, sure." He hesitated. "That's all you wanted with me, isn't it? I must fly on my mission of mercy."

"Carp, you really are on one—you oughtn't to talk about it like that."

"Marcia, you are like Miltiades, you think a good deed should be done gloomily."

"I wish you were more like him."

"If I had been you'd never have mentioned a combination wedding to me."

Marcia made a face at him and turned to go into the

house. The brother thought his sister charming. It was surprising how much better they were beginning to like each other than they ever had before.

"By the way, Marcia," he called, "A. Gray is coming around here some time this afternoon. I mention it so you can put on your war paint and sharpen your tomahawk."

"All right. I hope you find Ponny armed for a brisk skirmish."

This bucolic humor might have continued but a man riding along the road on a donkey attracted their attention. He was a gaunt, unshaven hillman, and he had to lift his long legs slightly so they would not drag the ground. He had on no shoes and in absurd contrast he wore a heavy blue army overcoat which swathed him and spread over the hinder parts of the long-eared little animal that bore him.

Polycarp and Marcia looked at each other and then pulled their faces straight. The hillman on the donkey was of preternatural gravity. He came to a halt in front of the yard and lowered his feet in the dust.

"Hidy," he said.

"Hidy," said Polycarp. "I'll bet I can guess where you got your coat."

The man looked at him steadily as if this were the most natural remark in the world.

"I ain't sayin' you kain't."

"And I am saying I can," returned Polycarp with equal seriousness. "You got it from Red Kilgo's wife."

"I ain't sayin' I didn't," said the man.

Marcia looked the other way. She thought she would better get into the house before she offended the donkey rider, but she could not tear herself away from such an exhibition.

"What did she charge you for it?" asked Polycarp solemnly.

"Didn't charge me nothin' fer it. I didn't git hit from her."

Marcia burst into uncontrollable laughter.

"Polycarp, that's one on you," she gasped.

Neither man paid the faintest attention to the convulsed girl. They continued looking at each other with the solemnity of owls. Polycarp said out of the corner of his mouth:

"Shut up, Marsh!"

The man in the greatcoat drawled with the aloof superiority of men over women, "Let her laff."

Marcia turned and went into the house with a mixed feeling of hysterical mirth and of a schoolgirl being stood up in the corner to wear a dunce's cap. When she was out of sight in the house she found her desire to laugh had gone. She went into the company room, stood on a chair, drew aside the pink-flowered curtain, and looked out.

The grotesque rider was still seated solemnly on his donkey but he was no longer funny. He was more nearly fantastic. It seemed that he might do or be anything. He and Polycarp were still talking; evidently, from the way they moved their heads, with the same laconic solemnity which she had heard. This, too, was no longer funny.

Presently, to her intense surprise, she saw the hillman fumble in his greatcoat pocket, produce something, dismount from his donkey by standing up and walking backwards, then he handed whatever it was to her brother. She wondered what in the world the thing could be. She decided it must be some curiosity he had found, probably an Indian relic of which the countryside was full. She tiptoed in her chair trying to see. She wanted to run out and ask Polycarp, but the man went back to his donkey, sat down on it again, and stayed on and on in the interminable leisure of the hills.

Marcia's calves began to ache so that she could tiptoe only now and then to see if he was still there. At last she looked after a long wait and saw the absurd little hind end of the donkey twitching off down the road under the blue greatcoat. She leaped from her chair and went flying outside.

Polycarp sat on his horse studying something.

"Carp!" cried the girl. "Let me see the Indian relic . . . what did he have?"

"It's not exactly an Indian relic," said Carp.

"Then what in the world is it?"

For answer her brother rode to the fence and handed it to her. It was a note. It read:

"To the Vadin boys—Gus Vadin pertended to hol ar hosses in the Catlin rade an' fit agin us. We hept Carp Vadin indurin the war and he hept kill two of ar men who hadent dun nothin 2 him. Milt Vadin got up the killin to skeer the niggers with. We dont like hit.

"LETHERWOOD GANG."

Marcia looked blankly at Carp and then at the note again.

"Was he one of the Leatherwood gang?"

"He said a man handed him the note up the road and asked him to hand it to one of the Vaidens."

"Why, Carp, I don't like this at all!"

"I can't truthfully say I'm fond of it myself."

Polycarp sat looking up the sunshot road in the direction the man had gone.

After her brother had ridden away, the note disturbed Marcia. She was moved to go in the kitchen and tell Rose, Augustus' wife, and her mother, but she was afraid it would worry her mother, and it would disturb Rose too on account of Augustus. Rose was endlessly fussy over Augustus. She watched what he ate, how he slept, whether a change in the weather caused his old wound to ache. And now, if anything even vaguely threatened Augustus, Marcia reflected that Rose would go into conniption fits. Rose never could get rid of the attitude that she was Augustus' nurse. She was like a hen with a single chick.

Naturally Rose's anxiety about her husband disgusted Miss Cassandra and amused Polycarp and Marcia. Miltiades never observed it. The only two persons who accepted Rose's devotion with entire complacency were old Mrs. Laura and Augustus himself. Mrs. Laura Vaiden fell right in with Rose's petting and she herself smuggled to Augustus' plate most of the present-day cream because he had been wounded and had suffered from gangrene four years ago.

Another reason Marcia did not go into the kitchen to tell about the note, she was afraid the others would put her to work. Marcia felt bitterly imposed upon if she had to do any work. She felt she had all she could do to dress herself, give her hair the hundred strokes night and morning, eat her meals, and spend the rest of the day thinking.

What she considered her thoughts had little definition and were more nearly moods than thoughts. Under her unguided reveries all things took on strange suggestive appearances. It seemed to her at times that some sort of dreamy meaning attached to all manner of things: a cloud, a pool of water beneath the willowed bank of a creek, or flowers. It seemed to her that flowers were conscious of life. The buds were children, the full blooms were maidens in love, and the withered blossoms were those that had known grief and care and were fading away.

Marcia had no physical objection to helping Rose and her mother in the kitchen. She fancied she might even like it if she could only spare the time from her thoughts. But she was always too busy.

So now, instead of risking the kitchen, she went up to her own room in the attic and began to dress for A. Gray. As she prinked before the mirror she began to wonder what it would be like, standing up with A. Gray in the church . . . being his wife in Florence while he ran a newspaper. There would certainly be no grand staircase up which she could sweep and glance back over her shoulder and smile. She thought, with a touch of superiority, that she would never in the world be as foolish about A. Gray as Rose was about Augustus. She was glad of that. . . . Then she wondered would she have been about Colonel Crowninshield. And abruptly all of her self-complacence faded out of her and she stood staring unseeing at her reflection in the mirror which, in turn, stared unseeing back out of the glass.

On days when she knew A. Gray was coming Marcia liked to walk down the road and meet him. To walk along the winding road, expecting to see him around any turn, made him, for the moment, something a little other than he was.

She walked on, touched by this illusion, for perhaps a quarter of a mile, when she heard the clatter of hoofs ahead of her. She slipped behind the bole of a tree to give her suitor a little surprise as he passed. And incidentally he would have to walk back to her home and let her ride.

The hoof beats grew louder, were right opposite her tree, and then she saw a man in blue was riding past. For a moment Marcia had an irrational impression that the donkey rider had expanded into a soldier in uniform.

Then the man saw her, pulled up sharply, and sat looking at her as if she had been an apparition. The rider appeared so whitened and emaciated that Marcia thought he must have climbed on his horse from a sickbed. His eyes were hollowed and blue. The fingers which held his reins were almost translucent. As Marcia stared back at him a sort of incredible recognition twanged through her heart. She could not believe what she saw.

"Jerry . . . Jerry," she whispered. "Jerry Catlin."

The man's face lighted up with a smile that wrinkled his worn features.

"I was coming to your home," he said in a faded voice. "I didn't hope to see you alone."

"Where have you been? What's happened to you?" She went to his horse's shoulder and held up her hands, partly by way of greeting, partly out of an impulse to take his wasted hands into her own.

The skinny smile flickered momentarily into his face again.

"I have been staying . . . with friends of yours."

His mirth horrified her.

"I don't know what you mean, Jerry."

"I've been in Tuscaloosa ever since you saw me last." He spoke in a weak, inattentive tone as he gazed into her face.

The dawning of horror came over the girl.

"How you have changed!" she cried pitifully.

The man gazed fixedly at her as if her features held some anodyne for his tremulous weakness.

"And you have changed, Marcia . . . to an angel." Then, without warning, and quite terribly to Marcia, his hollow eyes filled with tears. At this demonstration he apologized in his weak voice.

"Pardon me . . . I'm nervous . . . I'm terribly unstrung."

Marcia knew that during the war there had been a Confederate military prison in Tuscaloosa, but she could not connect Jerry's shocking appearance with that.

"Jerry, have you . . . been in prison?" she whispered in horror.

Instantly he was all right again.

"I was captured at Shiloh—I was in Prentiss' corps." He gave his faint heartbreaking smile again. "The men on your side were very persistent hosts to some very reluctant guests, Marcia. You know, lots of times I thought how our detachment had taken everything your father had to eat. I was sorry we did it. . . ." He sat musing on his horse for several moments. "The other prisoners would tell about their sweethearts in the North; it left me out. They knew they would go back to theirs if they ever got out. . . . We'd eat the salt pork and wormy bread and wonder if we would live to get out and see you all again. Then I would think . . . well, if I do, I probably won't get to see her after all."

Marcia knew nothing to say to this at all. She suddenly

realized that she had been in the thoughts of the soldier during his years of imprisonment.

"When did you get out?" she asked.

"About two months ago. I was sent here to Florence."

"That long!" ejaculated Marcia, wanting to be pleasantly cordial. "You might have come down to see us."

"I was looking too thin and bad when I first got here," said Jerry in his weak voice. "Really I—" he glanced at his emaciated hands—"I'm not very presentable now."

Marcia's heart failed again.

"Were you sick, Jerry?" she asked in a distressed voice.

"Well, we were all down with the scurvy," said the ex-prisoner.

Marcia was a little puzzled at this. She thought scurvy was a disease that affected the mouths of babies.

"Was it bad?" she asked curiously.

"The flesh falls off your shins . . . it made the prison smell horrible . . . about a third of us died from it."

"Didn't you have any nurses, or doctors?" ejaculated the girl in horror.

Jerry gave another of his mirthless wizened smiles.

"Nurses! We couldn't get anything to eat but salt pork. We tried to make money and buy something else. We cut brooches out of oyster shells and tried to sell them to the people who came to look at us."

"Jerry, you were sick—about to die—and cutting shells for something you could eat?"

His description called up a piteous lazar scene before the girl's imagination. She could not believe Confederate jailers could have been so callous to their prisoners. She knew the Northern prisons were horrible but she had thought the South . . . Jerry sat feebly on his horse before her, broken evidence of what those in the South had been like.

She caught his chilly fingers and pressed them in her warm vital palms.

"Oh, Jerry, I wish I'd been down there! If I'd only been down there to help you!"

He looked so tall and weak she had an impulse to take all of him in her arms and woo him back to strength with the mere outrush of her own vitality. As she stood with this feeling welling through her arms and torso the brisk clatter of another horse came from down the road.

She stepped a little aside and looked to see who it was. Jerry Catlin glanced backward in the manner of a man waiting for a third party to pass on by a private conversation.

Captain Lacefield came around the curve in civilian clothes. He looked twice at the Federal uniform, then lifted his hat gayly to Marcia.

"I've closed the deal for the roller press," he called.

For a moment Marcia loathed roller presses and hand presses and all the insensate and detestable paraphernalia that went to make up a printery. She had wanted to talk all the rest of the afternoon to Jerry.

When Captain Lacefield came up she introduced Jerry.

"Mr. Catlin was a private in the Yankee detachment that camped on your plantation, A. Gray," explained Marcia. "Jerry, this is Captain Lacefield, you may remember, the man I once told you about a long time ago."

After a little more talk, Marcia was elevated to A. Gray's horse, as was her wont at these meetings, and the three moved uncomfortably back up the road toward the Vaiden home. The Union soldier and the disfranchised ex-Confederate officer really had small margin for companionship. Marcia talked and laughed as best she could. She hardly remembered what she said from one sentence to another.

She was aware of the two men: Jerry on his horse, A. Gray walking at her bridle. Her fiancé was much the trimmer, of course the handsomer, and the more self-possessed. Jerry was crushed, after his long starvation and illness, at this slight untoward meeting. In A. Gray Marcia could feel a questioning, a slightly annoyed and somewhat amused questioning. In Jerry, a sudden utter grayness and hopelessness. She felt as if she were spiritually thrusting him back into prison again.

"Do you expect to remain in the army, Mr. Catlin?" asked A. Gray in mechanical small talk.

"I expect to be mustered out next week, Captain."

"It's pleasant to be your own master again. I've tried it."

"A man spoke to me about joining the Fenians."

Marcia turned around and looked at him.

"What are the Fenians, Jerry?"

"It's some men who are trying to give freedom to Ireland," explained Jerry simply.

Captain Lacefield stared at Jerry in his turn.

"You are not thinking about fighting for the freedom of Ireland after you've spent four years in subjugating the South!" A. Gray began laughing. "There were plenty of Irish in our army, Mr. Catlin—you might have helped General Pat Cleburn at Shiloh."

"Maybe he sees his mistake and is trying to make up for it," answered Marcia lightly.

Catlin rode a space in silence, then said, "Are any of your brothers at home, Miss Marcia?"

"I don't think there are, Jerry, why?"

"I had a message for Colonel Vaiden," said Jerry uncertainly.

"Could I take it?" asked the girl helpfully.

"Well . . . no. I wouldn't want to give it to you. I'm not particularly anxious to deliver it to anybody."

"What's it about?" asked the girl curiously.

"Well . . . there's an organization—the Klan, I believe?"

"Yes."

"Who is the message from?" asked A. Gray alertly.

"From General Beekman."

"I will deliver to Colonel Vaiden any message you care to trust to me," offered the captain.

Catlin thought a moment.

"Well . . . I shouldn't mind saying it to you."

Marcia laughed and said she would ride ahead and leave the two to their confabulation.

When Captain Lacefield caught up with Marcia again, Jerry Catlin was not with him. The captain said that Mr. Catlin sent his adieus and compliments.

Marcia knew that Jerry had not made use of either of these words. She felt oddly let down. Even in this brief renewed contact which she had had with Jerry, she received once more that impression of a reality in life which she had felt in him three years before. Now when A. Gray came back without him it was as if an illusory surface of things had taken the place of a sure, sad reality.

"He might have said good-bye," she mused.

A. Gray began talking enthusiastically of his presses again. He had ordered two cases of type, six fonts each . . .

"What was it he said?" asked Marcia.

"Who, Reynolds?"

"No. Who is Reynolds?"

"The man who sold me the presses and the type."

"No, I was talking about Jerry Catlin. What did he tell you that he couldn't tell me?"

A. Gray hesitated, then smiled.

"What he said was mainly foolishness."

"What sort of foolishness?"

The captain laughed.

"It's finally begun to dawn on General Beekman that he is in for a political fight."

Marcia was astonished.

"What's Beekman got to do with it?"

"He sent a message that if the Klan did not let the negroes alone he would institute reprisals."

"What sort of reprisals?"

"None, of course. It's a bluff—a Yankee bluff. What could he do?"

"I'm sure I don't know." Marcia was disturbed. "I wish he'd said."

"He doesn't know either," scoffed A. Gray, "or he would have said. . . . Reprisals—that's nonsense."

CHAPTER FIFTY-SIX

WHEN MARCIA and Captain Lacefield reached the Vaiden home, the girl said the sun had given her a headache and she would go up to her room for a minute or two.

A. Gray went into the kitchen and began telling Rose about his presses and type. Rose was heavy, strong, glowing, optimistic about everything except Augustus' health. She got on swimmingly with everybody, including even old man Jimmie.

Marcia went up to her room, lay down on her bed, and utter desolation came upon her. She amazed herself by lying face down and beginning to weep convulsively. She buried her face in her pillow to stifle her sobs.

After a while she sat up, drawing long sighs, then she got up and walked over to her mirror. Her eyes were swollen, her hair disheveled, and now she really did have a headache. She thought, with a momentary contrition, that the reason her head ached was because she had told a story and said that it ached when it really did not. She began rearranging her hair.

She asked herself silently why she should weep about something that was past, about something that was finished and done. But presently the thought of Jerry overwhelmed her again: he had been sick, unattended, with the flesh sloughing from his legs, his whole body a skeleton, while he feebly cut at a little shell trying to buy something he could eat.

She lay down on her bed again and wept and wept. It seemed as if all these horrible things had happened to her; that she had been penned up in a lazar house and starved and starved and starved . . . and now she had sent him back to his prison again.

She thought the words with the tears trickling silently from her eyes and wetting her pillow.

Her door opened and Rose came in. Cassandra never would have presumed to enter her sister's room without knocking and calling out, but Rose had a way of coming into rooms, of touching anyone, putting her arms around them, and nobody ever dreamed of forwardness. She had even stroked Cassandra's plain-combed hair one morning at the breakfast table when the older sister complained of not feeling well. That, of course, was not bravery, it was foolhardiness. But Cassandra had said nothing and did not seem to withdraw her tolerance of Rose.

Now the sister-in-law looked with dismay at Marcia.

"Why, honey, what in the world's the matter with you?"

Marcia thought swiftly for a reason for being disturbed. She considered it would be no story to tell Rose that she was uneasy about Miltiades, because she was. So that was what she told.

Rose inquired into this in the blankest surprise and learned about the note from the Leatherwood gang.

"What did the note say, honey?"

Rose was sitting on the side of the bed dabbing Marcia's eyes with her handkerchief which she had dipped in water.

Marcia could not remember the wording, but said it was full of threats and misspelling.

"Did they mention Augustus in it?" inquired Rose anxiously.

"M—m . . . I can't remember all of it," said Marcia, which she considered to be the truth for she could not remember *all* of it.

But Rose had found out that Marcia was one of those lit-

erally truthful girls and she subjected everything she said
to analysis. Now she knew Augustus had been mentioned.

"For goodness' sake," she cried, "we ought to do something about it!"

"Rose, you know if anything happens to anybody it will
be to Miltiades."

"What makes you say that?" cried Rose, who flew into a
pet as quickly as she flew into a kiss.

"Why, Miltiades is the—the leader in everything he
does."

Rose frowned and pondered. She was exceedingly sensitive about her husband because he never did anything at all.

"He hasn't got the heart of Augustus," she stated positively.

"What makes you say that?" cried Marcia, who considered Miltiades everything and Augustus nothing at all.
"Miltiades gave thirty dollars to ol' Pap's church."

"Pshaw, it's not what you do to be seen of men, but what
you really are that counts."

"Why, Rose!" ejaculated Marcia amazed. "You know
that Miltiades is—is the perfect one of our family!"

"I know Miltiades has less conscience than any man I
ever saw," stated Rose in an even voice.

By this time Marcia saw that Rose really and truly believed it and was not just defending Augustus. She looked
at Rose aghast.

"Why, you pretend to like Miltiades!"

"I do like him—he can't help being what he is."

"What has he ever done?"

"Nothing that I know of—a man doesn't have to do anything to have no conscience."

Marcia sat up, drew in and exhaled a breath of amazement at such an attack on the family idol.

"Miltiades is going to make a great success," stated the
sister firmly.

Rose smiled faintly.

"Don't you feel better now?"

Marcia looked at her sister-in-law with a betrayed expression.

"Did you start a quarrel with me just to get my mind on something else?"

"Listen, honey," Rose smiled enigmatically, "hurry and bathe your face and come on down. A. Gray has just about talked one of my arms off about his newspaper."

At this Marcia's spirits sagged again. She felt she could not endure another syllable of newspaper talk.

"Tell him my head still aches—it does, Rose, a little."

"But darling, you can't do him that way when he's come to see you!"

"Rose, that's reasonable. When we are married, I'm certainly going to stay in my room when I want to!"

"Honey, if girls started acting before they are married as they mean to act afterward, there wouldn't be any marriages."

Marcia began laughing.

"You say that—as soft as you are about Augustus!"

"Shoo, I acted a lot softer at the hospital while we were sweethearts."

"Then you must have run all over the place."

By now Marcia was quite cheerful again. Her headache was gone. As she followed Rose down the stairs she wondered a little why she had fallen into such utter grief over a tale that had been told to her.

When Marcia went below she found Mrs. Laura, Cassandra, and A. Gray all hard put to it to persuade old man Jimmie not to go out and start hammering at his blacksmith's forge. He was announcing in a voice that was not so round and booming as it once was that, by the gray goats, he was tired of wasting time, that his niggers wasn't doing anything, and his boys wasn't doing anything, and he wasn't doing anything, and that he was going to get out and make a living for the family at his forge."

The more Miss Cassandra commanded and old Mrs. Laura pleaded, the more determined old man Jimmie became to light his forge and start anew the labors of fifty years ago.

Young A. Gray said, "By the way, Mr. Vaiden, could you make some repairs on my presses?"

The old man paused in his preparation to set to work.

"Are ye presses made of arn?"

"Oh, yes, they are iron presses."

"I never did see a press."

"Well, I could bring you the broken piece. You could copy it, couldn't you?"

"I can hammer out any shape I ever did see, young man!"

"All right," agreed A. Gray heartily. "Just as soon as my press gets here and a piece breaks I'll bring it right down."

The white-headed old man nodded in satisfaction.

"And by the gray goats, Caruthers," he said, absent-mindedly giving A. Gray his father's name, "I want to tell you you won't get your press mended any cheaper anywhere in Lauderdale County than right in my shop."

After having taken this order, old man Jimmie's impulse to work was satisfied and he settled back in his chair.

When he had subsided, A. Gray said with a faint appealing smile, "Cassandra and I have been talking about something important, Marcia."

Instantly Marcia knew what it was and for some reason was disconcerted by it. She looked at A. Gray and then at Cassandra with her freshly bathed eyes.

"And when have you-all decided it ought to be?" she asked.

"Well, I happen to know that Drusilla and Miltiades have set theirs for the first of the month," said A. Gray with a lilt in his voice.

"The first of this coming month!"

Rose cried out laughing, "Why, of course, silly, the first of the month is the first of the month!"

"And where is it to be?" asked Marcia in an uncertain tone.

"Well," said Miss Cassandra, taking the arrangement into her own hands, "I don't know of any better place than here. I intend to stay here afterward with Mother and Father. And when Mother and I look into the company room, we would like to remember the—the triple ceremony. It would be a sort of—benediction."

Miss Cassandra said all this in a most matter-of-fact way, but at the word "benediction" Marcia suddenly began weeping again. The tears silently welled out of her eyes. She tried to hide them but everyone saw them and began sympathizing.

"Oh, it's that Leatherwood note!" cried Rose. "It threatened Miltiades and completely upset her."

"I thought it was the message General Beekman sent!" exclaimed A. Gray.

Rose had not heard about the Beekman message and A. Gray knew nothing of the Leatherwood note. The whole family began talking about the two threats from entirely different sources.

Old man Jimmie caught the drift of the conversation and cried out:

"Tell Milt to do like my daddy done—draw the injun far with a dummy an' then shoot the skulkin' devils!"

Marcia became composed again.

"We'll have to get some new curtains for the company room, Cassandra—I never did like those pink curtains."

"Maybe we can get our old lace curtains back from General Beekman," suggested Cassandra sarcastically.

"Just before the election, send him a bill for the curtains," proposed A. Gray. "I'll print it in my paper and it'll make good campaign ammunition."

Cassandra came back to the subject in hand.

"What will Drusilla think of being married in our house, A. Gray?"

"I think she will agree."

There was endless talk among the women about the wedding and the wedding arrangements. A. Gray maneuvered to get Marcia into the company room to look at her tatting. Marcia finally told him she had no tatting that day. The groom-elect bore this with the cheerful philosophy that the first of the month was only twelve days distant.

Aunt Creasy came out and said dinner was ready. It was the noon meal, the heaviest meal of the day. Rose had made a green-apple pie. She made extraordinary green-apple pies, just as Augustus had divined she would when he first saw her in the hospital.

There was only one drawback to Rose's pies: old Mrs. Laura would eat them. Invariably they upset her, and invariably the old woman would look at each new work of art Rose put forth, and she simply could not believe that such a crisp, brown, amber-filled pie would hurt anybody. Miss Cassandra would say:

"Mother, you know what green-apple pies do for you!"

"Yes, Cassandra, but look at this pie—this pie couldn't hurt a baby."

A. Gray began telling Rose of a series of editorials which he meant to write on Yankee misfeasance in office.

Marcia ate with her queer but customary feeling of being alone. It seemed to her that she was a solid person sitting among some images of people around the image of a table. After twelve days she supposed she would be transferred to a new set of images and semblances. She looked at A. Gray.

"One of these days," thought Marcia gravely, "maybe he will become aristocratic and kindly and beautiful, like his father."

After dinner old Mrs. Laura put a half spoonful of soda in a glass of warm water and drank it. After she had eaten of the pie what was left no longer looked as innocent as it once did. Then she said she thought she would lie down and take a little nap.

She always took her naps on a pallet, a quilt spread down on the floor. Miss Cassandra urged the bed, but Mrs. Laura could not get to sleep on a bed in the daytime—it was too soft. Neither could she get to sleep on her pallet at night— it was too hard. The resistance of her sleeping places varied, apparently with the light.

Marcia never saw her mother lying asleep on a pallet but what she was filled with tenderness. Old Mrs. Laura was the smallest one in her family of large children and a large husband. Marcia did not like other small persons but she would not have had her mother changed on any account. She felt she could love her more completely, being small. When she saw her lying asleep on her pallet, such a little thing, Marcia wanted to take her in her arms.

When Mrs. Laura had her nap the whole house became quiet. This was because old man Jimmie had his at the same time. If he had been awake he would have blared out and waked his wife.

Rose would sometimes step to the door of the living room, look at Mrs. Laura lying asleep on her pallet, and whisper to Cassandra, "No wonder I love Augustus."

Rose was the only one in the family who could speak of loving anyone without embarrassment. Her love was as outspoken as her friendliness.

After dinner everyone stayed out of the company room so Marcia could go in with A. Gray and show him her tatting if she wanted to. But to-day Marcia remained persistently in the big open hallway with the others. A. Gray finally fiddled with his watch and said he was afraid he would have to go.

Rose caught Marcia's eye and made a face at her. And Marcia thought pensively that she shouldn't have A. Gray ride down from Florence and then ride back without even a kiss. So she asked the captain if he had seen Cassandra's new book, a poem by a man named Browning. "I looked at it," she said, "but it didn't make sense."

Captain Lacefield had neither seen nor heard of a poem by Browning. He admired Byron intensely. So they went in together to look at the new poem.

When he shut the door behind them Marcia saw A. Gray's fingers tremble on the latch. Instead of putting his arms around her and kissing her as he always did, he took her hand, knelt down and put his face in her palm.

"Marcia," he whispered so as to be inaudible in the hallways, "I feel like a worshiper in a Catholic church and you are a saint. To think—in twelve more days—— Oh, Marcia, I love you! I have loved you all my life long! And Marcia—just twelve more days!"

He stood up, took her in his arms and kissed her. She could feel his cold lips trembling on her own warm mouth. His beard gave her face a faint tickling sandpapery feeling. It was not disagreeable. She thought they might live not unpleasantly together. She decided that she loved A. Gray—of course, not as Rose did Augustus, but that was foolishness.

In the hallway outside sounded a hurrying and a stirring. Then Marcia heard her mother sobbing. A pang shot through the girl. She said, "Oh! Oh! Mother's sick!" and she darted through the door.

Outside she saw a confusion in the door of the living room. Old Aunt Creasy was standing at the end of the hallway wanting to know what was the matter. Cassandra was looking into the door of the living room. Inside Rose's voice reassured everyone.

"It's all right," she laughed. "Mother hasn't got the colic, she's just had a bad dream, that's all."

"Mother," reproved Cassandra, "I told you not to eat——"

"But Sister Cassandra," excused Rose, "after all it's nothing but a bad dream."

"All the same it shows——"

But old Mrs. Vaiden continued weeping in the thin, broken sobs of an old, old woman.

"They shot Polycarp! Oh, they've shot Polycarp!" and she wept again.

"Mother! Mother!" argued Miss Cassandra. "You know it was that pie you ate—that and what Marcia told you about the note."

The old woman held up her arms to Rose.

"Put me in bed! Oh, they shot him from a thicket—just as he left the Johnson place! Oh, Cassandra—Rose——Oh! Oh!"

She went half bent in the arms of Cassandra and Rose, shaken with her grief.

They got the frail little woman in bed and brought her the camphor. She kept it dutifully and pitifully to her nose while she wept uncontrollably.

"Oh, Polycarp was my best boy! Oh, he nearly turned around to come back when he went away to the army—I heard him. He nearly turned round to kiss me good-bye!"

"Oh, Mother, honey, don't you know a dream doesn't mean!"

Outside in the road the group heard the growing sound of a horse running at full speed. The old woman suddenly stopped crying. She sat up with horror in her old face.

"He's coming to tell us Polycarp is d-dead!" she wailed.

And so the rider was.

CHAPTER FIFTY-SEVEN

Time, which had brought Death to Polycarp, now stood still amid the shock and pain Death had wrought. From the moment the horseman brought his news, while the men brought the body home in a wagon, while the robust motionless form of Polycarp lay on the bed in the company room, Time ceased to flow.

Columbus and Robinet went to the Vaiden burial ground in the pine grove on the side of a gentle hill and dug the grave. Negro George heard of his white people's trouble and came back to help Columbus and Robinet. Miltiades chose the spot and started the three silent black men to digging in turns. "From here to here," he said, "and this wide."

Old Mr. Erastus Ham and two more neighbors came to dress Polycarp and lay him out. As they moved about in the company room they talked in whispers, wondering who had waylaid their murdered neighbor. They examined the bullet wound to see if it came from an army musket or from the rifle of a Leatherwood bandit.

However even if they could have determined definitely whether it was Jerry Catlin or the hillman on the donkey or some person connected with these two harbingers of violence, it would have made no difference at all. If Polycarp were revenged one of his brothers would have to do it; or possibly the Klan.

The killing of Polycarp was not the sort of thing the

regularly organized government of the Union forces would investigate. Especially when half the chances stood that it was the regularly organized government's own blow at the Klan. There was nothing to be done unless Miltiades or Augustus should decide who was the assassin and exact their private revenge.

"If it had been Miltiades," whispered Mr. Ham, "Polycarp would have settled it off quick. Polycarp had pride that-a-way. The man who did this knew which boy to pick on—he must 'a' been intimate with the fam'ly."

Miltiades sent telegrams to all the brothers and sisters of the older set and it cost a good deal of money. They received an answer from Sylvester Vaiden, who was between Miltiades and Cassandra. The telegram said he would arrive on the second day following.

Marcia felt an irrational dread of Sylvester Vaiden's coming because she knew nothing of him. He had married and moved to Arkansas when she was a little girl. She had never seen him since and could remember nothing of him. Now she heard of his coming with a vague feeling of dismay. This presently was lost in the motionless bleakness of death.

The neighbors sent in wreaths of wild flowers and flowers from their yards, which were wilted almost by the time they reached the Vaiden home. These flowers were of all colors, but their formal shapes of crowns and crosses made them look sad and funereal.

One thing filled Marcia with the sharpest added distress. It was the remembrance of what Gracie had half confessed in the lane about her unborn child. For Polycarp to have been the father of the quadroon's child seemed to Marcia the most unforgivable of sins. She dreaded that God had condemned her brother for that. None of the family knew it except her.

After the neighbors had dressed the body she went down into the company room and looked at the pale changed features of her brother. And when she thought of what he had done, her heart broke. She wished she could go down to eternal torment in his place.

On the second day Sylvester Vaiden arrived. He did not look like any of his brothers, but still he looked like a Vaiden. He seemed much older than any of the children because Marcia was not accustomed to him and perceived his true age. Only Mrs. Laura, his mother, received him in complete and unestranged affection. She had never got out of the bed since Rose and Marcia had helped her into it on the day of her dream. When Sylvester entered her room, she held out her arms as if the aging man had stepped out of her presence only a moment before. Sylvester bent down and comforted her weeping as best he could. She asked Sylvester to lead her into the company room and let her look at Polycarp.

And so Sylvester became Marcia's brother again, and she loved him.

The funeral took place immediately after Sylvester drove up. There was no Primitive Baptist minister in the neighborhood at the time so old Parson Mulry held the services. Marcia was a little comforted by this. It seemed to her that if old Parson Mulry conducted the services, then God could forgive Polycarp, but if a Primitive Baptist had said the prayers, He could not.

Mr. Lacefield and A. Gray and Ponny BeShears and all the neighbors for miles around met in the pine grove on the hill and sang. The old parson read the Scripture and told of Polycarp's good deeds, his cheerfulness, his bravery, and how he died taking alms to the poor and distressed.

The funeral formed such a little, little group among the endless undulations of the hills. When it was over they moved weeping away and left the filling of the grave to Columbus and Robinet. These black men were supposed not to suffer at covering their lifelong companion with earth.

They were black.

CHAPTER FIFTY-EIGHT

IN EARLY September, at the beginning of cotton picking time, the white Democratic party in Lauderdale County scented a political victory in the approaching gubernatorial election. The Klan, which was responsible for this hopeful state of things, was full of that optimistic enthusiasm which always precedes an election in America. Few negroes would vote at the coming poll. Not many would brave the spectral terrors and the very solid horsewhips of the Klan.

The members of this organization congratulated themselves on knowing how to handle niggers. It was hereditary with them. Their fathers and grandfathers before them had lived by the management of niggers. Now, when the Yankees tried to hold the political reins of the South through the nigger vote, they couldn't do it because, by the living God, the Southern aristocrat still knew how to manage niggers.

Then as a great harvest of cotton began to spread its white abundance over fields long fallow, just as the dawn of a new freedom began to break on the white planters of the South, a very extraordinary and ill-starred thing happened in the railroad yard at Florence, Alabama.

Two long freight trains were backed into the siding, endless box cars filled with bacon and flour. They were billed to no merchant in Florence, but were taken over by General Beekman's men. Union soldiers were posted up and down the length of the yard. In the course of time the commanding officer himself drove down to the yards. On his way thither through the streets he told a dozen or so negroes to follow him. They did so dubiously, not knowing but what they would bring down on their heads the wrath of the night riders.

In front of his trainloads of provisions the general asked the black men if they were kept on the plantations and forbidden to vote in the coming election. All of them, even those who were not, said they were, moved by the African instinct to agree.

"Why do you stay on the plantation?" inquired the general.

"Because we's got to eat," said one of the group.

"Very well," responded the candidate for governor, "the Republican party realizes you must eat. They have spent blood and money to make free and independent voters of you black people. Do you imagine General Grant and the Union army are going to allow the white men now to starve you back into slavery?"

The negroes said they didn't know, it looked like they were.

"Certainly not," snapped the small blond man in a crisp businesslike tone. "The government will take care of you black men just as it takes care of the Indians. You don't have to stay on the plantations and nobody can keep you from voting. The Republican party will see to it that honest Republicans don't starve."

With this explanation the general opened a half-dozen box cars, exhibited them loaded with bacon and flour. He then asked all the negroes present how large their families were and how much they would require for a week's rations.

The black men stared at the trainloads incredulously, then at each other. Then they began laughing, slapping each other on the backs, bobbing about thanking the general and singing and shouting in ecstasy:

"Oh, my Lawd—sot free agin! We thanks you, Gin'l! We sho' come to Flaunce, settle down, an' be ready to vote fo' *you!*"

Soldiers handed out the bacon and flour.

As they went laughing and talking out of the railroad yards, other negroes asked what was the matter.

"Nothin' de mattah, niggah. We jest back frum de Lawd's secon' comin' in de railroad ya'd!"

Within twenty-four hours negro grapevine service flashed the incredible largesse all over the county.

On Wednesday of the following week, the Florence *Index*, a paper published and edited by A. Gray Lacefield, came out with the following scathing editorial:

It was headed, "Yankee Duplicity Toward Illiterate Negroes," and continued:

"Northern hands, reddened by the blood of Southern men, now seek to thrust the South into the abyss of poverty and despair by weaning the black laborer from his true friend, the Southern aristocrat . . ." and so on with an account of the free bacon and flour distributed by Beekman. Incidentally, A. Gray said this was rejected army provisions and that the flour was wormy and the bacon tainted: points over which the black folk were not hypercritical.

The negroes deserted the larger plantations almost instantly. They left the mules hitched to the wagons and the cotton-picking sacks half full in the cotton rows. When they reached Florence they were protected by Beekman's soldiers and were out of the power of the Klan.

The situation with the unpicked cotton became so desperate that the Klan finally appointed a committee to wait on General Beekman. Miltiades Vaiden, A. Gray Lacefield, Mr. Handback the merchant, and Ashton the attorney made up the delegation.

When they entered the general's headquarters at the Florence fair grounds Miltiades noticed a sad-faced dark-eyed woman and a little boy sitting at a table reading a paper in General Beekman's waiting room. As the general entered the woman laid down her paper as a silent mark of respect. It was several moments before Miltiades recognized

the woman as Gracie. He felt a movement of surprise at the
poise, the air of breeding, and the melancholy handsomeness
of the woman. The child, he supposed, was the son of Beekman, and a renewed contempt went through Miltiades for a
white man who would thus openly avow his relations with a
colored woman. All the white committee felt the same way.
Beekman's unashamed admission of his quadroon mistress
was a blow at the white caste in the South.

When the general asked what the committee wanted,
Miltiades protested against the government's course in
feeding the negroes and causing a sudden labor shortage in
cotton-gathering time.

The general was entirely unruffled.

"I understand undue influence is being used to keep them
away from the polls in November," he replied.

"Do you mean they will be fed all that time?" cried
Miltiades.

"The government will protect them to that extent in the
right of every citizen to cast his vote."

"You mean you will feed them to that extent so they can
vote for you," suggested Miltiades acidly.

"I imagine if they intended to vote the Democratic ticket
you gentlemen would see the iniquity of forbidding them to
come to the polls."

"Then you don't even pretend that it's anything more
than a scheme to forward your own political ends!"
ejaculated Ashton. "You don't even pretend to us it is for
the benefit of the negroes!"

Beekman smiled dryly.

"Why should you gentlemen be surprised that I should
try to get the most out of the negroes when you've been
working at the very same thing all your lives? But mark
you this, I give the negroes rather better terms than you
men do. If he sticks by me he can loaf and loiter. It's the
same thing over and over, gentlemen: in any historic struggle
an oppressed people can usually make shift to ease them-

selves somewhat. They offer themselves to the highest bidder in easements, and at present my bid is much higher than yours. Now, I'm not at all interested in the moral end of my actions down here, but it just happens that I am not particularly unmoral in making better terms with the freedmen then you can."

"But look here," protested A. Gray in horror, "the final upshot of this will be that you'll ruin the whole country. The niggers will produce nothing!"

"No, gentlemen, it won't be ruined, but it will be tremendously slowed down. From now on the South will have to proceed at the negro's tempo and not at the white man's. The control of the actual physical labor of the negro has slipped out from under white direction and now belongs to the negro himself. From now on he is going to work very, very slowly. You white men eventually will get everything he produces, but that won't be much. The South will cease to be the directing force in American politics because political power finally depends on wealth.

"And incidentally, gentlemen, from now henceforth you are going to have to obtain the products of negro labor by round-about methods, chicane, finesse, and not by simple force. In other words, you will cease to be gentlemen and become traders, landlords, and business men. In fact, you may fall to the low estate of Yankees and be forced to use your wits all the time."

The committee damned the general with all heartiness in this world and the world to come, and walked out of his office. In the following issue of the Florence *Index* an editorial began: "If General Cyrus U. Beekman were bred in hell and sired by the devil, he would be a disgrace to his country and a dishonor to his parent," and on and on.

CHAPTER FIFTY-NINE

After their revealing but unsatisfactory interview with General Beekman, Miltiades and A. Gray rode together to the Lacefield home in the Reserve. Their talk for a while naturally centered on the man they had just left. A. Gray said that he had never before heard a Northern man speak precisely what he thought. He said people really ought not to blame Beekman for his cold, heartless finessing, that all Northern people were like that—their climate caused it.

"And flaunting his mistress openly," observed Miltiades. "I wonder if he realizes how the son he is raising will be classed?"

"I don't suppose he cares," said A. Gray. " 'Whom the gods would destroy they first make mad.' " And A. Gray hoped he would remember to use that quotation in his editorial.

Presently they grew bored with bemeaning the general and Captain Lacefield said, "Drusilla tells me you and she have chosen another date."

"Yes, we want to make our wedding very quiet after Polycarp's death."

"Yes, of course," nodded the captain.

He looked across the flat Reserve landscape.

"I wonder, Miltiades," he went on, "if you could mention to Marcia something about our wedding—fixing another date. She seems so melancholy over her mother's illness and Polycarp's death I can't broach the subject."

"I'll do what I can, A. Gray."

"I have thought she was using that to put me off. . . . Don't breathe to her I said that."

"Oh, no. Marcia is a very sensitive girl."

"A lovely girl, a wonderful girl," seconded the captain heartily.

They were passing the BeShears home now and Miltiades caught sight of Ponny standing in the doorway. The black mourning dress she wore for Polycarp gave a softness to her full figure and made a foil for the glint of her blond hair. Miltiades called, "Good-day, Ponny," in a monotone that recognized his own and the girl's bereavement.

"Good-day, Mr. Milt," called back Ponny in the same muted voice.

"She's not like herself any more," said A. Gray.

"It was such a shock to us all. . . . I wonder who did that. You know, A. Gray, I feel like I ought to square the account. Polycarp and I were always so close to each other. We were more intimate than most brothers."

"Yes, you really were." Now that Polycarp was dead both men remembered a beautiful friendship between Miltiades and his brother, but the editor went on: "Yet, after all, what good would it do to shoot the fellow, Milt? Just another murder in our county, and God knows we have enough. Then he's skin and bones already. I saw him the morning of the day Polycarp was killed."

"It might be the other damn scoundrel that brought the note."

"I don't think so, but of course it might. It's half dozen to one and six to the other."

As the two turned off the main road at BeShears' store, Miltiades noticed the number of negroes idling about the store front. He recalled General Beekman's cynical observation that henceforth the negroes would work at their own tempo . . . and they would have to be traded with.

Inside his dark den the crippled storekeeper was industriously selling his wares to his new black patrons.

Two and a half miles further on, at the manor, the two men found the Lacefield family in process of packing their numberless belongings, making ready to remove their household goods to Florence. Almost the last negro on the plantation had deserted his work for General Beekman's free flour and bacon in Florence. Two black women and a black man were helping wrap the bedsteads and dining-room table in quilts to prevent scratching them. There was endless furniture in the various rooms, highboys, beautiful old writing desks, old prints, chairs, settees.

What they were going to do with it all in Florence was the despair of Mrs. Lacefield, with no place to put it. The house they had rented had only nine rooms, and, she told Miltiades, they were more like nine goods boxes than nine rooms. Later, Mr. Lacefield planned to build in Florence, but she didn't know how they would exist in the meantime.

As Miltiades passed through the dismantled hallway little Sydna came down the staircase with her eyes solemn in her oval face. When she saw Miltiades she paused on the steps and told him with childish concern that Mamma cry.

"Where is your mamma, Sydna?" asked the man.

"Upstairs."

Miltiades went up. He found Drusilla standing in her room with nowhere to sit except on crated furniture. The carpet had been rolled and the dusty floor was bare. The woman reached a weary hand toward her lover.

"Oh, Miltiades!" she sighed.

She was not weeping, but her eyes showed she had been. She gave Colonel Vaiden a wan smile.

"Isn't this terrible?"

He took her in his arms, kissed and petted her mechanically.

"Miltiades," she asked in a low tone, "do you think Father will be elected governor—the way things are now?"

"You mean after the niggers have got loose and gone to Florence?"

Drusilla nodded mutely, scanning his face for his real thought.

"I don't see exactly how we're going to keep them from voting," said Miltiades slowly. "They've got away from us— at present. I've been thinking and thinking, trying to study up some plan to put them to work again and keep them away from the polls—put them where they'll be of some use to themselves and everybody else."

He broke off and stood looking out the second-story window over level acres of cotton. Only five or six black figures dotted the white expanse where once regiments had worked. Drusilla stood with her small palm on the hand Miltiades had put around her waist. They stood in the peace of men and women who are physically and mentally sympathetic with one another and who have satisfied one another's desire.

The woman drew in a breath to start a sentence, then hesitated.

"What is it, Beautiful?" asked the colonel.

" 'Y—'Y—this, Miltiades," hesitated the woman. "I don't want to go to Florence."

He looked at her.

"What do you want to do, Drusilla?"

"Couldn't you—take the place—and run it, and—let Father and Mother go on if they want to?"

With an odd feeling Miltiades became aware that Drusilla was asking him to marry her at once and remain with her on the plantation. He pressed her waist gently.

"When shall we be married, Drusilla?" he asked.

"Then you will—right away, Miltiades?" She put her arms about his neck and began weeping silently against his shoulder.

"Of course I will, Drusilla, it is my dearest desire."

He bent and kissed her wet lashes, and patted the curve of the soft bosom he already had known.

"Would next Thursday be too soon?" she asked in a low voice.

"No, Drusilla, of course not."

She leaned back a little from him and gave him a faint questioning smile.

"Then we shall say next Thursday—at noon?"

He pressed her body to his with a faint touch of desire.

"Next Thursday at noon . . . and what preacher?"

"I always liked Dr. Landon, the Episcopal minister at Florence."

"He's to come here?"

"Oh, yes, of course."

He stood holding her close to him, his left hand about her shoulders, his right dropped down about the vase-like curve of her hips. His sense of touch recognized the Greek lines of her body. Her hips were neither large nor small. Her neck, her bust all held the inconspicuous harmony of beauty. A sudden prescience told Miltiades that Drusilla would remain physically alluring throughout the shapely middle age of well-bred women.

He fancied himself keeping the plantation with Drusilla, but he knew the stately days of the old manor were gone.

After a moment Drusilla herself came back to the great obstacle in the path of the continued idyl of their life.

"The few niggers you see out there, Miltiades, won't come regularly; just a day now and then. And Father has to pay them the most outrageous prices—some of them get a dollar and a quarter a day for picking."

"That's it—the more you pay them the less they'll work. When they make enough to run them a day or two, they'll quit."

"Do you suppose you *can* make them work, Milt?"

"We'll have to think up a new plan. Better wages will make them work less. What would spur on a white man will stop them."

They turned from the unpleasant subject. Just then Miltiades observed something.

"Why haven't you packed your dressing table?" he asked.

"It doesn't go very far. We sold that piece to Ponny. She always liked it and finally asked if we would sell it. Mother had so little space in Florence, she just let it go."

On his ride back to his own home Miltiades stopped at the BeShears place. Negroes still crowded about the dingy store, eating cheese and crackers, slices of store sausages, buying themselves bandanas, new brogans, and even store trousers. It occurred to Miltiades that Mr. Lacefield was paying for, and Alex BeShears was collecting from, this detestable expansion in negro luxuries.

At the BeShears residence Miltiades called on Ponny. Mrs. BeShears came to the door. She was a large woman and wore a checkered apron whitened in spots with smudges of flour. She began welcoming Miltiades with loud heartiness, then remembered Polycarp's death and subdued her voice. She rubbed her hands on her apron and opened the door of her parlor in which Miltiades could wait for Ponny. She pointed out a new sort of carpet on the floor.

"It's a Wilton," she said. "Ponny bought it from Mr. Handback in Florence." It had red flowers figured on a green background.

Miltiades said he thought it was a pretty carpet.

"Ponny! Ponny!" called the mother into the central hall-way. "Mr. Milt has come to see you! I'm uneasy about Alex," went on the large woman, plunging at once into her domestic troubles. "He broods so over what that Leather-wood gang done to him. I tell him I wouldn't brood so if I was him."

"I don't suppose he can help it," said Miltiades.

"Oh, I'm sorry I said anything about it. I guess the Leatherwoods are the ones who killed Polycarp—I declare I wasn't thinking of Polycarp—Ponny'll never get over that."

At this point Ponny herself entered the parlor and Mrs. BeShears went back to the kitchen.

Miltiades took the girl's hand and led her to a new sofa in the parlor.

"I thought I would stop by, Ponny, and see if we couldn't help each other," he said gravely.

Tears formed in Ponny's very blue eyes.

"Mr. Milt, it's mighty nice of you to come . . . Oh, me!" she leaned against the back of the sofa, closed her eyes, leaving her plump hand in Colonel Vaiden's fingers.

The black lace yoke of her dress let through a suggestion of the curves and dazzling whiteness of Ponny's smooth neck and bust. Her round, pretty face gave her an odd childlike quality. Her waist was constricted by a corset until it was not thick. Her thighs, vaguely outlined beneath her black skirt, were almost as large as her waist, yet they did not give Miltiades a disagreeable impression. She seemed not so much feminine as female.

She talked easily and endlessly and not uninterestingly as such girls do. She had heard about General Beekman's giving away flour and bacon. She had told her father that he ought to buy it from the niggers at half price and beat old Beekman at his own game. She told Miltiades that she had spoken for a dressing case from Mrs. Lacefield and really had wanted one of the Lacefield highboys, too, but they wouldn't sell that. She had looked for one like it at Mr. Handback's store, but she couldn't find any. She said she didn't know why she wanted to fix up her home like that after what had happened.

"Because you can't help it," said Colonel Vaiden, "it's your nature to make a home."

Ponny sat still a moment, a faint pink tinted her delicate complexion.

"Yes . . . I suppose it is," she said.

After another pause Ponny proceeded again. Her father didn't think the nigger working for wages was so bad. The supplies they got were either paid for in cash or were charged against the crop, and the amount certain to be paid in the fall. It didn't get to be a mortgage on the land and run on and on as it did under the old way.

Here she recalled that her father had attempted to foreclose such a mortgage on the Vaiden place and she paused and flushed again.

Miltiades was not offended, or even interested in the bygone foreclosure. There was about Ponny's talk, about her person and parlor, an air of ill-directed opulence. Her plump hand, still beneath Miltiades fingers, had the feeling of abounding physical vigor. Even if she squeezed in her waistline her feminine exuberance was in no wise impaired. She was like one of those trees planted near a pavement, whose lusty roots casually overturn the paving stones in their path.

When Miltiades took his departure he hesitated, but as a sort of quasi-brother-in-law, he touched his lips to Ponny's when he said good-bye.

CHAPTER SIXTY

L ONG after the Lacefield negroes had flown, Columbus
and Robinet stayed on at the Vaiden place, but the continued lure of free grub and the conviviality of hundreds of
other negroes finally drew them away.

They went after the manner of their kind. Columbus did
some small chore deliberately contrary to Miltiades' instructions. The white man corrected Columbus and told him
not to do that any more. The next morning both Columbus
and Robinet were absent. When Augustus told Miltiades,
the older brother said:

"Yes, I was expecting that. Last night he threw the hay
on the ground instead of putting it in the rack. That is
the nigger equivalent of a notice to leave."

The going of the two negroes placed the Vaidens in an
unhappy position. Part of their cotton was still in the field
unpicked, and the family had no money to hire outside
labor.

Rose suggested that if all the white persons on the place
would fall to and work, they could get the cotton out in a
week or two.

To Marcia the idea was fantastic. Even Gracie had never
had to work in the field. And Rose herself must have perceived it was impossible for Colonel Miltiades Vaiden, Grand
Dragon of the Ku Klux Klan, to be seen dragging a cotton
sack down a furrow.

Rose herself forbade Augustus working in the sun; it
might bring on a recurrence of his old attack in the hospital.

Old man Jimmie Vaiden determined positively in the midst of this family stress that he would light up his old forge and make horseshoes out of scrap iron. Scrap iron he could pick up for nothing, and horseshoes sold for ten cents apiece.

It is the misfortune of grown sons and daughters that they have no absolute authority over childish parents. Old man Jimmie acted very naughty against all their advice and pleadings, and presently a film of smoke wound up from the chimney of the forge and an occasional uncertain clink was heard on the anvil.

Then came some nights of full moons.

Miltiades got a sack, found an old pair of trousers, and went out into the field. While he picked in the hazy light he saw a dim figure on the other side of the field. At first he was disconcerted, then curious. He worked across slowly, identified the person as Cassandra, and picked back in the opposite direction until she was out of sight. It embarrassed the colonel keenly. It should not have embarrassed a philosopher like Cassandra. Whether it did or not, whether she was amused, or ironical or disdainful, Miltiades never knew. They never mentioned the incident to one another. But at any rate, during these moonlit nights the cotton moved slowly from the fields to the pens.

When it was all picked, Miltiades arranged for a hired negro to haul it to town. He would not be seen driving a cotton wagon into Florence.

The Vaidens had five bales of cotton and it was worth a dollar a pound. That meant about twenty-five hundred dollars. Cassandra called the family together and planned anxiously what to do with all this money. Rose thought they should get it in gold and keep it at home. Marcia thought they ought to buy everything they needed now before the money ran out. Cassandra thought they'd better put the money in the bank.

Miltiades had quite a different suggestion. He said he

was going to need a line of credit when he took charge of
the Lacefield plantation. He wanted to deposit the money
at Handback's store. It would draw eight per cent and it
would greatly assist him in getting credit with Handback
during the following season. In the meantime the family
would be out nothing. The common fund simply would be
deposited in his name, that would be all.

Rose said she would like to have hers and Augustus' share
paid to them in gold.

Miltiades was annoyed and asked Augustus what he had
to say, that he was the head of the family (Augustus'
family).

Augustus scratched his head and said he would have to
consult Rose privately before he decided what to do. As it
was very clear that Augustus already had consulted Rose
privately, Miltiades said:

"Very well, if you don't care to extend me a very great
favor which doesn't cost you a penny, I'll bring yours and
Rose's part back with me in cash."

Rose said he needn't trouble himself, that she and Augustus were going to drive to town on the day the cotton was
sold. She needed a few things, she said.

Marcia suddenly remembered what Rose had said to her
about Miltiades' lack of conscience and she grew very un-
friendly toward her sister-in-law.

The cotton was dispatched to Florence on the day before
Miltiades' wedding. The colonel, Augustus, and Rose went
ahead in the morning and the hired negro brought the five
bales on in a wagon. By noon it was in the warehouse of
J. Handback & Son. Rose and Augustus were paid six hundred dollars in gold and the balance of the money was left
on deposit in the name of Miltiades Vaiden.

With nineteen hundred dollars to his credit, Miltiades
did not feel so unkindly toward his brother for withdrawing
his share. Miltiades brought two brooches, just alike, one
for Drusilla and one for Marcia. Then he openly purchased

a hat and secretly bought some fancy silk underwear for himself.

As he rode home he began calculating what would be the probable extent of his credit with a preliminary deposit of nineteen hundred dollars. He thought it ought to be at least ten times the amount deposited. That would be nineteen thousand dollars . . . make it fifteen thousand. He believed he could get through the next season on eight thousand dollars. He pondered the price he would probably have to pay his negro labor—a hundred negroes at a dollar and a quarter a day. He saw that financing a plantation with hired labor would not be the same as financing it with slaves.

Rose had brought presents for Marcia and Mrs. Laura and Cassandra and they were all going home very happy.

Presently on the road old man Candy McPherson overtook them. He joined their party and began talking of this and that. Finally he touched on the governor's election.

"It looks like now," he began roundly, "that that thievin' Yankee carpetbagger is sure to be elected!"

"I suppose, if the niggers vote, it's a sure thing," conceded Miltiades.

"Well, the niggers are sure to vote. They kicked clean over the traces and out of their collar because that daggone Yankee's a-feedin' 'em."

"It's a shame! It's an outrageous shame!" said Miltiades. "We had the greatest difficulty in hiring labor to get our cotton picked."

Candy McPherson went back to his original theme.

"And besides the niggers, Lacefield ain't much of a candidate."

"What's your objection?" inquired the colonel quickly.

"Well, first an' foremost, he's broke and he hasn't got anybody to back his campaign with a little ready cash."

"That's a mistake," said Miltiades quickly. "J. Handback & Son are behind Mr. Lacefield's campaign."

"Well, that won't do no good!" cried Candy.

"Why won't it?"

"Hadn't you heard?" queried the old man blankly. "You-all must 'a' left town some little bit before I did. Why. J. Handback & Son is busted. That nigger sheriff, Trine, locked their doors up about two hour ago."

CHAPTER SIXTY-ONE

T HE involuntary bankruptcy of J. Handback & Son brought about the dissolution of the Vaidens as a family group. They did not have enough resources to support themselves during the winter and the two or three negro families necessary to make a crop the following year. Rose had the six hundred dollars which she had saved from the lost cotton.

When the family gathered in the fort-like living room, they were surprised and moved to find that Rose considered the six hundred as a common fund for the family. Cassandra, who was legal minded, reminded Rose that the money belonged to her and Augustus, but Rose said:

"No, it works out a hundred dollars for everybody all round, and maybe nobody will starve."

Miltiades laughed. The tininess of the sum touched his sense of the ludicrous.

"You may give my part to Marcia and Cassandra, Rose. I'm marrying to-morrow. A married man doesn't require capital."

"You are welcome to it if you want it, Miltiades," repeated Rose with a sort of cold, determined generosity.

She did not like her brother-in-law. In her heart she held the family losses against him. They had flung it all away trying to establish credit for Miltiades and the Lacefield estate.

Cassandra was furious at old man Handback. "The unmitigated scoundrel," she had cried out, "to accept our deposit when he knew he was toppling into bankruptcy."

"If he broke full handed," said Miltiades, "of course he would accept it."

"I hope you don't approve of him!" said Rose.

"Rose, how could he approve of him!" cried Marcia defensively.

"Just think," repined Augustus, "if we had only waited till the next day to haul our cotton to town."

Old Mrs. Laura from her bed murmured to Marcia that perhaps it was all for the best. Old man Jimmie thought a pack of fools had got what they deserved.

Rose began explaining her plans. She and Augustus were going to Florence to run a boarding house. There ought to be a big demand for rooms in Florence; everybody was moving to town. She hoped to run a high-class boarding house and charge her boarders as much as fifteen dollars a month for room and board.

That evening Miltiades found opportunity to speak to Marcia alone. He asked her should he tell A. Gray that she was ready to marry him.

"Brother Milt, you won't tell him that way, will you?" asked the girl, sad and embarrassed.

"Oh, no, he will mention it himself. He always does when he sees me. He has waited for you a long time, Marcia."

"Yes . . . that's true," said the sister.

She drew a long breath. She liked A. Gray. She was touched by his constancy. He really loved her in his straightforward, unappealing fashion. Marcia always felt between him and her a sort of psychic partition. Sometimes when A. Gray kissed her and had his arms about her she could feel something in him struggling to arouse something in her. But he never went any further than to create in her a sort of wistful loneliness.

She thought after her marriage this spiritual partition would melt away.

"You can tell A. Gray whatever you think best, Brother Milt," said the girl after a long pause.

"Marcia, do you love him?" asked her brother anxiously. "Don't marry on account of our present condition. That won't last always. I will look out after you, Marcia."

"Yes . . . I love A. Gray," said the girl.

She wanted to weep. She wanted to put her arms around Miltiades because all their money had been stolen from them; and he was so brave and uncomplaining, so hopeful and generous. She felt if A. Gray had been there she could have gone and wept in his arms. So she said again, faintly, that she loved A. Gray.

Here old man Jimmie Vaiden came up with an unsymmetrical horseshoe in his hand. His face was very red against his snowy hair.

"Look what I hammered out!" he quavered in triumph.

"And look how hot and shaky you are!" pointed out Marcia in concern.

"Pshaw! Pshaw!" scouted the old man. "Now, there's a dime I made."

Later that day, at sunset, Miltiades went to the stable to catch out his horse. Bridling and saddling his own horse always gave Miltiades a disagreeable sense of meanness and poverty. He had tried old Aunt Creasy, but the old woman was too feeble to bridle the horse. The actual work was nothing at all for the white man. The horse itself was very well mannered and always offered his head to the bridle.

From the erectness with which Colonel Vaiden rode down the rutty road he might have been on parade.

His thoughts moved incessantly back and forth among the actualities that made up his life. It was as if he were maneuvering his regiment on a battlefield.

He had no credit now and would be able to obtain none . . . the negroes were incorrigibly idle. It was as Beekman had said, they would produce little, but of course the white

man would get what they did produce. . . . Miltiades wondered what white man.

It flickered through the head of the rider that if the
negroes had become free legal agents, with the right to make
contracts and do business for themselves, then the man who
bought from them and sold to them would be the man in all
probability who, finally, would receive their earnings.

In his analysis the horseman forecasted that it would require a somewhat different man from the slave owner to
bring off this garnering; a man who could get along with
the negroes, who was not too scrupulous about his business
methods, a man, in brief, like J. Handback, who would
receive a deposit of money on the very morning of the day
he made an assignment. . . .

A twitch, almost of mirth, went through Miltiades. The
reins of power in the South would be transferred to tradesmen, to shopkeepers, to men like Handback, or even to such
a grub as Alex BeShears.

Indeed, the aristocratic planter stood in a bad way.
Beekman was certain to be elected Governor of Alabama.
He would soon bleed the state with exorbitant taxes and
official thievery just as the Northern governors had treated
every Southern state. The planters and their plantations
would be the shining object of their avarice. The very
honesty of the planters, the very code of honor that would
not permit them to stoop or defraud, would militate against
them.

Already half of them were bankrupts. Lacefield was a
bankrupt . . . he himself was a bankrupt. He had not a
friend in the world to turn to—indeed he had never had
friends.

As Colonel Vaiden weighed his condition, an extraordinary and unexpected sense of detachment and freedom filled
him. It was as if he were an immortal spirit dropped down
among these weapons and implements of flesh and stone and
earth, to take them up and use them with a sort of ebullient

certainty. Instead of being discouraged and depressed, he never felt more powerful or more confident in his life. It was a confidence that asked not the sympathy or friendship or approval of his neighbors.

He was suddenly a free soul. He would take up things as they were and do with them with the utmost wisdom he could summon for the benefit of himself.

As he pursued this line intently he thought again of Alex BeShears and, a half second later, of Ponny. His thoughts came to an abrupt halt at Ponny.

The image of the big, blond, comely girl, who one day would inherit whatever her grasping father had accumulated, brought the rider up at sharp attention.

The question came to his mind: if he meant to take up and use the most suitable weapon at hand . . . what of Ponny?

The mere notion of what he had in mind filled Miltiades with a kind of surprise at his own mental readiness and, at the same moment, it touched him with a vague, not unpleasant adumbration of the physical possession of Ponny, bred of his mood and the night.

At the Crossroads Colonel Vaiden drew up at the gate of the BeShears residence. He dismounted, stood at the gate and called Ponny. When he had called her twice the door opened and the girl came hurrying out into the darkness.

She came up to him, moved by his tones to some obscure excitement.

"What is it, Mr. Milt?" she asked in an unsteady voice. "I—I heard about the Handback trouble."

The man took her strong plump hand.

"Ponny," he said, "would you like to go to Florence with me?"

The girl moved her head, trying to see his face.

"When, Mr. Milt?" she asked more excitedly.

"Now."

"Right now?"

"Yes—at this moment."

The girl stared at him for an instant,

"Wh—what for, Mr. Milt?" she whispered.

"To stay with me—to live with me—to be my wife, Ponny."

At this odd sentence his voice softened involuntarily.

The girl shivered.

"M—Mr. Milt—I—I never exactly l-loved you, but I— I've sort of worshiped you, all my life long, Mr. Milt."

She began weeping, almost inaudibly. She felt as if Polycarp had returned from the dead in a glorified form. When Miltiades kissed her, her love and desire flowed out to him instantly in a tide of sweetness and anticipation.

To both Ponny and Miltiades, their ride to Florence, the arousing of the county court clerk and a minister was a long confusion.

At last, late that night, they were in the bridal suite of the old Florence Hotel. Ponny, after a long interval had finally gone to sleep at Miltiades Vaiden's side. She had dropped off to sleep after the difficulties, the painful adjustments and inconclusiveness of her new mode of life.

Miltiades lay quietly thinking, planning what he would do next; how he would move.

Now and then, in the interludes of his planning he would notice the lift of the quilts above Ponny's bosom and there would slip into his mind a memory of the exquisite and inconspicuous loveliness of Drusilla, of the tenderness and utter sweetness of her bestowal on him in her room at the manor; and he would feel again the wet, formless kiss upon his dry lips of her little daughter Sydna.

CHAPTER SIXTY-TWO

AFTER Rose and Augustus went to Florence only Marcia
and Cassandra remained at the homestead with their father
and mother and old Aunt Creasy. Presently Marcia herself
would go away. Her marriage with A. Gray was like a dim
rainbow on a rainy day: as she advanced toward it, it re-
ceded from her. Now she thought of her wedding with neither
pleasure nor aversion. Even Cassandra had quit casting her
habitual disparagements against suitors in general and
A. Gray in particular. Miltiades' marriage with Ponny Be-
Shears had been such a wound to her pride in the family
name that A. Gray was a solace. Her only comfort was that
Miltiades had made his marriage in revenge for Drusilla's
treachery to him.

And then, at last, the query had dawned on Miss Cassandra, with her family fading and falling like the leaves
of the harsh black oaks in the yard, would not marriage
with any other strain at all bring hope and life and children
again?

There was something melancholy and out of kilter about
the Vaidens. They clung to life too long. The first set of
children had scattered and gone long ago; now the second
set still cared for parents who, in the usual course of life,
would long since have been wept, interred, and forgotten.

On the old place only in Marcia still burned the fires of
the future. Where all the others saw only falling leaves, the
black oaks reminded Marcia that when winter had come and
gone they would unfold their spiky buds again.

With all these fading things around her Marcia moved about and had her being in a kind of symbol. Sometimes a spiritual ache invaded her for the symbol to shatter and let her find herself clinging to some sort of reality; but the log house with its small high windows and pink figured curtains maintained its immobile and tantalizing illusion.

She sat in her attic room curling her hair with a little iron over an oil lamp. She touched her tongue, tapped the iron, and faintly burned her finger every time she withdrew the curler from the lamp chimney.

She was not thinking of what she did. The curling went on mechanically while she exonerated Miltiades for jilting Drusilla. She told herself that Drusilla had flirted her brother and so Miltiades had paid Drusilla off in her own coin, and that she was glad of it. But she was not glad. It broke her heart that Miltiades could have done such a thing. And even if Miltiades had wanted revenge on the Drusilla who had misused him, there was no way to get it. That early Drusilla had vanished long ago and a sweet, kindly Drusilla had taken her place; and little Sydna was such a dear. . . .

From downstairs she heard the cracked voice of old Aunt Creasy calling up that a gentleman was to see her.

Out of habit she asked who it was, but she knew it was A. Gray.

Aunt Creasy called back quaveringly that she couldn't make out; she thought it was Mas' Polycarp.

The ancient's eyes and memory suddenly had failed. She never recognized anyone. Now she had forgot that Polycarp was dead.

The black woman's mistake set up an ache in Marcia's heart. It took away the faint comfort she felt in seeing A. Gray. Indeed, in Marcia's world Polycarp was still alive. He came and went and at times Marcia talked with him. And it seemed now that Aunt Creasy might easily have seen her sharp impressions of Polycarp's continued existence. He was as real as the other people of her shadowy world.

She walked slowly downstairs, glanced about the open hall-way, looked in the company room, then went into the living room, thinking that A. Gray had stepped in to speak to her mother.

Save for the sick old woman the house was quite deserted. From up the road she could hear the faint occasional clink of the anvil at the forge.

She listened a moment and finally went into the kitchen and asked Aunt Creasy where the man was. The old woman pondered, screwing her black face into a hundred wrinkles, and finally remembered there had been a man at the big gate.

Such a waiting place was unusual. Marcia went out of the kitchen across the windy yard toward the gate. A tall man, who was not A. Gray, stood outside the gate beside a buggy and a horse. He stood looking into the west. As Marcia drew near he turned around and a queer shiver went through the girl. She stopped and stood looking at him silently with solemn questioning eyes. Then she went for-ward a little and asked through the ancient obligation of hospitality:

"Won't you come in?"

"I know what folks have been saying about me; so I won't come in."

Marcia stood regarding him with a slow confusion of emotions rising up within her.

"Did you know," she asked in a strange voice, "that if Miltiades had been here he would have . . . shot you?"

"I didn't *know* that," stressed the man significantly.

Marcia became more and more affected.

"Why in heaven's name did you come here?" she asked in an aspirate.

"I'm out of the army. I'm going away. If you would see me, I wanted to say good-bye."

For some reason the sight of him always wrung Marcia's heart. Her old agony for him arose up.

"Oh," she breathed, "I wish you hadn't come . . . I do wish you hadn't come!"

The man's thin, colorless face went white.

"I knew I oughtn't to stop—I knew I ought to look at your home and go on by."

The girl could no longer restrain her tears.

"I—I don't know what's the matter with me," she whispered. "I—I must go back in the house."

"Marcia," said the man in his thin voice, "shorely—shorely you know I didn't——"

The girl composed her face.

"Of—of course I know it—it's what people say. Anything people say makes it a—a sort of reality. It's not as if they never had—accused you."

"No, I know that. But I just came to say good-bye." The man drew a long sigh. "I felt like I had to see you once more."

He stood a moment longer, then, still looking at her, tightened the rein of his horse and moved a step sidewise toward the buggy.

His movement filled her with anxiety.

"Listen, Jerry," questioned the girl, "where are you going?"

"Why, to the Fenians, Marcia. A man named Walker is raising an army to go into Canada."

"Jerry! Are you going to fight again?" she cried aghast.

"Well, what can I do? If I'm marching or fighting or in prison I—I can live; but when I'm turned loose to nothing at all—what is there left for me to do?"

"Why, anything!" cried the girl passionately. "You are so fine! They need men like you more than anything in the world—with everybody grabbing and deceiving and stealing." Her throat ached and she began weeping again.

"No, I'll have to go. I was born too far north, Marcia. If I had lived just a few miles down this direction—twenty—

fifteen, maybe—them few miles would have saved me. They'd 'a' let me into heaven."

He got into his buggy and moved his horse up the rutty road toward the hills.

It seemed to Marcia that her whole body was collapsing within her. The man in the buggy, moving away to some fantastic end, was so real that he was part of her. It was like the dearest part of her own body being torn out and dragged away up the road. She ran to the gate, fumbled an intolerable moment at the latch, then went flying up the road.

"Jerry! Jerry!" she wept. "You—you can't go by yourself! Jerry! Jerry!"

CHAPTER SIXTY-THREE

MARCIA was determined that under no circumstances would she run away and marry. She had the buggy turned back and told old Mrs. Laura and Cassandra that she and Jerry were going to be married.

"I'm not going to run away," she repeated warmly. "I'm sick and tired of elopements."

"What shall I tell A. Gray?" inquired Miss Cassandra, intensely displeased.

"Tell him I loved him," said Marcia, "but tell him Jerry needed me."

After they had gone away from the big house, Miss Cassandra told her mother a number of bitter things which she should have said to Jerry Catlin!

As the two went by the forge they found old man Jimmie shakily pumping his great bellows. The fire in his forge kept going out.

With an effort at the preservation of the formalities, Jerry Catlin asked the old blacksmith for his daughter. The old man loosed his bellows and stood by his forge looking at the tall thin hillman.

"I've heard o' you Catlins up in Tennessee long afore you was borned, and I never heard o' any good o' any of ye. You was abolitionists before the war, copperheads endurin' the war, and scalawags after the war."

"I would like your consent to marry Marcia," repeated Jerry grayly.

"Ask Polycarp," directed the old blacksmith bitterly; "if he consents, I consent."

The two walked out of the shop into the wind-swept road again. The sky was a moving field of clouds. Now and then a weak sunshine developed about the buggy and horse and faded into grayness again. The hills through which they rode were zoned in the dull smoky draperies of autumn. They passed fields of thin hill cotton with no one at work picking the poor crop.

Early in the afternoon the sunshine gave way to a uniform gray gloom. The more distant hills were lost to view. The air grew keener and the gray world seemed to contract around them.

A little later Jerry began to inquire at the cabins along the way for a place to stay all night.

The only obstacle to any traveler's staying all night anywhere in the hills was his appearance. If the wayfarer were well equipped, spoke correct English, and seemed of gentle breeding, then he was refused lodging by the hill folk through a combination of resentment at his station and embarrassment at his good manners. However, if he were rough, poorly horsed, and shabbily clad, such a traveler could find lodgment anywhere.

As Jerry shouted from the road, he was refused his keep time after time. Marcia noticed that the men and women who came out were uniformly wrapped against the cold in frayed blue overcoats. Finally she remarked about them and Jerry told her they were the relics of Buell's army on its long forced march to Shiloh.

"I heard the guns of that battle, Jerry," said Marcia. "Mother and Cassandra and I listened to the cannon all Sunday long and all day Monday. They prayed for Polycarp and Miltiades. I prayed for them . . . and for you."

By now night had fallen and the high hill road was bitterly cold. The cabins were blacker shapes along the dark trail. Before one of these Jerry drew up his tired horse and called hello at persistent intervals after the fashion of the hills.

They had a long wait. Jerry was on the verge of faring on when a voice in the woods on the opposite side of the trail called out to know who was there.

Jerry told who he was and said he had with him a girl whom he intended to marry in Lanesburg on the following day. She was a Miss Vaiden, he called, the daughter of old man Jimmie Vaiden who lived in Alabama near BeShears Crossroads. He kept on, giving all the points of identification he could think of because he had to allay the suspicions of a hillman.

In the middle of this the hidden voice said:

"Let the gal stan' up in the buggy so I kin see her."

Marcia loosed the robe tucked about her legs and stood up. Everything was perfectly dark to her. She could see nothing at all. After several moments standing in the apron of the buggy she sat down again. A voice close to them apologized.

"You-uns must excuse me fer bein' over-particklar, but when I hear a hollerin' in the dark I make shore an' certain who it is before I pass the time o' day."

"Why?" shivered Jerry curiously.

"I want to make shore an' certain it ain't ol' man Alex BeShears."

An odd feeling went over Marcia. She peered in the direction of the voice.

"Who are you?" she asked.

"My name is Kilgo, ma'am," said the voice.

"And why do you have to make so sure?"

"Why, a lot of us fellers, ma'am, burnt the ol' man's feet an' made him give up his money endurin' the war. So ol' man Alex has been gunnin' fer us ever sence. I un'erstan' he kilt Johnson and Sloane and one of the Vaiden boys who lived down thar clost to him. He allus thought Polycarp Vaiden hep burn him, but he didn't. Polycarp jess hard [hired] me to take what news he found out spyin' on the Yankees to a rebel officer in Corinth."

The two travelers sat silently in the buggy for several moments, then Jerry said in a queer tone:

"And you expect old man BeShears to come up after you?"

"Yes," said Red Jim, "I'm shore he'll come fer me. I'm not gwine down in Alabam' to git him, but when he fin'ly comes, I'm a-gwine to do what I kin to kill him fust."

The hillman said this very simply and with complete detachment. It was a commonplace in his life.

"You-uns get out an' come in," he invited. "Yore gal kin sleep in the bed with my ol' womern an' the baby, an' me an' you kin sleep on the floor."

CHAPTER SIXTY-FOUR

OLD man Jimmie Vaiden steeled the surface of his heart against the loss of Marcia. She had not run away but she had gone off against his will. She had made her bed and now she could lie on it.

The old man clinked away at the cooling iron on his anvil, filled with a persistent anger at Marcia. Behind this anger spread a sense of desolation which only the anger could mask. The big house and the black oaks, which he could see from his forge, took on an inimical appearance now that he knew it sheltered only old Mrs. Laura malingering on her bed, old Aunt Creasy mumbling her stinking cob pipe, and Cassandra, moving and speaking in chill, unrelenting logic.

These were what were left of all his struggle.

The niggers he had brought with him from South Carolina decades ago were free, voting, running for office, electing governors of Alabama. . . .

In the silence of the forge he began a quavering, ironic laughter which, abruptly, the bitterness of Marcia's marriage, recurring like a round song, estopped.

A penetrating chill filled the November morning. Then he saw the fire in the forge had died out again. He had some matches. Marcia, before she left, had bought him a box of new-fangled matches. They were behind the crosspiece on the flat dusty top of his billows.

He reached for the box, fumbled at it, became irritated because it did not open smoothly. He jerked at the container, tore the pasteboard open and scattered the matches over the earthen floor. Some were ruined in the dust-covered water in his cooling tub. Some were lost in the chinks between the stones of his forge.

Old man Jimmie was appalled at the calamity. All of his matches were gone. He could not distinguish the matches from the shavings and débris scattered on the floor. Without his matches he could work no more. He wondered whom he could get to find them for him. Cassandra would not look. She would say his hammering and forging were bad for him. Old Aunt Creasy was blinder even than he. Marcia would have found all his matches—or bought him some more —but Marcia was gone. She had gone off against his will with a Catlin.

He hunkered down, feeling for the matches Marcia had given him. As he searched he quavered his old imprecations: Where in the thunderation . . . He'd have to get somebody with eyes to look. . . . Dad blame a man's eyes, goin' back on him!

He pulled himself up by the horn of his anvil. He moved shakily to the door of his shop.

"George! George!" he creaked.

He stood looking up and down the old road in the cold sunlight.

"Where in the thunderation is that nigger!" And then he remembered that Nigger George had been sent to Montgomery, to the legislature. He had run against some other nigger—he couldn't remember who.

The grotesqueness, the idiocy, of the world shook at old Jimmie's reason. He saw a blur down the road toward the big house: some person or some animal at the ancient gate of the big house. He began calling in shaky impatience:

"Cassie! Marsh! Crease! You dad-blame lazy heifers——"

He clutched the door facing of the forge in a fury that

the person did not hear him and come to him at once. The door itself seemed to sway. The old man clung to it and it seemed to topple over with him, sprawling him inwards on the earthen threshold of his shop. Pain pierced his breast. He gasped for air.

The road, the cold sunlight seemed to rush toward him and recede and rush forward again, cutting off his breath.

Then he saw a woman and a little child flying toward him along the wavering road.

"Pap! Ol' Pap. What's the matter?" cried the woman. "Ol' Pap, are you sick?"

The prostrate ancient looked at the woman.

"Is—is that—Gracie?" he gasped.

"Yes, ol' Pap, I—I come back. The governor wouldn't take me to Montgomery if I kept my baby. So I kept it and—come back home."

"Home! Home! You runaway nigger, you ain't got no home here!"

The child, a little gray-eyed white boy, stared at the old man and began whimpering with fright.

"Hush, Toussaint," soothed the quadroon shakenly. "Can I get you some water, ol' Pap?—some whisky?"

An overpowering weakness rushed over the old man.

"You—haven't—got—time. I'm—— Where's Marsh?"

"She's gone, ol' Pap."

"Lef' me—went away an' lef' me. I wanted to die in my daughter's arms."

"Oh! Oh! Ol' Pap—you are, ol' Pap!" sobbed the woman, holding him up and looking into his ashen face.

"What do you—mean?" he gasped.

"My mammy—old Hannah, you remember—the woman you owned in South Carolina—she told Aunt Creasy I was your daughter."

The old man made a great exertion, put up a hand and pushed away the face of the woman who held him.

"You—nigger," he panted, "lay me down—lay me back down—in the dirt——"

When he ceased breathing Gracie got up, took her child by the hand, and hurried to the heavy, silent, fort-like house. She needed help from her half sister, Cassandra, to bring their dead father home.

THE END